Three Contemporary German Novellas

The German Library: Volume 88

Volkmar Sander: General Editor

THREE CONTEMPORARY GERMAN NOVELLAS

Lenz

A Runaway Horse

The Sunday I Became World Champion

Edited by A. Leslie Willson

CONTINUUM · NEW YORK

2001

The Continuum International Publishing International Group Inc
370 Lexington Avenue, New York, NY 10017

The German Library is published in cooperation
with Deutsches Haus, New York University.
This volume has been supported by Inter Nationes, and a grant from the funds
of Stifterverband für die Deutsche Wissenschaft.

Printed in the United States of America

Library of Congress Cataloging-in-Publication Data

Three contemporary German novellas / edited by A. Leslie Willson.
p. cm.
Contents: Lenz / Peter Schneider — A runaway horse / Martin Walser — The Sunday I became world champion / Friedrich Christian Delius.
ISBN 0-8264-1213-0 (alk. paper) — ISBN 0-8264-1214-9 (pbk. : alk. paper)
1. Short stories, German—Translations into English. 2. German fiction—20th century—Translations into English. I. Willson, A. Leslie (Amos Leslie), 1923- II. Schneider, Peter, 1940- Lenz. III. Walser, Martin, 1927- Fliehendes Pferd. IV. Delius, Friedrich Christian, 1943- Sonntag, an dem ich Weltmeister wurde.

PT1327 .T47 2001
833'.91408—dc21 00-060146

Contents

Introduction

The literary prose form called *novella* stretches back several centuries. It received its name because of its newness, and because of its freshness and its brevity it found immediate acceptance because it entertained and fascinated the few who could read and had acccess to it at the time. Giovanni Boccaccio popularized the form with his *Decameron* (written 1349–53). Chaucer's *Canterbury Tales* (written in the last decade of the fourteenth century) contributed to a growing tradition of humorous, often erotic and objective short fictional narratives based on local anecdotes, presented in a structured and focused form.

The form spread with amazing speed throughout Europe and began to flower, contributing to the development of the novel in the eighteenth century and the short story in the nineteenth. Johann Wolfgang Goethe defined the genre with his *Novelle*, emphasizing its concentration on a singular event (made up or adapted from real incidents), often with a single emblem (person, animal, object) as a metaphor for the work's theme (a falcon in Goethe's novella). In his *Conversations of German Immigrants* Goethe also exemplified the form for his contemporary readers.

Masters of the form in the nineteenth century include Dostoyevsky, *Notes from the Underground* (1864), Leo Tolstoy, *The Death of Ivan Ilich* (1886), Henry James, *The Aspern Papers* (1888), and in the twentieth century Joseph Conrad, *Heart of Darkness* (1902) and the prime example of the form, Ernest Hemingway's *The Old Man and the Sea* (1952). German-language writers were drawn to the novella from early on, ranging from Heinrich von Kleist and other authors in the nineteenth century to twentieth-century masters such as Gerhart Hauptmann, Franz Kafka, and Thomas Mann.

Through the centuries of its existence the novella has matured and evolved. The use of a frame often sets the occasion for the novella (a device used from the beginning). Novellas have discrete plots, are often shot through with irony, are usually restrained emotionally, and mostly avoid subjectivity. As time goes on, the novella retains its vigor by adapting to the age in which it is written, unified always by mood and style.

This volume contains novellas by three contemporary masters of the form: Peter Schneider with *Lenz* (1973), here for the first time in English; Martin Walser with *A Runaway Horse* (original publication, 1978; English, 1980); and Friedrich Christian Delius with *The Sunday I Became World Champion* (1994), also appearing here for the first time in translation.

Peter Schneider (born in 1940) uses Berlin (East and West) as the setting for his novels. In *The Wall Jumper* (published in English in 1983) the Berlin Wall is an object of contempt and separation that challenges the wiles and resourcefulness of various East and West Berliners (jumping the Wall is a two-way street) who seek to escape their plight and yet reforge their national identity long before the Wall fell. In *The German Comedy* (English in 1992) he depicts the difficulties of unification for a generation split by politics and ways of life. The tragicomic novel *Couplings* (English in 1996) follows the engaging yet sobering fate of two Berliners whose escapades with women friends force them to examine their own behavior and attitudes. Schneider's bestselling short novel, *Lenz,* depicts a slice of Berlin life during the period of international student unrest and rebellion—1968. The titular hero, who begins to doubt his leftist icons and pillars, cavils and complains, even flees Berlin for Italy, but experiences moments of epiphany and finds unexpected comfort and serenity. The novella captures the incontrovertible dilemmas of an era filled with paranoia and hope and determination, a time fraught with deadly silliness and infused with contradictory realities that define a greater truth.

Martin Walser (born in 1927) has been called the dean of contemporary German writers of fiction because of his publication through the years of novels that mirror the vagaries of German society, the struggle of individuals to find their niches and the conflicts that arise in their lives. His skill as a narrator and his incisive delineation of character and incident have won readers' hearts and minds. His works in English translation (at this writing, all out of print) include *The Unicorn*, *The Inner Man*, and *Breakers*, as well as the novella republished here. *A Runaway Horse* is classical Walser, a masterful tale of the reunion of two friends, long separated and now met again with their wives while on vacation. The challenges and vagaries of a generally mundane existence are thrust onto a laggard teacher and a brisk and optimistic yea-sayer of life. An encounter with a runaway horse and the later plight of a disastrous gale-tossed sailboat on a lake convince the teacher that strategies of survival do not merge without peril. It all depends on whether you face life head on or back into it.

Friedrich Christian Delius (born in 1943) also takes advantage of the unique qualities of Berlin and its picturesque and maddening residents in many of his novels, such as *Adenauerplatz* (1984) and *Amerikahaus und der Tanz um die Frauen* (1997). His novella *The Sunday I Became World Champion* is a departure from most novella forms in that it is deliberately subjective (with a nameless hero narrator, an eleven-year-old boy). The novella portrays a small postwar German village through the delicate eyes of a boy on the verge of adolescence who is caught in contradictory feelings for his stern pastor father and the Father to whom he prays. The boy's bewilderment and lack of self-confidence is exacerbated and emphasized by his inability to speak without a stutter. Then one Sunday, at the turning point of his young life, in front of a radio his estrangement from language and world becomes irrevelant as he listens to the national German soccer team vie for the World Cup. The team's victory marks the startling and triumphant moment when a guilt-ridden nation and a struggling young boy both come of age.

The three novellas have in common an effervescence of spirit, a fast-paced ironic and even comedic esprit, mixed with nostalgia and daring. The prose urges the reader on, pulls the reader along and, though at intervals risking a perilous and impudent twist, sets the reader down gently and contented at the end.

A. L. W.

LENZ

Peter Schneider

"He walked on indifferently. The path was not important to him, now upward, now downward. He felt no weariness at all, except it was at times unpleasant that he could not walk on his head."

Georg Büchner, *Lenz*

AT MORNING LENZ WOKE UP out of one of his usual dreams. With L. he had ridden in a mine cage for kilometers through a building without doors and windows. All around them, nothing but walls. Then he had fallen down a dark shaft, many hundreds of meters deep, without crashing. A conveyor belt had received him, transforming his plunge into a horizontal flight forward. He was caught at the end of the conveyor belt. He had been expected: women with gigantic breasts, sorcerers, clowns, somersaulting children, the whole messed up Fellini troupe. A man in a flickering costume pressed a kiss upon his mouth. Lenz became infuriated. He jumped out of bed.

For some time he had already been unable to endure the sage face of Marx over his bed any longer. He had hung it turned to the wall once already. In order to let the intellect drip off, he explained to a friend. He looked Marx straight in the eye: "What were your dreams, old know-it-all, at night, I mean? Were you really happy?"

While he ran the water into the kettle for coffee, he was struck with the desire to call L. It is still too early, Lenz thought. She'll say "hello" with that sleepy child's voice and then give me what-for that I'm already calling again. He forgot to set the kettle on the fire and went to the telephone. He picked up the receiver, listened to the dial tone for a long time without dialing, and put it back down. He left the house. It was still early—the birds were clamoring. He bought himself a newspaper and looked at the people streaming into the S-Bahn station. Men with great strides and briefcases, women wearing flat shoes, always somewhat more in a hurry than the men. They were going to work, Lenz thought. He did not connect any mental image to that statement.

He went to the ticket window, got a ticket, and took the escalator with the others up to the platform. Halfway up he turned around and amidst the curses of those standing behind him on the steps forced his way back down. "Someone like him needs his face smacked to wake him up!" "Shut up!" Lenz yelled to the rear. Nothing better occurred to him. He went into a telephone booth and dialed L's number. No answer. Back up to the platform, which had meanwhile emptied. He took the next train and rode into the Western part of the city. For a while he imagined that the houses and streets were rolling past him on rails. He was surprised by the brightness that especially emphasized every object. The windows in upper stories, the treetops, which from up here looked like bushes, the freeways below the train, everything, as though he were seeing it for the first time. Very briefly a song of the Doors was in his head, first the melody, then the words: *people are strange, when you're a stranger, faces look ugly, when you're alone.* When he opened the newspaper, he saw the teeth of the zipper on his coat. They seemed to him to be too big. He read a headline that went across the entire page: SEX FIEND ARRESTED, TURK ABUSES 13-YEAR-OLD. Next to him a woman about sixty, with a big nose, which she hung over his shoulder so she could read along with him. Lenz had no desire to keep reading; he waited until she was finished and turned the page for her. He looked at the worn faces of his neighbors, who were reading the same headline. Then again the old, childish idea: The publisher's skyscraper collapses in flames.

After a few stations Lenz changed trains. The station was old, almost a ruin. Between rails that were no longer in use, grass grew rampant. Bushes grew high beside train cars on sidings, foliage hung over tops and windows, in the air a heavy odor. Like from chestnut trees in the spring, thought Lenz, then saw that chestnut trees were actually there. He saw a steep street ahead;

it was the city in which he had grown up. On his bicycle he rode through it under the chestnut trees. The branches formed a roof over the street, and the forbidden smell of semen, which he washed off his hands mornings after he got up, streamed down from the leaves and pursued him to the school gate. The incoming train tore him out of his fancies; someone had called out his name.

He rode for a long time, he didn't know where to, then he got out and left the train station. When he looked back, he saw the train moving away on a bridge; it seemed to him as though it were carrying him away. Then he let himself be borne away by the stream of people hurrying out of the train station. He was in the center of the city; different people were around him. The abrupt forward movement of cars when the traffic light turned green bothered him. It was one of the first warm days in the year, and like a strike of a gong that droned through the whole city women came out on the street for the first time without stockings and in lightweight pullovers. Everywhere next to him, in front of him, behind him was the tapping and pattering of high heels; the women's legs were incredibly white, and a few of the young men already had begun walking with springy pushes of their toes. For the first time there was a jouncing and jiggling under the pullovers; Lenz had an uneasy feeling that begins somewhere in the stomach and goes to the fingertips but doesn't stop there. At first he resisted it. He knitted his brows as though he were pondering. But it was one of those days when every person made every other person aware of the fact that among other things he had genitals.

From an open door came fairly fast music; while he was passing, it almost pulled him back. He stopped and pressed his nose against the display window behind which a lovely tall girl was just putting a few things in order. The girl flipped her fingers against the window at the very place where Lenz had his nose. Lenz recoiled, the girl laughed, and because he had recoiled she looked over again and gestured to him that he might as well come in. That made Lenz so happy that he simply continued on his way.

* * *

On another day Dieter arrived, the student who for a few months had been working with Lenz in a factory group. When Lenz saw his beaming face, which was a constant with him, he at once fell into a bad mood.

"Do you already know where our group will meet tomorrow, before the demonstration?"

"I'm not going," replied Lenz.

Dieter looked at him in disbelief. "You helped write the circulars, helped distribute them, and now you don't want to go with us?"

"Right," said Lenz, "in the rows of the working class that is being formed by us, this time I'm leaving a yawning hole."

Dieter pressed him hard; what had happened to him? He didn't recognize Lenz anymore. For quite a while he had noticed that Lenz was cutting himself off.

"It's just that I'm not going with you this time, that's all."

He would have to clarify his standpoint, say something more; he couldn't convey that to the others that way.

"Convey, convey!" yelled Lenz, "I'm having bad dreams."

Dieter became enraged. Lenz should explain himself, at least voice his criticism. Lenz didn't want to go into it.

The next morning Lenz rang the doorbell of a girl he had met at a party a few days before. The only things he knew about her was how she moved while dancing and that her name was Marina. When she opened the door, she was surprised that Lenz was standing there. Lenz asked whether he could have a cup of tea with her. She was pretty confused, she didn't say no. She went right into the kitchen and put on the water. While she was busy in the kitchen, Lenz felt how the air in the room was becoming very heavy. He opened the window and looked at the fat green leaves on the trees, then he looked for a piece of furniture to put his legs up on. Marina set the tea on the table and took a seat opposite Lenz. Because nothing came to mind that he could say, he reached straight for the teapot. She took the teapot away from him because the tea had to steep first. How had Lenz gotten the idea of visiting her? Lenz replied that he had gotten the idea that morning, right after getting up. He had wanted to visit her, talk to her, and so on. He barely avoided asking her about a book she had talked about at the party and that at the moment was of no interest to him at all.

Then she began the customary interrogation of him: what he did, in what group he worked, what he thought about the other groups in which he did not work. At one statement or another about the relationship of political work and personal difficulties, it occurred to Lenz that he had made exactly the same statement a few days before without ever having met with any contradiction. He interrupted himself, he was just blah-blahing, saying nothing but uninspired, pre-chewed stuff. He fancied her, that's why he had come. He went to her and grabbed her. She didn't even know him yet, she said.

"You don't get to know each other with this asking and answering," Lenz replied. "There are only a few ways of getting to know one another: if you work together, if you do crazy things together, if you grab one another."

She resisted at first, then no more. It bothered Lenz that everything happened so fast. They tore the clothes off their bodies without really looking. Then it was very nice, there's nothing more to say about it. Later, when they were lying beside one another, her tenderness hurt Lenz physically.

"Tell me what you do," he said.

Another day Lenz presented himself in the office of an electric firm. In front of the personnel manager's room there were several men waiting whom Lenz watched mistrustfully. Lenz distinguished scraps of sentences in Greek and Turkish. He had learned Greek once on vacation; he made out a few words. One of the men waiting told him that he had come here for the third time and had been waiting already for two hours. If he didn't find work, he would be tossed out of the workers' hostel. Lenz did not understand exactly what he said about the rent he was paying. The personnel manager opened his door and cast a short glance at those waiting. He told Lenz to come in. Lenz hesitated, the others looked at him as though he had conspired against them with the personnel manager. The personnel manager repeated his summons. Lenz obeyed, not to be conspicuous, but realized then that in doing so it was only to the personnel manager that he was not conspicuous. He offered Lenz a position using an automatic adding machine. Lenz declined, he preferred to work on the production line. The personnel manager called his attention to the fact that he would earn considerably less then. Besides, it wasn't customary that men worked on the production line. At any rate, piece work would also come into consideration. Lenz dodged the question about what occupation Lenz had worked at before—he could see that he had an intelligent person before him. He insisted on being engaged as a temporary worker. The personnel manager handed him an agreement that Lenz filled out with wrong answers as far as he possibly could. Lenz was hired for 4.20 marks per hour.

Going out, Lenz was addressed by one of the Turkish workers, who asked him about the result of his negotiations with the personnel manager. The Turk told him how, in a train in which there was not even a place to sit, he had traveled three long days to Germany. Earlier, in an examination by German doctors, he had moved an arm that he had just broken as though it were sound.

"You pretended to be healthy to be able to work?" Lenz asked. He had to resist the thought that he had taken a job away from the Turk.

The Turk then told about a small accident that he had had with a friend's car. In a blood test an elevated alcohol level was found. He was sentenced to two months in jail. Since he had lost his job, his residence permit lapsed and he was afraid of being deported to Turkey. For a week he had tried in vain to find work. All the personnel managers demanded an exact account of what he had done in the time he had been in Germany. Lenz had a hard time listening. Mostly he looked at the Turk's eyes and at his powerful, boxerlike arm movements. He had the strong desire to see the world through his eyes. For an instant it seemed to him as though he had to embrace him, make him a friend. Lenz let himself be taken along to the Turk's room. They sat down on the bed and started drinking right away. A second, unmade bed stood empty. His colleague was at work, the Turk explained;

when he came back he would have a meal ready for him. Could Lenz cook?

Later, Lenz took the guitar that was hanging on the wall and played a song, the words to which he had forgotten. The Turk asked what kind of song he was playing. Lenz replied it was a song about a man who gets to America for the first time and thinks that he's blowing his mind. He hurriedly took his leave; he promised to come again.

In the middle of the night Lenz woke up. He had the feeling that he was not alone in his room. It was as though L. were lying next to him and bending with her hair over his face. When he thought he felt her touch, he turned on the light. He realized clearly that he had been living alone for three months. Then again it seemed completely incredible to him that he slept alone in this room. He believed he could sense L.'s aroma in the room. His cock stood large and annoying under the blanket. He began to stroke it but quit when he perceived that all his fantasies involved experiences in the past. He felt an unpleasant power arise in him that paralyzed his body He struck the wall with his head and fists. At the same time, the way he was behaving seemed to him foolish. He wanted to free himself from the images with violence. He began to roar, but then realized that he was only imagining it.

He got dressed and left the house. It was just getting light; in the dawn the city looked as though it had just emerged from the sea. The streets were smooth and slick, as though covered by blue ice; a few newspaper pages lay motionless in the gutters; only a few cars were standing there, dead insects that had fallen from the walls. When Lenz looked up at the walls of the buildings, nothing moved, no curtain was pulled back, no window opened, a light nowhere. At first he walked with long, heavy strides; his limbs dragged; it was as though he had lead in his fingers and toes. Then he began to run, at first slowly with even breaths, then faster; in the entrance to a building, startled, a couple broke their embrace, the man leaped out into the street and looked back to see whether he could be of aid to a pursuer. Lenz ran on; a sheet of newspaper got caught on his shoe and flew in tatters onto the street; the building walls and display windows jumped back from him. Once, when he looked up the street, it seemed to him as though the city ended there, as though an unknown landscape opened up beyond, but he couldn't go on; he stopped, gasping for breath. An alarm clock somewhere, windows were opened, radio music came out, in a backyard a motor was started. When Lenz returned, his fear was gone; he felt relieved.

The next morning at six-thirty Lenz began his work in the factory. The foreman showed him his work station and explained to him briefly what he had to do. He greeted Lenz amicably, as though he already knew him. On his head he had only three hairs, which he constantly brushed from his brow. Lenz's task consisted of welding electric tubes together. When the foreman had left him by himself, he watched his neighbor to learn his work more quickly. The woman next to him stretched both arms out as though in flight, drew them in and, angling her arms as though she would touch the material to be welded only by chance, took it in both hands, bobbed up and down, while she picked it up, with her body forward, to step three four times on the foot pedal—the first part was welded. Then again spreading her arms, taking it up with a swoop, the same sequence until the second welding operation was completed. Then stick the finished welded tubes in the screen and start over again. At first Lenz fell upon the tubes and picked up them as fast as he could. Then he realized that he worked slower than if he structured his movements and kept a certain rhythm. The tempo depended solely on the machine; his task consisted of bringing his body into the same rhythm. The less he resisted the prescribed rhythm of the machine, the more quickly the screen filled up with completed tubes. When he began to master the work procedure, he enjoyed for a time sensing every moment that passed.

Out of the corner of his eye he saw next to his elbow the rhythmic up and down of the arms at the neighboring machine; he heard the short telegraphiclike messages that flew back and forth between the machines; they were short, precise messages about lunch, the hair dresser, marketing, children. All motions and sounds merged into a basic movement and basic sound that dominated the whole hall and the purposes of which were of no interest to Lenz. He sensed no compulsion to compare anything that he now perceived with something else that he had earlier perceived. He had only an irresistible urge to delay. He would like to have stopped the whole world with a hand lever on the machine, just to see how it started up again. After eight hours, when the signal bell sounded, he went home weary and satisfied.

On another day on his way home Lenz met his friend Walter. They had not seen one another for several years. They embraced and walked for a while aimlessly through the streets.

"I totally forgot your face," said Lenz, "what do you look like, anyway?"

Walter thought it was an empty phrase; he turned his head aside. He had lived in Spain for a year; he had bought a piece of land and a horse. He became embarrassed.

A horse? Surrounded by cars it seemed pretty crazy to Lenz that Walter had ridden through the area for a whole year on a horse.

Then Walter said that he hadn't come directly from Spain rather from a psychiatric clinic in Hanover. He had been expelled from Spain because in a coffee shop he had called General Franco a fascist and murderer. He had argued with the waiter, and when the waiter threatened him with the police, it got the better of him. It had been pretty idiotic of him.

Lenz wanted to know how he had come to be in the psychiatric clinic. Again, it was hard for him to listen. He looked at Walter's shoes; the sole was hanging down on the left shoe and slapped against the sidewalk before he set his foot down. While Walter walked along beside him with a hanging head, Lenz saw him running through Hanover. Walter had run out of money during the trip. At first he had tried to hitchhike to get to his family in southern Germany. Then he had run back into the city and begged for a mark. He wanted to call up friends who would send him money. The people whom he asked always said the same sentence over and over: that no one needed to beg these days.

Then he had only cigarettes left and in a cigarette shop asked for a light. The salesman refused to light up the shop flame; he offered Walter a box of matches for five pfennigs.

"You will still give me a light," Walter said.

The salesman replied he should pay five pfennigs like everyone else.

"But I need a light right now, for this cigarette, and I don't have five pfennigs now."

"It can't be," the salesman replied, "that there's anyone who doesn't have five pfennigs," and he should leave the shop.

He then walked for hours through the streets; it's all too ridiculous; it's almost impossible to tell it; he could have asked someone else, but he had already been too weary and hungry to come to terms with the fact that someone had refused on principle to give him a light. Then it got dark; he broke down a door to sleep in the entry hall of a building; a neighbor called the police, a radio car came; in his overwrought condition he thought the car's headlights were searchlights; he tried to shatter them with rocks; the policemen grabbed him by the arms and legs and beat him. They took him to the station in handcuffs and charged him with resisting arrest. From there he had been taken to a locked section of the psychiatric clinic, out of which he came six weeks later.

"Let's buy a pair of shoes," said Lenz. "I need shoes and you do, too."

It occurred to Walter that he had a hole in one of his socks. In a department store they swiped a pair of socks; then they went into a shoe store and were shown a dozen shoes. Walter could not say which he liked and which he didn't like, he thought they were all equally attractive.

"What kind of shoes do you have in mind?" asked Lenz.

"What kind of shoes do you want?" asked the saleslady. Lenz urged her to wait on another customer.

Walter couldn't manage to describe the shoes he had in mind, neither the color nor the height nor the type of leather.

Lenz asked Walter for his jacket and gave him his coat. Like that, each in an article of clothing of the other, they walked around in socks in the shoe store and watched the customers trying on shoes. Lenz asked Walter which shoes in his opinion would go with the coat he now had on. Walter chose a pair of medium-height boots made of white leather, which somehow gave the impression of being second-hand, with round flecks of leather sewn on the sides like on track shoes. They bought the shoes. Lenz asked for his coat back. Walter asked what he was supposed to do with the shoes without the coat.

"They don't go with the coat, they go with you," said Lenz.

They said goodbye until another day.

On a weekend Lenz had time to finish a letter that he had begun in the factory restroom on one of his first days at work. The constant pressure of the machine had squeezed his body like a wet sponge. The thought of L. excited him so much that he thought his body would explode. He had gone to the restroom several times during work to sit down to release himself among grunts, whistles, and farts from the neighboring cubicles. He was upset for being by himself with his arousal. He would like best to have torn down the partitions that separated him from his neighbors to bring about a collective ejaculation.

"Have I ever made a declaration of love to you? I didn't get to that because of all the back and forth. It's so that I have your aroma in my nose the whole time. Every time a woman passes me, I first have to look closely before I see that you walk very differently. I check every pullover that approaches me to see whether it has the same folds as yours. I'm fed up with it, feel like a nut case, dogmatically hardened. It has already gotten to the point that I don't see anything anymore without making it have some connection with you; I recognize you everywhere, imagine what you would say about this. I only call up men now, so I won't confuse a woman's voice on the telephone with yours. I didn't know how horrible it is to desire someone so much. I'm not talking about fucking; I believe it's your caresses that I'm not strong enough for. If I only knew what makes me so afraid. Maybe it's that in these sensible conversations with my friends I can't find anything that makes me so dependent on you now. After all, no one takes hold of someone without it immediately meaning something else; we never tried that. Recently I got weak in the knees only because a man whom I don't know very well simply put his arm over my shoulder. You know, I'll have to become a lumberjack to be prepared for your touches and afterward to get my feet on solid ground again . . ."

At first he was completely in agreement with the letter. But then it occurred to him that it was serious, that L. really did not want to hear anything from him anymore. Maybe he had described his feelings for the first time, but how was it with L.'s feelings? They weren't mentioned at all in his letter. Now a thousand sentences came to him in which L. made it clear what she expected from him. He read the letter through again and then added it to the other unmailed letters.

The thought that he would not be able to communicate drove him out of his house. It had rained, right into sultryness. The wetness made the houses smaller; the sidewalks moved closer together. One time he saw the face of a passerby with such clarity that tears came into his eyes. Tell me your story, I won't string you up. In the dusk Lenz sat down on the bank of a canal. The bushes cast long shadows into the water, and in the dark, unmoving mirror Lenz saw the lights of streetlamps and houses coming on, one after the other. A barge lay at the wall; it seemed to Lenz that it must be freezing. Several times he tossed stones into the water and then waited until the houses stopped wavering. When he looked up, he could no longer recognize the boundary between roofs and sky. As far as he could see, nothing but immense blocks, above him the pale bell jar of light in the sky, and everything so cold, so stony. He became terribly lonesome, he was alone, he wanted to talk to himself, he couldn't, he scarcely dared to breathe.

He got up quickly and went into a bar nearby. A few customers were sitting in the open on damp garden chairs. Lenz was still too cold even with his coat on; he went inside. There, yellow, smoky light, a juke box, the old songs, the old posters, the old conversations. Lenz saw only hideous faces. At the counter he ordered a double schnapps. Someone next to him insisted on having seen him before.

"If you did," said Lenz, "what would follow from that?"

He turned aside; he didn't want to talk. As a diversion, he watched how the people coming in entered the room. A man came in, both hands in the back pockets of his pants. As though inadvertently he looked around left and right, in the expectation of being called out to by someone. When no one called to him, he walked to the back of the room, looked around more closely at the tables, at which he certainly didn't expect anyone, turned around brusquely, and walked full of scorn out the door. Another man entered the room with a "Hello," which was answered at once by a man at the first table; he smiled promisingly but walked on to call out "Hello" again, directed the question to someone as to whether he had seen Charlie, walked on without waiting for an answer, then turned around and took a seat at the first table. Yet another man entered the room, looking neither to the left or the right, walked straight over to the juke box, pressed two numbers, listened to the first three bars, threw a long glance at the people at the tables, suddenly turned and left the room.

Someone placed a hand on Lenz's shoulder; it was the girl he had recently been with. It was unpleasant for Lenz to find her here; he felt caught out. He looked at her; he couldn't think of her name. But her joy in meeting him was infectious. They sat down together at a table. They drank; Lenz got to talking; suddenly he was telling his story about L. He talked fast, as though he had to catch up with something; gradually he became calmer. He stopped; it was to him as though a splinter was pulled out of his eye:

"She's hiding behind her frailty, behind her vulnerability. When I assailed her because she had some fault to find with all my friends, because with each one she invented other reasons why I shouldn't meet him, she felt sick. I could never criticize her without her punishing me with one or another physical reaction, without her making me into a butcher. Then it was my fault that she almost got run over by a car, that she suddenly could not lift her arm anymore, that her throat was inflamed. When I said once she would rather kill me than let me near her and let on to her weakness, she seduced me to shut me up. And she succeeded, too. And now, while I'm talking about it, I have the feeling of being a traitor again."

Someone had selected a song by Eric Burdon. The song had a strong rhythm and penetrated Lenz's body. For the first time he understood the lyrics, he was surprised that he had never listened, and translated for Marina what he understood:

My Captain says to me
Go on, jump in the water
And the water was cold
And the weather was winter
And then a sailor
Really nice said to me
Best thing is not
To take it so seriously
And I didn't take it so seriously
But the Captain yells Lazybones

Marina told Lenz that she liked him much more this evening than the last time. She had felt herself ambushed.

"Maybe it's like this," said Lenz without answering her. "You love the feeling you have for someone you love just as for the one who produced it. Maybe I suffer more from the loss of this feeling than from the loss of L."

Marina got up to get some cigarettes. At the next table Lenz recognized an acquaintance. He was sitting there with his wife, with whom he had lived for three years in an enduring separation. Right away Lenz greeted him, then the woman got up and left the room without a word. For a moment Lenz had the feeling that it must be his fault. His acquaintance turned deathly pale, looked at Lenz dumfounded, and went after her. After a while he returned alone and ordered a schnapps. Lenz got up and left with Marina. They then stood on the street, leaning against one another, waiting for a taxi.

They parted at the door to her house.

The next morning, in the factory, Lenz felt watched by everyone. He looked down at himself to see whether something was not in order. He found nothing. A woman who passed by his workplace with a colleague, lightly touched his neck with her arm. The two women poked one another with their elbows and laughed; Lenz believed he heard his name. At the other end of the aisle he saw the foreman standing with his hands in the pockets of his white smock. Lenz had the impression that he was continually looking at him; he tried to work faster. A telephone rang on the table at the front by the entrance to the hall. Lenz had to hold himself back from standing up and picking up the receiver. The two women returned with paper cups in their hands; one of the two shot him a mocking look. A young skilled worker whom he had known for a few days poked him in the back with his fist.

"You're working like a world champion," he said in passing.

Lenz was uncertain about whether he should explain himself. Now Lenz saw the foreman again as he put his fat hands on the bare arms of a female worker to give her some direction or other with a smile rich with insinuation.

Lenz felt a new, unfamiliar hate rising in him. He looked up and down the aisle; he saw the arms and legs of the women move as though pulled by invisible threads, over them their stiff, tense faces, then again the foreman, who had turned around and just greeted another white smock. With a watch in his hand the white smock took up a position beside one of the women and timed her. He asked her to stand up and showed her how to perform one movement more quickly. The woman followed his directions; the white smock seemed not to be satisfied yet. The other women acted as though they were not noticing him, but they worked faster. The sounds in the hall now seemed to Lenz to be unendurably loud and violent; he believed he could hear their tempo constantly increase. Out of the scraps of sentences that he caught, he heard only accusations. One woman talked about her chronic tendonitis, another complained about her back pain, a third had experienced a dizzy spell a few days ago at her machine. During the break Lenz participated in the conversations of the women.

He inquired about the increase in the number of pieces over the last months and asked about the corresponding increase in wages. With his questions he forced the women to list the reasons for their back pains and the soreness in their shoulders. When he confronted them again with what they said, it seemed strange to them. The women looked at him curiously, they wanted to know who he was, what he had done before, how long he would be staying. Lenz hesitated. A student who had likewise worked in the factory had in the same situation claimed that he was a watchmaker. He hoped in this way to win the confidence of his colleagues. The result was that his colleagues brought him their broken clocks from home one after the other, and he spent many nights learning the trade of a watchmaker. Lenz replied that he was a student; he was working here to learn about the situation of the workers. They looked at him; what he said made sense to the women: each one should quietly take a look at that. But then when he continued speaking, they listened to him patiently without interrupting him. He had become intense while talking; everything fused seamlessly together; he succeeded in deriving the depressions of the women from one point. He made suggestions about what was to be done; he had forgotten himself completely. It seemed to him that he could do something good, be rid of an unknown guilt. He did not see the glances they gave him.

One afternoon after work Lenz was picked up by Marina. Lenz was glad that he suddenly belonged to those who had someone waiting for them outside. She had bought two bottles of wine. In her car they drove out of the city. They stopped at a bridge and walked down a narrow path that led through bushes along a canal. It was still hot; the air flickered above the water. The smell of stinging nettle, the lush sticky leaves on the bushes, everything seemed to Lenz so exaggerated, so intrusive. He looked around. Behind them a couple of smokestacks trembled in the hot air; on the other bank the watch towers and barbed wire; farther away a few houses that looked uninhabited. He didn't want to go farther.

The girl pulled him into a cornfield; the stalks towered over their heads. She undressed him and made a bed out of his things. When they were lying on the ground, a sort of dizziness overcame Lenz; there was a pricking and stirring under him; the odor of the earth was strange and repulsive to him, and high above him those ridiculous stalks that actually did rustle like a cornfield. He wanted to go back, back to the car, among people, feel asphalt under his feet. He seemed to himself so like a schoolboy. He had the feeling the field glasses in the watch towers were directed at them. Then when she aroused him, he forgot his fear, he became calm. Then she told him about Greece, where she had lived, about the light there; she described the path that led from her house to the sea, the stony landscape. Lenz could listen as forgotten desires were awakened in him. When they were driving back to the city, he would like to have torn up the asphalt. He talked about learning karate.

On another day, on the way home, Lenz noticed a gathering of people in front of the Greek embassy. Someone called to him out of the crowd and pressed a circular in his hand. The demonstration was directed against the dictatorship in Greece and against the deportation of forty Greek workers who had joined the strike because of salary cuts and had been fired on the spot. Lenz mixed with the others and with them pressed against the barbed-wire barricade with which the police had sealed off the embassy. Surrounded by smoke flares, the police stood in front of the barricade and waited for the command to use truncheons.

Someone whispered to Lenz that he should move to a group at the end of the procession and urge others to do likewise. The demonstrators were to storm the nearby Amerikahaus unexpectedly before the police could be there. They formed a group of about sixty people. At a given signal they started running as fast as they could. The sudden movement at the back of the gathering produced a kind of suction, most people turned around and ran with them. Before the police, who were looking bewildered from under their helmets and sweating, understood what was going on, hundreds of demonstrators were running across the empty parking lot to the Amerikahaus. It took a fairly long time before the police decided to run after them or to get into their police van. When Lenz looked back, the sight of the pursuers, running along in their stiff uniforms with truncheons at the ready, reminded him of a hundred meter relay hopelessly fallen behind.

Cobblestones lay along the way, piled carefully into small heaps, which first some people and then more and more picked up running past, and then the first window panes smashed, first two, then three, and then more and more—it was a brief, massive ceremony of a breach of the peace. When the first patrol car turned the corner, not a window pane was whole, and far and near no one was to be seen.

A bit later Lenz met a very young acquaintance who told him with a beaming face that he had for the first time thrown a stone in a demonstration. He described to him exactly how he stood with the stone in his hand in front of the Amerikahaus, first just swung his arm to and fro loosely as though he didn't have a stone, let the stone drop, startled at the sight of a passerby, how then with intense rage—he didn't know whether it was rage at his indecisiveness or at the Americans—picked it up again and fired it at the window pane. Afterward he felt free as never before—he couldn't possibly describe what a feeling that was.

Lenz remembered that a very similar thing had happened to him when he threw his first stone. He then tried to explain to him that the time for this kind of demonstration was past; the demonstrations had to become the expression of a much broader and longer-lasting task, and their methods would change accordingly—it was dependent entirely on the political situation, whether it was politically interesting and useful to conquer his personal fear of applying the use of force.

"Oh, I did it out of anger, and I'm still angry today," said his acquaintance. Lenz felt like a spoilsport; he wondered whether he really had become richer because of his perception or poorer because of the anger.

While shopping Lenz met a writer who had once been his patron. Lenz noticed a kind of sadness in his face that characterizes people whose wishes have all been fulfilled and who now ask in astonishment what they have to accomplish in this world that has become a post-world to them. Lenz accompanied his erstwhile patron on the way home and was at once swept up in a conversation by him. Lenz realized that his patron's arguments had all already been published somewhere.

Had Lenz really come to his senses? The student movement had been important and useful, society owed important impulses to it. But now other social groups had taken over the best initiatives of the students while they still believed the whole world turned around them. It was necessary to recognize this process and take part in it instead of whining about the inevitable losses to which the ideas of the students were exposed on the way to seeping into society. The students were happy with the role of the prophet in the desert; they were afraid of getting their hands dirty with practical work in institutions; they had a self-destructive fear of success.

It bothered Lenz that he did not have an opposing opinion to all the points of his erstwhile patron. Involuntarily Lenz had often nodded. Still, he felt impelled to contradict everything and everyone. After a few unsatisfactory attempts at contradiction, he realized he wasn't so very angry about the statements of his patron, rather about his dignified tone and about the suit he was wearing. To gain some distance in the conversation, Lenz inquired about his companion's work and about his plans. But he wouldn't be moved from his theme, he demanded that Lenz take a position. In doing so he shoved him with his rather extensive belly into a building entrance and did not notice that he interrupted Lenz so often that Lenz couldn't manage to answer him. Lenz tried several times to slip under his arm, with which his erstwhile patron had propped himself against the door frame, but he was able to speak only when a resident asked to get by.

"Didn't you say the same thing before the rebellion of the students even started?" asked Lenz. "I remember that you warned against going astray when no one had yet set out for anyplace at all. While others took to the street and were fighting with the police, you raised your index finger in warning, separated what was right from wrong prudently, increased your printings, and established publishing houses. But it's not the same thing when someone who never picked up a stone instead of a ball-point pen now condemns stone throwing in the same sentences with which someone else describes the discovery that it has become senseless to throw stones. In practice, the same sentences will not have the same meaning, don't you think?"

Fine, they didn't have to argue about that, replied the erstwhile patron. The important thing was the result, what Lenz would do now. He was ready to help him find his way to a practical political activity. Then he sketched what he understood by that. Lenz was too ill informed to be able to follow him in everything. He got stuck on the phrase *mountain of butter.* The European *mountain of butter* had to be leveled. And while his erstwhile patron was already talking about the disappointing behavior of a finance minister, Lenz was still seeing his patron with a spade in front of a gigantic mountain of butter.

Lenz wanted to know in more detail exactly what his erstwhile patron understood by practical political work. But he had an appointment. He invited Lenz to look in sometime, if he needed advice.

On Tuesday evening, as every week, Lenz went to a meeting of a factory group. He was received amicably. He was well liked. The room was full of smoke; he could recognize the faces only indistinctly. A text by Mao Tse-tung was read. Lenz could not concentrate on the text. He hated the men because they weren't women and the women because they weren't L. He always heard the same words: sensory cognition, consciousness, proletariat, strategy. The stately, seamless melody of these sentences took root in his ear; it bothered him that there were no pauses, no new starts, no allusions. All of it seemed to him to be so fetching, so nice; he would have liked best of all to praise the speakers by patting them on the head. He imagined that other groups were meeting at the same time at other places and saying the same sentences in the same tone of voice.

He saw himself jump up, sweep the table bare, drum a strong rhythm on the tabletop, jumping backside-first into the smoke and the face before him. He abandoned this mental image when he realized that there was nothing to say against the text: "You see, in the process of their practical activities people at first see only the appearance of things, their individual sides, and the outer relationships between things . . . That is called the stage of sensory cognition, the stage of feelings and impressions."

He looked at the faces of the individual workers one after the other. He wondered what he might know about them. Where were their wives? He reviewed what he knew about that and concluded that they all were unmarried. Only fat K. was married, who three weeks ago had come back into the group again because his wife had gone on a trip four weeks before. He started over again from the beginning. How long had they been in the factory? It was clear to him that most of them were strangers in town and had worked only for one, at most for two years in the factory. What had they done previous to that, what did they do after work, what kind of plans did they have? L., the apprentice, still lived with his mother and wanted to be an engineer. He would come here only until he had reached his goal because the group rejected his wish for advancement. C., the skilled worker, had at one time tramped through the world for two years with his friend A. He improved his earnings with a small trade in hashish. A. dreamed about buying a farm in Italy. How would he view the group, if he had it? The tall guy, D., was gone because his fiancé, who wanted to be rid of him, had accused him of a minor theft in the factory, whereupon he was thrown out of the factory. M., at the age of thirty, was still living with his mother; no one had asked him up to now why he was never to be seen with any other female. Once over a beer the Italian, G., had told Lenz that on the weekend he always exchanged German marks for East marks on the black market and spent them in East Berlin with Polish female guest workers, who earned some extra money with West Berlin male guest workers. There was nothing special about any of that, but it became special because it was kept separate from work as though it were a crime.

It seemed to Lenz so funny at the moment that all these comrades with their secret wishes, with their difficult and exciting life stories, with their energetic asses wanted to know nothing more of one another than these clean sentences from Mao Tse-tung—that just can't be true, thought Lenz. Didn't they also want just to be together, to exchange their pleasures and problems, to simply stop being alone? Would these needs, which were considered hindrances in their work, not take place behind the backs of the group and hinder work through their suppression? And what about the students? Lenz tried to listen: "In the continuation of social practices, things that elicit feelings and impressions among people in their activities are repeated many times. Then a change in the process of cognition occurs in the human brain and concepts come into being . . . That is the second stage of cognition."

Where did the concepts of the students come from? On the basis of what impressions and feelings had the transformation into concepts in their brain come about? M. once wanted to become a filmmaker and had then given up the continuation of his studies. S. had two tries at studies behind him. K. was lovesick and swore from now on to approach matters of love in a proletarian way. What influences did these and other feelings and impressions have on the students' formation of concepts? "The most ridiculous people in the world are the know-it-alls who, after they have snatched up fragmentary knowledge somewhere, appoint themselves the top-notch authority in the world, which is merely evidence of their boundless conceitedness. Knowledge belongs to science, and in that area even the slightest dishonesty and arrogance is not allowed—the very opposite is certainly required, honesty and modesty." Cool, how clearly the Chinese saint could express himself. He had the right word ready for each one at the right time.

Lenz gave up being annoyed by the text; he was annoyed about the hypnoticlike condition that he was swept up in. He looked at the pants of men and found out on which side their cock lay. He imagined their cocks erect and then the series of changes in their bodies that would have had to take place before they could all sit down and talk again. He began with a counter hypnosis; he heard himself speak: "I am now placing my hand on your brow. You close your eyes. You stop talking. You climb, while I am speaking, onto your chairs, you hold one another by the hand. You begin to rock the chairs. You don't fall down. You begin to rock with closed eyes. You begin to yell while I am talking, rocking with closed eyes. You open your eyes and yell at one another. You yell at one another until you begin to hit out at one another. You hit out at one another with your arms, as hard as you can, without touching one another. You begin to strike one another with your blows. You get tired, stop hitting, begin to speak."

He began to speak. He put forward an objection to the argument that in an economic crisis the consciousness of the masses would grow. He had the feeling he was saying real sentences, he hated the way he was speaking. He was startled by the strange look with which he was regarding everyone. He came to a conclusion; he said, "I can't concentrate on the sentences that are said here. I understand them, I just can't connect them, at least not what is meant by them. For example, in the words 'the complete removal of the darkness in the world,' I get stuck on the word *darkness*.

"I don't know whether this is familiar to you. I remember a dark, foggy night, I think it was New Year's Eve. After an argument with my girl friend I was about to drive home, and in the middle of the darkness we had a blow out. We didn't have a tire jack, and we weren't successful in stopping another car to get the tool to change tires. Finally, after half an hour, we found someone who helped us. The waiting and freezing in the darkness, the searching and walking back and forth until we found someone to help us, made our argument completely unimportant. Afterwards, sitting in the car, we made up and didn't even know anymore what we had been arguing about. And then it occurs to me that I've been alone for three months, that since then I've often walked alone through the streets, and that my mood was pretty dark.

"By this I mean to say that the text releases something in me, but just something that has nothing at all to do with its meaning. Either it's my fault that just now I react merely to provocative words, no matter what text is involved. Or the text is so far away from our immediate experience that we fill it with completely strange and arbitrary experiences, independent from a personal condition. What do all of you think, for example, about this sentence or about other sentences? Can you understand them as they are? Can you imagine using these sentences against opponents or helping friends with them?"

The group was silent. Most of them looked overwrought at the floor. Then a few begin to speak. How would he actually imagine a group task if each person were to begin to publish his personal thoughts as a scholarly text? How could a mutual activity come into being from that!

"I'm not making a suggestion," Lenz replied, "I'd just like to know whether you have the same or similar difficulties at a reading of the text." The question was wrongly put, the work of the group was not determined out of their difficulties but out of their tasks. It was useless to tackle difficulties, if there were no method of solving them. "So I must already know the solution of difficulties before I express them!" Lenz exclaimed. "How then can we ever find the method for their solution?" The discussion was broken off; after two hours the discussion about the chapter read was closed; they sat down to have a beer together. The young skilled worker whom Lenz had bumped into in the factory turned to him: "What you said really doesn't belong here. But it surely belongs somewhere. Come visit me sometime; I think you're really good."

One afternoon Lenz walked through the city's shopping streets. He needed to put on a different pair of pants after work and wanted to buy himself a pair. His bright coat was reflected in the display windows; he saw himself approaching from several directions. He looked at the displays in the windows. He was amazed that every month new cars, fur coats, shoes, TV sets, evening gowns, and suits were still displayed. There were still lounge lizards like those that three years ago climbed out of red sports cars, there were still salesgirls who bought much too expensive shoes at Bally, still James Bond films, still people who waited for the new VW model with the same impatience that he and his friends waited for political news. It seemed to him as though the display windows must have been emptied in the last two years, as though the passersby meanwhile had had to walk past them in the same clothing and with new wishes.

The changes that had taken place in the wares displayed over the last two, three years seemed to him to be ridiculously small, hardly perceptible to the naked eye. He stopped at a VW showroom. He saw that nothing had changed in the essential components of the VW: It still had the same form, four wheels, two doors; it had not become larger or smaller. At the same time, something had changed. He did not understand the significance of the lines that he noticed in the shape of the fenders and the front window.

He watched the passersby who were standing in front of the display window and observing the VWs displayed there as he was. He heard statements that described the new things about the car. Referring to invisible details, the observers commented on the changes in the motor, itself not visible, of the new model. They compared the cubic capacity of the new motor with the cubic capacities of the older motors; they talked about changes and reenforcements in the body, in the ground group and in the undercarriage, about a revolution in the interior ventilation, and they insisted that the car runs and runs and runs. Lenz deduced from their descriptions that great changes must have taken place. He realized that the same changes that had seemed comparatively unimportant to him were perceived by most observers as large and decisive. He wondered what had prevented him all this while from being interested in those changes, and whether conversely the sociatel changes that had been perceived by him and his friends as great and decisive would be looked upon by those observers as unimportant.

He walked on. He became uneasy. He felt shut out. As the streets became more and more shaded, everything seemed to him so unreal, so repugnant. The buildings towered up before him like mountain ranges. A peculiar anxiety seized him; he would like to have run after the sun. He wrapped his arms around himself to warm himself. He clung to all the objects; shapes moved rapidly past; he pressed up to them. Again and again he thought he recognized the gait or the hair of L. He was deceived every time. He started running. It seemed to him suddenly that he was sticking in the city only with his feet, at the most up to his knees; as though he were walking on enormous stilts through the streets and the rest of his body had grown taller than the buildings; he yelled, he sang, he wanted to make himself smaller.

He went to the apartment of the young worker whom he had befriended since he worked in the factory and with the factory group. Wolfgang lived in a shared apartment; his room was furnished in the same manner as most rooms in shared apartments that Lenz knew. On the wall a homemade bookcase with a few blue- and red-backed books, three mattresses shoved together in a corner to make a bed; an unfinished door on wooden sawhorses served as a table in front of the window. Posters on the wall, calling for a demonstration, sprightly young faces looking unfazed into the future under red flags. Wolfgang showed Lenz the stereo that he had bought at a ridiculous discount of 20 percent in the sales shop of the firm where they both worked. He asked whether Lenz would like to hear a song by a black blues singer whom he had just rediscovered. Lenz declined; he didn't feel like it.

He tried to describe to Wolfgang how he had just run through the streets. "You must have time on your hands," said Wolfgang. Lenz felt he hadn't understood him.

"I see what's up with you," said Wolfgang, "except, the way you tell it, they don't see it. The thing is, you'd like to make yourself intelligible to me, and not only in a political way. You'd like to believe that we workers are people, too, whom you can talk to, but you don't believe that yet. In reality you imagine someone like me whom you'd like to be like. Partly, anyway, 'cause you wouldn't like to slog away all your life. You haven't learned to defend yourself vigorously, so I must be big and strong and go right to work with my fist, if I don't like something. You have only your love affairs in your head, so I can't have anything else on my mind but work and exploitation. Since you are always vacillating, I have to be firm and unshakable and have nothing else to do but build barricades. But the feelings and desires that you have, I'm not allowed to have; you keep those for yourself. You're right, I don't have the same feelings that you do, and I'm glad I don't. See here, I want to tell you how things have been going for me lately with you and your friends."

Wolfgang asked Lenz whether he remembered that they had recently gone to see Polanski's *Fearless Vampire Killers.* A few days later Wolfgang's awareness had changed remarkably. He noticed it the first time when he was riding home on the bus after work. The man sitting across from him took a newspaper away from his face to turn the page, and Wolfgang suddenly noticed two tiny vampire fangs protruding a bit over his lower lip. When he turned the page again, Wolfgang took a good look—they had vanished. But right after that, when the man put the paper down to show his ticket, they were back, sharp and conspicuous. Wolfgang was surprised that the conductor noticed nothing, but then he understood why. The conductor, too, had developed little white vampire fangs, which only Wolfgang noticed, however, because he looked so hard.

When he got off the bus, everything was in order again; there was nothing wrong with the teeth of passersby. But when he stepped into the dark entry of his apartment building, they were there again in throngs: At least six or seven fully grown vampires were standing in the corner, avariciously baring their fangs. Wolfgang at once climbed three steps at a time; the vampires panted along behind him. Wolfgang got to his apartment door first, unlocked it and locked it behind him, but when afterward he was lying on his bed in his room, they came grimacing from behind the wardrobe and fell upon him. Wolfgang kept them at bay with furious blows of his fists. He gave one of them, the smallest, such a blow on his teeth that the lower jaw flew off. That seemed to help. Anyway, the vampires beat it and left Wolfgang in peace. For a few days Wolfgang had nothing more to do with them. It had become boring for him to stare with a mistrustful look at every set of teeth that approached him.

But the following Tuesday when he went to the factory group, the circle of vampires had gathered in full force. The largest and most brutal fangs were in the face of the student M., who showed them most uninhibitedly when he addressed the circle. Even in the faces of the girls, who hovered wonderfully tender and pale over the books, as soon as they even opened their mouths, strong, knife-sharp incisors came into view. Only the female student K., whom Wolfgang had known for quite a while and who had brought him into the group, showed him a perfect set of teeth. Lenz's vampire fangs were not too big; he constantly made an effort to hide them. But as soon as he got to talking and quoting, they grew larger and exceeded Wolfgang's worst expectations. Even when Lenz tried again and again to hold his hand in front of his mouth, it did not escape Wolfgang's sober glance that he was just as much a vampire as all the others. Later, drinking beer, the fangs of all the members of the group shrank to a bearable length. But when Wolfgang early in the morning talked with the foreman in the factory, everything started all over again.

Earlier he had given the foreman his frank opinion: If something didn't suit him, he had treated him just like any other colleague one couldn't tolerate. They knew his hackneyed expressions and made fun of them, they looked to see whether as usual he had parted his three small hairs. Now the foreman was no longer Mr. So-and-so but the agent of a hostile class; everything he said and did had a very specific significance that Wolfgang now saw through clearly. Wolfgang no longer talked to the foreman just the way it came out, he reflected on every word; with every sentence he had the voices of the students in his ear who affirmed or warned him.

With growing clarity he saw the two-faced attributes of his colleagues. All are dissatisfied with their work in the factory; they talk about being exploited, but they put up with it. He began to mistrust his colleagues; he began to weigh every word they said. When recently a colleague threw his tools down at the foreman's feet because he had carped at him, he felt real scorn at such a ridiculous act. But the students, too, seemed to him to be unreliable. It was easy for them to talk, they had an answer for everything, but what did they do? They had no relationship to work, and when they did work, then they didn't like doing it, as did Wolfgang, for example, who sometimes really liked his work. The worst thing was that in recent times he also could not really screw right; he constantly tried not to look into his girl friend's face because he saw that she also had vampire teeth.

"Somehow I have the feeling," Wolfgang concluded his tale, "that all of you are sucking the blood out of my bones. And you, Lenz, however harmlessly you sit there, you're a blood sucker, too!"

Lenz asked Wolfgang what he was doing now about the vampires.

"Waiting and drinking tea," replied Wolfgang. "Now I'm not the first to strike a blow when they visit me. I simply lie there peacefully and let myself be torn to pieces. Then they become more and more listless." And what did he intend to do if the vampires wouldn't leave him alone? "You're not the first I've told about this. My colleagues here in the factory have advised me to go to the dentist. And if that doesn't help, then I'm going to the nearest insane asylum, and at the latest in two weeks I'll be back."

Wolfgang then told Lenz that the most voracious of the vampires was a GI whom he had met previously. Wolfgang had grown up in one of the cities occupied by the Americans. As a fourteen-year-old he had been provoked by a Black GI in a bar. He pushed him away with his shoulder, the GI got reinforcements. Under the table his friend slipped him a steel rod that Wolfgang smashed into the GI's face. When the others saw the bloody lacerations on his face, they ran off. Later on he read books by Malcolm X and Eldridge Cleaver. At the time, the GI's face, streaming blood, appeared frequently in his dreams. Before, Wolfgang was never afraid of striking the first blow. Only since he had been forced by the factory group to reflect did he learn to be afraid.

Wolfgang asked Lenz whether he would like to come with him in the evening to *Ten Years After*. Lenz did not want to decide.

"You're taking your quirks too seriously," said Wolfgang. "If you and the others, if all of you, wouldn't talk such rubbish so much, we could get quite a lot done. You've ruined me, and I guess I'll have to punch you in the face before we can really do something together."

On a Saturday evening Lenz went to a party. He knew that it was the kind of party that could actually no longer take place, and yet still did. Immediately on his entrance Lenz was heartily embraced by a poet who could stand him even less than Lenz could stand him. Lenz looked around. Prematurely aged poets, augmented by a few revolutionaries, who wrote poetry furtively, and student functionaries. Otherwise it was the usual. Red velvet curtains at the windows, slightly melancholic to fat faces, the women in beautiful gowns, new on the walls some tasteful political posters. The host greeted every arriving guest as though he were the very one on whose coming he placed sole value.

The Germanist and critic Neidt, whom Lenz had not seen for a long time, came up to him. After they had expressed their surprise to one another at having met in this very place, the critic wanted to know what Lenz was up to. Lenz asked about a new publication that he had just found out about. The critic made a scornful gesture as though he wished to say that he was turning his back once and for all on new publications and everything connected with them. The critic repeated his question.

"I'm running around and looking at the buildings," Lenz replied. "Have you ever noticed that the number of windows of the next-to-best buildings always results in an odd number when added to the number of floors?"

"Fine, fine." He hadn't inquired about Lenz's private life.

"Doesn't it interest you?" asked Lenz. "You used to write poetry. And now you read only Willi Bredel and are quite objective? How was such a rapid development possible?"

The poet talked about childhood diseases overcome. What was Lenz busy with, had he been at the last demonstration? He had come here because he wanted to dance, Lenz replied. The critic took that as an evasion. He had heard that Lenz was working in the factory. Did Lenz think he could change his nature by throwing himself into the arms of workers?

"I'm working more out of curiosity," was Lenz's answer, which caused the critic to remark that he was operating with a very remarkable category, curiosity. Lenz said, "I can follow an idea that I've come upon only if I add to it by observing the feeling that corresponds with it. How do you do that, where do you take your emotions from?"

The critic instantly developed a train of thought according to which it was opportunistic to work in the factory as an intellectual. Lenz did not contradict him. He answered by always precisely amplifying his conclusion, which necessarily followed the argumentation by the critic. In doing so, he paid attention above all to the critic's voice and to his gestures. When he spoke, in each instance he took the tone level and gesture of the preceding sentence and tried to exaggerate them. When the critic's glance swooped past Lenz into the distance at the phrase *working class,* Lenz gestured with his arm in the direction of the critic's glance as though the working class were at that moment running past. If at the word *opportunist* hate flashed in the critic's eyes, Lenz made a fist in affirmation. Finally the two arrived at the point where in a chorus they declared war on *opportunism* and all its varieties. At once Lenz looked around for an object that he could use as an example. Lenz pointed to a wall of books that was filled up to the ceiling with opportunistic writers. He tore a few volumes by Goethe out of the bookcase, demanded that the critic grab an art nouveau vase, and pointed to a picture on the wall that depicted Che Guevara as a suffering Christ. The critic was horrified. The fight against bourgeois ideology had to be led in an organized way; it was not accomplished by such spontaneous actions.

Finally the critic asked why Lenz did not contradict him.

"Because I feel nothing when you speak," Lenz exclaimed, "because I feel nothing when I contradict you. All of you," he said then, not speaking directly to the critic, "have everything that less-privileged people only wish for, even if not actually everything. You have fast cars, big apartments, beautiful wives, as long as they are unfaithful to you. And since you didn't work for these advantages, you rightly have a bad conscience. Full of dismay, you discover that you're completely superfluous. This discovery bothers you so much that you quickly try to seize the actual movement that infringes on your privileges, and make yourselves its leader. Without setting your own image before yourself and your class, without enduring your aspect for even a second and changing yourselves, you fabricate for yourselves an ideal picture of the worker whose most important task is: He should not be the way you are. Since you are bursting with egotism, he must burst with solidarity. Since you begin to feel repulsed by your tender hands, he must have callused fists, best holding a screwdriver in them. Since your theaters are emptying, he is not to want to know anything more at all about culture, even about his own. Since you can't do anything with yourselves, he is supposed to be completely lost without your leadership. If once, as long as you were getting along better, you seized the fruits of society's work for yourselves, now, when you can't do that so easily, you seize the theory of the elimination of exploitation for yourselves. The joke is that the exploited class you dream of now really begins to liberate itself, only it is doing so without regard for your offended ideas about that liberation. Do understand for once that you can best support that movement if you begin the struggle against your own class—you can't lead this movement. You aren't that important."

The critic asked Lenz what he was driving at, what goal he was following. Lenz fell silent; he realized that the reproaches he had uttered against the critic were directed at himself. He wanted to move, to be rid of the rigidity that he again felt in his body; he began to dance. At first he let himself be distracted by the movements of the other dancers. His host danced with an apologetic smile on his lips that at once took back every one of his movements. "I'd rather be judged by my writings," he seemed to want to say to his partner, "dancing is not one of my strong suits." A progressive poet stomped angrily from one leg to the other; for him, the music was a reason not to let himself be shaken out of his rhythm. A student leader executed grand movements that filled the room; he bumped into everybody and each time laughed gaily.

Lenz closed his eyes; he didn't want to resist any longer; he danced with wide, furious movements; everywhere in his body he felt knots and sticks. "You're not dancing fiercely enough," he told his partner because she didn't say it to him. "You're not dancing your hate out. It has to hurt before you can feel your body. Don't hold back. Be uglier, dance more clumsily. You will become beautiful only when you are completely kaput and breathless."

Gradually he became mellower; he let himself be tickled and pushed by the music; his brain did not stay in his head but slid down into his arms and legs. When he stopped, he had a wonderful feeling that begins in the belly and makes the whole body porous—he had become bigger. He looked around. It did not bother him anymore that most of the guests were still standing in the corners and conversing in a monotonous sing-song about revolution and literature. He looked for the critic. He had the desire to dance with him or at least hold him by the arm.

One afternoon Lenz had a date with L. She wanted to meet in a coffee shop where they had often gone together before. Lenz took a seat at a table outside on the street. At the table next to him sat two carefully dressed old gentlemen, one of whom was reading aloud a letter that concerned a legal battle in a matter of an inheritance. Lenz was so restless that he could not manage to read a newspaper. Reluctantly he listened to the text of the letter, which told of a relative described as insane. At an advanced age that relative had come into an inheritance of 40,000 marks and now was frittering the money away through the acquisition of dozens of toy electric trains, roller skates, expensive dolls and the like. The letter was trying to convince the recipient of the letter that the relative in a short time would waste the whole inheritance and should be declared incapacitated.

When Lenz saw L. coming from a distance, it gave him a shock. She actually does look just like I imagine her all the while, she moves that way, too, thought Lenz—I'm not imagining it. He was glad he had a chair under his backside; he knew for sure that his knees would quake, if he had stood up. It was a feeling similar to back when he had seen her for the first time. She was standing at a bus stop and along with Lenz was waiting for a bus. When he looked at her, at first he didn't trust his eyes, and then he felt like he had been hit by a lightning bolt. When he had talked about it later with a friend, they had been amused by it because there was no reasonable explanation for this feeling of recognition. What actually happened then, when it went through you—wasn't that your imagination? But then he had read in a book that the people in Sicily described such an event precisely with that word—they called it *a bolt of lightning,* and when it happened, they all reacted in the same way. It was self-evident that the family and the friends of those involved did everything to bring the two together.

L. took a seat; she pulled a few letters for Lenz from her purse, which had been sent to their mutual address. Lenz looked at the return addresses, as though there were nothing more important at the moment, then he pocketed the letters. They had not seen one another for months, but they behaved like a married couple who had parted only at breakfast. L. had just been to the dentist; the dentist had inquired about Lenz. L. said how hard it had been for her to give an unconstrained answer. Lenz inquired how it had been at the dentist. Holding her mouth open with a finger,

L. showed him the filling she had had put in. When Lenz looked into her mouth, his curiosity about the filled tooth seemed so silly to him that he would like to have bored around in it. L. herself seemed annoyed about their intimacy. She leaned back and asked Lenz why he had called really, had broken their arrangement.

Lenz had laid a few things out in advance. Meanwhile a couple of formulations had occurred to him, which in his opinion would revolutionize their relationship. But now, so close to L., all of that seemed to him to be hollow and contrived. He was seized by a rage because after such a short time his arms and legs seemed as if bound. He wanted to say, it's certainly not because I don't want you—any blind man can see that I stick to you like a barnacle. Every day and every night I have to think of you. I am so unspeakably tired of seeing your body before me. I'm being enslaved, castrated, incapacitated by these thoughts of you. I'm bursting with longing. Why can't you understand that it's not a matter of binding us more strongly with one another, rather of admitting a greater distance between us so that we don't mutually become a single organ through which we perceive the outer world.

He said nothing of the sort. With a matter-of-factness that disgusted him, he suggested that they should see one another more often; he found it absurd to live here in the same city without seeing one another; it would be unavoidable that they made one another into a myth; they ought to try to talk about their work, about their everyday existence, and finally form an—Lenz could think only of a standard expression—emancipated relationship with one another.

"You're talking only about yourself," L. said, "I'm not even present in what you're saying."

That was by no means a new suggestion, he had already made it umpteen times. He could stick it, it wasn't anything for her.

Lenz couldn't think of anything else he could say. He knew only that he was fed up with everything, L.'s obstinacy, his suggestions, the whole hopeless situation. He looked at the new pullover L. was wearing and naturally, once again, at the shameless, high-positioned breasts beneath. It occurred to him that he had not bought a single article of clothing since they had been apart, because he had grown accustomed to L. selecting things for him. She was actually the first to teach him how he could best dress; she knew best what looked good on him. He was incensed that, in contrast to him, she had managed to buy that pullover and who knows what all. He saw her now before him, entering a shop, being shown an expensive French gown, many dresses, standing in front of a mirror; the salespeople behind her in amazement; everything seemed made just for her; there was nothing that didn't look good on her. Then she undressed again, bought the pullover for 12 marks and put it right on, wearing additionally a simple skirt, bought used and hemmed herself. She needed nothing more. She tried on these expensive things only because she enjoyed dressing herself up for a moment.

He was now obsessed by the idea that he would never again be able to buy clothes without L., that he would never have an appetite without her, that his room would remain empty and dead, a waiting room in a train station from which you could only head out. He was unable to suppress the question of where and with whom she had bought the new pullover. For his part, he ought not to sound her out, make it even harder for her; he had finally to realize that for two years they had mutually repressed their needs. Lenz knew what was coming now; they were in part his own words or those of his friends, that splendid formula that put into words all their dependencies. And with its use it was always the same: If he rejected this formula of declaration because he could not fulfill it with his emotions anymore, L. put it up like a wall between them. When she could not stand it, he took it out of the drawer:

A young intellectual falls for a beautiful girl from the folk. He has previously had few social experiences. As the obedient son of his class he has principally taken a theoretical look at life, and then, when he found the political concepts for it, rejected bourgeois life that observes the struggles on a social basis from the safe distance either of possessions or of theory. For the first time he meets a person who has lived through everything directly and practically that in his own mind existed only as wish and idea. His beloved becomes the key to the world for him; he throws his entire need to catch up into this relationship and begins, using it as a spring board, to conquer the world with his senses. On the other hand, his beloved sees in the relationship with the intellectual finally a key for her indistinct experiences and new beginnings. She wants to arrive finally. She looks for protection and assurance, and the intellectual, who through opportune deliberation and judgment avoided the mistakes and errors that she made, must, she believes, be able to give her that. But the intellectual feels threatened by her demands. For the first time he has begun to live and he's supposed to again wall himself up, marry, and have children. He believes that he owes it to his self-awareness to manage his discoveries with his own strength. Now that he has discovered his own taste, he wants to go dancing alone, travel to America alone, alone captivate a strange woman without improving his chances at the start through the general admiration for the beauty of his girl friend. But as soon as he has put such a solitary way into practice, the old anxiety and inability is there again. He recognizes that he has begun to live only through the power of a stranger. The intellectual conceals this experience from himself and his beloved. The hurt with which she reacts to each of his attempts to take an independent step makes it permissible for him to press her into the role of an obstacle. Not his education, his life up to now, but his beloved prevents him from liberating himself from his impediments. He begins anew to tear himself loose and hurts her by reproaching her for that hurt; she reproaches him for his inability to decide in her favor, and so on.

"And that's actually all there is," said L., "you need this freedom to begin with. I need closeness and love to begin with, which you can give me only when you have conquered this feeling of missing something. We've been demanding too much of ourselves with these needs for two years. That means, I see our affair as finally ended. We cannot mutually fulfill our needs; what we do instead is create hang-ups for one another." She didn't want to meet him anymore because at the moment she couldn't stand to see even the tip of his nose.

For Lenz it was as though he had been hit on the head. Is that really everything, he wondered, that I made the impossible attempt to overcome the contradiction between the ways of perception and ways of life of the classes privately through a love story? And, if that's so? How does that insight help me, if it won't let me sleep at night? They talked on a while in a quiet tone. L. told Lenz how she was living, what she was planning. It was incredible to Lenz how little his ideas about what L. was doing without him corresponded to the truth. For a moment it was as though a veil had been lifted from his eyes; these reproaches and nightmares, the idea that L. would not be able to live without him, had little or nothing to do with L. They were feelings that came only from himself, he didn't know where from. He realized that L. had begun to develop for herself the abilities that she had admired in him. When they parted, he was relieved; he knew it wouldn't last long.

A couple of days later, when Lenz met Marina again and walked her home, she took him by the arm, without wasting any questions, and pulled him up the stairs. Lenz didn't particularly want to, but on the other hand he was tired of sleeping alone for months. Then, when they were lying beside one another, he didn't want to stir; each of her touches somehow hurt him. He looked at her, but that didn't improve the way he felt; everything seemed to him to be a betrayal; her breasts were too small for him, her legs too short, her fingers had something fumbling, uncertain, that drove him crazy. To him, it was as though he had a splinter in his throat. He was glad that he got the hiccups. He suggested that they sleep on the floor; the bed was so narrow, he couldn't get used to the new situation very quickly. She became furious. He oughtn't behave like that. He could take a running jump with his little complaints. She was tired of beating the ghosts out of his head. She wouldn't think of scrapping with him like that, he could just sleep on the floor, he belonged there, he didn't want it any differently. Lenz did not contradict her, but then when he was lying on a mattress next to the bed, it was terrible to hear her even breath. She soon went to sleep; Lenz stayed awake until it got light. When the birds began with their choruses, he got up, dressed quietly, wrote a few lines, and left the house.

* * *

After work the next day Lenz went to his friend. B. was sitting at his desk, working at the moment on a translation. They went into the kitchen, sat down at the kitchen table, smoked a cigarette, and waited for the water to boil. B.'s ten-year-old daughter came running into the kitchen to show Lenz a picture story she had just drawn. The story was about two little girls who had gotten lost in the woods and then had fallen into the hands of guerrillas. The girls fell in love with the guerrillas at once and asked whether they could stay with them. They didn't want to return to their parents at the emperor's court because it was much too boring for them there. The guerrillas explained to them that they were still too little to fight with them and wanted to take them right back. B.'s daughter asked Lenz how the story should continue. Lenz thought about it; nothing came to him. He pondered; he felt caught. B. took up the thread and developed a continuation of the story. His daughter left to keep on writing the story.

The water was boiling and B. got up. He filled the teapot with water, poured the contents of the teapot into the sink, with his hand scooped up the old leaves that collected on the sink strainer, threw them into the garbage pail, with the same hand put new tea leaves from the tea canister into the pot, and brewed the tea. Lenz felt uncomfortable that not a word was spoken during this activity. He wanted to say something or other to reduce the importance of the process, but he didn't know what. The quiet purposeful movements of B., the kitchen, in which every object was in its place and had its story, all of that gripped him.

B. asked Lenz what he was doing. Lenz looked at him at a loss—he was getting along fine, he was working in the factory. B. wanted to know what kind of work he was doing in the factory. Lenz explained his work routine sketchily to him. How long and with what goal Lenz wanted to remain, what he wanted to do afterward. They got into a discussion about the political work of the intellectual. After a short time Lenz again felt a hatred for the ready-made phrases that he and B. were using. His replies became more and more impatient, more and more vehement. He suggested they break off the conversation, it was all just talk, it was too strange.

B. invited Lenz to play ludo with him and his daughter. Lenz agreed, and they all three sat down on the floor in the living room. Lenz saw the fields on the game board melting; again and again the rules had to be explained to him. After a while B. asked him what was wrong, why he couldn't concentrate on anything. Lenz explained that he was in a terrible state, everything was going to slip away from him, he had the feeling of having fallen off the world.

Lenz ought to explain himself more clearly.

"For example, today on the bus," Lenz replied. He didn't have the correct change to buy a ticket; the conductor had demanded that he get off. Lenz had turned to the nearest passengers and asked whether they couldn't help him out. In a chorus they had repeated the conductor's demand and shouted: "Get off, get off!"

Why had this small scene struck him so, B. asked.

"Because it is so cold, so unreal!" exclaimed Lenz. "No, that's not what I mean. That's too ridiculous. I mean something else."

Several days ago in a Spanish restaurant he had watched a Flamenco guitarist, who for his part was watched by a German. The German had asked the singer to give him a second guitar and played along with him. The Spaniard had regarded the German's playing with curiosity and also a bit flattered, you could see the pride in his face with which he measured the German's variations on his own playing. The German, on the other hand, had locked his eyes on the Spaniard's hands; in his face an indescribable joy and longing was expressed, so grand and old that it had stung Lenz. At that moment he had felt incredibly poor.

B. asked what Lenz wanted to do now; he was communicating only observations and realizations that left him inactive and helpless.

"It's true," Lenz replied, "I have an evil eye. I see everything as though through a magnifying glass, which shows me only disgusting things. Always torn to and fro between neurotics and theoreticians, looking for passions in some and salvation in the others."

B. badgered him, saying that he had talked with friends from his group; they were annoyed by Lenz's unreliability; he was wasting his life; he ought to stick to one goal, and stuff like that.

"And you with your advice," Lenz exclaimed, agitated, "then tell me what you like, what you love. I don't mean an idea, a view of the future, but something that you have now, anything. Can you tell your wife that she is lovely, if you find her lovely? And when you say that, can you feel it, too? Does your face change when you look for words for your feeling? Can you defend what you find beautiful and put up with the effort that it costs to admit that something you liked doesn't please you anymore? Can you tell your wife what you find abhorrent about her, and can you then feel it while you describe it? Can you tell her that you can't stand the way she smells anymore, without blaming capitalism for that? I know that none of you can. You can only say generally, in concepts, what you hate or love because you're all afraid that something might please you, because you're afraid that then you can't fight on anymore. You can't fight anymore then. Since you always read the objectives of your battle from the lips of your opponents, an abatement never comes, not even when your opponent is beaten. Since you haven't first looked for and discovered new pleasures in order to strike the opponent who denies them to us and the masses, you achieve at most the pleasure that comes from the defeat of your opponent. You don't know what to call what you're fighting for, or you do know it, but you don't have it inside you. Because you're not fighting for your own happiness, you don't defend the happiness of other people. You're not open to attack—because you have nothing to defend—but only to attackers. They can knock you dead, but you're not vulnerable."

B. was out of sorts. Lenz left; he felt miserable.

During the evening Lenz went with his friends to drink a beer. They built towers with beer coasters, then began throwing them at one another. When the beer coasters were lying all over the place, they threw ten-pfennig pieces at one another. One started tossing the coins among the people at the table opposite them. They paid no attention at first, then threw them back. Now even larger coins were thrown at the heads at the other table. Finally someone took a fifty mark bill out of Lenz's wallet, wadded it up, and threw it across. That was too much for Lenz; he became angry, but then he had to laugh. He was amazed that such a thing was simply possible; you just had to do it once. This time the bill did not return. For a long time there was quiet, fragments of a consultation about how they could meet this attack could be heard. At Lenz's table they waited to see whether a smaller, a larger, or no bill at all would fly back. Finally the waiter was called to the opposite table. Wine was ordered for both tables, the others came over, they got acquainted, and parted from one another after several hours.

The next morning—Lenz had again hardly slept; sleeping pills worked like stimulants—Lenz came to a quick decision. He went to the personnel office and without giving an explanation demanded his papers back. He took his guitar to a pawnshop and paid two months' rent in advance. He sent off two telegrams, onc to L., onc to B., in which he informed them of his decision. He arranged a meeting with Dieter, a student from the factory group, to tell him what he was planning.

"After all, it's summer," said Lenz, "and in three weeks you will go on vacation, too."

The group had put together the task this time of traveling together so that their private relationships would keep up with their political steps.

"Task, task, do you all want to do this?" asked Lenz. This time Lenz had the feeling that Dieter found Lenz's behavior not as strange as he pretended. They parted amiably, and because Dieter made no reproaches to him, Lenz suddenly had a bad conscience. He choked it down and went and got his stuff. At the train station he purchased a one-way ticket to Rome. As he was sitting on the train, he was amazed how quickly everything had taken place.

During the first hours of the trip he paid no attention to the landscape that streaked past the window. The names of the cities that the train left behind were of no importance to him. He needed to be aware of as little as possible. He wanted only to ride, ride. The moving images outside the window merged with the much slower images from the factory in which he had worked, the streets through which he had walked, the groups in which he had spoken and listened. The train swept everything away.

In the evening the train approached the Alps. Lenz woke up and looked around in his compartment. The compartment had filled up with new passengers, who looked at Lenz hostilely. As they traveled into the dark mountain range, Lenz was overcome by a senseless fear. He forgot the people around him and stared out the window. Broad expanses spread into the valleys, few trees, nothing but stony strata and jagged peaks and, farther up, the stony ravines. He remembered how as a child he had looked back at evening at the black peaks after a mountain climb with his parents and imagined that he would have to climb again alone as punishment. He held tight to every detail; he tried to distinguish houses and paths between the hills, find any living thing. Sometimes he saw a light, very high on a peak, but then it moved on and he did not know whether it was a house or an airplane. Then he saw only his eyes in the window, staring into the darkness.

Lenz woke up early. At a train platform the name of an Italian city was called out. He kept only the melody of the call in his ear; it pleased him somehow. When the train started up again, Lenz stood in the corridor of the car and let the villages and the landscape whiz past him. In the windows and in the yards, in the narrow streets strung from house to house, wash was hanging out to dry everywhere. On the walls were drawn children's mottoes and political slogans that Lenz understood only when a foreign word was included. The paint of the houses, rusty red and ocher yellow, was flaking off everywhere; the walls shown in so many shades that it seemed to Lenz they had been painted like that intentionally. He liked the bright green window shutters with the arch at the upper end. He did not know himself why window shutters were suddenly so important to him. In the much brighter light the vegetation appeared insistently luxuriant and colorful; the light was like an index finger that pointed expressly at every object. Lenz missed the designations for most of the trees and shrubs. He wanted to be able to say more about them when a German neighbor said to his wife: "Look there, the trees there!" and "Man, are they red!"

Later, after Milan, he walked through a few cars. There were conversations in the corridor everywhere, children running around, sandwiches being unpacked, bottles of red wine passed around. After a time Lenz grew tired of watching; the vitality of the people was too much for him; he sat down again in his compartment.

A look-conversation developed between Lenz and a young woman, whom Lenz could see only in profile because she was sitting right next to him. Just like Lenz she was staring at a traveler who had just boarded, who immediately after boarding went to sleep on his seat. At regular intervals his head slid from the headrest. He looked so remarkably like a pig's head that Lenz was sure that the woman next to him must have thought of the same term at the same time he did, except in Italian: *pig's head.* Whenever his head slid down, they looked somewhere else first, but whenever he had reached the lower part of the headrest again, they simply had to look back, until he sagged and, giving a snort, brought himself back to the starting point. When they had watched him a couple of times, the young woman nodded her head as though to give a sign that the pig's head was about to sag now. Finally they looked one another in the eye, as though each wished to test the other by how they they were looking; they had to laugh.

A young man asked Lenz in Italian whether he was actually the actor So-and-so, whom he resembled almost identically. When Lenz answered in the negative, he asked him whether he at least was the boxer So-and-so, he was certain he had seen him once somewhere. He did not wait for Lenz's answer and told him and the young woman why he was missing four teeth. The young man said that he had been a boxer until the misfortune with the teeth. He demonstrated how he had fought in a deciding round against his opponent, in the course of which he forced Lenz into the role of the opponent. With precise movements, which he designated with various expert labels, which Lenz knew in part from the reference book section on traffic, he demonstrated an exchange of blows that had cost him his teeth. While he executed blows against Lenz that began ferociously but stopped just before they landed, he tried to show Lenz at the same time with which fist he now had to strike which spot. He desisted only when Lenz with a straight right — "la destra, la destra," he yelled, because Lenz tried it first with his left—had touched his lips, at which he uttered a triumphant cry. He then talked to Lenz and the young woman for a long time. Lenz slowly dozed off.

When Lenz stepped out onto the platform in Rome, the impact of the foreign noises and voices was so strong that for a moment he remained standing, dazed. He set his suitcase down beside a telephone that was mounted on a column of the train station hall. More through signs than through words, he informed him that to telephone he needed certain coins, which were to be bought in the tobacco shop. When he had inserted the coins and dialed, the train station hall seemed suddenly much smaller. No one answered.

He put his things into a locker and went out onto the street. He had often heard it, but it amazed him nevertheless that he encountered no difficulties in crossing even the busiest street. The cars drove faster than in Germany, but they also braked quicker. It didn't seem to matter who had the right of way, the pedestrian or the car, you just had to head for the nearest gap; then they made accommodations. Lenz went into a coffee shop and ordered a coffee and a grappa. From a juke box came the Italian version of a song that Lenz knew in English—it was a deep, powerful woman's voice, accompanied by a dilettante rhythm group, with the addition of an organ and violins, a mixture of blues and Puccini. He liked it that the singer made no attempt to mimic the English original.

When he had walked around for half an hour, he came to a rather large square on which hundreds of street dealers were offering their wares. He stopped in front of a chinaware booth. It took him a while until he understood the trick with which the salesman enticed the public. He treated the chinaware as though it were unbreakable. On a glass plate he piled up five cups, tossed one piece into the air and caught it at the last second, then slammed the whole tower on the table so that the spectators thought it would certainly break, slapped three more saucers on top, and while he named his price struck the table so violently with the flat of his hand that the tower of chinaware clinked and wobbled and was bought from him, actually only to keep the chinaware from falling over. Lenz was swept by the stream of buyers from booth to booth; he was grabbed and pulled along everywhere; he was addressed in all languages to get him to make a purchase. Gradually it became irksome to him that he could not simply stand there and look on without being a disappointment to the seller. He took a taxi and rode back to the train station.

Friends in Germany had given him the address of a guest house in the Alban Hills above Rome. A woman about sixty, with an immense bosom and a voice that filled the whole house, showed him his room. She gave Lenz to understand that he could live in the whole house, the kitchen, the living room, and the garden. Lenz put his things in his room and threw himself onto his bed. He looked around. A wooden ceiling, a wide bed that was too wide for someone alone, a narrow chest that his few belongings would still leave empty. Outside on the path he heard the hooves of a mule. The strange sounds impressed on him that he was actually in this room. What was he doing here? How had he come to be here?

He imagined that he would awaken tomorrow alone. He ran out into the wind. The clouds flew dark and dashing like the ghosts within him. He ran down the slope. It seemed to him as though the hills rose and sank; he wanted to touch everything, every bend, every corner, but not running, rather skimming over it in flight; the wind tore at his limbs, nothing could be held on to.

He forced himself to return to the guest house. Then he sat for a long time in the garden, contemplated the balcony with the wooden railing, the empty bottles in the shredded, woven basket, the clay vases filled with ashes, then again the iron supports under the balcony, everything all too obvious, as though under a magnifying glass. He went up to his room. He looked down at the interior courtyard, a jumble of chimneys and balconies; children in underpants were called to supper by fathers wearing undershirts, a torrent of noises, cooking pots, birds, ping-pong balls and, added to that, the sounds of Italian that were called out at every range of loudness from balcony to balcony or toward the interior. Everywhere something was enlarged or extended; every balcony was something like a wrinkle in the face of the family that resided there. He didn't feel alone anymore; he became more at ease.

After a week, German acquaintances arrived, traveling through. Lenz was as happy as a child. Greedily he listened to all the news from Germany; at everything that was reported, he nodded as though he had expected nothing else. He didn't know an answer to the question of how he was getting along. He spoke in a disjointed fashion about the pig's head on the train, his landlady who was married to a policeman and was at the same time a Communist, the small children in the village who were permitted to hit their mothers without being punished. In passing, one of his acquaintances mentioned that he had met L. on the street before his departure. Lenz asked if she had been alone. She had been in the company of a young man whom he didn't know. Lenz talked on for two hours more, but from then on he talked and listened as though in a dream. His thoughts clung tightly to the remark about L. He sought an opportunity to return to it. On what day had his acquaintance met L.? L. had asked him to tell Lenz nothing about the meeting, it now occurred to the acquaintance, she didn't want Lenz to have anything more to do with her. Lenz took this news as an enlightenment. His sick fantasy now reviewed all his mutual friends and acquaintances with the sole purpose of whether they were suitable as a lover for L. As though she had said it yesterday, Lenz had in his ear a remark by L. about the student leader W. She had made fun of his thin lips and laughed about them for a noticeably long time. Lenz was now certain that behind that laughter an incident was hidden. He saw L. before him as she sat down in front of the student leader and with an outrageous exactitude gave him directions about where he should caress her.

Lenz dreamed then at night how in a high building he scanned fifty nameplates for L.'s name. On the second floor he began to ask for L. The residents gave contradictory statements. They sent him to ever higher stories; each one seemed to know and to conceal L. Finally Lenz discovered L. on the lap of a Black, while the student leader W. was carried out with pale lips, mortally weary or really dead.

In the middle of the night Lenz woke up. In the adjacent room he heard a woman screaming. He sat up, he considered whether he should go over there. When he had really become awake, he realized that the woman was screaming in passion. He was relieved; after a while he became impatient. Isn't that going to stop, he thought; do they have to do it right next to my room, where I'm lying alone? Hardly had he fallen asleep again, than it started all over again. He listened more attentively this time. Why am I hearing something only from the woman? he wondered. The next morning, when he was eating breakfast with the others, it was incredible to him how he had gotten worked up by his fantasies. It seemed to him as though the whole time he had been hanging on an invisible band that became more taut, the farther away from L. he traveled.

A few days later Lenz drove down to the sea. He ran across the sand for a long time. The waves, which broke on the beach, splashed further in his mind. The wind was blowing holes in him. Above him the airplanes from the Leonardo da Vinci Airport shot steeply into the sky. The beach was full of cans, plastic sacks, scraps of newspaper, condoms, shoes, bottles—the wind blew the refuse toward him. A dead dog lay on the beach; the waves dragged at its body and moved it, as though it were dying. Lenz went into a trattoria that stood on wooden piles in the sea. At the juke box he picked a few Italian pieces at random. The heavy, festive beat of the songs met with the whistles and thunder of the rising airplanes and the splashing of the waves. The light was dazzlingly bright; his eyes were too narrow to take everything in. With his eyes he traced the shining path that the afternoon sun drew over the sea to the point where it met the sky. Then suddenly it was as though his eyes had taken on a different focal length, and everything—the huts, the cranes on the mole, the children who, black with sand, were looking for mussels in the sea with small nets—stood sharply and clearly before him. A girl standing by the juke box told him which songs he should choose. They started talking. Lenz gathered that she was from Rome and worked in a hospital. They walked along the beach for a while; she snuggled up to him; they did not speak much; he accompanied her to the bus. Then he sat for a long time on one of the white stone piles on the mole on which the fishing boats were moored. With his eyes he followed the thick bend of the strap, which itself was wound from many thick ropes. He followed the soft, tugging movements of the strap, that were created by the steel cable that was tied together by the strap. He followed the movements of the steel cable that transmitted the movements of the boat that pulled on the steel cable and transmitted the up and down of the waves to the cable. He did not remember anything; he did not think for a second beyond the moment. He walked to the bus stop and rode back to Rome. When he got off, he was sick of all the looking and running around.

Lenz felt pretty awful. For hours he sat in a coffee shop in the Roman inner city and stared at the headlines of the newspapers on the kiosk opposite him. Like at an eye exam he put the letters together into words and tried to guess their meaning. When once he found the word POLICIA and BERLINO on the first page and a photograph of a street battle, it flashed through him like an electric shock. He called friends in Berlin at once and inquired about the details. In response to their questions he raved to them about Rome and assured them that he was getting along splendidly. He wrote many letters to L., all of which he tore up again before he finished them. He often went into telephone booths and leafed through the telephone books as though he were about to call someone. He sometimes felt clearly how he was merely organizing everything. He then looked at himself with a stranger's gaze; he kept talking to himself; he treated himself like a sick child.

When in the park of the Villa Borghese a young man spoke to him, because Lenz supposedly resembled someone, he fell into a conversation. The young man claimed to be a film producer who lacked only the leading actor for his next project. When Lenz refused the offer, he suggested Lenz take the role of director. To prove that he meant it seriously. he took a roll of film out of his pocket and held a piece of film up to the light. Lenz saw only black film, but the young man unrolled the film more and more, Lenz would see. He asked if he might accompany Lenz on his stroll. Lenz did not refuse. When the young man indicated with a glance at Lenz's coat that he was cold, Lenz helped him put it on. They reached the Spanish Steps, and Lenz used an appointment as an excuse to get rid of his companion. He held his hand out for his coat, which his companion grasped in astonishment, as though he were about to say that a handshake was not customary in Italy. Lenz now vigorously demanded his coat back, the young man acted as though he didn't understand him and pulled the film roll out of his pocket, as though it were that which Lenz wanted. Lenz grabbed him then by the coat collar and began to unbutton the coat, laughing furiously. With his elbows the young man forced Lenz's arms aside and likewise laughed. He pulled more film out of his pocket and tossed it around Lenz's neck. Some passersby began to notice and asked the young man what was going on. Lenz did not understand the curses with which the young man responded to their questions; he caught only the word *porco* in numerous compounds. In his excitement Lenz was speaking German, while the young man fended off Lenz's unbuttoning hands. Finally, an elderly passerby got involved and pulled Lenz's arms away from his coat so that he held only a button in his hand. The young man fled, still looking back outraged and cursing, in Lenz's coat and with his wallet.

While Lenz was standing there without his coat and his wallet, he suddenly felt cheerful. For the first time he looked more closely at the people approaching him and passing by. Some of them were wearing a summer coat. And each one had a wallet in his pocket, thought Lenz. That seemed remarkable to him now. In a display window Lenz saw a pair of shoes that he liked. He went into the shoe store, had the shoes shown him, took off his old ones, and when he sent the saleslady off for a pair of different shoes, he had already put on the new ones and, leaving behind his old shoes, ran out of the shoe store. He ran around a couple of corners and was glad that the shoes didn't pinch.

In his pants' pocket something still clinked. When he reached inside and pulled out a couple of telephone tokens, he thought of calling an actress who lived in Rome and whom he had met a few years before in Germany. Maybe she could lend him some money. When he had found her number in the telephone book and had dialed it, he was surprised when she answered at once. Lenz listened more to her voice than to what came tumbling out in Italian. He recognized her voice again immediately. Sometimes it was indistinguishable from a male voice; in the same sentence she could switch to the highest soprano. She asked him how long he had been in Rome and why he hadn't called long before. He himself did not know why. Then he became aware that he hadn't thought of calling her because he had been afraid that she didn't want to know anything about him. Pierra then asked him where he was and in elaborate detail described to him the department store in front of which she would wait for him. She had to buy herself a few pairs of stockings anyway.

He remembered that they had once bought stockings in Berlin together. There before his eyes he saw her rather fat legs in the newly purchased net stockings. She really wanted him to bargain down the price; he did not succeed in making it clear to her that such a thing didn't happen in Germany. She insisted that he try, and when he had no success, she was still convinced that he had just not done it right. He remembered that he had been relieved to examine Pierra's comical legs in detail without losing his desire for her. He had been relieved that he did not compare his awareness of a woman's body with a previously formed conception.

When he was standing in front of the department store, he looked at the legs of all the women because he was certain that at the moment he would best recognize Pierra again by her legs. Pierra came with a girl friend and from the distance pointed at Lenz, gesturing as though she couldn't believe that it really could be Lenz. For a second the uncertainty of what changes in him would strike her first struggled in Lenz with the joy of seeing her again. When she moved toward him he suddenly became as stiff as a board; he couldn't move from the spot. Only after she had slung her arms around his neck and whirled him around twice did he feel an enormous joy. Pierra asked Lenz no questions—what he had been doing the last three years, how he had come here, how he was getting along—she just stared at him and immediately told her friend everything possible about Lenz, which he didn't understand. They completed their purchase and parted from her friend.

When they arrived at Pierra's apartment, she tossed her shopping bag onto the bed and pulled Lenz into the kitchen. Her voice and her outward appearance changed. Lenz noticed that she had gotten plumper. The movements of her face had become slower, as though they had met with an obstacle. Pierra pressed Lenz against the wall and patted down his body. He was surprised, he stayed quite still. He had the feeling that she wanted to remember him with her hands. She let him go and now began to ask him questions. Lenz answered reluctantly; he wanted to know whether she found him changed. She replied histrionically that he gave the impression of a warrior who had been drawn into battle and returned from it wounded. Lenz did not want to know what she meant by that; it was irksome to him that he could not hide his true feelings at all.

Pierra realized that he did not want to talk about himself. She made tea; they sat down on the bed. She took his hand and from it read him the answers to the questions she had just asked. It annoyed Lenz that he had to concur with most of her assertions. Where had she learned that? Did she believe in palmistry? That didn't matter, he should just say whether she was right. The simplicity with which Pierra set his life before him, everything traced back to a few precepts that propelled his life, impressed Lenz. Pierra made fun of Lenz's consternation; why, he believed more in palmistry than she did. Lenz wanted to know what experiences she had with it, what evidence of the truth were in it. She explained to him that the left half of the hand expressed the outwardly directed energies of a person, while the right half showed the powers that are at work in the unconscious, that the most important lines are distinct even at birth and at death disappear from the palm of the hand.

She then took his left hand, compared it with his right, made a concerned face, looked at them again, and pushed them between her legs. While doing so, she looked into his face curiously. At first, Lenz was too surprised to react, then he felt a quiet lust; there was a ringing in all his limbs and in his head; he had the desire to sit on the floor beneath her and gradually work up her body. When he was about to push into her, he was startled. She screamed "No, No," and swore at him. But when he stopped, she swore at him for that. This was repeated several times. Finally, he understood that she wanted a struggle with him; he did not avoid it. Later, they lay quietly next to one another; they had no more need to touch one another or to speak to one another.

Old, sunken images surfaced again—the portion of a street through which he had driven with L., the smell of furniture in a room in which he had lived ten years ago, a path in the woods on which he had strolled along as a child, everything in reverse motion as in a film that you play backward. Then curse words occurred to him that he had not used for years; he cursed his father, his teacher, the critic, finally L. for some trifle or other, but with words that made them sink through the floor. So he climbed from curse to curse until he was again with Pierra in the bed.

At night they then sat in the Coliseum and looked across the steps down to the stumps of columns that rose from the bottom of the arena. Pierra explained to him the whispering and laughter that came to them out of the corners and niches of the Coliseum. At night, when the tourists had left, the Coliseum became the meeting place of all the sexual minorities: the gays, the lesbians, the transvestites. Then she told him how, before she became an actress, she had sat in a dark chamber in a cellar and sewed for other people. While she was sewing and sewing, a mountain of wishes towered up in her that she was now leveling as an actress. When Lenz had met her, she was living in accordance with the principle of grabbing and making every wish real as soon as it appeared. She brooked no objections, neither by those from around her nor by those from her conscience. At the time she found it right to sleep with as many men as possible. She did that until it became boring. Afterward she had lived with a woman who managed a factory, but who within her four walls submitted completely to Pierra's wishes and whims. Later, she happened upon a masochist—she didn't know whether she made one of him or whether he was one from the start. Her relationships always came to an end when she had made her partners dependent upon her.

She had been convinced that women were stronger than men, that every real woman tried to destroy the man with whom she lived, and that the struggle to the death began all over again with every new man. Later she realized that she was always on the lookout for a man who managed to make her dependent on him and to suppress her. She was enthused by SS uniforms, by Mao Tse-tung, by de Gaulle. She wanted to be thrown against the wall by a man, made his servant, and become dependent on him, but in reality she always arranged it so that the opposite happened. Finally, she didn't want to start with anyone; she had to puke when she had slept with someone. The human ruins she left behind her began to overwhelm her.

A girl friend introduced her to a lady analyst, and now she submitted with the same decisiveness to the interpretations of the analyst with which she had earlier submitted to men. She was so charmed by her analyst that she tried to convince all her former friends, male and female, to go to her for treatment, which mostly came to naught because of the analyst's appointments schedule. On the analyst's couch it became clear to her that she had played the role of Brunhilde not from strength but out of fear. She had been raised a strict Catholic and fatherless, but her mother had let her participate in her affairs and had put her lovers at her disposal even when she was a young girl. She had learned to consider herself a victim and was now of the opinion that out of vengeance she had taken the role of oppressor, which as a rule men played in regard to their women. She had conquered all the men with whom she had been together up to this point, but now she no longer wanted to be victorious, finally she wanted to be vanquished. She could perhaps live with Lenz, but he was looking for a woman who did not exist, who only haunted his mind.

Lenz did not want to answer. The lewd whispering in the corners, the beam of the floodlights that illuminated the walls of the Coliseum and threw a reflection on Pierra's passionate face threw him into even more confusion. He did not want to go home with her. When they parted, Lenz suggested that the next day they travel to the sea.

The next day they took the train to Ostia. It was a windy day, the clouds hung low in the sky but broke up into irregular masses, now large and black, then again bright and diaphanous; the wind blew them landward at a high speed. Occasionally the sun broke through and cast in rapid change a beam of light on a settlement or on a strip of landscape. Under the low sky the landscape made a flatter impression than usual; everything increased in breadth as in a concave mirror.

For one reason or another the train had to stop on an open stretch. When the brakes squealed and the train came to a halt, Lenz remembered a train halting on an open stretch where it was approached by dive bombers; the people ran across a field to a small woods to take cover there, but someone in the compartment advised Lenz's mother to stay in the train car—the woods was a better target than the train; many dead were already lying around in the woods. They waited until the attack was over; gradually the people came back out of the woods; no one knew whether they were all there; the train went on its way.

Then it occurred to him that he had ridden in trains through the whole war and had remained nowhere longer than half a year. He told Pierra about that; she wanted to know more; he didn't want to discuss it any further.

"Maybe that later I always felt more at home when I was underway than when I stayed somewhere and tried to settle down is really connected with those early trips, that constantly being underway. Now, when the train is stopped, I realize that in situations in which I had to be tied down for a rather long time—signing a two-year lease for an apartment, taking on a job that was to confine me for years—I had a very similar feeling: that it's like a train stopped on an open stretch that must soon continue on its way."

Pierra definitely wanted to introduce him to her analyst; Lenz refused. They did not stay long at the sea.

Friends of Pierra invited the two of them to come along to a party. They stuck Lenz into a suit, the pants legs of which were a bit too short for him. Lenz protested, but they insisted—he couldn't get in without a suit. They were picked up at the Piazza del Popolo. They drove to a house that was in the middle of the city on a small square that was accessible only through a narrow lane. The cramped square, the narrow entrance gate betrayed nothing of the grandeur of the house. You rode in an elevator one story up and were standing in a gigantic salon. The hall would have sufficed to contain the workforce of a medium-sized factory. In its center stood two columns of red marble that obviously supported less the ceiling than the lifestyle of the host. Between the columns at a distance of five meters apart were set two sofas covered with velvet from which guests could make themselves understood only by shouting. When Lenz sat down on one of the sofas with Pierra, the white piece of leg that was visible between the end of his sock and his pants cuff glared at him and at everyone who sat next to him and opposite him. In these surroundings that piece of uncovered leg had the effect of a flash out of a Hitchcock film, a corpse's leg that suddenly emerges from the water. Lenz jumped up.

When he was walking through the salon with Pierra, he was surprised that in all the bits of conversations that he caught as he walked was talk of politics. A pale young man, who Pierra said was a millionaire, was talking about his dissertation on the early writings of Marx. A Swiss-franc millionaire was enlightening a lire billionaire about why he could no longer reconcile his membership in the reform Communist Party of Italy with his political conscience. It seemed to Lenz that the glances and gestures accompanying their remarks suited totally different sentences than those they were saying. When, for example, a lawyer said that the bombs in Milan fit the plans of the government so perfectly that they could have been laid personally by the president, the laugher that followed seemed to Lenz to be excessively loud. He could account for it only if the lawyer were laughing about something entirely different. In the reply of the laywer's conversation partner Lenz again did not understand why she slipped into a tender tone. When the lawyer took her arm with a seductive gesture, Lenz thought he heard flattery. But when he recalled the lawyer's words to mind, they were only a statement about a public prosecutor. Now the lawyer really complimented his partner on her dress. But in doing so, he looked at her scornfully, as though he meant to say, "Don't you see how ridiculous you're making yourself? Hanging such a beautiful dress on your uninspiring frame?"

Always, when Lenz listened to what was being said, he did not understand the gestures that accompanied the words; if he paid attention to the gestures, he did not understand what was being said. The guests seemed to him now like deaf mutes, who accompanied the movements of their mouths reflexively with the much clearer speech of their facial expressions and their hands.

"Why are they just saying things they don't mean at all?" Lenz asked Pierra.

The more Lenz looked around the hall, the more everything seemed of no interest to him, the result of efforts in which these people definitely were not involved. Out of the loudspeakers came the muffled songs of the Rolling Stones. No one was dancing. Lenz saw pictures hanging on the walls in which the suffering and struggles of the working masses were depicted. Pierra mentioned the name of the artist, Guttuso, and estimated the cost of the pictures. They were affordable only to people who shared responsibility for the sufferings depicted there. And the long hair that the men wore was not their own. It had been originated by people who had been scorned as hippies by their present imitators. The clothing and shoes were distinguished from cheaper clothing and shoes mainly by seeming to be used, although they were new. In most cases it was a matter of copies of pieces of clothing that had served as used and work clothes, manufactured out of expensive material. Film directors in stylized sailor jackets greeted authors who waved to them in a uniform of the Red Army or in luxurious blue jeans.

Lenz joined in the conversation between Pierra and a young film actor whose dungarees were the exact reproduction of the work clothes of a gas station attendant. He was saying that he was preparing for the leading role in a film about Che Guevara. Pierra was so enchanted by his tales about the *Diary of Che Guevara* that Lenz was not successful in drawing her away from him onto the balcony. When, on the occasion of the host's birthday, a small fireworks display was set off there, Lenz retired to a corner of the balcony. While the fireworks were shooting into the sky, Lenz simply took a couple of flower pots standing there and, one after the other, let them smash on the car tops below the balcony. The guests, whose eyes were directed to the sky, ascribed the bangs to the rockets and firecrackers and clapped their hands every time. Lenz took Pierra's arm and left the party with her. Pierra just didn't understand why. When he told her the story later, she became furious at Lenz and Lenz at her.

Lenz met Pierra as often as she had time. It was fun for her to take him along everywhere, to show him Rome, to ask him about his impressions. She led him only to places with which she connected a personal experience. When he asked her occasionally about the history of a palazzo or a square that attracted his attention, she referred him to her friends. Lenz would never have thought of such questions by himself. But Pierra's passion to trace her present back to her childhood corresponded somehow with the character of the buildings and squares that for their part constantly put their past on display. Lenz was amazed that the people in this city stuffed full of monuments and ruins seemed to him to be more vital and imaginative than those in the cities with no history that he knew in Germany. A similar feeling bound him to Pierra. Although she related everything that happened to her with some event or other from her past, she seemed to him to live more intensely in the moment than he did himself. Lenz shared this observation with her. He said that for the first time he could imagine that this carefree living together with the past made it easier to adapt to the present.

Their relationship changed. The tension that had come about between them in the first days dissolved into a more siblinglike relationship. Pierra immediately passed on to him the advice she had received from her analyst and in doing so forced him to differentiate himself from her. She worried about him with a kind of remote-controlled care that Lenz put up with. She told him what and how much he should eat, she showed him maps that indicated how he could get to this or that place in the city, she sewed on his buttons, she refused to sleep with him.

The friends with whom she brought him together had likewise to do with theater or film, and when they weren't at the moment being analyzed, they were preparing to be. With what false profundity they could go after the meaning of a chance sentence or gesture soon got on Lenz's nerves. They took nothing literally. When Lenz complained about headaches, they considered it an evasion. They kept questioning him until he admitted that something else was depressing him, but that didn't make his headaches go away. He then ostentatiously took a headache pill. When one got mad about the acrimonious remark of another, they did not take sides with the one or the other, rather asked him first what the remark made him think of. When they talked about a film or about a play, they talked only about the scenes and characters in which they recognized themselves. Whenever they discussed politics, then it was only about individual politicians about whom they formed an image. They were not interested in social processes but felt responsible for their dreams.

Unlike Pierra, who was completely at the mercy of her analyst, this constant return to one's own past in the case of most of her friends seemed to Lenz like a parlor game in which the participants concealed their boredom and lack of interest in their surroundings. Lenz was annoyed that he had told so much about himself in the beginning. The lack of resistance with which each one talked about himself and his problems seemed to him more and more a way of postponing a solution. One, who at every opportunity talked about the harm his parents had done to him, rejected the suggestion that he finally moved away from home as absurd. Later on, Lenz found out that he was living on money from his parents. Another described in great detail his dependence on his wife, which he traced back to a disturbed relationship with his mother. But in his refusal to break off with her, Lenz saw more and more his need to continue the dependency.

Lenz proceeded to confront his conversational partners with events that had absolutely nothing to do with them. Partly out of defiance, partly out of interest, he began to read newspapers systematically and to provoke Pierra's friends with questions about the reasons for the innumerable demonstrations. He explained to Pierra what he was feeling. Her friends, he claimed, moved in a similarly closed world as the political groups he had not been able to endure any longer. Whenever the former traced every conflict, even the most private, back to the contradiction between capital and labor, the latter insisted upon deriving every conflict, even the most social, from the family situation. He didn't know which of the two groups was crazier, only which one he preferred.

Later, B., who was negotiating a book with an Italian publisher, arrived in Rome. Lenz picked him up at the airport. It was annoying to Lenz that, hardly had they said hello, B. asked questions in German that Lenz had almost forgotten: "How are you? What are you up to? Have you gotten ahead with your work?" Lenz had never been able to stand these questions, but now—when he had not heard them for so long—they were doubly annoying. Not only that, you replied to them mechanically, as a rule, without establishing any contact beyond that with your conversational partner. You were forced to take up some event or other without being able to make it clear to yourself or your conversational partner how you even got there. So answers such as "Yes, I'm doing fine, yes, I'm getting ahead" were actually always false, even when they were right. You yourself didn't know what you meant, and naturally, your conversational partner didn't know either. But if you gave a negative answer such as "I feel awful" or "Not a bit, I'm just going backward," the questioner didn't want to know why anyway. Later, when they were sitting in a taxi headed for Rome and B. was commenting on the way Italians drove, they fell into a conversation.

B. stayed only two days. He proposed to Lenz that he drive with him and an Italian student to northern Italy; he had been asked to give a lecture at the university in Trento. The idea of racing in a fairly new big Fiat on the autobahn to northern Italy pleased Lenz. The next morning the three of them were in a car, looking for autobahn signs in the direction of Bologna. B. wanted to know how Lenz had spent his time in Rome. Lenz told him a bit about the people he had met at the party in Rome. It annoyed him again that B. already seemed to know everything that Lenz told him. When Lenz was surprised that so many rich people were in the Communist Party, B. replied that it was clearly because the Communist Party protected their interests. When Lenz described how the people at the party were dressed, B. asked whether Lenz perhaps believed that the bourgeoisie could produce anything like its own culture. It was impossible for Lenz to share any observation that might have in the least way been surprising for B. B. asked why Lenz had gone there anyway; Lenz replied that what B. knew about the bourgeoisie had been known likewise by him, but he had gone anyway and still had been surprised. To annoy B., Lenz quickly invented a few discoveries:

"I discovered that I'm susceptible to the privileges of the bourgeoisie. I am susceptible to the effect of a beautiful dress, but it bothers me that the woman wearing it shows off not only her beauty but also her social position and the associated prerogative of spending three hours daily on putting herself together. I don't have anything against a big house, I'm simply against the people who have it. I like driving a big, fast car through the countryside, but I don't want to belong to those who own it. I'm not indignant about the presence of luxuries, but that they are reserved for people who did not produce these luxuries, and I mean by that not the luxuries but the need for them. But you fight not only against the privilege that the ruling class has regarding these luxuries, but also against the luxuries themselves; you deny that it has anything to do with pleasures at all. Admit that it's nice when you are brought breakfast in bed in the morning; what makes us furious is that the one who brings it doesn't as a rule enjoy the same pleasure himself."

When they passed the toll booth on the autobahn, Lenz wanted to know where the money went. Paolo explained that in Italy most autobahns belonged to private owners. The length of the stretches depended completely on the capital of those private firms. In the northern part of the country, Paolo said, for that reason there was a stretch that for years had not been finished because two competing firms were fighting over the contract. As a rule the large firms limited themselves to getting the contract and putting up the capital, then they let smaller firms compete for contracts to carry things out. In order to increase competition among the small firms, the large firms gave contracts for only one or two kilometers, which the small construction firms carried out with the help of cheap labor from the south. Through this system the large firms had succeeded in taking possession of stretches of 100 and 200 kilometers without themselves buying a single sack of cement. Suddenly it seemed crazy to Lenz that there was a man somewhere in Italy who could drive on this stretch and say: "This belongs to me."

Paolo pointed to the billboards set up along the side of the autobahn. Some of them held only a single letter—because of the speed with which they drove past the letters fixed at ten-meter intervals, they became one word. Paolo was prompted by the name Pirelli to tell Lenz and B. about the struggles that had taken place there during the last three months. At a new company name that appeared at the side of the autobahn, he interrupted himself and began a tale connected with it.

Once they saw a mighty, elephantlike outline of an animal in front of a large complex of buildings. Paolo explained to them that several large consumer concerns had merged to form a new enterprise that they called Mammoth. It concerned a chain of gigantic consumer malls that came into being all over the country outside of cities. Lenz became nervous when Paolo's and B.'s questions and answers were no longer to be stopped, when from Mammoth they started talking about the concerns that belonged to Mammoth, from the concerns to the strategy that they followed with this enterprise, while they finally started talking about similar enterprises in France and Germany, while the visible impulse had long since disappeared behind them.

Lenz enjoyed looking outside and observing everything—in the rhythm of the trip. He did not want to transform what he saw into concepts so quickly, not immediately reach the point where you saw only the essence of the things but no longer their exterior side.

"Oh, just shut your mouth," he exclaimed to Paolo and B. "I just can't understand so much all of a sudden," he said then to B. "Oh, well, of course I can, but I don't have any wish to."

B. wanted to know what he meant by that.

"Sometimes it seems to me now," Lenz replied, "as though I have found the right tempo for my concepts, for the connection of my concepts with my perception. Now, when this landscape is pleasing to me, it occurs to me that formerly I was always able to look at landscapes only with revulsion and anxiety. I liked it best of all when I traveled through on the express train, and the trees or houses flitted by close to the window so that you couldn't retain anything exactly. I never understood how someone, with his hand on his brow, could stare for long minutes at some hill or other or a mountain and say: 'There, today you can see it very clearly.' It seemed to me then as though I wanted to cling tightly to a firm point. But also when I was walking down a street or sitting in a coffee shop, I experienced my surroundings as though they were flying past at 100 kilometers an hour. When I was eating, I ate in a hurry, as though someone were going to take the plate away at once; I never really inhaled the smoke of a cigarette; when I was sitting down, I had the feeling that others were sitting more than I was. I paid attention to details only when they were odd or unusual. If someone had a harelip, I could note his face and his name. I then combined everything that he did or that I heard about him with that feature. If someone was famous, he was just famous. If someone was especially handsome or intelligent, then that was the concept that I associated with him. Actually, I rushed through my surroundings always at an excessive tempo and noticed only those characteristics that in my haste I could seize and hold on to for myself.

"Later, when I learned to think politically, the direction of my perception changed, but nothing changed regarding my haste in taking a detail for a concept. When the workers struggled for higher pay, in my eyes they were already struggling for the abolition of hourly wages. When they used violence against a strike breaker, then they finally endorsed proletarian violence; when they called a union member a traitor, they had grasped the betrayal of the unions. I could take a detail seriously only when I transformed it into a concept, when I could say that this detail meant the same thing as that detail. Here in Italy, where I'm bringing more patience to details, I'm gradually becoming aware of the fear that makes you quickly swallow up what you perceive and change it into concepts."

Paolo pointed to a Motta sign, suggested they eat something at the next rest stop. Five kilometers later, they turned off the autobahn. The two buildings of the rest stop were connected to one another by a bridge across the autobahn, on which there was a restaurant. They found a table by a window. It was fun for Lenz after riding to look out of a quiet window at the landscape they had just driven through. When he looked down at the uninterrupted stream of cars, the same feeling started up that he once had in a swimming pool hall when after swimming he was drinking a coffee and through a glass wall watching the swimmers among which he himself had also just been. It was somehow comical to see himself in the others. Only now was it clear that you had just been swimming, that you had been doing that and nothing else.

"Everywhere, not just on the autobahn," Lenz said to B., "there surely are places where you can watch others doing what you were just doing yourself. What was missing for me the whole time was that someone was watching what I was doing and that I could have watched him. I preferred to go away on a trip because I thought my friends capable only of giving advice but not that they would have been able merely to repeat what they noticed while looking on. They always perceived only a part of me because they perceived only a part of themselves. I simply didn't credit them with the fact that I would get to know myself through them because I didn't recognize in them the feelings and perceptions that drove me through the streets."

Paolo described the city they were driving to. It lay in the Alps; the old people ran around with goiters on their necks; in the good air, for which the city was famous, goiters and churches flourished. During the war the city and the mountains had been a center of the partisan struggle against the fascists; throughout the mountains, weapons still lay concealed. The students were considering now whether they should go and get them. Paolo then developed odd connections between Christianity and Marxism; he seriously asserted that with his weapon in his hand Che Guevara was furthering the work of Jesus Christ. Lenz and B. objected. Then Lenz remembered how in Rome the new streets and buildings were built around the old ruins; in Paolo's statements he recognized the same inclination to use the past instead of rejecting it.

When they were sitting in the car again, Lenz threw his arms around B. from behind and kissed him. Lenz realized how the fright, which he himself had had to overcome, shot through B.'s limbs. He had known B. for many years, but such an intimacy had never taken place. At the most on the way home or at a demonstration they had once locked arms or laid an arm around a shoulder. For the first time Lenz smelled B.'s skin. He didn't like the odor. He did not know whether it was because he had never been conscious of B.'s body physically. B.'s body was as strange to Lenz as the suit of an astronaut. B. must have felt the same way. He did not move, then turned his head and looked at Lenz helplessly.

"I just wanted to try that," said Lenz. "Before, I noticed how you got into the car. You sat down in the seat as though it wasn't there for you. Although, I believe, you're not afraid of riding in a car, you sit there like you're expecting an accident, your hands clasped in your lap. And now, as I say that, it occurs to me that I've often been aware of you like that, sitting there, except there was no form of communication between us that could have made such an observation communicable. We've always taken what we said and did seriously. We never paid attention to whether that was consonant with our movements, our voices. When you are speaking, you seem optimistic. When I see you sitting, you seem somehow resigned. Why shouldn't I take the second as seriously as the first?"

It had become dusk. When Lenz looked out, he saw the trees congeal into a dark mass. It was revolting to him how in the twilight the objects gradually lost their contours; it was still too light to turn on the headlamps and already too dark to make out clearly what was outside. All the objects far away were dark; only the mountain close to him formed a sharp outline. Lenz had the feeling that something was being snatched away from him. He resisted falling back into this blackness where you could deal only with yourself; he didn't want that anymore.

Suddenly B. started speaking. He said that underway minor matters that previously had not seemed important suddenly became important to him. He described one fellow from a group who was so inhibited that he could hardly speak; all the others acted as though they did not notice his inhibitions and paid attention only to what he was saying. In retrospect he found this objectivity brutal. Then B. told about a meeting that, for reasons he did not understand, took place under conspiratorial circumstances. They had parked their cars outside a village so they would not be standing at the meeting place; they had walked half an hour through the rain to meet in the back room of a tavern; they had broken up because it turned out that someone had mentioned the meeting place in writing in a letter to another person and had thus perhaps furnished a tip to the police. B. had never been so afraid in his whole life, because the others had acted so conspicuously afraid of being discovered that it was almost inevitable that someone would notice them. And all the while the whole incident concerned nothing more than getting ready for a demonstration that depended on the broadest possible publicity. To B. this fear of pursuit seemed to be a need to be pursued, so as in that way to excite attention that was not achieved in practical work. Someone had recently given him up for lost because in the middle of the Viet Nam war he had managed to paint his kitchen. B. talked then about the faces, the chanting, the ritual slogans.

To Lenz all of that seemed so far out that he did not want to hear about it. "Meanwhile, it doesn't matter to me whether that can be generalized," he said. "Anyhow, I'm not prepared to suppress the minor matters you speak of in the name of some major matter or so, unless we are forced to. When I tackle something with someone, then I'd damn well like to know whether I can tackle him, too."

In the middle of the night they arrived at Trento. Before he fell asleep, Lenz drove back over the whole stretch again in a doze.

The next morning, after they had gotten acquainted with Paolo's friends, they rode in the cable car 500 meters up over the city. Broad expanses of mountains shrank from a great height into a narrow, long valley; a river meandered through it; beyond it great masses of cliffs again spread downward. No sound, no movement; everything stood quiet and fixed there in the light; the quiet did not make Lenz fearful. The city below—there was a flash of gleaming brightness on many windows and roofs, so that you had to look at them; others lay dull and drear there; cars moved slowly and steadily, pulled by invisible threads. Paolo and his friends pointed at the buildings that dominated the city: the churches, the police station, the townhall, department stores, two factories on the edge of town, and the low apartment buildings.

They pointed out the route the last demonstrations had taken, from the slums through the center of town in front of the townhall. Then the square, now empty, on which 8,000 workers and students had gathered, the streets from which the police had moved forward, the points at which barricades had been erected. They directed the glances of B. and Lenz to the steep slopes outside the city on which farmers grew their crops on small fields without the benefit of technology. They told about a demonstration with which farmers had protested at the high profit margins because of middlemen, told about the banners they carried with them.

Then, farther to the east, a valley that was almost completely hidden by a chain of hills. Lenz saw only specks, skeletons of cottages strewn on the hills, linked together by narrow, winding paths. He learned that a year ago the valley had turned into a volcano; the whole region had been shaken. The valley had been dominated for about a hundred years by a family whose largest enterprise, a textile factory, employed about 5,000 workers. One morning, when new piece rates were announced through posted notices, the hate of the populace for their feudal masters, which had been dammed up for years and decades, erupted. The unions declared a twenty-four-hour general strike that remained without results. The employer replied to a second, spontaneous strike with a lockout of the workers. The workers gathered on the street with their wives and children and, first of all, toppled from its pedestal the bronze statue that the employer had had set up in the center of the village. They forced their way into his department stores and carried off the merchandise. They set fire to his taxis and occupied his factory. The farmers supported them with foodstuffs until the most important demands of the worker families had been met. The valley was named Valle del Agno, which means, The Valley of the Lamb. "The lamb has turned into a lion," the workers wrote on the walls of the textile factory. This motto appeared again a hundredfold on factory walls all over Italy.

Lenz liked all of that. He listened closely, he asked about many things he had not understood. The motionless landscape below him came to life with scenes of the struggles he had just heard about. As he was standing above and looking down, the struggles that he was carrying out in the arena of his soul appeared to him to be unimportant and ridiculous. He felt how the direction of his attention was changing, how his eyes stopped looking inward. He did not want to remain up here, he wanted to be down there, to become again one of those many specks that moved down below.

They rode down; they were expected in a restaurant. Lenz and B. were told what battles the students had waged up to now, how they moiled in the residential districts and in front of the factories, what clashes loomed, according to what principles and to what slogans they were organizing their actions. He was able to make suggestions and ask questions in regard to everything. The theoretical knowledge he had acquired before suddenly seemed to Lenz to be indispensable; he was surprised that they had earlier so often seemed to him to be empty talk.

During the afternoon B. gave his lecture in an assembly hall of the university. He talked about the connection between the struggles in Germany with the freedom movements in the Third World. The curiosity of the listeners was transmitted to Lenz; now, when he sat among the others as a listener, he wondered why he had not yet asked B. about that with the same curiosity. Afterward they were bombarded with questions; they had to tell all they knew; nothing seemed unimportant; they were squeezed out like lemons. Since B. and Lenz did not control the language well enough, everything was interpreted. The pauses that came about between the individual sentences gave Lenz time to consider each sentence beforehand. What he said seemed to him remarkably new and convincing. But when he listened to himself, he had to admit that his sentences became new only through the curiosity of the listeners and that he then said things about which he didn't know he knew.

Later, when they were sitting together eating, someone said to Lenz:

"Everyone wants you to stay here. Why don't you stay for a while?" Lenz had time. But he was a foreigner; he spoke the language too poorly; he didn't know the situation well enough.

"That's all well and good," they interjected, "but why don't you let us decide whether that's a cause for hindrance. Why won't you try it with us, if we want to try it with you? You'll find out in time from us, if we can't use you anymore."

Lenz talked with B. about it. B. advised him to stay. "Why don't you give it a try?" he repeated. "Why do you come up with some sort of imagined duty now, now when you perhaps have an opportunity to perform a political task out of desire that up to this point you felt only as a necessity and compulsion."

The next morning B. took his leave. Lenz promised to write him.

In the mountains it was colder than in Rome. Lenz noted only now that it had become autumn. More and more frequently he was asked in the evening whether he wasn't freezing in his light clothing. Warmer clothing was offered him from every side. From one person he received a coat, from another a pullover—in a short time he was newly clothed and distinguishable from his companions only by his halting speech. He was taken with the candor with which they treated him and one another. He grew accustomed to everyone touching everyone else, when they had a mind to, without there being any kind of innuendo attached.

He took it for granted that they were interested in his doubts and insecurities as much as they were in his standpoints. Since without further ado he could talk to most of them about L., about a dream, about his anxiety; it no longer seemed so important to him to talk about them.

He observed that personal conflicts were often solved on their own without having need of a plan to work them out. A girl who seemed particularly stiff and seldom opened her mouth was constantly involved in wrestling matches all in fun with her acquaintances and was pushed around until she defended herself and protested. Later Lenz found out that she had been raped by her father and raised in a Catholic girls' school. Most of her acquaintances knew nothing about that; but they acted as though they were aiming to have her thrash them soundly in her father's stead. A stutterer who had an unfortunate love of unpronounceable words was often interrupted when he got in a muddle. They did not act as though they didn't notice his stuttering; they were bothered by it, mimicked him until he either got the word out or fell into a rage. All of that occurred without an arrangement, without a plan—it just functioned that way.

Often after the meetings the guitars were brought out and, if none were to be found, a rhythm was beaten with hands on tables and benches, to which all began to dance. Someone turned out the light, in the darkness someone grabbed the microphone and began to moan and groan, then to curse and yell. He was spurred on by shouts out of the darkness; he improvised, half in earnest, half in fun, a confession of the misdeeds he had committed as the obedient son of his parents; he switched to a tongue-lashing of the listeners; he was called names until someone turned on the light and everyone stood there for a moment surprised and uncertain.

Lenz stayed. He wrote no letters and no longer telephoned to Germany. He had no longing to return or to go anywhere. Like a child he learned to speak through mimicry and observation. No one noticed any longer when he asked about a word he didn't understand. He went to meetings and spoke there as though he belonged. Since every day he saw clearly before him the needs of the students and the workers with whom he became acquainted, he had no doubt about the terms with which he expressed them. He again read a lot. He participated in carrying out the work of the students from the university out into parts of the city and the factories; he made enemies. Sometimes, when he looked out of his window at the mountains, he remembered with some unrest a trick that had made an impression on him as a child. With a long staff in his hands, a tightrope walker balanced uphill on a wire cable that was stretched from a building to the church tower.

He felt good when he walked along the few streets in the center of the city. He saw everything and was seen. Every day he was informed by the merest acquaintance of those small changes that in Germany only long-trusted friends noticed about him: how he looked today, that the pullover didn't suit him, what was wrong with him; he seemed this time so unenthusiastic. Every emotion was caught in the act and taken to task; he learned to develop the same attention toward his new friends. He wondered how it was possible that as long as he was by himself in Italy, he walked around with the feeling that he could not make a single woman in the world sure about himself, and as long as he had that feeling, it was so—while now he had the feeling that he could talk any woman he liked into anything, and since he had that feeling, that was right, too. He made an effort to fulfill the expectations that were put on him. He felt clearly that he actually had taken on duties and that the hate at a personal failure was his own hate. Not because he was afraid that the others would upbraid him but because they would have been sad and disappointed.

There was no reason to conceal anything at all from himself. Perhaps that is why he very unexpectedly experienced scenes out of his childhood. Once he was hauled out of bed during the morning to help push a Fiat that wouldn't start. Two of them had to push the car several times until it finally went forward in jerks. The unexpected effort, while he was still half asleep, exhausted him so that he got dizzy and had to sit down on the doorsill. As he was sitting there, the rift came again, so strongly, that it couldn't possibly have come from that strain. Lenz was falling and fell inexorably, back through many years.

When now he looked up with half-closed eyes at the mountains, which stood sharp and cold in the sun, he again saw the mountains among which he had grown up. It was wartime. His ten-year-old friend showed him his mother walking up there on the scree with a man who was not his father. He held the field glasses up to his eyes, described to him what was happening up there so exactly that he thought he could recognize his mother and the stranger. He felt an unbearable anxiety that his mother would leave him with that stranger.

Then in quick sequence he saw other images that were connected to the first. He remembered how as an eight-year-old boy he had prowled with a friend through the woods and villages in the area throughout the night and had come home only in the early hours of morning. One morning, when it was already daylight, his mother had waited for him in her nightdress with a stick. She had beaten him bloody, and the next morning she had driven away to his father, who lived in another city, and had died there. The face of his mother, distorted by rage and hopelessness, had been the last he saw of her. He had taken the news of her death indifferently. Only much later did he feel the rift that it had made in him at the time.

Then he thought of how years later he had run desperately through the woods searching for something or other, for what, he didn't know. He thought about the feeling of triumph he had when at night and late he returned to L. and she came running in fury out of the house. It seemed to him that he had again and again gotten her into situations that hurt her, as though he wanted to prove that being the murderer of his mother didn't matter to him.

At evening, when Lenz told his friends in key words about an experience, it no longer seemed too important to him. They listened to him full of curiosity. What he talked about did not seem odd or bizarre to them, but in his telling everything moved far away. He realized that the experience he described was thus left behind through his describing it.

* * *

Lenz made friends with a worker with whom he had gotten acquainted on one of the first days. He was frequently invited by Roberto for a meal; he accompanied him on his strolls through the city; in the afternoon or on Saturday morning he went shopping with him, went visiting, went to gatherings. Lenz noticed that Roberto's apartment was different in every way from the apartments that Lenz frequented. The furniture was not more expensive, but it was kept meticulously clean—every piece of furniture had its firm place. Lenz noticed that the chair he had set beside a cupboard once weeks before to reach things was still standing next to the cupboard. In the meantime it had occurred neither to him nor to the students with whom he lived to return it to its old place. In Roberto's apartment there was no pile of laundry in the bathroom and no five-day-old dirty dishes in the kitchen. Meals were not improvised, and when Lenz accompanied Roberto's wife shopping, he noticed that Anna, though she mostly shopped as cheaply as possible, sometimes bought a particularly expensive wine or a particularly good cut of meat. It occurred to Lenz that his student friends likewise bought expensive as well as cheap things, but that the alternation was fairly unintentional—they thought of what they wanted to eat at the moment they saw the goods. The cost did not surprise them for they assumed anyway that the grocery stores sold their goods at exorbitant prices.

One evening Anna asked him how everything tasted. Lenz answered with the customary clichés, but suddenly he found this thoughtlessness insulting. It meant that Anna had taxed her imagination for naught. He thought about why he could not say whether her way of preparing meat was more preferable to him than another, why that had seemed to him like a superfluous set phrase. He had given up paying attention to eating because the exaggerated significance that eating had among the bourgeoisie actually represented a disregard for other, more important things. Lenz had a similar experience in his relationship to books. Roberto showed him his favorite books; with each one he asked Lenz if he knew it. If Lenz did not know it, he urged him to take it along, he just had to read it. Lenz admitted that for a rather long time he had read hardly at all, at least, any novels.

Didn't Lenz have any time for it? Lenz replied that earlier he had read too much. How could anyone read too much, Roberto asked; he didn't understand that.

Frequently Lenz went with the two of them when they visited a friend or went to a gathering. At every street corner someone crossed their path whom they greeted; they knew the tobacconist, the waiter, the women who were carrying their shopping bags home; they constantly stopped and exchanged a few words. Regarding each one, they knew which party he was sympathetic to, what he had been doing ten years ago; they made use of every opportunity to exchange opinions. Lenz asked Roberto whether the people knew he was a Communist and that the state was engaged in several suits against him because of the instigation of a railroad blockade, of resistance to state authority, of being the ringleader at the occupation of a factory.

"Of course they know it," Roberto answered. "Everything was in the paper. But I grew up here; everyone knows me; I supported my colleagues even before these actions, and they know that I'm one of them. Even if many are not now in agreement with my views and with much that I've done, they tell themselves that I must have had my reasons. Someone you've known for so long can't have gone crazy from one day to the next."

At the workers' gatherings there was talk mostly about the daily events in the factory. Lenz was surprised at the amount of anger and recklessness with which the workers again and again criticized the decisions of the unions without using the term propagandized by the students, "the long arm of the employer" and such. Lenz asked his friend how he could reconcile these attacks with his role as the local functionary of the Communist union.

"Naturally, I'll stay in the union as long as I can," he said. "Why should I do you, Lenz, and all of you, the favor of voluntarily quitting the field? Naturally, I have more problems here than all of you do in your groups, but I also have more influence. We can use you: You can explain things to us that we don't understand; you have shown us forms of struggle that we had almost forgotten; you can help us write leaflets that would not come into being without your help. But how long are you going to stick with it? Your enthusiasm for our cause—where does it come from? You don't have the same problems that we do because you don't have to do the same work we do. As long as we follow your ideas, everything will be fine. But what will happen when it is of no more use to us to follow your ideas, if we must disappoint you? When we are pleased about a success that seems too insignificant to you? We know our interests because we have to defend them daily. But your interests—do we know them? Do you know them? What are you suffering from? What do you want for yourselves? We'll take note of that, but as long as I don't know, why should I trust you more than a union functionary who, I at least know, wants to keep his job? I like all of you, because you're brave. But you're hiding something."

One morning when Lenz was sitting in his coffee shop drinking a cappuccino, he wanted to ask the waiter for a coffee spoon that had been forgotten. He couldn't think of the word for *spoon.* He had already stood up to run after the waiter. But then he remembered that he had already asked what the right word was many times and each time had forgotten it. The idea of having to make the waiter understand with gestures what he wanted was so repulsive to him at this moment that he returned to his place and had to gulp down the unsugared cappuccino morosely. He could speak with fair fluency. In the ten hours daily that he was together with the students, he had learned to say the most difficult things in Italian. Without hesitating he could talk about alienation, double exploitation, sexual repression, but he still didn't know the word for *coffee spoon.* Suddenly it seemed to him that he was sitting beside himself, watching himself sitting there. His brown corduroy pants belonged to the stutterer Massimo, he had his coat from a Marxist-Leninist with whom he got into arguments more and more frequently; a worker friend had taken the pullover one evening out of his own closet.

"What are you doing with all these strange things?" Lenz asked the one sitting at the table drinking unsugared cappucino.

* * *

At noon, on the way to a gathering, Lenz was addressed by two men wearing suits. Was his name Lenz? When Lenz started to ask the men what their intentions were, they locked arms with him on the left and the right. More flying than walking he landed in a car on a side street. It concerned his residence permit; the matter would be settled immediately. On the drive to the police station the two men asked Lenz questions. They knew who his friends were, at which gatherings he had been, what viewpoints he had expressed. At the police station they let him wait for a few hours. Then another man came and laid a document with a seal before Lenz. Lenz was not permitted to pick up his belongings or to telephone. He was taken to the border. On the trip no one spoke to him; he also did not attempt to speak. They drove into the mountains. Lenz saw a train traveling down to Italy. During the rapid drive with its the many curves, Lenz got sick. He had to get out and throw up. Afterward his head was suddenly quite clear. He looked out quietly; the mountains were all the same to him, no memory, not a trace of anxiety.

A few days later he walked with B. through the old streets. What he saw made him impatient. The same people were sitting in the same coffee shops, still the same songs from the boutiques, the same headlines in the same newspapers, the publisher's skyscraper was still standing. And what else? The factory group was still fiddling around on the same text, Lenz found out. Dieter, the student, still had the same beaming look; students were still founding new parties.

"How and why should all that have changed?" asked B. "Maybe because you weren't there?"

Lenz realized later that he had been too quick. Dieter, the student, had grown tired of repairing clocks at night, had quit his job and was preparing for his exams. Was that something new? No matter. From one day to the next Wolfgang had packed his suitcases and given up the room in his shared apartment without a word of explanation. It was fun to furnish his own apartment. The couple who had lived apart for three years had separated. New groups had come into being, which also sometimes listened to music together. Lenz was envious by now that these changes had taken place without him. B. told Lenz that he had to move out of his home. He had no desire to explain that to Lenz; anyway he wanted to go on a trip, far away, preferably to Latin America. What did Lenz want to do now?

"Stay here," Lenz replied.

Translated by A. Leslie Willson

A RUNAWAY HORSE

Martin Walser

Translator's Acknowledgment

William Vennewitz, my husband, has given me unstinting assistance and advice throughout this translation, and I am deeply grateful to him.

Leila Vennewitz

For Franziska

From time to time one comes across novellas in which certain persons expound opposing philosophies. A preferred ending is for one of these persons to convince the other. Thus, instead of the philosophy having to speak for itself, the reader is favored with the historical result that the other person has been convinced. I regard it as a blessing that in this respect these papers afford no enlightenment.

—Sören Kierkegaard, *Either/Or*

1. SUDDENLY SABINA PUSHED her way out of the tide of tourists surging along the promenade and headed for a little table that was still unoccupied. Helmut had the feeling that the chairs in this café were too small for him, but Sabina had already sat down. Nor would he ever have chosen one in the front row. Sitting that close to the crowds moving past in both directions, you really couldn't see a thing. He would have chosen a spot as close to the building as possible. Otto had also sat down. At Sabina's feet. But he was still gazing up at Helmut as if to say that, as long as Helmut was not yet seated, he regarded his own posture as temporary.

Sabina promptly ordered coffee, crossed one leg over the other, and regarded the sluggish back-and-forth on the lakeside promenade with an expression of enjoyment intended solely for Helmut's benefit. He switched his gaze back to the people strolling too closely past. There was little enough to see. But of that little, too much. He felt a kind of hopeless craving for those brightly, lightly clad, suntanned figures. They looked more attractive here than back home in Stuttgart. He did not feel the same way about himself. He felt ridiculous in light-colored pants. When he wasn't wearing a jacket, the most noticeable thing about him was probably his stomach. After a week he wouldn't mind. But on the third day he still did, just as he minded his hideously sunburned skin. Another week, and Sabina and he would be tanned too. As for Sabina, all the sun had achieved so far was to puff up every little wrinkle, every tiny flaw in her skin. Sabina looked grotesque. Particularly now, as she gazed delightedly at the passersby. He placed a hand on her forearm. Why on earth did they have to sit here looking at this thrusting tangle of arms and legs and breasts? What's more, in their vacation apartment it would be much cooler by now than on this concrete, treeless promenade. And every second passerby wafted such an air of adventure under one's nose that watching them turned into swiftly mounting unhappiness. They were all younger. How pleasant it would be now behind the straight iron bars of their vacation apartment windows. They had been here three days, and for three evenings he had had to follow Sabina into town. Each time to this promenade. She found people-watching interesting. So it was. But intolerable.

He had planned to read Kierkegaard's diaries and had brought along all five volumes. And may the Lord have mercy on you, Sabina, if he gets through only four. He hadn't the faintest idea what Kierkegaard had entered in his diaries. Unimaginable that Kierkegaard could have jotted down anything private. He yearned to get closer to Kierkegaard. Perhaps he was only yearning so that he could be disappointed. He visualized those many hours of daily disappointment while reading Kierkegaard's diaries as something enjoyable. Like a rainy day on vacation. If these diaries permitted no proximity, as he feared (and still more hoped), his yearning to get closer to this man would increase. A diary devoid of anything private: what could be more fascinating? He must tell Sabina that, starting tomorrow, he would be spending all his evenings in the apartment. He could have trembled with indignation! Sitting here on this inadequate chair, staring at people, while in the apartment he . . .

He did not want to take Kierkegaard down to the lake. That was something he had done as a boy of fifteen. He had read *Zarathustra* while lying on his stomach. Snob that he was, he had read the French translation. *Ainsi parlait Zarathustra.*

Sabina's enjoyment of the passing throng had meanwhile produced a smile that remained fixed. He felt embarrassed for Sabina's smile. He touched her arm. They should probably be conversing. An aging couple sitting mutely on café chairs and observing such a lively scene is an odd sight. Or a pathetic one. Especially when the woman is still wearing that long-defunct smile. Helmut did not like people around them to have ideas about himself and Sabina that were accurate. Never mind what people thought about them both as long as it was wrong. To succeed in promoting mistaken conclusions always made him feel good. *Incognito:* that was his dearest image. In Stuttgart he had to accept the fact that knowledge about him was increasing among neighbors and at school—among his fellow teachers as well as his students. The nickname "Kiwi" had stuck to him. This showed him that he had been perceived, unmasked, and tagged with almost inimitable accuracy. Whenever, in school or in his neighborhood, he saw evidence of being recognized for what he was, of familiarity with attributes to which he had never admitted, he wanted to escape. To run away, away, away. They made use of a knowledge about him whose accuracy he had not conceded. Made use of it to deal with him. To subordinate him. To make him perform. They knew how to manipulate him. And the more they knew how to manipulate him, the greater became his longing to be once again unrecognized. As long as someone knew nothing about him, all things were possible. Unfortunately he had not always fully realized that, which was why he had not prevented those familiarities. Now all that was left to him was escape. Once or twice a year. His vacation, in fact. On vacation he would try out faces and manners that seemed to him appropriate for shielding his true person from the eyes of the world. To be inaccessible, that became his dream. And he found it difficult not to allow the slender, pointed, steep-sided rocky fortress to become a permanent image. A kind of super-Neuschwanstein seemed to be burning itself into his imagination. And forests. Always he saw forests. Saw himself trotting through forests. Without moving he would trot along, penetrating farther and farther into the forest which, fortunately, never ended. Forests without end, that must be perfection.

Had he in fact really wanted to become a teacher? Does anyone really want to become anything? Might this longing to remain unrecognized harbor the wish to be younger? On taking up his first post he had published a short paragraph in the school newspaper that he still knew by heart. When he said the lines over to himself, he grinned as if he had to listen to a joke that offended his sense of decency:

A Teacher's Enthusiasm

I refer to a circumscribed subject which the teacher does not fully master but which he presents with the utmost vigor. The students will be better informed on the subject itself from other quarters. But in listening to the persistent words of this teacher they have learned something of which they were not aware. His absurdity is a lesson that will last them a lifetime. They will look back at it reverently. The deeper the teacher fades into the past, the more exalted will the students' reverence become.

Probably he was grinning because of the scruples that prevented him from simply suppressing such thoughts.

How pleasant it was to arrive at the Zürns' house, where for the past eleven years they had occupied the vacation apartment for four weeks; to be aware of automatically producing the role that one acted here.

His behavior toward Mrs. Zürn had taken shape during their first stay eleven years ago and could subsequently be deemed fixed. She regarded him as cheerful, talkative, in need of a rest, fond of flowers, devoted to animals, crazy about children, with a heart of gold. . . .

He had not invented the vacation role that Mrs. Zürn expected of him. All he had done was adjust his behavior to accord with his notion of what Mrs. Zürn liked best. The result had agreeably little to do with him. True, the smile that Mrs. Zürn produced as soon as he and Sabina appeared might also have nothing to do with her. So much the better. In eleven years her husband had not had a single real conversation with him. With Sabina, yes. He and this Dr. Zürn continued to pass each other as two mysteries of equal status. He had already told Sabina that he found this Dr. Zürn more likable than anyone else. Didn't they even resemble each other? Round shoulders, round stomach. And heavyset. In the slightly exaggerated courtesy with which they were treated by the Zürns, Helmut perceived the degree of reserve that was most agreeable to him. He did not wish to know what kind of a doctor Dr. Zürn was, or why the Zürns were still renting out an apartment in their beautiful lakeside home, any more than the Zürns wished to know from them why in eleven years no other vacation spot had suggested itself to them. The most splendid thing about this vacation relationship was its annually increasing but totally detached familiarity. They had never progressed beyond the basis that eleven years ago both the Zürns and he had owned a young spaniel. Now the Zürns as well as they themselves owned an old spaniel. In spite of all this, he could think of no one with whom he felt more at ease than Dr. and Mrs. Zürn. Toward their four daughters, on the other hand, he maintained the same reserve as toward the rest of humanity. Oh, if only they could be out there now at the Zürns'!

Sabina said: "You're not getting impatient, are you?" She was not looking at him as she spoke. Anyone watching her from a distance would have deduced from her expression that she had said to her husband: Sitting here with you is just fabulous. He said: "Impatient? Whatever makes you think that?" She said: "Are you hungry?" "Hungry," he said in a solemn, melodramatic tone. "Shall we go?" she asked. "Back to the apartment," he said. "No, to have supper somewhere," she said. "Are you hungry?" he asked. "We shouldn't have eaten all that cake after lunch," she said. "You baked it," he said. "I know," she said guiltily. "If only you wouldn't make such good cakes," he said gloomily.

There's no salvation anyway, he thought. He had no idea why he thought it. Save mankind, he told himself. Go ahead and save it. Maybe Sabina can enjoy this people-watching. He didn't think so. She would have to be quite different from him. But she isn't. They have affected each other. They now have an uncanny resemblance to each other. Just look at her smile. Probably, without being aware of it, you are at this moment wearing exactly the same precipitous smile. Anyone seeing you like this is bound to take you for twins. And just then Sabina said: "I think we both already have spaniel faces." This happened over and over again: She would make a remark that was like an answer to what he happened at that very moment to be thinking. On this occasion it annoyed him. Shut up, he thought, and immediately felt acutely embarrassed at having been so harsh with Sabina in his thoughts. "Don't fight so hard," Sabina said, placing her hand on his. He withdrew his hand and stroked Otto, saying: "He's insulted, and no wonder, because you said we resembled him, whereas you're the only one who resembles him, I don't at all." "Separatist," she said. "Are you having a good time here?" he asked. "I could watch people forever," she said. "I couldn't," he said. "Too bad," she said. "I'm leaving now," he said furiously. "Just one more minute," she said. "By all means," he said, and looked at his watch.

2. SUDDENLY A SLIGHT, trim young man was standing by their table. Wearing blue jeans. A blue shirt, open down to his rawhide belt, which was decorated with branded symbols. And beside him a girl divided into two distinct halves by the seam of her jeans. Just as she, wherever one looked, was all soft and round, he was all vertical, athletic, without an ounce of spare flesh. On his deeply tanned chest grew only a few golden hairs, but from his head sprang a blazing blond mop. Probably one of his former students, thought Helmut. Unfortunately it happens all the time, former students coming up and speaking to you. And more often than not it's the ones who did their utmost to make your job as a teacher unbearable. The very ones who used to make your life thoroughly miserable now suddenly stand there in front of you, grinning, holding out their hands, introducing some wild female or some stunning girl like this one; maybe even a few merrily shrieking kids who paw you with sticky fingers; then they proceed to rattle off their fantastic life stories and confess their remorse, insisting that it took them years to realize what a *super* teacher you had been . . . These sentimental gushings from his former tormentors aroused only revulsion and disgust in him. While they were talking, he would keep his eyes fixed on the toes of their shoes or their feet. Just as he did in school. Hence the nickname "Kiwi." It must have been the girls who had induced this posture of head and body in him.

With their pitiless blouses and pants. On one occasion his power of dissimulation had deserted him: he had reached out; fortunately the girl in question had regarded it as inadvertent.

No, the man in blue with the blaze of golden hair, with such white eyeballs and such white teeth and his bare feet and beautiful pristine toes, was no student, he was Klaus Buch. And Klaus Buch refused to believe that his classmate and boyhood pal and fellow student Helmut did not recognize him. Helmut could merely reiterate his apologies. His memory for faces and names was professionally exhausted, he claimed; he had had to remember far too many faces and names. Klaus Buch—he lied his way along—of course, now both the name and the face began to seem familiar. And so that's Sabina, Helmut's wife. And this is Helene, known as Hella, Klaus's wife. As he shook hands with Hella, he sensed that Klaus expected a compliment. This woman was like a trophy. At least Helmut should now have told his former friend Klaus how puzzled he, Helmut, was because Klaus looked more like a student of Helmut's. Although now forced grudgingly to admit having had a friend whose name was Klaus Buch and who had looked like the young man confronting him, he was totally unable to relate this person to the Klaus Buch who was gradually surfacing in his memory, simply because by now *his* Klaus Buch must also be forty-six, whereas the man confronting him must surely be closer to twenty-six. Like his girl. Above all *because* of his girl. Helmut said nothing of all this. No compliments. That'll get you. He looked down at their feet. Her toes, too, lay straight and snugly side by side. The two were talking away. Still talking, they sat down. Seated, they went on talking. Helmut thought of Kierkegaard's diaries. Sabina supplied all the information required by Hella's and Klaus's nonstop talking. Helmut nodded. Suddenly Klaus Buch jumped up with a shriek and waved one hand about as if it had been burned or pierced by a bullet. Helmut and Sabina were baffled. Fortunately Helene Buch laughed. After regaining control of himself, Klaus Buch looked carefully under the table. "Is that animal yours?" he asked. "But he has never yet bitten anyone," said Sabina. Hella said: "With his paranoia about dogs, the slightest touch is enough to set off a trauma." Sabina said: "Down, Otto!" She apologized profusely to Klaus Buch and promised to keep an eye on Otto.

Well, would you believe it, for three years they've also been coming here for their vacation. And staying out at Maurach. "That's less than a mile from where we are," said Sabina. They, Sabina and Helmut, had been staying out that way for the past eleven years. They, Hella and Klaus, were fed up with the Mediterranean. What a joke, for three years they had been spending their vacations side by side and had never bumped into each other. Well, if that isn't a joke, Helmut! Say, Helmut, what do you say to that? Sure, he also thinks it's a joke. Hella and Klaus go sailing a lot. Sabina and Helmut prefer to laze around by the water, or just sit around. It sounded as if she were complaining to Klaus Buch about Helmut. Helmut nodded. He knew Sabina wasn't really complaining. It happened to suit her to pretend that she was. Perhaps it was a kind of compliment directed at Klaus Buch. She became all enthusiastic about the enthusiasm that this meeting had aroused in Klaus Buch. That he should be so pleased to have met her husband again apparently made her feel good. She looked at Klaus Buch in a kind of bliss. As if she had been waiting for him for a long time and was now hanging on his every word. This Klaus Buch couldn't stop enthusing about his boyhood friend Helmut. Had read *Zarathustra* at fourteen. Way ahead of all of them. Puberty with a crown of thorns. A sort of ingrown single-mindedness. From the very beginning. Right? Klaus Buch phrased his sentences in such a way that, in agreeing or disagreeing, one merely agreed or disagreed with his phrasing, not with the content. Helmut had always been the prophet in suspenders, hadn't he! Saint Frantic in person! Simply inflamed. Barefoot and inflamed, that's the only way he knew his Helmut. Quite often the inflammation had switched from the mental to the physical. Once a month, for four or five days, all one could do was look up at the windows of the room where—and behind horrible russet drapes at that—Helmut was letting his inflammation burn itself out. Helmut interrupted him. He wanted to get away from here. By this time other people must be listening in. Besides, he felt that Klaus Buch's wife must be bored listening to these phrases that didn't in any way concern her. But he wasn't going to let them escape, said Klaus Buch. He herewith invited the Halms to dinner and wasn't going to listen to any kind of refusal.

This fellow really does remember my name. After about . . . Helmut stood up and as casually as possible asked when they had last met. "You don't remember?" cried Klaus Buch. He refused to believe it. It was exactly twenty-three years, almost to the day. He, Klaus Buch, had then left Tübingen after getting himself that post at Edinburgh. After the farewell dinner Helmut had insisted—remember?—that Klaus take a dip in the fountain on the market square. Accustomed to doing whatever Helmut said, he did as he was told. Surely Helmut couldn't have forgotten that? Helmut pretended to recollect every detail of all that Klaus Buch was scooping up with such largesse as if out of a puppeteer's box. But he remembered nothing. If the fellow hadn't mentioned *Zarathustra* and the frequent attacks of tonsillitis, it might have been a case of mistaken identity. Even the russet drapes seemed stagy. Had they had russet drapes at home? And what do horrible drapes look like? On no account must he let on what a total stranger this Klaus Buch seemed to him. True, in the darkest corner of his memory something was nibbling away that might be the name of this person. And this blondness, this nimble, trim elegance, this laugh that seemed to ring out for the benefit of his teeth . . . that might have been. That jutting jaw, those perfect teeth and almost obscenely mobile lips, they might have been there in his youth. But then again they might not. On the other hand, the fellow knew so much about mutual friends that Helmut recognized that a mistake was out of the question.

Perhaps Helmut had erased this Klaus Buch from his memory. Hadn't he at one time envied someone who had obtained a lectureship at Edinburgh? He believed he had. And there had been a young Klaus who seemed to have everything. So this was the fellow. That house with windows as tall as church windows, with stained glass, that had been their house; behind dark trees; somber. He had never been inside. He had been afraid. Only once, when he knew they were all away at the North Sea, had he climbed over the wall and, from behind the bushes, studied the garden and that tall house. Didn't it have a bay window that with the aid of a separate pointed roof seemed to be trying to turn into a turret? Suddenly he had had to bolt. In terror.

"Didn't you have a bike with balloon tires?" Helmut asked. "Ri-ight!" cried Klaus Buch. "At last! Jesus, I was beginning to wonder whether you didn't want to know me!"

Klaus said he would take them to the Hecht for dinner. "With the greatest of pleasure," said Helmut

3. IT BEGAN TO DAWN on Helmut that by this time Klaus Buch had run out of witnesses for certain cherished years of his life. And these were the very years he apparently wished to preserve intact. In order to revive the past, he needed a partner who, at least by nods and looks, would confirm that it had been thus and so. Without this partner he would be quite unable to talk about those days. Helmut realized that it was a case of the war-buddy syndrome. Personally, he lacked this fanatical desire to resurrect bygone days. Every memory of the past depressed him. He felt a kind of loathing when he considered how much past history had already accumulated in him. Put the lid on it. Keep it closed. Don't let any oxygen get at it or it would start to ferment. Klaus Buch was different. When he found a thread, he wanted all the others connected with it. He wouldn't give up until he felt sure of having the entire fabric of an afternoon twenty-five years ago once more before his eyes. Or at least the design. Or the colors. Or at least the idea. Generally speaking, however, this Klaus Buch was so well informed about past happenings that Helmut was staggered. According to him, there had been boxes of geraniums around the edge of that fountain and, before Klaus Buch had been able to take the dip ordered by Helmut, they had removed two of them. The girl studying theology—remember?—the one with the Grace Kelly face and the embroidered blouse—had turned her back as Klaus Buch started to undress. Don't you remember, with sort of shoulder-length hair turned under at the ends and a braid on top that disappeared into her hair on either side of the part . . . .

Helmut felt a burning envy. He had virtually never lived. There was nothing left over. Behind him there was practically nothing. If he tried to remember, he saw motionless images of streets, squares, rooms. No action. His memory images were pervaded by a lifelessness as if in the wake of a disaster. As if the people did not yet dare to move. In any case, they stood silently against the walls. The center of the images usually remained empty. He felt that, in him, adventure had once and for all come to an end. In fact, everything worth telling. Sometimes, it was true, he would sit down and, in a kind of panic, summon a parade of all the people he had ever known. The names and faces he evoked would appear. But for the condition in which they appeared to him, the word *dead* was much too mild. Probably his memory was no worse than other people's. And, like most people, he was fascinated by his youth and childhood. But then the silent, odorless, colorless scenes would mean nothing to him. For a time he had persisted fanatically in attempting to resurrect the past. At one point he had even started to write down everything he remembered about his father, who had been a waiter at the Hindenburg Center. Helmut was disgusted when he found himself gluing together scraps of memory, coloring them, breathing onto them, inventing texts for them. He was too old for this puppet show. Surely to breathe life into the past meant resurrecting an event in a pseudo-vividness that simply denied the pastness of the past. The picture of his father that subsequently appeared on paper was a denial of the charnel-house condition in which the past existed within him. It was this very deadness of the past that interested him. Klaus Buch evidently preferred to recount the past in drastic terms. Is there anything less compatible than "past" and "drastic"? Klaus Buch was simply churning with sounds, smells, noises; the past heaved and steamed as if it were more alive than the present. Those doing the remembering became manikins pointing up to Heaven, where the giants were lustily doing battle. Helmut saw only fragments, holes, wreckage, destroyed items. For many years he had done little but prepare himself to live with what had been destroyed. Nothing attracted him so much as things that had been destroyed. Someday or other he would do nothing from morning to night but surround himself with what had been destroyed. His aim was to transform his own present into a condition resembling as closely as possible the destroyed nature of the past. Already he wanted to belong to the past. That was his objective. Within him, around him, before him, he wanted everything to be as fragmentary as in the past. After all, a person is dead far longer than he is alive. It is really grotesque how tiny the present is in relation to the past. Hence this relationship should duly minimize, grind down, distort to insensibility every second of the present.

Klaus Buch and his wife ordered only steak and salad, and they ate the salad before the steak. And they drank only mineral water. They spoke so enthusiastically about their practice of drinking mineral water that they seemed to want the Halms to follow suit at once. And what connoisseurs they were, even of mineral water! Helmut had already noticed at the promenade café that they hadn't ordered coffee. They had drunk mineral water there, too. But there they had not enthused about it. Out of the goodness of their hearts they rebuked Helmut and Sabina for their reckless eating and drinking habits. It was Hella who directed her reproachful concern at Sabina. Helmut and Sabina were drinking the heaviest, most expensive Pinot Noir, of which Helmut had five large glasses and Sabina two. Helmut felt himself lapsing into a delicious, somber state of languor. Far away, Klaus Buch was rehashing memories and almost fell off his chair with delight when, out of sheer politeness, Helmut went so far as to mention that the girl with the narrow braids, the theology student, whose footsteps Klaus Buch had dogged for a whole semester, had come from Worms. For this enabled Klaus to hear her voice and accent ringing in his ears again. However, in the midst of reveling in those reborn sounds, he once again let out the shriek he had uttered on the promenade; this time, since they were sitting in one of the Hecht's old, lowceilinged rooms, the sound was so dreadful that even Helmut leaped up, that even people at other tables, even in the other rooms, leaped up. Sabina slapped Otto's nose. Klaus Buch dashed out to wash his hands. Sabina said with a sanctimonious smile: "That's the first time he's ever done that!" Although this was true, she obviously didn't believe it herself.

On his return, Klaus Buch failed to find the thread to lead him back into his orgy of memories. For a while he and Hella looked on silently as Sabina and Helmut emptied the cheese platter, ate white bread, drank red wine. When for the third time Helmut looked up and registered the Buchs' wide-eyed horror, he said that being watched by Hella and Klaus reminded him of a scene in the life of the great Swedish philosopher Emanuel Swedenborg. Already over fifty and a famous man, he had once been having dinner alone in his room in a London hotel. Suddenly he had noticed a man in a corner of his room who at that moment called out to Swedenborg: "Don't eat so much!" And how did the great philosopher react? asked Hella. From that hour on he partook only of a roll soaked in hot milk. And a lot of coffee. But with far too much sugar. "There you are!" said Hella. "Swedenborg, Klaus—don't forget that name, he interests me. One roll per day or per meal?" "I'm sorry, I don't know," said Helmut. "That reduces the value of the diet considerably," said Hella. She seemed quite put out in her disappointment. "You've remembered everything," she said, "last name, first name, occupation, nationality, scene, location, ingredients, and then you forget the quantities. Klaus, can you understand that?" "Helmut has always been interested only in quality, never in quantity," said Klaus Buch. "But without exact quantities it's impossible to achieve quality!" cried Hella. "Don't eat so much," said Klaus Buch. Then he looked at his watch. "Good God, almost eleven!" he said. Helmut would have liked another glass or two of that wine. But Klaus Buch was already on his feet, and had paid for all of them, and, while Helmut was still protesting that he shouldn't have paid his and Sabina's share, was already announcing his plans for the next day. At six-thirty A.M. he and Hella would go for a run, at seven play tennis, then go for a sail, then have lunch then a snooze, by three o'clock they would be rested up and ready to meet Sabina and Helmut. Of course, if Sabina and Helmut wanted to play doubles with them at seven, that would be great. Helmut declined with a shudder, Sabina with a smile.

They would have liked to give Sabina and Helmut a ride back to Nussdorf, but they had come on their bikes. Helmut felt compelled to say that he and Sabina were looking forward to the walk back. As soon as the others had left, he suggested taking the bus. But the last bus had gone. Glumly, Helmut traipsed along beside his jaunty wife toward Nussdorf: Fortunately there was a strong west wind riffling the treetops and the waters of the lake. This harmony of sound pleased him. Unfortunately Sabina was talking almost nonstop. About Klaus Buch. Although she too thought it odd that they should play tennis at seven in the morning and spurn wine and not smoke, she found the two of them refreshing. In order not to fail Sabina entirely, he said he was also quite glad they had met them, otherwise he wouldn't have had such a good wine this evening. He had never enjoyed his cigars so much as at the moment when this Klaus Buch had refused the cigar Helmut offered him, remarking that he mustn't fall from grace. "That sounded as if smoking were a crime," said Helmut, "and somehow the consciousness of committing a crime by smoking made the cigar seem to course through my veins with even greater intensity."

That was a lie. When he noticed their concern as they watched him smoke, his cigar had not tasted as good as usual.

For a moment Helmut wondered whether he shouldn't suggest to Sabina that they quickly undress and dash into the waves for a dip. They had done that before. But he was afraid Sabina would take the suggestion to be an effect of this Klaus Buch. She had criticized him for always saying "this Klaus Buch." What, then, would she prefer him to say? he had asked. Well, he was his friend, wasn't he? Had been, said Helmut. From age eleven to twenty-three, as he had discovered today. That meant nothing to him anymore. Even so, surely it was ridiculous to keep saying "this Klaus Buch" instead of "Klaus." "Right," said Helmut, "quite ridiculous in fact." "From now on you'll say 'Klaus,' " she said. "Yes," he said. "From now on I'll say 'Klaus.' " Sabina punched him lightly. She evidently believed they were now agreed. That was fine with him.

Because he had eaten too much and maybe also had too much to drink, his sleep was restless. Sabina also often lay awake beside him. Both were surprised that the red wine had not had a more soporific effect. Helmut said he was going into the next room to look something up. He sat down at the table and wrote: Dear Klaus Buch, I can see a misunderstanding developing. Perhaps it is already too late. That would be disastrous. I must warn you both. As soon as someone seems friendly, I have a feeling that I can no longer be as friendly as before. I believe that I now seem friendlier than I am. Sometimes I regret that I am not as friendly as I seem. If someone seems friendly, I feel as embarrassed as a meat-eater among vegetarians. I won't talk about all that has happened because that would mean soliciting empathy. I like the idea of keeping quiet about something. My ideal is to be able to look on silently when I am being misunderstood. To agree with the misunderstanding is something I would like to learn. To prefer so-called enemies to so-called friends is something I would like to learn.

Helmut stopped. He realized how absurd it was to write this letter. If he was serious about even a single sentence in this letter, he must not utter it. But he could not stop writing. So he went on: And I want you to know that I am not interested in finding out something about myself, let alone saying something about myself. That is why we should not meet again. Yes, I am running away. I know. Whoever tries to stop me will . . . I don't want to put everything into words. My heart's desire is to maintain privacy. This is a wish I share with the majority of all living people. We consort like battleships. According to less than intelligible rules. The point of these rules is their pointlessness. The more someone else knows about me, the greater would be his power over me, hence . . .

Helmut stopped. He felt relieved. The letter had acquired a tone that made it impossible for him to send it. It was only when he had pursued the tone of the letter to the point of incommunicability that he was able to stop. Now he was looking forward to bed. He felt the self-sufficiency of the negative surge through him. How wonderful that a person who has ceased to want anything is sufficient unto himself: How easy everything becomes as soon as one is alone. Not only spiritually. Every step. A glass and a hand. No problem moving. He could walk back and forth across this medallion design in the rug forever. As soon as he is alone, the tension in his shoulders is gone. Above all, the tension in his face is gone. His features relax. Lie naturally. His mouth benefits the most. It simply does what it wants. As soon as the mouth knows that we are alone, it behaves like a dog. Lies motionless for long periods, then feels like moving about, playing games. Apparently it now wants to be conscious of itself. Marvelous. Let it.

4. BY WHISTLING, stopping to look at trees, and commenting on the Birnau church lying up there so loftily and, according to him, holding out its breast to the sun like a young ox, Helmut tried to prevent their walk to the Hotel Seehalde from looking like a pilgrimage to Klaus Buch. He was trying to make something out of the walk itself. Sabina's remorseless insistence that Otto be left behind in the apartment had shocked him. That was a gesture of surrender. He had groaned, and cursed yesterday's moment of discovery by Klaus Buch. "Now come along, it'll do you good," Sabina had said. "What?" he had asked back. "To be dragged out for a change." "Dragged out of what?" "Out of your rut." "You call this a rut?" he had exclaimed, rut! This jam-packed sequence of fraught moments, every one of which in turn exacts from us a whole cluster of decisions. Shall we act up, if so, when; shall we have breakfast, but what; shall we dress, if so, how; shall we go down to the water, if so, where shall we lie down, and how . . .

As Klaus Buch hastened toward them, Helmut put on as inscrutable an expression as possible. Klaus Buch said that, since the Halms fortunately didn't have their four-legged nuisance along, they must go sailing. Helmut looked at Sabina as if to say: Serves you right! He said it was a wonderful idea, but unfortunately he and Sabina weren't dressed for sailing. Klaus said: "Off with your shoes, no problem!" Sabina simply agreed. Helmut let her see that he was surprised. Didn't she know how ridiculous they would look in a sailboat?

Helmut and Sabina were told to sit on the floorboards of the boat, which rocked violently as they stepped in. Cushions were slid beneath them. With their toes pointing skyward they sat there ill at ease, trying to dodge the expert movements of the Buchs. Klaus Buch had insisted that Sabina and Helmut also take off their stockings and socks. Otherwise they might slip and break some bones. Helmut held out his socks to Sabina while making a face in which he let despair get the upper hand. Klaus cast off, Hella tended the jib, the west wind caught the sails, Sabina was alarmed, the Buchs, who were sitting on the gunwale, laughed. Helmut felt he and Sabina were being treated like a couple of grandparents. Klaus Buch performed at the tiller as if expecting a stream of compliments. Helmut restrained himself. Gradually Sabina found that she had never imagined sailing to be so wonderful. This gentle, skimming glide, no, really! And the view, Helmut, just look, from the lake the hills leaning against each other were even lovelier than when seen on a walk. She behaved as if she had never been on the lake before.

"Doesn't it look like a herd of hills camped around the lake for a rest?" she cried. Evidently she was trying to compete with Klaus in picturesque speech. Helmut also responded to the gentleness of the hills they were sailing past but took care not to say so. Klaus Buch said it. He knew his Helmut, he said. No one could tell him that he, Helmut, would remain untouched by the green contours rising and falling in the dazzling sunlight. At school, Helmut had always written the most soulful mood-prose. But his cleverest trick had been to read aloud the most outlandish phrases in a totally dispassionate voice.

It pleased Helmut to be enthused over so inaccurately. For Sabina's sake as well. He noticed that his feet were ice cold. It was a hot day. Discreetly, he tried to move his feet into the sun.

All he could think of was to ask Klaus Buch about his career. He hoped that, in talking about himself, Klaus Buch would moderate his language. Indeed, when he talked about himself it was less flamboyant than when he had talked about Helmut. But the way he characterized himself also grated on Helmut. Whatever that fellow did was wrong. Blithely Klaus Buch confessed that he had not found himself equipped by nature to be an educator. Had he become a teacher, he wouldn't have had the willpower required to keep out of a rut. A run-of-the-mill bourgeois, that's what he would have become. A narrow-minded, disintegrating concentrate of uric acid, that's all. Without challenge he couldn't exist. If he was not overtaxed, he wasn't alive. He needed to be stretched to his limits to be aware of himself. So he had become a journalist. A specialist in environmental problems. And in ecology, a specialist in nutrition. On television too. Sabina said at once that they hardly ever watched TV because they spent their evenings reading. Klaus envied Sabina and Helmut. To read in the evenings, beautiful. It comforted him to think that such people still existed. Hella said: "In your *All Things Green* you say: 'Readers are mankind's green lung.' " "Hella," he said, "fancy you knowing me by heart! I believe you do still care for me a little." That was his favorite among all his books, his *All Things Green*. But what do the Halms read, in the evening? "De Sade," said Helmut quickly, before Sabina could reply. "And Masoch," Sabina chimed in sulkily. "What a pair you are!" exclaimed Klaus. Helmut said: "That's right." "Ready about!" cried Klaus. "Ready!" cried Hella. "Hard alee!" cried Klaus. Sabina and Helmut ducked.

"You know, Klaus," said Sabina—Helmut was annoyed because she always addressed Klaus Buch as Klaus; he had persisted in calling Hella Mrs. Buch and, on being ordered by her husband to call her Hella, had avoided her first name altogether—"for years Helmut has been intending to write two books, but the school simply ties him down; now he has reduced his plans to one book, but even that, he has to keep postponing." "You know what, Hella," said Klaus, "we'll present the Halms with our inoffensive little books." "Yes, do!" cried Sabina. "Helmut, maybe that will encourage you to make a start."

Helmut was thinking that, although it might be a kind of vice, surely it was the sweetest of all feelings to find that even your own wife was totally in the dark about you. Naturally he nodded to everything that Klaus said, that Sabina said and, as a sign of intellectual respect, raised his eyebrows to the very top of his forehead. So Helene Buch has also written a book. You don't say! On herbs. And Klaus has published quite a number. On food in general. Well, well. And there are seventy-five thousand people eating according to his theories. That's the way it is. But he has remained modest. He claimed no merit for it. He had just put into words what was in the air anyway. Hella's book on herbs had far greater merit and thus a much smaller readership. Hella protested. "I would never have written a book, if he hadn't insisted. Besides, I didn't really write a book, I merely translated Pastor Künzle into modern German—I mean, whenever he mentions God I've replaced it with Nature. I expect you know *Herbes and Weedes?* No?!" Well, that was why the Buchs had been coming to this area for three years, to gain more insight into Pastor Künzle's ideas. Spiritually, too, as it were. Pastor Künzle had suddenly become more important to them than Byzantium or Ravenna. Meanwhile Klaus had become so enamored of the area that he was planning a big book about Lake Constance, to be called: *Let Europe Drink Thy Waters.*

Klaus Buch said it was time to put an end to that fraud over there. He pointed to the prehistoric lake dwellings of Unteruhldingen, which they happened to be passing. "What do you mean, fraud?" asked Helmut. He thought he remembered reading in the brochure that these pile dwellings in the lake were, quite frankly, built in 1929 or 1930. "The fraud," said Klaus, "is that there never were any lake dwellings there," whereas these phony lake dwellings were meant to give the impression that at one time there had been. Did he know for sure, Helmut asked, that there had never been any lake dwellings at this or some other nearby spot, perhaps off Goldbach or Süssenmühle? At no time and at no place along or in Lake Constance had there ever been any prehistoric lake dwellings. Helmut said with a smile: "My dear Klaus Buch, there were no lake dwellings here during the Stone Age?" Generally speaking, the indigenous Celtic population had not gone in for pile dwellings. Wouldn't the barbarous Alemanni hordes have immediately swept them away? Helmut had no idea. But Klaus Buch's tone goaded him to contradict. "Yes yes ye-es!" cried Klaus Buch. "That's exactly what that swindler would like to hear! The man who invented it all, and as a result was made a professor forty years ago, could hug himself because his clumsy and hence successful inventions must have long since made him a millionaire. Mind you, it's pure envy on my part, I admit that. If I felt the urge to achieve something, it would be a fraud with a solid foundation, a real live proposition." "But haven't you achieved that?" laughed Hella. "The seventy-five thousand people who eat according to your books are pretty real, aren't they?" For a moment he looked at Hella aghast—his tongue was working against the inside of his upper lip, bulging it out as if the tongue were imprisoned there—then he laughed, louder than Hella had laughed. Then he said that was what you got for marrying a callow young thing like that. His first wife could never have been so devoid of instinct as to take seriously an ironical remark that he had made about himself and then turn it against him. Herta had made a lot of mistakes, but not that one. Never. But unfortunately she had never developed and for that reason had begrudged him his own development, that was why he had had to leave her, if he didn't want to wither like a plant in a pot that was too small for it. Klaus Buch directed these explanations at Sabina. Then he turned to Hella, and said in a deadly serious, utterly hopeless, tone: "You don't care for me anymore, do you?" She laughed at him, leaned across and kissed him. He quickly turned his head so that her kiss landed on his mouth. Then he ran his tongue all around his lips so as not to lose one particle of Hella's kiss. Helmut found it hard not to look only at Hella. He had to look carefully past her because the others might have noticed how insatiable his eyes were. But then, of course, he was an expert at looking past people.

His feet still felt cold, although they were now lying in the sun. That was to say, only part of his feet. Only the heels. But they were as cold as if lying in snow. He should have moved about. He and Sabina were sitting there like a corner-grocery couple who had been talked into taking much too arduous a boat trip to celebrate their golden anniversary. They must look a scream, sitting on little cushions on the floorboards, their bare feet stretched out in front of them. The misshapen toes. The horribly reddened skin.

At first, the separation from his children had been a real body blow, said Klaus Buch, raising his face into the wind and screwing up his eyes so that the golden eyelashes met intrepidly. His wife, a fanatical bourgeois, had set the kids against him to such an extent that they refused to have anything more to do with him. Hella, he was glad to say, thought the way he did: No kids on any account. To screw only to produce children: How square can you get—right? He was sure that Helmut, who, even as a boy, had been past master of the bizarre, had developed a gorgeously lurid, heavily ritualized art of screwing. It was a good thing that nowadays everyone could screw to his own taste. Hella and he, for instance, were into bouncing. That had literally nauseated his first wife. Man was no doubt a mistake on the part of Nature, but bourgeois man was the elevation of this mistake to a program. Uptight like Hitler, stupid like a Bavarian prime minister, and wicked like Stalin. Hella and he could hardly wait for the day when they could finally turn their backs on this bourgeois country. The income from one more apartment building and they would put out to sea. Set their course for the Bahamas. There was simply no hope for the Germans. Take his first wife, for example: an admirer of Pius XII. At fourteen, a Holy Year pilgrim, with her father, an audience with the Pope. She never recovered from that. Favorite book: *Richard Wagner's Letters to Mathilde Wesendonc*. Next most favorite: *The Song of Bernadette* by Werfel. And knew on Monday morning which blouse she would wear on Friday. Hella looked at her Klaus with compassion. Sabina said as ironically as she could: "How enviable!" Klaus Buch shouted: "Ready about!" Hella shouted "Ready!" Klaus Buch shouted: "Hard alee!" Sabina and Helmut ducked.

Suddenly Hella removed her top, tucked it away saying that with this wind Klaus could manage alone, and lay down on the bow. Resorting to his professional glance, Helmut observed her breasts as he looked past them. The breasts looked as if they were inquisitive, too. Fortunately Klaus Buch had gone on talking as if nothing had happened. Did the Halms have any children? Helmut said: "Sabina, do we have any children?" Sabina said that if he were to ask their two children whether they had any parents, they would probably answer: "Parents! For God's sake, never had any!" When he had seen their dog, said Klaus Buch, he had taken them for a childless couple. "Why don't you two have a dog?" Sabina asked. They avoided anything that might interfere with their independence, said Klaus Buch. If one morning they should feel like flying to Tenerife, they must be in a position to leave their little house in Starnberg at noon and land in Los Rodeos that evening, otherwise he would simply feel like a cockroach. And that wasn't a pleasant feeling. At school he had often felt like a cockroach. In those days, Helmut had been pretty good at making him squirm. Just because his parents had had a big house on the hill, with a garden full of plum trees and a blackberry patch, Helmut had refused ever to set foot on the Buch property, and had even tried, sometimes successfully, to incite the other kids not to walk home with Klaus Buch. He had been all for the class struggle, said Klaus Buch. "Not anymore," said Sabina dryly. "Too bad," said Klaus Buch. At that time, of course, he hadn't been able to understand Helmut's secret hatred for the Buch property. He had thought it was directed at him personally. If during their group masturbation he hadn't been able to prove that his penis was the equal of any other, he would really have been desperate. My God, what would he have done if it hadn't been for that masturbating in the school toilet and on the construction sites. Those had been just about his only chances for rehabilitation. Since he had been shorter than most of the other kids, they had naturally assumed that everything they had was longer than what he had. But he'd shown them up nicely. Did Helmut remember, when the new bank was being built, on the top floor? Objective: Who can manage to pee through the skylight opening? And who was the first to do it? Little Klaus Buch. Yes, indeed. What those bean poles lacked was either pressure or firmness to produce the necessary range. No amount of math could produce that parabola. But the one who got the biggest laugh had been Helmut, Klaus Buch cried ecstatically. Helmut shuddered at his tone. For in those days Helmut had had—something he surely no longer was bothered with—a knotty problem with his foreskin. A real little cauliflower of a foreskin at the orifice, that's what Helmut had had. Needless to say, that had interfered with a fine, long-range jet. Only a sort of intermittent gush. Pulling it back was unfeasible. Much too painful. So what does our Helmut do? Takes his thumb and forefinger and pinches the skin in front firmly together. Lets his water come. Holds on tight. The skin-balloon fills and fills. And when it's about to burst, our HH fires away.

But unfortunately in the wrong direction. Sheer ambition has made our HH aim steeper than steep and he squirts the whole lot into his own face. Klaus Buch laughed and laughed and repeated the more dramatic bits. Sabina had merely let out a shriek. Helene Buch laughed her high-pitched, penetrating laugh. Helmut commanded himself to laugh loudest and longest. He succeeded.

"One of the finest moments of our erotic dawn," said Klaus Buch in an even more brimming voice, "occurred in the cellar of—remember?—Rolf Eberle, d'you remember, on Rothenwald Street, when we tried again. The rest were all rubbing away nicely, it was dark of course, we couldn't turn on the light, or talk, so we thought we all had the delicious agony of our lust well under way when suddenly we heard Helmut's voice saying very, very softly: 'Now I've got to the real thing.' "

Again he burst out laughing. Hella said: "How adorable!" Sabina said: "You were a fine bunch, I must say!" Helmut laughed an operatic, full-throated Ha-ha-ha-haaa! Klaus repeated the words Helmut was supposed to have said and explained that everyone in that cellar had immediately grasped that for the first time our HH had managed to pull back his foreskin over the glans. *Ecco!*

Sabina said she was simply amazed that Klaus should remember everything in such detail. "Aren't you, Helmut?"

"Congratulations, Klaus," said Helmut. "As you see, you've already convinced Sabina that what you've been describing actually happened."

"Didn't it?" asked Klaus.

"Not that I know of," said Helmut and was annoyed at the level tone of his voice.

"Oh how disappointing, Helmut," said Klaus Buch, "to find you trying to deny these touching childhood moments."

"I tell you, I simply don't remember a thing about them," Helmut said. "I couldn't tell you it was like that or it wasn't like that. So you can say whatever you like, I can only listen and marvel. I'm sure you didn't have an easy time with us in those days. You were a bit isolated, I seem to remember. Ever since you had the bike with the balloon tires, I think. That may have stimulated your imagination. An entirely normal process, actually. Everyone tends to compensate."

Sabina yawned pointedly.

"Helmut, that's a point I'm going to have to tackle you on," Klaus Buch said. "It doesn't have to be now. But trying to turn the most sacred moments of our childhood into figments of my imagination—I'm not going to let you get away with that. Those childhood flickerings can't simply be stamped out."

Hella said as if from a higher plane: "Sailing over the water and reviving old memories, how absolutely out of this world! I never knew how well they went together. Water and memories. Now really, Helmut," she said, punching his shoulder, "the reason these dear little vignettes have surfaced in Klaus's mind today is because you are here. I never knew about the five-finger exercises of those little men. By himself, he wouldn't have either. Otherwise he would have told me. He tells me everything, you know. Everything he has been telling us was prompted by you. And now you want to take it away from him again. Don't tell me you're a sadist, too?" Meets Klaus's eyes. Then: "Forgive me, darling, I didn't mean to say that. It just slipped out." Helmut said: "Never mind, I'll let him have his puppet show." Hella rewarded him with a kiss on his temple. Sabina said: "Don't spoil him." "How glorious it all is!" exclaimed Klaus Buch. "God, who would ever have thought life could be so beautiful! And the most beautiful part, to my mind, is that it could have been different, too. Something had to be done to make it as beautiful as it is at this moment. At this very moment, dear friends, we have reached the peak! And if from now on anyone in this boat uses anything but first names, overboard he goes. According to the law of the sea, the captain's orders must be implicitly obeyed. Ready about! Ready! Hard alee!"

With the change in course, Helmut's feet were in the shade again. He stretched them out into the sun. His heels remained ice-cold.

When they had docked, Sabina said that the effects of going sailing surpassed her wildest dreams. Seen from the shore, sailing often looked as if nothing at all were happening out there. Now she felt drunk. But in the most agreeable way. She felt so light and yet so heavy. And how aware she was of her skin! Never before had she been so aware of her skin. She felt as if she had been on Mount Olympus for a massage and was now returning to earth, growing heavier by the minute. "Regards from Apollo the masseur," said Helmet. But he agreed with his wife that the effects of such a sail were unimaginable for a non-sailor. He, too, felt as if he had been thoroughly worked over. Only he couldn't yet say by whom or what. It surely hadn't been Apollo. But it might well have been a god. At any rate he would like to thank Hella and Klaus Buch most warmly for having put up with him and Sabina so patiently in their boat, and he hoped they would both thoroughly enjoy the rest of their vacation. Klaus Buch would not accept that. Parting company? What? What's that? Oh I see, one of those typical HH-notions. Is that how it was meant? "He's a sadist, we know that," said Hella.

"Sometimes he tries to overdo it," said Sabina.

"I see we're agreed," said Klaus. "Man, was that ever a shock! 'We hope you will both thoroughly enjoy . . .' I've a good mind to beat you up." Half in fun, half in earnest, he started pummeling Helmut.

"Very well then," he said, "since Helmut quite rightly feels that whenever I watch him eating I want to keep saying 'Don't eat so much,' we'll meet after supper . . ."

"Hey, wait a moment, what was the name of that fellow with the rolls?" cried Helene. "Swedenborg," said Sabina. "This time I'll write it down myself," said Hella. "That Klaus has a memory like a hole." "Like a sieve, if you don't mind, I don't let the big pieces through," said Klaus. "No sweat, then you'll remember Swedenborg," said Helmut. "Okay, eight-thirty then," said Hella. Helmut drew Sabina away.

"We'll be there to pick you up!" Klaus Buch called. It sounded like a threat.

"Ye-es!" Sabina called back. It sounded like an endearment.

Helmut and Sabina tramped off to their apartment. As soon as they get away from those Buchs, life becomes humdrum, dreary, the fire goes out. Nonsense. You should say the very opposite. Helmut swore. That wretch Sabina: Why hadn't she helped him ward off the attacks of that dieting, sailing athlete?

Sabina feigned surprise. Hadn't Helmut, just a few moments ago, lavished praise on the afternoon? Surely he wouldn't have done that if he had disliked the Buchs, or would he? "I would," he said. "Yes," she said, "you're quite capable of that."

5. HELMUT BULLIED Sabina into being ready in good time. By eight twenty-five they were standing outside the low garden gate. Beside the garbage cans. So it must be Monday evening. In all those eleven years he had never once managed to carry out the garbage cans. Whenever he went to do so, Mrs. Zürn had already carried them out. He would have liked at least once to carry out the Zürns' garbage cans with their own. To seem helpful would have pleased him.

"You're always in such a rush," said Sabina. "Now we're standing here like two bumps on a log." He couldn't tell her that under no circumstances would he allow Klaus Buch and Helene to set foot in their apartment here at the Zürns'. If they were ever to set foot in that apartment he would never again spend his vacation here. Why, he didn't know. That was why he couldn't discuss it with Sabina. To apologize for his seemingly senseless haste, he quickly ran his thumb along the hollow of her neck. Her head drooped toward her responsive shoulders, her eyebrows rose, her body relaxed into an S.

The Buchs drove up, jumped out, greeted them as if they hadn't seen each other for years. Back in the apartment, Otto barked and howled. "Poor thing," said Helene.

"You're right," said Helmut.

"Klaus, if you would watch your hands a little more carefully, we could take him along," said Helene.

"Thanks a lot, and I can always wear gloves, of course," said Klaus.

"Because of you the poor dog has to spend all evening—"

"Okay, okay," he interrupted, "by all means bring him out!"

"No!" Sabina cried.

"Well said!" exclaimed Helmut, and ran into the house to fetch Otto, who was jumping for joy.

"Otto!" cried Sabina. "Down, Otto, down!"

Helmut congratulated Klaus on his self-control.

Before very long, Helmut managed to steer the stroll along the promenade into a wine tavern. He confessed that he had never had anything else in mind: The idea of having to spend an evening without wine simply paralyzed him.

"So we're not enough for you," said Helene.

Helmut hesitated, looked at Hella a shade too long, and said with a quiet shake of his head: "No."

"Prosit!" said Sabina in a conciliatory tone.

The Halms drank wine, the Buchs drank water. Helmut couldn't understand how, in the ensuing discussion about wine and water, the Buchs could become so animated. He always drank his first glass rather quickly because, until he had had a drink, he didn't feel the slightest desire to open his mouth.

Suddenly Klaus Buch yelled: "No!" Sabina said: "Now it's happened." Helmut shouted: "Otto, down!" Klaus Buch stood holding up one hand with the other as if it were seriously injured.

Hella said: "Oh for God's sake, Klaus!"

Klaus, still clutching his hand, said: "He's got such a cold, wet tongue, Christ you've no idea. And always me, why always me? Can you explain that?"

Helmut said: "No."

Sabina said: "This is the last time we take him along. That's it." And down to Otto: "Bad dog!"

Hella said: "Poor Otto. I really feel sorry for him."

"For whom?" Klaus Buch cried.

Hella said: "For you too, of course, darling."

Helmut said brightly: "There is nothing one can't feel sorry for."

Klaus Buch said: "All right, now I'm putting my hands on the table; if anyone sees me taking a hand off the table by mistake, please tell me immediately."

It struck Helmut that, in relation to his almost fragile build, Klaus Buch had noticeably heavy wrists. And his forearms: manifestly more powerful than his own. And the hands, broader. The fingers, stronger. No question that he also had a larger, more efficient penis. Nevertheless it was Helmut's impression that Hella would have enjoyed poking fun at her husband's obsession with his physical fitness.

And invariably when she looked across at him with a less than lovesick expression, he would immediately say in a despondent voice: "You don't care for me anymore, do you." And she would invariably pucker up her lips and blow him a kiss. Helmut had the feeling that in blowing the kiss she didn't care where it landed. But it was enough to see their tanned arms and hands, and Helmut's and Sabina's arms and hands, lying on the table to know who belonged to whom. Helmut noticed that today his cigars and wine were less enjoyable than the day before. He was afraid he would not be able to defend his habits against this couple. They attacked him ceaselessly. Both of them. They were getting him down. It was enough to sit at the same table with them to feel in the wrong. Meanwhile Hella was cradling Klaus Buch's hands in her own; in fact, she was cradling all of him. He was somehow snuggled up under her arm, his head against her breast. Helmut and Sabina noted simultaneously that Klaus was falling asleep.

"Ssh," said Sabina. "He's asleep."

Hella explained that every morning for the past few days Klaus had run five times around the track at the marina, she being the timekeeper; his best time was 5:11, which meant Klaus must have considered himself a superchampion runner; 2,000 meters in 5:11, that equaled, say, the best Russian time of that year. But this morning Klaus had been told by some horrible old gymnast that the track was not 400 meters long, as one had a right to expect, but only 300, so that Klaus hadn't run 2,000 meters but only 1,500. She could have killed that cynical old gymnast. Couldn't he have kept his stupid remark to himself? Klaus murmured: "Helmut, please, do tell me, what was it our physics teacher used to call out on the first floor?" Helmut didn't know. "Come on, Helmut," groaned Klaus, displaying an agonized face, "our physics teacher who always shouted: 'The lower floor belongs to me!' Something like that. 'The first floor is my domain!' Some such thing. I need the actual words. If you don't get every single word right, you have nothing. One word in the wrong place, and the whole sentence is hollow, dead. As soon as you get the word in the right place, *Open Sesame!* There stands our teacher, shouting his head off, there you stand, clear as day. Won't you help me, Helmut?—please!"

"For God's sake help him, can't you see how he's suffering?" said Hella. "He's turning blue in the face from lack of memory-oxygen. Helmut!"

Helmut said automatically: "The whole lower floor belongs to physics." "Right, Helmut, right!" shouted Klaus Buch, whereupon he leaped up, fell on Helmut's neck, and continued to whimper "Right." And blissfully repeated: "The whole lower floor belongs to physics." Helmut looked at Hella over Klaus Buch's shoulder, trying to convey that she alone had dredged up the words of a long-dead physics instructor from the depths of thirty years. Klaus murmured happily: "Call the waitress." Helmut shouted in positive alarm: "The check, please. All on one!"

Klaus held his hand horizontally across both eyes. He was playing the role of someone who refuses to witness a disaster. Hella, as she stroked her Klaus with exaggerated motherly concern, said that now the Halms had really and truly offended her Klaus. Without the slightest warning she had lapsed into a grotesque Swabian accent. Klaus straightened up and covered his ears. Hella intensified her grotesque accent as she informed them that it was really torture for Klaus when she imitated his native dialect. Klaus Buch sprang to his feet, whereupon Hella, in an equally grotesque Bavarian accent, said that Klaus was a loony mutt and shouldn't carry on like that, if she had a piano now she would leave him in peace. With her Bavarian accent her face acquired, as if demanded by the dialect, an angry expression. Klaus was now standing in front of her as if to hypnotize her. She said: "Don't you look at me like that, my boy!" and ran her fingers across his eyes. Klaus said: "You don't care for me anymore, do you." She kissed him. They could leave now.

The Buchs tried to talk Helmut and Sabina into a game of tennis. That was successfully warded off. All right, then they would all go on a hike together. The Buchs would be at the Halms' place at eight— "Nine!" Helmut cried shrilly. In their car. Since the Halms had been coming to this area for eleven years, they must know of some good hikes, so it was Helmut's job to come up with some inspiration overnight.

As Helmut lay behind the wonderfully straight bars on the windows of their ground-floor apartment, he felt happy again. Fortunately Sabina had immediately reached for her *Wagner—My Life*. Fortunately she had made no attempt to touch him. He hoped she was lying beside him as he beside her. That would be life's crowning achievement. For each of them. If he could have been sure that Sabina had reached the same point as he had, he would now have said how pleasant it was to be lying in this isolated apartment. He would have liked to give vent to the thought of how terrible it would be to be lying under the same roof as the Buchs. But then Sabina would have asked, Why? And then it might have turned out that Sabina had not yet reached the same point as he had.

Helmut recalled a night twelve years ago, during the last vacation they had spent in Italy. In a hotel in Grado. They were just about to come together when from the next room he heard a noise as of a bed being struck by a giant hammer. Every blow went clearly through all the springs and ended up hard. The amazing thing about this noise, in view of the presumed force of the hammer blows, was the speed, the incredible speed, with which the blows fell. Helmut had guessed at once that he would never find his own rhythm as long as that fellow next door kept hammering away like that. He had noticed that Sabina was also listening intently. Surely she must, must, *must* reproach him for not being that kind of a hammer. They both lay there, just listening to what a man is capable of. Helmut wouldn't have believed it possible. Should he count the blows? He was suffocating with heat. He was dreadfully embarrassed. He was at fault. The fellow next door was in tune with the times. That's how a man must have felt in the old days of the pillory. Anyone falling short of the sexual demands of this age and of society was, so to speak, permanently pilloried. There were enough publications to take care of that. With words and pictures. Now to escape. Where to? To kill. Her. Strangle her. But his hands didn't move. The hammering seemed to be going on indefinitely. It simply never stopped. He gasped for air. He found he had been holding his breath. Later he told himself that the whole thing could have lasted no more than eleven or twenty-one or at most twenty-nine minutes. But as long as it lasted, it seemed as if it would never, never stop. If at least he could have thought of some words to release Sabina and himself from the spell of sheer listening. He could think of nothing. Spellbound, they had been forced to listen until it was over. If they were now sleeping in the same hotel as Klaus and Helene Buch, Sabina would be sure to imagine what the Buchs were doing, and involuntarily Klaus Buch and that episode in the Italian hotel would merge, blend, and Klaus Buch would then be that other fellow. The Buchs were into bouncing. Whatever that is, thought Helmut, it doesn't concern me. But Sabina. Sabina was the point at which he was vulnerable. Did he want to be able to compete? When he read about the level of performance required in order not to be considered impotent, he felt pilloried. For months he had not felt inclined to give way to his sexuality. The mere fact of those people publicly prescribing to each other how often they had to crawl onto their wives in order not to be considered impotent was enough to arouse his aversion and disgust. Whenever he felt the urge to have sex, he had only to think of that terrible propaganda to calm down again. He hoped all this would soon be behind him. But until he had discussed it with Sabina, nothing was behind him. He should have told her long ago what it was that interfered when he wanted her. The moment he thought of her, wanted to touch her, something in his mind prevented him. Then it seemed utterly ridiculous to roll across to her, or to send his hand on ahead, or to ask Sabina outright, or to start a seductive conversation. Nothing would then seem as unbearably comical as any activity determined by or directed toward sexuality. And he had a feeling that this had something to do with the way in which these activities were publicly recommended. To desire it, yes. To do it, no. That the day would come when he would no longer desire it was more than he dared hope. It would probably always remain a kind of open wound. He would at least have to tell Sabina he couldn't lie quietly beside her unless he was sure she was lying quietly beside him. He wanted to give her a sign. So he carefully moved his hand toward her and let it lie close to her shoulder. He didn't envy Klaus Buch what he was no doubt at this very instant actively engaged in. Or did he? He had no definite opinion about these profoundly stirring sensations, much less a categorical, or categorically negative, one. As a teacher he was an eloquent supporter of society's insistence on greater sexual freedom. Wasn't he considered progressive? This was an area where he could hang on to his incognito. He was considered very progressive. He invoked the right to freedom of opinion as his justification. Surely in his domestic and most private life he didn't have to put into practice the pretense he maintained in school. Wasn't society's insistence on greater sexual freedom conceived to make each person responsible for the measure of his own lust? Just as marks you get in school are your own responsibility. As a teacher he felt justified in condemning sexual indifference, which is how society wanted it, whereas at home he felt justified in trying to condemn sexual pleasure, which is how he wanted it. No criticism implied of the national or popular dailies, parliament, and school. How were people supposed to get through life without pretense? Didn't he know how difficult it was to escape the dominance of pretense even for an instant, or even to a minute degree or even tentatively? Immediately you feel pilloried. So, quick march back to the pleasure front, the leisure front, the pretense-production front. But again and again this temptation to escape. Apart from Sabina, no one must notice it. She even had to help him, otherwise he wouldn't get away. In school he would continue to produce the required pretenses. But at home he would let himself go. He had already given a name to the state which he would then attain: martyred inertia. It was his favorite mood. There he perceived his entire sluggishness, but with approval. That sluggishness, sweating a bit. With approval. Sluggish and sweating and pale. The color, too, he perceived with approval. Color of a corpse. With approval. Himself a sluggish, sweating corpse, that was his favorite mood, martyred inertia. How to involve Sabina? She was probably still living under the full force of the dictate of pretense. She must be given an inkling of the opposite. Self-indulgence, she would say. Sabina with her social commitment; that's to say, the commitment serving the production of social pretense. He noted that revulsion was channeling his thoughts. He had nothing to worry about: He had his revulsion. His position behind the position. He had his pleasure in being misunderstood. Deception, wasn't that the essence of all that was required? The goal of producing pretense! With his well-developed talent for deception and the pleasure he took in deception, wasn't he a paragon of all that was desired here and now? So much for solitude, self-indulgence, remoteness! Representative, that's what he was! Quintessentially typical, that's what he was! He was the prototype! Fine. Had he attained it, was he enjoying it now, his martyred inertia? Almost, yes, almost.

Unfortunately, this glorious mood was very susceptible to temperature. It had to be warm. He had to feel warm. The slightest hint of cold was enough to destroy everything. The fact that his feet were still cold bothered him. One must be aware of no unpleasant sensation, then one was there. He couldn't understand why his feet simply wouldn't get warm. They were painfully cold. He put on his socks. Sabina, who was still reading her *Wagner—My Life*, asked what was the matter. "Cold feet," he said bluntly. But the socks made his feet colder rather than warmer. "Goddamn synthetics," he said, ripping his socks off, and went to get his wool sweater, in which he wrapped his feet. When he touched one foot with the other, he noticed that both feet were warm. Even so, in each separate foot he felt a chill that was painful.

Sabina put aside her book and stretched out a hand. He gave it a quick squeeze and tried to give it back to her. But she immediately stretched out her hand again. "No, let me," she said, in a tone to which, in his opinion, she was no longer entitled. So he let her hand lie on his shoulder. He had withdrawn his own hand. He would turn away imperceptibly so as to get rid of her hand, which now bothered him. But Sabina noticed his intention. Apparently she was concentrating fully on the hand lying on Helmut's shoulder. This hand was her float that signaled whether she had a bite. He wouldn't bite. What was she thinking of anyway, suddenly trying to start something again at this point? Surely he could assume that the tentative state he had so happily achieved had been reached not entirely without her consent. If she continued to maneuver her hand like that, he would have to ask her to account for her backsliding. He really had no alternative. She wouldn't stop. And if he said nothing, she would assume she was making progress. And if she allowed her expectations to grow, he would have to pay for it. Maybe this was the time for that overdue talk. "What's got into you, Sabina?" he said quietly. She responded with sounds he would rather not have heard. Outside in the darkness there was thunder and lightning. A thunderstorm. That's all we need. She probably considered a thunderstorm an encouraging sign. Or even—if she was that far gone already—an open invitation. But then Sabina wasn't a Wagnerian. "Okay, then I'll ask Klaus if he'll sleep with me," she said. For God's sake, woman, he thought, don't say that. Very slowly and as gently as possible he went: "Sssssssh." Then he stroked her head. Just her hair. Unmistakably soothing. Distracting. Suddenly the rain came splashing down. He considered that a deliverance. Slowly, slowly he withdrew his hand. He pulled up his knees, sought his knees with his chin, made himself as small as possible. He had the feeling that for the last few years he had been living alone. Sabina, he thought, can you hear me? He had hurt her, a moment ago. He was incapable of movement. He lay rigid. With fear. They were so close to one another that every hurt he inflicted on her felt as if it were being inflicted on himself. It was only much later, when he could be sure that Sabina had fallen asleep, that his body relaxed. He could think about falling asleep himself.

He dreamed he was turning over in his coffin and that, in spite of the complete darkness, he sensed that one side of the coffin was missing. This impression was so vivid that one of his hands began to grope toward the side that seemed to be missing. Sure enough, it wasn't there. Immediately, an upward movement followed, faster now. The coffin lid was there. But where the side was missing his hand kept groping apprehensively. It touched a step. He had to push himself up and came to lie on the step outside the coffin. He mustn't stay there. Involuntarily he rolled down on the other side of the step and lay where he landed. But now he realized that he was in a hall from which it was possible to get out. This suited him. He knew he would emerge into daylight, among people. And he knew there was only one condition: If even a single person recognizes you, it's all over, forever. He woke up in terror and thought: the new life.

6. AT FIVE MINUTES to nine, Helmut and Sabina were standing on the porch, watching fat bumblebees crawl into the delicate blossoms. Helmut joked about the bumblebees' little polleny pants. He was trying to bring a smile to Sabina's face before the Buchs arrived. He didn't succeed. Not until the beautiful old silver Mercedes 230 coupe pulled over did she smile. The women had to find room in the narrow back seat. Helmut said it did him good to see the women squeezed in like that. "Must've read too much de Sade last night," said Klaus Buch. "That's why you haven't left your four-legged torturer behind, too." If that creature was going to snap at Klaus's hand when it happened to be changing gears, a disaster was inevitable. "At last a disaster," said Helmut. "We'll leave him behind," said Sabina. "Stop griping and get going," said Hella.

"You don't care for me anymore, do you," said Klaus in his despondent voice. "Where are we going anyway?" "Up onto the Höchste," said Helmut, and gave him directions.

But Klaus wouldn't reach for the gear shift for fear that Otto would take the opportunity to lick his hand. "We'll leave him behind!" Sabina almost screamed. Hella, her voice even shriller: "I'll drive!" Klaus Buch had to sit in the back. Now Hella found she hadn't brought along her glasses. Sabina offered hers. Hella tried them on. To everyone's joy, they were suitable. "How beautifully they distort you," said Klaus. Hella stroked Otto. Helmut liked that. "The countryside inland," he said, "is a paradise."

He promised them a hike through magnificent, silent forests. Then a view ranging from the Vorarlberg to Bern. He could feel his voice verging on the rhapsodic. Walking in the forest would be like walking in a cathedral. Only that the light would be more vivid and the air better. The most important thing about these forests was that they could still evoke that old feeling of infinity.

In Limpach he told Hella to stop and jumped out of the car. Suddenly he was seized by an eagerness that surprised even him. He couldn't remember whether this was the spot where he and Sabina had started out on their hike, but he tried to pretend that he was quite sure and made them all get out. That's right, they would start walking from here. Into the forest. In the forest he turned off the paved road. After five minutes the undergrowth became impenetrable. Otto ran off out of the forest. They followed him. Meanwhile it had started to rain. Since progress between forest edge and meadow was also laborious, they ran—Helmut again took the lead—across the meadow toward a clump of trees where there was a crucifix. Helmut hoped to be able to wait out the rain here and then continue their walk along a field path. Beneath the trees there was a bench onto which they sank down with relief. Helmut had no idea where they were. Klaus Buch reminded them that, on leaving the car, he had asked what they would do if it rained. We would be walking through the magnificent, cathedrallike, luminous, aromatic infinity-forest, Helmut had intoned. And now, where was that forest, so magnificent, tall, luminous, aromatic, and filled with infinity? Farther up they would come to a forest like that, said Helmut, shouting rather than speaking. He was, quite simply, aroused. How much farther up? Three hundred yards maybe, did they have to argue about every foot of the way, with the rain about to stop anyway? *Was* it now, said Klaus Buch, and where did he think the weather was coming from? They all looked at him. From the west, Helmut said in a voice conveying patient indulgence toward the questioner.

"Not so!" cried Klaus Buch, in a voice that implied: Ha! "Helmut says it'll stop any minute," said Klaus Buch, "because he's looking only toward the west, where the sky is clear. But the least he could do is lick his finger and hold it up into the wind, then he'd know that today the weather's coming from the east. Now listen to me: We'll start running right now, in ten minutes it'll be raining so hard that we'll have no protection here." "But where do we run to?" asked the women. And it was Klaus Buch they asked. Over there, he said, behind some trees he had glimpsed a farm roof. And he was already running ahead. The women followed. Otto scampered after Sabina. So Helmut had no choice but to follow.

Wet with rain and sweat, they paused for breath under the overhanging barn roof. Klaus Buch, having arrived long before the women and Helmut, greeted them with a laugh. He didn't seem in the least out of breath. Well, there were worse things than a forest in this rain, he shouted, for it would soon be raining harder than ever. Over there, that wall of cloud, there was more to come. The only thing to do was to strip to the waist and run up the hill, so they would have something dry to put on when they got to the top. As he spoke, he was already undressing. So was Hella. Helmut hoped no one would come out of the farmhouse. Since Hella wasn't wearing a bra, she was naked to the waist after taking off her jacket and blouse. Here her breasts seemed even more inquisitive than on the boat. Again Helmut looked at them by looking past them. He and Sabina maintained that they always walked fully dressed in the rain. They were so used to it. Was there anything nicer than a warm summer rain?

Klaus started running. They reached the paved road and headed as fast as they could for the hilltop restaurant. By the time Helmut and Sabina arrived with Otto, Klaus Buch was already standing at the door, fresh as a daisy, his hair combed. Helmut was soaked with sweat as much as with rain. He was panting. Sabina was also a pitiful sight. Klaus Buch laughed and said it was a good thing Helmut had been the one to plan the hike. Helmut said as breezily as possible: "Oh, it was me, that's right." "It was your idea to come up here," said Klaus Buch, "wasn't it?" Helmut looked at the grinning face with a smile and thought, If he had even the slightest inkling of my hatred, he would run away. At the same time he gave Klaus Buch a friendly pat on the shoulder and said: "Of course it was me. Weather, direction, everything that happens externally, turns into a disaster where I'm concerned. If the Israelites had had to rely on me, they would still be in Egypt." Thank God, he had himself under control again.

While hurrying through the rain he had been thinking with disgust of the few seconds when he had been unable to hide his annoyance. There was nothing he loathed more than this state of being exposed to another person. In fact, something approaching zest for life could really develop in him only when he experienced the difference between the internal and the external. The greater the discrepancy between his true feelings and his facial expression, the greater his enjoyment. Only when he appeared to be someone else, and was someone else, did he really live. Only when he lived a double life did he live. Any directness, whether on his part or on the part of others, seemed to him unhygienic. When he gave way to an outburst—whether of anger or joy—he was usually immediately overcome by an almost uncontrollable depression. He felt at the end of his tether. Then anyone could do what they liked with him. In the apartment they could sometimes hear Dr. Zürn shouting through the house. He sounded as if about to expire from the effort required by all that shouting. Each time Helmut would think—as a kind of exorcism—Not that! Oh God, not that! He had rehearsed emergency measures against outbursts of any kind. What he had practiced was a sort of cheerfulness that might still have seemed a bit forced. This is what he now resorted to at the entrance to the restaurant.

Klaus Buch showed Helmut and Sabina the way to the restrooms. Suddenly they heard a piano being played. Quite forcefully. Klaus Buch stopped in his tracks, bringing Helmut and Sabina to a halt too. His face was working. Especially his mouth. His tongue bulged behind his lips, trying to break out somewhere, especially through the upper lip. Sabina said: *The Wanderer Fantasy*. Klaus Buch ran outside. Helmut walked into the restaurant. Hella was sitting at the piano and playing. Sabina finally walked over to her and said something. She stopped playing. As she passed him Helmut said: "Beautiful." Sabina and Helmut followed her outside. They saw Klaus Buch dashing wildly off. Clear across the meadows. Suddenly he stopped, changed direction, ran toward a tree, leaned against the trunk, put his hands in his pockets, and stared straight ahead. Hella said: "You two go inside, we'll be with you in a minute." Then, almost too firmly and without taking her eyes off him, she walked toward Klaus.

When Helmut and Sabina came back from the restrooms, Hella and Klaus had not yet returned, but they arrived before the

Halms had finished their soup. They were both smiling, walking close together, a happy couple. In their case, their soaked condition looked heroic. When they had all finished their soup, Klaus Buch wanted to know how much farther it was to the Höchste. Helmut told him they were already there. This made Klaus Buch laugh so uproariously that he had to stand up. "The Höchste!" he kept shouting. "The Höchste, Hella, would you believe it, we're on the Höchste—'the Highest'—by God, I'd call this hill the All-highest!"

Helmut was embarrassed by this display in front of the staff and the other guests apparently spending their vacation up here. He was also embarrassed for Klaus's sake. Helmut had the impression that Klaus wasn't nearly as amused as he pretended to be by the fact that this hill was called "the Highest." He was trying to find it more amusing than he actually did. Hella had let herself be carried away by Klaus, but her high, ringing laughter sounded even more artificial than Klaus's.

The Halms must *please* not get them wrong, she said. For herself and Klaus, a hike was something not to be accomplished in less than six hours. To find themselves at their destination after an hour simply seemed terribly funny to them. Helmut said that in fine weather the view from here was pretty unique. When Klaus Buch was about to laugh again, Hella cried: "Klaus, please, it makes Helmut quite sad when you laugh like that."

He tried to send her a look that she would find impossible to decipher. He wished to look mysterious. And tough. And inscrutable. He knew he was not succeeding because suddenly he found himself looking only at her nose. What a nose. What an adorable little nose. He was not going to go out of his mind. When he was twenty, he had gradually come to believe: I won't go out of my mind, ever. He noticed that Sabina was aware of his profound preoccupation. He nodded to her from the depths and said: "How's the schnitzel?"

Klaus Buch swore at the food. To begin with, his schnitzel was too thickly breaded; secondly, it was pork instead of veal; thirdly, the salad was a limp mess. He did not spare the waitress. She stood there with a heavy, putty-colored face under a towering coiffure, looking miserable. When, weighed down with reproaches, she finally turned without a word and plodded off, Hella said in a low voice that the waitress's old-fashioned miniskirt was really something to behold. "A pretty unique view, I'd say!" said Klaus Buch, and burst out laughing, which made Hella follow suit. They both laughed so hard that they dropped their knives and forks on their plates. Helmut and Sabina felt no urge whatever to laugh. Sabina at least tried to put on a knowing expression. Helmut made a great effort to sound jocular as he said: "Come on, kids, behave yourselves!" Hella gave him an ecstatic look and said: "Yes, daddy." Helmut tried to continue in that vein with: "Or you'll get it," and he looked at her a shade longer than was warranted by so short a sentence.

Sabina said: "The weather's clearing up."

Before Klaus Buch, who was now obviously at the point of dissolving into laughter at the slightest provocation, could burst out again, Hella said: "Ssssh!"

Helmut called the waitress and asked for the bill. The food had been excellent, he told her. It came to fifty-four marks twenty; Helmut said: "Make it sixty." He sternly rejected Klaus Buch's attempts to pay his share of the bill.

Helmut wanted to offer them some forest at least on their way back, and as soon as they left the restaurant he turned aside from the road. They entered a spacious forest. Helmut would have liked to hear someone say something about the tall tree trunks or about the green light or about the fragrant forest air.

When Otto suddenly disappeared and did not respond to Helmut's and Sabina's calls, Helene Buch stuck four fingers in her mouth and whistled so that the forest reverberated, and Otto came back at once. Helmut felt that Helene Buch understood the forest. Couldn't she make it resound like that again? However, shortly before entering the forest, they had passed a wheat field, and Klaus Buch was still carrying on about the farmers, who this year, in Baden-Württemberg alone, would be collecting 650 million marks in drought subsidies, and just look at these fields, those stands of wheat, one ear plumper than the next. Had any of them, on their way up from the lake, seen any drought damage anywhere? He hadn't. These crooks did nothing but collect. Oh well, he was just saying that because he was envious. Six hundred and fifty million marks in swindle subsidies, and not a single mark in it for him; it was enough to fill him with grief and despair. He simply couldn't see a crooked deal without being tormented by the desire to participate in it. Don't forget, he happened to be the son of a patent attorney. Really, these German farmers, said Hella Buch in a tone that emphasized rather than hid its artificiality, knew how to milk the taxpayer. On their trips through the Middle East, she and her husband had noticed time and again that there was such a thing as agriculture that could get along for years without water simply because the peasants had adjusted to producing drought-resistant crops. A Turkish peasant would never dream of trying to wangle a drought subsidy.

Helmut asked whether it wasn't demanding a bit too much of German farmers that they switch to drought-resistant crops, considering that a drought occurred only every ten or twenty years. He hoped that, in speaking these words, which unfortunately he had been unable to refrain from uttering, at least his voice had sounded pleasant. The plain fact was that he was annoyed because no one was enthusing about the forest. After all, it really was a perfect forest. And in this wetly shimmering forest this Klaus Buch was venting his spleen on drought subsidies about which, by his own admission, he had read for the first time in the morning paper. And she ignores the forest and immediately tries to bolster her husband's obviously weak position. And he himself is still naïve enough to criticize them instead of enthusiastically agreeing with the rubbish they are spouting. Only by agreeing can you escape. Theoretically, you know that. My God, how marvelous it could be now, alone with Sabina. They spoke very little when they went on a hike. At most, Sabina might put into words what they both saw anyway. She would say "a bench" when they stood beside a bench. And just when he was wondering whether the weather would hold, she would say: "I don't think we'll have any rain." And then it didn't matter one bit whether they had any rain or not, because it also didn't matter one bit what one of them said or had said or ever would say. Usually he would speak up at that point and say: "Oh my love. my one and only. Sabina."

They passed through Unterhomberg. A herd of young pigs came running up across the patch they had finished grazing. Otto was convulsed with rage. The hikers, prompted by Helmut's example, pulled up some grass outside the fence to feed to the slim little pigs. The pigs crowded against the electric fencing because the hikers were not pulling up enough grass and couldn't toss it far enough over the fence. This meant that the ones in front always got electric shocks on the pink bulges of their little snouts. The pink bulges reminded Helmut of Helene's nipples.

When they were just beyond the village, they heard behind them shouts, cries, echoing hoofbeats. They immediately ran to one side. Through the village came a horse. In headlong flight. The houses looked small compared to the horse. Perhaps because it was bounding in such huge leaps. With its head held stiffly, obstinately, to one side, it came thundering out from between the houses. Its front legs rose and fell so simultaneously that they seemed to be shackled together. One man had already tried to stand in its path but, since the horse did not slow down for him, he had been forced to jump aside at the last moment. Suddenly the horse stopped. About halfway between them and the village. Two men who had been running after the horse caught up with it. One, probably the owner, reached it first, spoke soothingly to it, approached it from the front, and tried to seize it by the halter. But at that moment, just as his hand came close to its head, the horse reared and raced off again. It raced past the hikers at full tilt, farting explosively. It was all Helmut could do to restrain Otto. Probably his barking added to the horse's frenzy. It was a splendid roan with a white blaze, enormous even on the open pathway. Klaus yelled at Otto: "Shut up, you mutt!" Tossed his jacket at Hella and ran after the horse. Hella called weakly: "Don't, Klaus . . . Klaus!"

When the horse came to a halt again, some distance away, and started grazing at the edge of the meadow, Klaus slackened his speed. The closer he came to the horse, the slower he walked, approaching it in a wide arc directly from the side. Finally he was seen to grab the mane, and the next moment he was sitting astride it. The horse galloped off again. But Klaus kept his seat. A small, compact figure. As if part of the horse. Since the path turned downhill into the trees, the two were now out of sight. Meanwhile the men from the village had caught up with Helmut and the women. One of them said the kid shouldn't have done that. Now for sure the roan wouldn't give up. He would run till he was worn out. The kid would never be able to make him stop. Most likely the roan would brush the kid off somewhere.

The farmer obviously assumed that Klaus, whom he had seen only from a distance, was Helmut and Sabina's son.

Hella had turned her back when Klaus jumped on the horse. That was how she was still standing. Sabina walked over to her. At that moment, around the bend under the trees, Klaus appeared with the roan. And when he reached them, the roan stopped. Both were sweating. Hella ran up to him. They all ran up to him. Except for Helmut. Otto was barking furiously again, so Helmut had to keep him as far away as possible. Klaus handed over the horse. The farmer said: "You could have killed yourself!" Klaus said with a laugh: "No way! He's a fine fellow. Probably just a horsefly that made him bolt." The farmer shook his head, as if still disapproving of Klaus's interference. Then they parted and went their separate ways.

When they were on their own again and all expressed their admiration of Klaus, he said, putting his arm around Hella's shoulder: "You see? If I hadn't stopped that horse in Merano, I would have been scared of this one." The horse in Merano, he explained to Helmut and Sabina, had only been a Haflinger, a smaller breed. "And Hella tried to hold me back. You know, if there's something I can identify with, it's a runaway horse. That farmer made the mistake of approaching the horse from the front and talking to it. You must never stand in the path of a runaway horse. It must have the feeling that its path remains unobstructed. Besides: You can't reason with a runaway horse."

Klaus spoke with fine, sweeping gestures and great aplomb. Hella now seemed smaller than he. Helmut agreed effusively. "You're right!" he cried. "How right you are!" Sabina said: "How would you know?" "Ah," he said, "I suppose you've forgotten that I'm a horseman from way back."

It was beginning to rain again. Since Helmut could no longer promise them any sheltering forest, Klaus Buch, stripped to the waist again, ran ahead to get the car.

Helmut was walking between Hella and Sabina. Hella and Helmut: Suddenly these two names seemed to him like two parts designed to be fitted together. He would call her Helene if he had something to say to her. They walked through a gang of workmen who were carrying on with their blacktopping in spite of the rain. Helmut had a fleeting hope that this asphalt would only *look* like the real thing and would soon disintegrate again into slag and gravel. What he was hoping was that these men were also producing only pretense.

When they were sitting safe and sound in the car, Sabina said: "Klaus, you saved our lives." Klaus said to Hella—this time gaily, cockily, by way of parody: "You don't care for me anymore, do you." She kissed him and agreed that he had indeed saved all their lives. Helmut chimed in, and his praises of Klaus Buch were even more vociferous than the women's. Klaus was now no longer afraid of Otto's nose. Helmut could understand that.

Helmut couldn't go on listening to the others. He was about to lose the ground from under his feet. Once again he found himself forced to view his situation as a painful image. What a person sees reflects virtually nothing of what actually is, he thought. He saw himself lying on a rock under a cascade of water. He, Helmut, can find almost nothing to hold on to. But the deluge of water simply won't subside. The end is no longer in doubt. Nevertheless, he keeps clawing his fingers into the rock. And this, since the end is certain, merely prolongs the agony. He can clearly see himself gasping open-mouthed, rolling his eyes heavenward, as in a nineteenth-century picture. As soon as he exhausted this image, he saw himself sweating and shivering. He didn't know how it was possible, but he was shivering and sweating at the same time. He couldn't have said whether he actually was sweating and shivering or whether he was merely imagining it to the point of physical perception.

As Sabina and Helmut were getting out of the car, Klaus thrust two paperbacks at them. One by him and the other by Hella. Helmut said it could now rain pennies from heaven as far as he was concerned, he was so eager to read these books, that for the next few days he wouldn't stir out of their apartment.

"You won't get rid of us that way!" said Klaus Buch. First they don't meet for twenty-three years, then Helmut wants to give them the slip right away. "Fine thing," said Klaus Buch. They would pick the Halms up at eight-thirty tonight. And tonight he would be in charge. No argument.

They drove off. Helmut ran inside, threw himself on the sofa, and stared up at the ceiling. He could have wept. Sabina pretended not to understand. He wouldn't believe her. He was glad to find Otto frantically eager to be petted and patted by him.

On noticing that Sabina was about to say something, he jumped up and said: "I'm going under the shower for an hour."

When he emerged, Sabina showed him Klaus's book and asked if he knew that Klaus wrote his name with a C.

"Terrific," he said.

7. JUST BEFORE eight-thirty, Helmut and Sabina were standing on the porch contemplating Mrs. Zürn's riotous medley of a flower garden with an absorption that Mrs. Zürn, had she suddenly appeared, would have found most gratifying. Mrs. Zürn had once told Helmut that she was embarrassed about the bars over the apartment windows, which was why she had planted phlox, foxglove, rose campion and, especially, those tall hollyhocks. Helmut had replied that once you had become used to the bars you didn't see them anymore, whereas the glorious show of flowers was a daily miracle.

He did not mention the fact that every day he noted the straight, unadorned bars at the windows with deep satisfaction. Every year, on their return to their little house in Sillenbuch, he missed the bars. Unbarred windows then seemed desolate and empty.

As soon as the car with the Starnberg license plate drove up, Helmut and Sabina hurried to the garden gate. Helmut wanted to prevent Klaus from even setting foot on Zürn soil.

Everything Klaus had recently been wearing in blue had now been switched to faded pink.

Only belt and sandals seemed to be the same.

Helene was naked and had draped something black over herself. The Buchs had reserved a table at their hotel. They were sitting right above the water. But behind glass. All the tables were occupied by little groups like theirs. The waitresses moved about. What a beautiful void, Helmut thought. Now to drink and sink to the bottom. But Klaus Buch was determined to find out whether there was any justification for his suspicion that his romantic-bizarre HH had turned into a workaholic. Helmut nodded. "Oh come on," said Klaus Buch, "I can't believe that." "Sabina," said Helmut, "what would you say?" Sabina said that Helmut worked nonstop, though in a way that wasn't apparent to everyone. He always had his nose in a book. It looked as if he were studying, but she was more inclined to regard it as living, meaning that it produced no tangible results. Maybe that wasn't even his purpose. Mind you, he did change as a result of his reading. After reading a page he wasn't the same man as the one who had turned it. Helmut gave a low whistle. Of approval. In any case, he was constantly progressing, that much she could see. At any rate, considering the tempo that Helmut had gradually set himself, she had long despaired of keeping up with him. Yes, he was welcome to give another whistle. He interjected that although he would love to accompany her aria with sixty-four violins, all he had was two parched lips to which even Klaus would not refuse a drought subsidy. Unperturbed, Sabina said that sometimes she found his tempo pretty ruthless. He gave the impression of no longer caring whether she could keep up with him or not. Helmut said, as if he didn't mean it: "Doesn't she lie beautifully? And all the time she knows she's lying."

Klaus Buch said: "She's raving about you. Hella, why don't you rave about me for a change?"

"You take care of that yourself," said Helene.

Klaus Buch first said Hella didn't care for him anymore, then he said he was so happy to see that Helmut had not become a bourgeois.

Helmut thought: If I'm anything at all, I'm a bourgeois. And if there's anything at all I'm proud of, it's that. He decided that as a bourgeois the best thing for him to do at this moment was to smile and drink a toast to Klaus Buch, but on no account try to start discussing this designation with him. It had been a pleasure to hear Sabina talking so totally wide of the mark about his reading and living. If he imagined her saying those things when he was alone with her, all he could do was laugh. Alone with him, none of these performances would be possible. They were presentation pieces. What they expressed was a need, not a reality. She wanted to say something impressive about her husband. Perhaps she was trying to tell him something.

It turned out that Klaus Buch had asked about Helmut's attitude toward work because he liked telling people how he and Hella felt about work. They worked as little as possible, he said. "Right?" he asked. She said: "Yes, we don't need work in order to feel good." That sounded rehearsed. Klaus Buch said life was too short to waste it on work. She said, now quoting him openly and perhaps even critically (or was that wishful thinking on Helmut's part?): "Only people who are sexually inadequate need work." Now Klaus took over completely. Work was a substitute for sex. It also meant the annihilation of sex. On the other hand, sex, when taken seriously, meant the annihilation of the will to work. Anyone wanting to live must not be distracted by work. Work made a person incapable of love. Right? Or don't you care for me anymore.

She kissed him and said: "He tends to talk about it a bit too much. But that's his only fault."

"Does that mean that otherwise I'm pretty good?" he asked insatiably.

She laughed and said: "So-so."

"You admit it," he insisted stubbornly.

"Yes, I admit it," she said, laughing and kissing him.

"You're eighteen years younger than I am. Have you ever had reason to complain?" he asked relentlessly.

She put her hand over his mouth.

"I'm serious," he said.

"So am I," she said.

"You don't care for me anymore, do you?" he said.

"He has to keep talking about it," she said, without having kissed her husband. "Can you understand that? I'm not that keen on this craze for verbalizing. But no doubt that's just envy because I'm not so good at it."

"You don't care for me anymore, do you?" he said.

Now she kissed him. Then they both drank some of their mineral water. For the first time they seemed to be bothered by the smoke from Helmut's cigar and Sabina's cigarette. As on the previous evening, Helmut again had difficulty enjoying his wine and cigar. He drank quickly. He wanted to get drunk as quickly as possible. Should he admit to himself that he was in love with this girl Hella? What would be the point? And was it really true? Wasn't he completely indifferent to her?

Klaus Buch suddenly began to tell them about his father's ninetieth birthday, which he and Hella had just celebrated. They had picked him up from his exclusive retirement home in Degerloch. He had been amazingly strong and amazingly feeble. But all there. Interested in everything. Name of the federal chancellor, the federal president, even the president of the federal parliament, knew them all. . . . Helmut loathed being told about old people. Incontinent, mind you, but can still reel off his multiplication tables! Probably Klaus Buch was merely anxious to demonstrate that he had another forty-five years, significant years, ahead of him. Helene said: "My mother is seventy-one and still enjoys life without restriction." Restriction, thought Helmut, with a little shudder. Trips to Africa, Persia, every year, said Helene. Nowhere, her mother had recently written, had she felt as happy as in Bali. Shouldn't it be *on* Bali? thought Helmut. "Where are your parents?"

Helmut turned his thumb straight down. Klaus said: "Show them the photos." Helene said: "The Halms won't be interested." "Go ahead, show them the photos. There's nothing more interesting than pictures of old people."

Helmut said he wouldn't like to get older than seventy.

He found this remark just as mendacious as it was true. Hence nonsensical. But wasn't everything he could say here nonsensical? Only what Hella and Klaus said really made sense. They wanted to grow old. There was every likelihood that they would grow old. They were looking forward to being able to grow old. They were doing everything in their power to grow old. They had the strength for it. Their thinking was such as to enable them to face up healthily to a ripe old age. And anyone who thought otherwise was talking nonsense. The only thing that made sense was to live to a ripe old age. A person who lives longer than someone else is more successful than the other person. The longer you outlive the other person, the greater your victory over him. Helmut wasn't sure whether that was exactly what the Buchs were trying to tell him, but that was how he interpreted the way they vied with each other in describing seventieth and ninetieth birthdays. They had celebrated by going on long drives with their respective parents. Eaten blood sausages and liverwurst on mountain meadows. Taken them to the movies. How the old folks had laughed! Look at him. And her. Just look. Poking their withered noses into bouquets. Look at that one. Sniffing up rapture from them. Just look. A continuous round of pleasures. Nothing is more beautiful than that. And the most beautiful part of all is that it never stops being beautiful till one's dying day.

Helmut said he was more grateful to the Buchs for this evening than everything else. No one, as long as he could remember, had so fortified him. So uplifted him. So richly rewarded him.

He felt his eyes filling with tears. He pretended to be embarrassed and quickly left the room. As a matter of fact, he was ready to burst into tears.

He was drunk.

Tomorrow Hella would be making her rounds of the villages, so the Halms could go sailing with Klaus. Hella would love to take Sabina along on her rounds, but she knew from experience that with two visitors the little old grannies would be twice as unapproachable. Oh, hadn't they told the Halms anything at all about Hella's new book? Klaus explains: It's going to be called: *From Grandma's Lips*. Hella drives around the villages inland, asks the mayor for the names of the five oldest women, then for the names of the three most talkative ones among them, then proceeds to drive to their homes to tape whatever good advice they can still remember. She already has thirty-seven tapes full of grandmothers. Hella says she only hopes that this book, which again is Klaus's idea, will sell better than her herb primer. "I don't know what you're talking about, my sweet," cried Klaus Buch. "Your primer is a slow burner that will feed us in the Bahamas until we're ninety years old. All right then, we'll cast off tomorrow afternoon at two-thirty." Sabina begged to be excused. She had an appointment with the hairdresser tomorrow in Meersburg. She went there every year on the same day. It was an appointment that couldn't possibly be changed. In that case, just Helmut. Klaus Buch is delighted. It'll be an orgy of reminiscing for mature men. Ciao.

Helmut and Sabina, heavy with wine, traipsed homeward. Helmut said: "Lucky you!" "My God, they're energetic!" said Sabina. "What a blessing they can't ruin more than our vacation," said Helmut. "Starnberg is too far away." Sabina took Helmut's arm and said: "Don't be so negative." "But I like being negative," said Helmut. "Are we going to have another thunderstorm tonight, Mr. Negative?" she asked pointedly. "Ask Klaus Buch, Mrs. Positive," he said. "Wicked man," she said. "I'm asking you, from now on I'll ask only you, I'll talk only to you, I'll forget every other language in the world except yours, now there!" "I was hoping that was already the case," he sighed. So he, Helmut said, had indeed progressed farther than she had, since he had long given up trying to understand anyone except her. He put his arm round Sabina and squeezed her until she squeaked a little. That made him think of Helene Buch. For the moment there was nothing he could do about that. "I'm drunk," he said. "We are," she said. "I am," he said. "We are," she said. "Who cares?" he said, running ahead of her. But she quickly caught up with him and didn't let go until they reached the apartment.

He complained once more about the way she had got out of sailing tomorrow. He couldn't understand it. She talked about this Klaus Buch like a flower in love with the wind, and then she backed out. Tomorrow wasn't her hair day at all. She was, she said with a nasty little giggle, afraid of falling in love with Klaus—whom Helmut, in spite of his promise, had again called "this." Helmut wondered whether he should rape her and throw her into the lake and prevent her from coming ashore again. "I'll forgive you this lapse and the next," he said. "I won't be offended till the third, and the one after that will be fatal, absolutely fatal." "It makes me shiver when you talk like that," she said. "That's fine," he said. "I feel warm when you shiver when I talk." "Then there will be a thunderstorm," she said. "Oh you little naturalist!" he said. "Here we are on the brink of disaster, and you talk like the weatherman. We've both been a little bit seduced at the moment," he said. "We'd better watch out. After all, we're farther along than they are," he said. "Maybe you are," she said. "Fine," he said, "I know, you aren't. Nor am I. Fine. You must resist this seduction by the Buch family, my girl. Even if what they are doing is the right thing. Let's stick with the wrong thing." "Why?" she asked. "I don't know," he said. But, he went on, it had never been so important to stick with the wrong thing as now. The wrong thing is the right thing. This evening, Bina. Tonight. If they were to get close tonight, she would be thinking of Klaus and he of Helene, and the very idea of that was enough to unman him. "Idiot," she said. "Yes," he said. "Spoilsport," she said. "Yes," he said. "Moron," she said. "Yes," he said. "Asshole," she said. "That'll do," he said and, bending down to her, kissed her carefully and said: "Oh my love. My one and only. Sabina."

Only when she had fallen asleep did he breathe easily. Although it hadn't ended up as the talk he owed Sabina, they had touched places in each other that they had never touched before.

Beautiful, he thought, clothes that have been made over, how beautiful.

8. KLAUS BUCH pushed open the door for him, Helmut got in; Klaus, in greeting Helmut, let his hand lie a shade too long on Helmut's shoulder. Helmut regretted that he didn't feel the same way about this as did Klaus Buch. It would be nice if there were someone whose hand one wouldn't mind having a shade too long on one's shoulder. He should have apologized for his inability to reciprocate emotions. Today Klaus Buch was all in white. The blue of his eyes had never been so blue. He pushed and pouted his mobile lips even when he was not speaking. He

was aroused. Nothing against the women, of course, but for Fate to present them with a day all to themselves was just great, didn't he agree? "Man, Helmut, just us two, that's really wild!" He stepped on the gas, then immediately had to brake, they were already there. Klaus Buch went into the hotel to pick up a bag. This time he had brought some canvas sneakers along for Helmut too. Helmut doubted they would fit, but Klaus reminded him that they had always worn the same size shoes. Helmut had to help hoist the sails. Klaus Buch would insist on merrily calling out each instruction two to four times, as if Helmut were an idiot. Even so, Klaus Buch frequently had to come skipping across to show Helmut where to put his hand.

At first there were still some extended patches of moderate wind. Then the whole lake was as smooth as molten lead. Everything visible had only one color. They had emerged from Lake Überlingen and were now drifting outside, somewhere between Hagnau and Kesswil, Helmut estimated. Klaus Buch cursed Lake Constance. That it was an impotent old bag, could only do it once a day, and then so feebly as to be barely noticeable. Just look around: a landscape of muggy, floppy rags, just look, those houses over there, and those hills, just look, the sky, everything hanging, hanging, hanging, we're in for an afternoon in the Hereafter, my friend. What a shit of a lake. Frankly, if it weren't for the research to be done for Hella's book, he would never come here to sail. It might be all right for old fogies for whom the fever of life is over. Just take a look around you, this whole area, gone to its eternal rest. I swear it. Nothing happens here anymore. We are in the realm of the dead. Dreary isn't the word for it. The waters of Lethe, Helmut. Sorry. I was looking forward to a good stiff sail with you. Not a chance now. So all we can do is chew the rag. Let's chew the rag then.

He said this with incredible ferocity, his loose lips and unruly tongue moving in an obscene parody of speech. Helmut had to laugh. That put Klaus Buch in a good mood.

Christ, how they used to sail in the Aegean. They had to tie each other to the boat or they would have been washed overboard. Twelve hours at a stretch without leaving the tiller for a second. Once the boreas blew so hard that for three days they couldn't even get out of the harbor. Once they sailed from Thasos to Rhodes more under and through the waves than over the top of them. The one thing he was looking forward to was the Bahamas with their steady trade wind. Couldn't Helmut see himself joining them? Far be it from him, Klaus Buch, to wish to poke his nose into Helmut's affairs, but he had the impression that it might do Helmut good to simply clear the decks, burn his bridges, and set out for a new world. "Life needs stimulation," said Klaus Buch, "otherwise it peters out. While you're still alive. You see, it's different from ethics or morals, the world of the spirit simply exists of itself, maybe it can generate its own tension, I really don't know about that, you're the expert there. On the other hand, I know that living matter needs an impetus. In fact, what living matter needs is something totally new. Nothing can be new enough for it. The newer, the more alive. The totally unpredictable reaction, if you follow me, that's life. Tell me, Helmut, how often do you screw your wife?"

Helmut must have given him such a look that Klaus Buch did not insist on an answer. "Or to put it another way," he said. "Are you quite sure you still love your wife? Please, don't misunderstand me, Sabina is really a wild woman, I envy you Sabina, but even the wildest woman can be a threat to men of our age. If she doesn't have it anymore. Hella could also be a threat to me. If she didn't have it anymore. But she still has it. And how! Hella is a challenge for me. She's too much for me. I can't cope with her. It's a constant struggle. Day and night. It keeps you in shape, that's for sure.

"After you've been in bed for a month, you can't walk half a mile, that's how far gone your muscles are. It's like that with *everything,* Helmut. I'm truly fascinated by life, Helmut, believe me. When a raindrop splashes onto my skin, I could scream with delight. When I look up into a tree, I could shriek for love of chlorophyll. But I'm scared of my mind going to seed, Helmut. The danger exists, I know that. I'd like to stay brilliant, you know? Bright. Outstanding. And noble. Noble through and through. Like untearable silk, that's what I'd like to be. Raw silk, of course. I am a worshiper of myself. To some extent Hella also worships me. Because she considers me more intelligent than I am, you know. I go on pretending to her. I keep her smaller than she is. I persuade her to do things that are beyond her. Just in case I can't cope with her, you know. What I really need is a person like you, Helmut. I mean it. When I saw you sitting there on the promenade, *ecco*, it was a vision. My old HH, forever gnawing away at problems, reading *Zarathustra* in his swim trunks—Helmut, if you come along to the Bahamas, it'll be the salvation of both of us. There you can do anything you like in your swim trunks. What would you be giving up here? What school are you at anyway?"

"Eberhard Ludwig," Helmut said, doing his best not to sound proud.

"Oh," said Klaus Buch, "congratulations—oh well, you were always tops, of course. Even so, I make so bold—imagine, me, old cockroach, never been anything, never become anything—I make so bold as to offer you—a Ph.D. and revered teacher at illustrious E.L.—some far-reaching propositions. I maintain that it's necessary. You need to be saved. You need me, Helmut, I can sense that. Hence my question, how often do you screw Sabina? I don't mean to humiliate you, man. I'm not trying to make like the Body Beautiful. Christ, Helmut, toward the end I used to screw my first wife only once a week. That's the kind of shape I was in. *We* were in. So there. Feel free to talk to me. If you want to. I simply feel that, before we reach fifty, we two should launch out again. And without you I am in danger of mental stagnation. I'm quite aware of that. You are truly a challenge for me. You and Hella, then things will start to hum. No problem."

Helmut nodded as often as he could. Klaus Buch must be under the impression that Helmut was seriously considering these propositions. That stimulated him to even further suggestions. Since Helmut had not yet shown any readiness to speak, Klaus Buch said, he could only continue to bare his soul in an effort to provoke Helmut into abandoning his reserve—a reserve so threatening to himself—so that they could at last jointly pursue their joint salvation. Helmut was—and he, Klaus Buch, felt this quite clearly—acutely aware of the danger of stagnation. Maybe Helmut had even resigned himself to it. But he, Klaus Buch, didn't think so. He was more inclined to think that Helmut was temporarily playing at resignation but that, as soon as he realized that it was no longer a game, he would try desperately to escape from that resignation. Then it really would be too late. Or at best a panic action. But there was still time for them to plan their second launching together. And in such a way that it would succeed. Without anybody getting hurt. That was the crucial point. He could say that the separation from his first wife had come to pass without either of them getting seriously hurt. Precisely because he hadn't waited for panic to set in. So, as far as he was concerned, the offer was unconditional. He suspected that Helmut might already be suffering the first damage inflicted by the unappealing routine of finality. *Might* be! he had said. And his offer, far from being prompted by compassion, was downright selfish. The more Helmut made use of him, the more emboldened he would be to make use of Helmut. And, after all, they were such old friends that they could be quite ruthless about offering mutual assistance. No inhibition must come between them. Helmut could consult Klaus Buch, if he wanted to know how he could split up with Sabina with a minimum of damage—provided that was what Helmut wanted, of course, he was only mentioning it as an example because every man who still has life in him wants to split up with his wife, only the dead are faithful. But Helmut would be just as welcome to consult him, if in need of reassurance as to the length of his penis; this, too, he was merely mentioning because every man who still had life in him was interested in any chance to test his own competence. If for once two men were to join forces they would carry off a tremendous victory. If each of them remained alone, each would have to wangle his own miserable way through life, seizing loot, securing loot, consuming loot, seizing more loot, and so on. "Helmut, man, let's aim for the top. Not settle for less. Remain great. Become greater. The greatest. We two are the greatest, I swear it. Life is calling us. I'll get you out of your doldrums, kiddo. I'll fix you up again. You'll see, in a year you won't know yourself. You're on the point of going under. I refuse to watch. I'll turn you on, man. I'll put such an appetite into your belly, you'll go straight up in the air, want to bet? First off, you'll come to us in Starnberg. Just for a few days. That'll get the whole thing rolling.

And it'll just keep rolling, I'm convinced of it. Helmut, man, in Starnberg, you know, I often sit naked on the terrace from four to seven in the morning, listening to the birds. There's no sound in the world like it. I have some huge trees in my garden, that's where the birds start up even before the sun has properly risen. But not first one and then the other: Like in an orchestra, all the ones that belong together start up at the same time. Some come in gently, some clamorously. And the next moment a positively inconceivable number of birds are singing. But you don't see a single one. So the trees themselves seem to produce the sound. And you can no longer tell that this chorus comes from individual birds. It might just as well be coming from a giant pipe organ. Or from a few hundred organs being played on their highest registers. And it doesn't sound in the least like outdoors, more like an echo chamber. Like a giant echo chamber resounding, reverberating, with birds' voices. It's as if the whole world were reduced to the nave of a church. And the fantastic part is that the chamber itself, the nave, just imagine, doesn't stay in one place, it rises, you can hear it, it rises up into the air. But it doesn't budge an inch. That's the most staggering part. It hovers. It really does. It hovers. In the air. The chamber just keeps on growing. And echoing. A vast chamber consisting of nothing but birds' voices. A bird-cathedral, formed by a reverberating multitonal sound. My dear Helmut, that's when I have to go indoors, but on tiptoe, as silently as the first ray of sunshine; and although I'm in the mood to shout and stomp, to leap in the air, dive onto her, no, I snuggle up to her and caress her awake, but even before she is quite awake I have the seduction already in place so that, when she opens her eyes, when her lips part, she already desires me. Capito?"

A squall hit the boat and with a resounding crack blew the sail to the other side.

"Hello there, we have a visitor!" cried Klaus Buch, grasping the lines and the tiller.

Helmut had not been able to look very long at Klaus Buch's mouth either bulging out or split open by a tongue run riot. He had fully understood the haste with which Klaus Buch had been speaking. While Klaus Buch had been talking as if for dear life,

Helmut had kept his eyes quietly on the surface of the lake, the surface of the sky, the gradually materializing shoreline. Almost imperceptibly, colors had reappeared. In the sky, inky patches of every shade of blue had flowed together. In the course of the afternoon, everything had grown more definite. At some places in the inky streams there were now even distinct silvery borders. Only the western sky still consisted of an endless transparency. A real pink. Helmut was reminded of "the real thing." The water had absorbed all these colors and concentrated them in a dense blend. In the water one could see all the blues, the silver, the pink; together they produced a blue of increasing steeliness flooded by a violet gold. And it was into this that the thundery squalls ripped their black scars.

"Storm warning!" cried Klaus Buch, letting his tongue break through his mouth and pointing enthusiastically across to Switzerland and back to the German shore. At many places, yellow warning lights were flashing. A color otherwise not present. The squalls came from all sides. Klaus Buch swore. "It's gone crazy!" he shouted. He meant the wind, he said. He looked around belligerently, not to be caught napping by the approaching squalls. "We need headway, then the squalls can't hurt us," he cried. Squalls with no wind; he had never seen such a thing. Helmut was to tend the jib sheet. When Klaus Buch called *let run,* he was to pay out the line but never let go entirely; when Klaus Buch called *haul in,* he was to take in the line. While he was still speaking, a gust passed over them that Klaus answered with a leap to Helmut's side. "Boy oh boy, was that ever a handful!" he cried. He explained what Helmut had to do when they came about. Helmut asked whether they were now heading for the German or the Swiss shore. For the time being they would be sashaying with these totally crazy squalls, said Klaus Buch. As soon as those were followed by a wind from one direction, something that was to be expected even on Lake Constance, they would carry on with their afternoon sail. Helmut pointed to the storm warnings. He was afraid. Among the darkened colors, the many glaring lights flashing away at various points looked ominous. Klaus Buch pointed to the darkest part of the sky: an advancing thunderstorm, that would give them just what they needed. Helmut said he would rather they tried to reach land as quickly as possible. Switzerland seemed closer to him. Why not make for Utwil or Kesswil and phone Hella from there, maybe she could pick them up with the car? "And us at the roadside with the sail under our arms, right?" Klaus Buch laughed. Helmut said they could also wait out the storm ashore. Probably the German side was easier to reach after all, since the wind was coming from the southwest.

Klaus Buch said it was high time for Helmut to stop evading life. Another squall hit them, Klaus Buch called out: "Let run!" But Helmut let go too late. Since Klaus Buch had luffed the mainsail in time and compensated with the rudder, they survived the squall nicely. But it was immediately followed by the next. Helmut shouted: "Klaus, we'll have to head for shore!"

By now the lake had turned into a light green, whitely hissing surface. Klaus Buch shrieked with delight. Helmut thought: Maybe he really is crazy. Klaus shouted to Helmut to sit on the side of the boat. Helmut moved up. They were now racing full tilt toward Switzerland. Theirs was the only boat left on the lake. Close to the shore, they could see boats without sails making for the harbors, probably with their engines.

Klaus Buch behaved more and more like a rodeo rider. He talked to the wind. Gave every approaching squalI a new name. "That's Susie, trying to crush us between her thighs, attaboy, let run! There she goes!" Each time they righted themselves after a gust, he would give Helmut a happy laugh, pat the hull, and shout: "Good girl, *Seabird*, good girl! "

Helmut saw that it was becoming increasingly difficult to cope with the wind pressure by maneuvering and shifting ballast. Flying spray had long since soaked them to the skin. He was holding his jib sheet by the very end. "Haul in!" roared Klaus Buch. Helmut shouted: "You're nuts!" He was convinced the boat would capsize as soon as any strain was put on the jib. The wind was producing a sharp, machine-gun rattle with the flapping jib. "Full warning!" Klaus Buch shouted triumphantly. True enough, the lights were flashing twice as fast. "Head in now!" yelled Helmut. Klaus Buch shouted: "Coward!" Helmut couldn't take the excessive heeling of the boat anymore. The waves were already washing aboard. So this Klaus Buch was a madman after all. By leaning their weight as far out as possible and keeping the sheets completely slack, they now managed to hold the boat on the very verge of capsizing. But the storm increased. The boat began to heel still farther. Helmut simply let go his sheet. The snapping and rattling became ominous, as if someone were hammering away at them. Klaus Buch shouted: "To make you happy, we'll re-eef!" He turned the boat straight into the wind. The boat righted itself immediately. Thank God. Helmut could breathe again. Klaus Buch called out: "Get over to the tiller! Hold it between your legs! Keep the boat heading straight into the wind! Don't be such a sissy, man! Grab ahold of it! As if it were part of you!" He laughed and skipped over to the mast. Helmut had no idea how, in the midst of all the roaring and snapping and rattling, he was supposed to achieve anything with this ridiculous piece of wood. It seemed like midnight to him. Suddenly he felt a pressure on the tiller. The boat was no longer heading straight into the wind. He jerked. But in the wrong direction. The mainsail swung clear across. Klaus Buch yelled something. Rushed at Helmut, grabbed the tiller out of his hand, bent down for the lines. Helmut felt sure the boat was about to capsize. Certainly it would, if Klaus Buch hauled in the mainsail again and the boat was once more at that appalling angle. When Klaus straightened up, working with the tiller and the sheets to bring the boat under control and the boat started to heel over again, Helmut shouted: "Don't!" Klaus Buch shouted back: "We're taking off!" And laughed. Preposterously. And hung terrifyingly far out over the side of the boat. He was practically lying on his back. The boat had resumed its appalling angle. It was obviously going to capsize within the next few seconds. "Come along, sweetheart," Klaus Buch yelled. "I need your weight!" Helmut positioned himself on the hull but kept most of his weight inside the cockpit. Now Klaus Buch was even tipping his head back as he shouted, "*Lucy in the sky!*" When Helmut saw that the waves washing aboard were about to pour into the cockpit, he kicked the tiller out of Klaus Buch's hand. Then everything happened at once. The boat shot back into the wind. Klaus Buch toppled backward into the water. The boat righted itself. The wind caught it from the other side. Helmut ducked just in time as the mainsail whipped across. Then he cowered beside the mast and looked around for Klaus Buch. The instant before Klaus hit the water, Helmut had received one look from him. The mainsail had torn loose. Mainsail and jib were flapping before the wind, which was now coming from behind. In spite of the clattering of the sails, it was suddenly much quieter. Helmut cautiously got to his feet, his eyes scanning the white crests and the dark troughs. "Klaus!" he shouted. Louder and louder: "Klaus! Klaus!" When he realized that he was now shouting only for his own benefit, he stopped. Be quiet, he thought. Don't try anything now. Just keep quiet. Klaus should be able to take care of himself. A sportsman like him. If they should ever capsize, Klaus had lectured, the thing to do was let yourself be carried by the waves. Never try to reach a nearby shore against the waves. It was absolutely no problem to swim three miles with the waves, but impossible to swim five hundred yards against them. Absolutely no problem. So there. Idiot. Forget about it. You didn't mean it to happen! You *didn't*! So there. Then why are you on the defensive? You didn't mean it to happen. Stop it! Klaus can look after himself. But you can't. That's the way it is. He would cling to this boat. If it sank, he would go down with it. But maybe it wouldn't sink. Klaus Buch had said something about buoyancy tanks. He looked around for places to hang onto. He refused to look out of the boat. But to judge by the snapping and rattling he must still be making headway. By now it was almost dark. It was raining. Klaus . . . Oh Sabina, if you only knew. Had he ever felt so utterly shattered? He gave a great wail. During those last few months, when he had still been having sex with Sabina, he had experienced exactly the same sensation, that of being destroyed. Each time it was as if he had committed an irremediable error. Each time he had wailed like that. A long-drawn-out, steadily rising wail. His life was to be endured, he had felt, only if he continued, and never ceased, to emit those high-pitched, infinitely prolonged, muted screams. But he wasn't allowed to. Each time this happened, Sabina was so alarmed that he had to break off at once. He had told her he only did it for fun: She could see for herself, his eyes were completely dry, he enjoyed uttering these little cries. But Sabina had said, if that were so, she didn't want to live, those sounds were so terrible.

Now he was free to scream as high and long as he wanted. Once again he had committed an irremediable error.

Only when the keel suddenly scraped the gravel along the shore did he stop crying out. He jumped into the water, waded ashore, and headed for the nearest light.

People were alarmed. They called for an ambulance. They urged him to drink tea laced with brandy. He was in Immenstaad, they told him. They notified the water police so that action could be taken immediately to rescue his friend. They telephoned Sabina. They telephoned Helene Buch. Helmut thought he had better remain apathetic. In Unterhomberg Klaus had said you couldn't reason with a runaway horse. He had agreed.

9. HELMUT STOOD at the window, looking through his binoculars at the foxglove blossoms where the ants, ten times their real size, were crawling over the aphids and milking them. "Voyeur," said Sabina. "Shouldn't you phone Helene Buch?" he said. "If she hasn't heard anything by now, she won't hear anything," said Sabina. "Have you noticed, the red lily opened up during the night?" he said. "I'm sure she would call us if she'd heard anything," said Sabina.

Helmut walked up and down on the Kirman rug. "Why don't you call her," he said, "just to be on the safe side?"

Sabina got up and, reluctantly, went over to the Zürns'. It was all right for her to do that. In all the eleven years he had never used the Zürns' telephone.

Once when he had been walking around on this pale Kirman with the dark blue medallion, he had been obsessed with the notion that clutching his right hand was a person the size of a seven-year-old child, and that this person was Friedrich Nietzsche, aged forty but reduced to the dimensions of a seven-year-old. And his terrible fear of Otto made him cling to Helmut's hand.

Klaus Buch had later had exactly the same fear of Otto as Helmut had observed in his miniature Nietzsche.

Helmut was in the habit, when walking up and down on the Kirman rug, all alone, of talking unconsciously to himself. "Quiet," he would say, "quiet, quiet." And after a certain interval: "All the dead, move up one; all the dead, move up one."

It was a very old habit, this *Quiet*, and *All the dead, move up one*. As soon as Sabina had left the room he now said: "Quiet, quiet," and, after a pause: "All the dead, move up one; all the dead, move up one." But he had a feeling that today he had started to speak not automatically but consciously.

Sabina reported that Hella still had no news. "Aren't we going down to the lake at all today?" he asked. She couldn't bear the sight of the lake today, she replied. Mrs. Zürn had told her that, according to the newspaper, three people had been drowned in yesterday's storm. One had drowned although two motorboats had reached the capsized sailboat and thrown ropes to the yachtsman, who had been clinging to the hull. The waves had torn him away from the boat and, unable to reach the ropes, he had disappeared before the very eyes of his rescuers. Helmut nodded as if he knew what it was like. Sabina put her hands around him and nestled against him. Helmut responded as far as he was able. He would go down to the lake anyway. Maybe she would come later. "How did Hella sound on the phone?" he asked. Her voice had been very low and miserable; she had hardly said anything. Just Yes and No. Helmut picked up the first volume of Kierkegaard, quickly left the house, and walked down toward the water. Otto was happy and scampered along with him. They were greeted outside by the Zürns' spaniel Florian, who always wanted to start something with Otto. But Otto, a bitch, invariably fought off the advances of Florian, a male dog of the same age, as fiercely as possible.

Today the lake presented itself as edgeless. Serene. And innocent. Helmut liked that. In that softly blue, shining, edgeless expanse, not a soul would have recognized the hissing monster of yesterday. A haze, in itself invisible, made everything visible look blue, indirect, mild, insubstantial, airborne. No limits anywhere. No contrasts. Only blending. Wasn't this a day when one might apply the word *endless*? Might have, if . . . He could feel his heels. Ice cold. As if lying in snow. All night long he had kept putting his hands around his heels and been surprised each time to find that they felt quite normal. The moment he released them, though, they signaled a pain that he perceived as icy cold. The first time he had had this feeling was on their first sailing trip . . . That's right, just carry on. Last night, when they had finally driven him home and all he had wanted was to get into bed as quickly as possible, a huge insect had lain on the mat by his side of the bed. A beautiful green grasshopper. Helmut had almost stepped on it. He tried to pick it up but, in its death throes no doubt, it had fastened its claws into the fabric of the mat.

He had to use a little force to pull it off. One of the two long antennae was drooping. Otherwise the beautiful green creature was completely intact. Its hemispherical eyes apparently could not be closed. Helmut had thought: Carry on. Wings like a tailcoat, he had thought. A green neckplate like a Regency collar. Or like Klaus Buch's golden, collar-length shield of hair. Suddenly the creature had drawn up the long lower half of one hind leg and then let go again. Then the whole hind leg had started to twitch. It was actually jerking back and forth. The other hind leg was twitching a little too. The long belly was quivering. He couldn't bear to watch. He placed the little green, horselike creature on the windowsill between the iron bars, crawled under the quilt, and tried to make himself tremble. He actually did. For quite a while. But then he had to yell at Sabina. Her whimpering made everything that much worse, he shouted. Whereupon Sabina wailed without restraint. But after that she quieted down. By morning the grasshopper was gone.

He opened his black Kierkegaard book and began to read: *During my sojourn here in Gilleleie I visited Esrum, Fredensborg, Frederikevaerk, and Tidsvilde. The latter is known chiefly for St. Helen's Spring, to which the entire local population makes a pilgrimage on Midsummer Day.* Helmut shut the book. He did not know how to face the situation.

Suddenly he felt that from now on ceaseless attacks were to be expected from all sides. Not a single innocuous minute was left.

Suddenly everything was unpredictable. He couldn't go on lying here. One thing was certain: Reading was the least feasible activity. He had to move. He should. If he could. Oh God, don't lose your mind the very first day, one can cope with much worse things, self-defense, my God, self-defense. You didn't mean it to happen. If he'd carried on with his crazy rodeo, we would have capsized. And neither of us would have survived. It's in the paper, isn't it, stop-stop-stop, you mustn't think like that, go ahead, admit it, let your conscience safely graze, what does that mean, I ask you, to let your conscience graze, must be a contest in verbal prostitution, stop, admit you can't cope with it, your memory serves you as never before, no trace of charnel house. Intense is the word, you actually *lived* in that instant, you went out of yourself, HH, for an instant you failed to maintain your pretense, this is the instant you are stuck with, will be stuck with, when the rupture of that instant can no longer be closed.

He got up, ran back to the house, and said he wanted to go for a jog through the forest with Sabina. Sabina was taken aback. A nice easy one. No athletic ordeal. Just a suggestion of a long-distance run. "Long-distance run, Sabina, d'you know the expression? I love it. Long-distance run. Just start off very gently. Running shoes. We've no running shoes. Look, I'll make a quick trip into town and get us some running shoes, track suits, running shorts, running shirts. Please, don't laugh, don't cry, it's all so meaningless, we have to get moving. If you don't want to swim, we'll run instead. Let's behave like opportunists. Come on, Sabina, jogging for the masses. D'you want to come into town with me? We can borrow a couple of bikes. From the Zürns. Would you do that? Please, please, Sabina, do go and ask them if they can lend us two bikes, no wait a minute, we'll buy some, yes, at last things are starting to hum"—too late, the Klaus Buch expression had slipped out, and Sabina had recognized it as such—"we'll buy two bicycles, across from the Löwe, the shiniest bikes they have, then we'll ride into town, buy our outfits, and ride into the forest, then we'll park the bikes and go for a jog. Let's go."

Sabina had to be pushed. She tried to nod. She was probably thinking of Klaus Buch. But she did not say his name. They walked into the village and bought the best available bicycles. In town they bought their outfits. Then they bicycled back along the lake road to the apartment. The cycling was fun right away. They were less awkward than they had feared. Helmut said: "Oh Sabina, am I glad we thought of bicycling! That's the right way to begin. How easy it is. A real success situation, don't you agree?" "Yes!" Sabina cried. "Just wait," he cried, "once we've changed our clothes it'll be even better." He felt that nothing could stop him now.

Back in the apartment they changed with undiminished haste. By now Sabina had been infected by Helmut's urgency. They both moved effortlessly. They decided they looked funny in their track suits, but not ridiculous. In fact, she looked most intriguing, said Helmut. Like a woman athlete from one of the Trans-Ural Soviet republics. "You," she said, "look like a top American executive on a Saturday." He is a bit worried, though, that he might have bought his running shoes a size too small. "At last I recognize you," she said. But he would tolerate no delay.

Just as they were reaching for their bicycles, up drove the old silver Mercedes. It was Helene Buch. She wasn't in the least surprised to see the Halms holding bicycles and wearing track suits. She herself was dressed in a way that the Halms had never seen.

Ancient, patched jeans, and a navy blue, double-breasted pinstripe jacket over a T-shirt that had once been black. And her hair close to her head. Now it could be seen that her neck was almost curved. Now it could be seen that she needed this lovely long, gently curving neck to lift that gentlest of little noses high into the air.

She hadn't been able to stand it another minute in the hotel room, she told them.

The Halms put away their bicycles and went indoors with Helene. Sabina made some coffee and asked Hella what she would like. Hella said she'd be happy to join them in a cup of coffee. Sabina said with a query in her voice that she also had some homemade cherry cake. "Yes, I'd love some," said Hella. They each had two pieces of the cake. Hella said it was the first piece of cake she had eaten in four years. It was the best she had ever eaten. A cup of coffee and a piece of cake, what could be better, said Helmut. Without them, he said, life wouldn't be worth living. He hoped Hella and Sabina realized that he was spouting all this nonsense just so the silence wouldn't be unbearably prolonged. As soon as no one had anything more to say, this cake-eating became a repulsive ritual.

Sabina then cautiously asked whether Hella would mind if she smoked a cigarette. "No, of course not," said Helene, smiling a bit like a convalescent. She felt she could use a cigarette today too. Sabina offered her one.

The most remarkable sight now was Helene smoking. She inhaled deeply, tranquilly. Like a person making very sure.

At one point she said: "I'm intruding. It would be nice, you know, if you could behave as if I weren't intruding. If, for instance, you were to read now, I'd know I wasn't intruding. I just don't want to be alone, not right now."

Sabina asked if she should make another pot of coffee. Helene nodded with gentle eagerness. "We could also offer you a twelve-year-old Calvados," Sabina said. Helmut frowned and said brusquely: "Sabina!" They were to do whatever they would normally be doing, said Helene, otherwise she couldn't stay here another second. Sabina was welcome to put down a glass of Calvados beside her, then she would feel less of an intruder. Sabina poured a Calvados for each of them. Helmut said: "Not for me." Helene said: "Why aren't you smoking?" Helmut waved away the idea. "I like it when you smoke a cigar. My father used to smoke cigars too."

While they were sitting there, Sabina and Helene drinking their coffee and Calvados and smoking, Helmut said: "I don't know, Sabina, would it be better if I talked about what happened, or would it be better for us not to discuss it now? I simply don't know. Hella, you must tell me what is . . . more acceptable to you, it's up to you." Helene looked up. He had actually said "Hella." Perhaps for the first time. Instead of answering, she started weeping convulsively. A loud, long-drawn-out wail. Helmut sprang to his feet and paced up and down, his steps jerky and angry-looking. Helene also stood up, forced him to stop. Then she started weeping again, this time leaning her head against him. He could feel the sobs shaking her. He led her back to her chair. Sabina was wailing too. Helmut could not prevent his own eyes from filling with tears. Suddenly he remembered Sabina having said she couldn't go sailing because she had a hairdresser's appointment. Helene must have noticed long ago that Sabina hadn't been to the hairdresser.

Helene drank the Calvados that Helmut had refused. Sabina filled all three glasses again. Helene was the first to reach for the refilled glass.

"Do please smoke your cigar," she said. "I'm quite sure you would be smoking now, if I weren't here."

Sabina also gave him an encouraging nod. Helmut said: "No, really. Not at the moment. Maybe later." Helene, again ostentatiously, placed a third glass of Calvados in front of Helmut, then raised her own glass to him. He shook his head. She and Sabina drank. Helene said: "God, this Calvados is good! Six years ago I spent a semester studying at Montpellier, and I used to drink Calvados quite often. With thick, thick walls all around." Helmut could not help thinking of the thin walls of the hotel at Grado. He looked across at Sabina and saw that she was thinking the same thing. That annoyed him. "Montpellier," said Helene, "was the most beautiful time in my life." This statement sounded funny.

She finished her drink. Sabina poured her another. "Now I'm the only one drinking," she said.

"Cheers," said Sabina and drank, too.

"I'm leaving tomorrow morning," said Helene.

"For Starnberg," said Sabina.

Helene nodded.

Helmut had a feeling he would never be able to move again. And that he would ever speak again also seemed unlikely to him.

"Klaus," she said, half to herself, "would probably say that life must go on."

Obviously she was on the verge of tears again. Obviously this time she would fight them. She bit her lip." It's just that I don't know how," she said.

She continued to fight back more mounting sobs. She finished her glass. Sabina filled it.

"Klaus once told me," she said, " 'You only have to care for me as long as I'm alive.' And now I have a feeling I'll never be able to believe he's dead. I can never get that into me. Never. For me he's still alive."

She drank up her Calvados and held out her glass for Sabina to fill. "Cheers," she said. Sabina drank too.

"He didn't have much of a life," Hella said. "It was just one long grind. Every day ten, twelve hours at the typewriter. Even when he couldn't write, he still sat at the typewriter. 'I must be at the ready,' he would say then. Everything he did was a terrible effort. That's why he tried to give everyone the impression that he didn't work at all, and that whatever he did was for the sheer pleasure of it, effortlessly. Yes, without effort, he wanted to seem to do everything without effort. And then always the feeling that whatever he was doing was a fraud.

"That one day he'd be found out. He often used to cry out, at night. And more and more often he would break out into a sweat, in the middle of the night. That's why he kept saying: 'We'll clear out to the Bahamas.' When we were alone he used to add: 'And join the other crooks.' He was absolutely convinced that he was a crook. Needless to say, we didn't have the slightest prospect of moving to the Bahamas. We could hardly afford even this kind of a vacation here. Even in the hotel room, he kept on working every day. And I was supposed to collect grandmothers' sayings. That's over now. That's the one thing I'm sure of. Never again, as long as I live, will I touch another tape. Never again a typewriter. I couldn't tell him how little that appealed to me, forcing my way into quiet villages, asking the mayor, interviewing those dear old women, explaining how and why and what a microphone is. But he was so thrilled with his idea. He was a child. Or wanted to be a child. 'A person can do anything.' That was another of his sayings. He should have become a gym teacher. Or an explorer. But not in this day and age. A hundred years ago. Captain of a sailing ship. Adventurer. Someone who surmounts every obstacle. As long as it's caused by Nature. In the face of Nature he was always courageous, ingenious, invincible. Only with people. . . ."

She made a plunging gesture.

"He was fantastic with his hands. The cottage in Starnberg was a chicken coop when we bought it. A refugee had wanted to start a chicken farm and didn't make it. Klaus did it all himself. And how! A terrace, you've never seen anything like it. Of red sandstone. That red terrace is his monument. It will survive, I know that. But actually he was finished. I mean it. He was in the wrong boat. And he forced me into that wrong boat, too. That's how I know what it's like to be in the wrong boat. It's hell. By some idiotic chance he got into this lousy journalism. And on top of that into this environment stuff. Then he believed he had to take the whole thing seriously because it's our bread and butter. He was so uptight about it. Toward the end he had rows with everybody. And I do mean everybody. He hated the editors and publishers' readers he depended on just *because* he depended on them. If one of them showed the slightest trace of criticism, Klaus would tear up his own manuscript before their very eyes. That was really wild. Ridiculous, too, of course. He always had a copy. Everyone knew that. He was just waiting for them to stop him. They would just grin."

She finished her drink, held out her glass, had it filled, said "Cheers," and drank. Sabina drank too.

"And the way he insulted people he depended on, that was really wild. Just because he depended on them. And his publisher, the way he bugged him. For a while he drove regularly into Munich, and what he used to do to that publisher's car . . . I'd hate to tell you. He really was finished. Totally and utterly finished. That's why he was so happy that we bumped into you. 'Now we'll make a go of it,' he said after our first evening. He was a fantasist. Right away he started about the Bahamas again. Off to the Bahamas with Helmut. That was his latest idea. Life with him wasn't that easy, I can assure you. Because he was so touchy. Because they let him feel they didn't need him. Once they had let him feel that, it was all over. That's when he began, a hundred times a day, I swear, a hundred times a day he'd ask if I still cared for him. He saw himself more and more as the lowest form of dirt. And it was my job to keep proving to him that he wasn't the lowest form of dirt but a supersupersuperman. And convincingly, too. I mean it."

She jumped up. Walked up and down. Holding the glass. Having it filled. Drinking.

"It had become practically impossible to talk to him. Gradually I was coming to realize I wouldn't be able to stand it much longer. More and more I felt as if I had to hold a drowning man above water. When I could no longer do it, he would drag us both down. I realized I wouldn't be able to go on doing it forever. That's why I was equally happy we bumped into you. You see, we were totally isolated. Totally. Please, don't get me wrong. You know I don't want to say anything against Klaus . . . I want . . . I just have to say . . . I must tell you . . . I must tell someone, how . . . I am . . . I was hardly . . . if I could say this just once . . . I wasn't allowed to live, he didn't permit it. I had to show far greater interest in what he was doing than he did himself. As if I had been his daughter: What he couldn't achieve, I was supposed to achieve. I was his pride and joy. On the other hand, he resented it when someone praised something I had done. He was crazy. Because he realized that no one needed him, he had reached a level of egotism that can only be called pathological. I was studying music when he met me. From one day to the next I had to give that up. We'd known each other for less than three months when he decreed that I would never make it as a real musician—give it up, you'll only make yourself miserable. Basta. There. Then he started indoctrinating me with his interests. I was twenty-two. And a fool. I was such a fool, you know, the Matterhorn is nothing by comparison, that's how great a fool I was. Of course I also know he can't help it . . . but why me . . . why should I be the one to pay? I had to sell my piano. Believe it or not! He developed a fanatical hatred for music. It was either him or music! One more year, and I would probably have succumbed. Then I could have stood it forever. Cheers. Isn't it amazing, the things people can put up with! I have him to thank for that. I've learned that once and for all. I can stand a lot. I . . . d'you want to bet that I can stand more than the two of you together? Come on, let's have a bet. I'd like to win. It's been so long since I won anything. I feel I . . . you've no piano here in your fancy apartment. Not even a violin. What a lousy deal. A vacation apartment with no piano. And no violin. And for eleven years. Eleven years with no piano or violin. You can put up with a lot. You must be pretty hardened by now. Let me feel, Helmut. Are you hardened? Your soul? Let me feel. Your earlobe. Don't you know? Like earlobe, like soul. Hm, you have a rather flabby earlobe, I would say. And you, Sabina dear? The fact is, women do have fuller earlobes than men, you find that over and over again. And talking of women, mmm! I tell you, there are some women with such fullness, you can forget about men. What is a man, Sabina? Full of hot air, okay. What else? Nothing. Klaus had . . . ah Klaus . . . Somehow I seem to be floating in a liquid. And I'm also drinking some of the liquid I'm floating in. I must say, it really is a bit out of this world. If only it doesn't suddenly come to an end. Helmut, you'll see to it that the phone doesn't ring all of a sudden—Mr. Stahlhagen calling from Munich to say he won't be wanting anything more from us . . . I'll be forever in your debt for all you two have done for me, I mean it. You really are the greatest. And by the time we meet up with you it's practically too late. What rotten luck. Helmut, you can't imagine how happy Klaus was to have run into you. 'It's like finding buried treasure,' he said. You—he felt that—you with your quiet, determined manner could have made him whole again. That's what he lacked, your common sense, your sense of proportion, your inner calm. Oh you two dear things, you can give me a little bath now if you like. I'm staying here with you. And you'll give me a bath. With a big sponge. You don't have a bathtub? You just have a shower, like us. A bit on the skimpy side, wouldn't you say? Never mind. Would've been rather nice if you had given me a bath. But that's the way it is. I, creature of luxury that I am, would like to get into a tub. But there isn't any tub. Just like in the Sahara Desert. There's just a chance I might get sad now. But please, don't take it to heart. A hot bath is the best thing for sadness. It must be good and hot. When I'm lying in a hot bath I always start singing. Although otherwise I haven't been singing at all recently. I tell you, it faded away so quickly, my singing. To practically nothing. Sometimes I sit there exuding silence. And there I sit, in that silence. Like under a glass cover. Then, ladies and gentlemen, it gets to me. *It* gets to me. Depression, I mean, the resentful, self-devouring kind. Because now I'm worth no more than something you throw at the wall to smash it so completely that you can't tell from the pieces what it was or what it was meant to be. That's really the most important part, for the destruction to be thorough enough. If they were to only partially smash us all, there would be a wave of sympathy in which we'd all be sure to drown, and that would be the end of the world. But as people who have been smashed to smithereens, we go on living without feeling. I thank you.

"And now, without further ado, we'll start. We've already wasted too much time. Ladies and gentlemen, as an artist I am not as well prepared as I would like to be. But in a different way I am much too well prepared. So I take the liberty of asking for your attention. I shall now play for you the *Wanderer Fantasy* by Franz Schubert."

She played the notes in the air, sang the notes, punched out the rhythms, drew lines with her fingers. She walked up and down, stopped, turned around. She performed the piano piece as if reciting a text. She didn't omit a single syllable and explained exactly how she meant it.

There was a knock. Helmut ran to the door. Mrs. Zürn. A gentleman had come to pick up his wife.

Past her, past Helmut, Klaus Buch walked into the apartment.

Helmut gave Mrs. Zürn a quick nod, then closed the door, ordered Otto to heel, and kept his eyes on the dog.

"Klaus!" screamed Sabina.

Helene, abruptly breaking off her music, said, as if wilting, expiring: "My Klaus, my dear, dear Klaus. There, what've I been saying all along? He's alive, I said, and what is he? Alive. And how late he is! That's just like him. He simply wanted to know what we do when he's not around. Right? You devil. Didn't I tell you he was a devil? Klaus, do find yourself a comfortable chair, I just have to finish playing the *Wanderer Fantasy.*"

She found her place and resumed. But not for long. She looked at Klaus and, keeping her eyes on him, poured herself a Calvados and said "Cheers," then drank it down and looked at Klaus again.

Klaus said: "Come along now."

She said: "Didn't you like it? Forgive me, there you stand, freshly rescued, and I'm playing the piano: It wouldn't surprise me if you were to classify me as an egoist. You who have been snatched from the waves. He always triumphs over Nature. I told them that in advance, didn't I?"

Klaus said: "Come along now."

Helene said: "But Klaus, do let's stay with our friends for a while. There's no bathtub in our room anyway. They don't have one here either. So we might just as well stay here. Either way, we'll play out our fate of being without a bathtub. No problem."

"I'm leaving now," said Klaus.

"Has someone upset you?" she asked. "I can see, you're offended. Klaus, quick, tell your Hella who offended you. Whoever it was, I can see he really hurt your feelings. I can see that. Eeeeh! They've really, really hurt our Klaus's feelings. I'll put new life into you, lover boy, and before very long too, I swear."

She lit another cigarette, took Helmut's straw hat from its hook, and put it on. "May I borrow it?" she asked. And then she said: "Let's go, genius, onward and upward."

Waving to Helmut and Sabina, she went out the door, somehow taking Klaus with her. All the time he was there, Klaus Buch's and Helmut's eyes had not met. Helmut realized this now. So he was to preserve the look in the eyes of the man toppling backward. Klaus had probably seen through him at that moment as no one had ever seen through him before. And the man who had seen through him like that was alive. They did not move until they heard the car driving away.

Sabina said: "Hold everything."

Helmut sat down, lit a cigar, poured himself a Calvados, and said: "Cheers." And drank. Sabina did not drink. "Do you know what got into him?" Sabina asked. Helmut ignored the question. "Helmut, what's got into him?" asked Sabina. "Something's the matter. Instead of wanting to celebrate, he arrives . . . like Doomsday personified. Can you explain that?"

Helmut picked up his black Kierkegaard book and said: "If you're looking for your *Wagner—My Life*, it's over there, shall I get it for you?" Then he opened his Kierkegaard book and read: *During my sojourn here in Gilleleia I visited Esrum, Fredens-*

borg, Frederiksvaark, and Tidsvilde. The latter is known chiefly for St. Helen's Spring, to which the entire local population makes a pilgrimage on Midsummer's Day.

He closed the book again. Sabina had not stirred. "Come on," she said. "We wanted to go for a bike ride, remember? Into the forest. A jog through the forest. Let's go." Helmut stood up and said: "I can't wear these things." He started to change. While changing, he told Sabina they could give the bicycles to the Zürns. They would simply leave them behind; they could always use them again, if they ever came back here for a vacation.

He said: "Please, Sabina, you change too. Please."

He spoke again in that firm, compelling voice with which he had insisted on buying the sports outfits.

When they had both changed, he said: "What would you say if we started packing now? Or maybe I'll pack, you find Mrs. Zürn, pay her for the four weeks, and whatever you do, don't accept a reduction, say something about special circumstances, and if we come back next year we'll let them know in good time, and so on. Please, please, Sabina. I'll tell you all about it when we're on the train. Please."

Sabina sat down and said all this was much too fast for her. In a withering, utterly convincing tone of sheer blackmail, he said: "Then I'll have to go alone." "Is that so?" said Sabina. "But I'd like to make a speech, too," she said. "When do I get to make my speech, if you don't mind? Perhaps you think I'm not entitled to make a speech, is that it?"

"Oh Sabina. My one and only. Sabina," he said.

"Don't," she said.

"You're right," he said. "On the train, Sabina, on the train."

He began to pack. Gradually she joined in. When she was on her way to the Zürns, he called after her: "A taxi, in fifteen minutes." Trim Mrs. Zürn and two of her tall daughters stood at the door waving as Helmut, Sabina, and Otto drove off. Dr. Zürn, fortunately, was away in the Algäu. At the ticket counter Helmut said: "Two and a half, one way to Merano." "Merano," said Sabina, shaking her head. "Why Merano?" "Just a moment," said Helmut to the clerk, "my wife doesn't agree. Where else then?" Helmut asked. "To . . . to Montpellier," Sabina said, exhausted.

"Two and a half to Montpellier, one way, first class," said Helmut. "I hope you won't find it too hot there," said Helmut. "If the walls are that thick?" said Sabina with a little grin.

Helmut kissed Sabina carefully on the forehead. Otto made a sound as if he were suffering. Sabina gave Helmut a look that made him say: "You're looking right through me as if I were an empty jam jar. Wait a bit. On the train." Sabina said: "Last night in my dream I was supposed to know the word for a number that is not divisible by any other, and I didn't know the answer. Everyone else did. Including you. But even you wouldn't help me." He ruffled her hair a bit contritely. The train was arriving. Helmut said to the locomotive, which was brown with a white stripe and reminded him of a father confessor: *"Qui tollis peccata mundi."*

When they had found a compartment to themselves, he said: "Sabina, now we don't have to move till we get to Basle."

Sabina said: "I'm a bit afraid about the heat after all. What will we do if it's too hot down there?"

"Oh," said Helmut with a shrug, "sew shadows together."

For a while they sat across from each other silently, like strangers. She facing the engine. He with his back to it.

"What really happened yesterday?" she said.

An express train rasped by.

"It's rather a long story," he said, looking out onto the Rhine. "The Rhine," she said. She stretched a little. She was sitting in the evening sun. He in the shade. He intensified his voice as never before and said: "Oh Sabina. My one and only. Sabina." He could see that she liked the sound of it. This encouraged him to soar to heights that he felt bordered on hyperbole.

"Suffused in light, my Sabina," he said, "with your strength of which you are unaware. Looking out from the years as from a bower of roses, that's what you're like."

"Very nice. And now?"

"Now I'll start," he said. "I'm sorry," he said, "but it's just possible that I'll be telling you all about this fellow Helmut, this woman Sabina."

"Go ahead," she said. "I don't believe I'll believe all you say."

"That would be the solution," he said. "So, here goes," he said. "It was like this: Suddenly Sabina pushed her way out of the tide of tourists surging along the promenade and headed for a little table that was still unoccupied."

Translated by Leila Vennewitz

THE SUNDAY I BECAME WORLD CHAMPION

Friedrich Christian Delius

for M. and for Ch.

It leads down to the harbor, I hope,
I fear it goes on into the world.

Wolfgang Koeppen, *Youth*

THE SUNDAY I became world champion began like every Sunday: The bells pounded me awake, chopped my dreamy pictures asunder, beat on both ear drums, hammered through my head, and flailed my body, which turned defenseless toward the wall. Only a few meters from my bed stood the church tower, and no bed covers, no pillows helped. The peals of the bells pierced the windows and doors, beams and walls. They filled the room, vibrated in lamps, glasses, mirrors, and although they rang out to the village, the valley, and the forests all around, they seemed to have no other target than my ears and no other purpose than to destroy every other sound and reduce every thought to rubble. From on high, they sent reverberating, hefty assaults against me, ripped away the pale face that I saw hovering in a hilly landscape, and tore us apart mercilessly with their noise, as if something forbidden, something tender were to be forced out of my head.

Bright and early at seven o'clock, Sunday morning was rung in, for fifteen long minutes I was subjected to the bells. I did not want to accept it and tried holding tight to the vanishing pictures. Aside from the weightless face, a girl perhaps, I thought I saw my grandfather standing on the sea without his U-Boot, holding his arm up in the air. I did not know whether he was threatening or asking for help, the film had torn, the picture sequence destroyed, I was on land, was awakened.

I ducked down under the familiar racket, tried to ward off the inevitable and find something to like, peal for peal, about the swinging, hefty triple-toned ringing, tried to discover something like music, to discover in the metallic tones a melody or at least a rhythm. The large bell hammered the deep tone in a slow cadence, the small bell jumped in between with light, quick jingling, and the mid-sized bell added a clear background, a conciliatory tone. Three tones incessantly, one after the other and then simultaneously in changing, yet soon predictable order. I wanted to numb myself and be carried off, to swim away again on the sound waves, following the girl, the one sunken in the green landscape, following my grandfather, whose uniform had remained dry despite the high seas. Rocking in pictures to the rhythm of ringing bell tones, I was still unable to find the dream's trail and reconstitute what had been destroyed, to rescue the vanished face from the green and my grandfather from the sea.

I had only one chance: to become accustomed to what I was experiencing as an attack. I wished I were up there, on the tower, where those stronger boys were, two or three years older than I and unreachably distant in their position as confirmees, up on the ringing platform above the nave and altar tugging on the three bell ropes, waking the village, rattling the windows and sending the sound waves kilometers away, up there is where I wanted to be, where the wind blew through open window arches and embrasures. I would rather make the noise than suffer it. Already past the dangerous roof beams, stairs, and ladders, there I helped pull the ropes, just as I tried to do occasionally—when it was time to ring the bells on Saturday evenings, at weddings, or funerals—I cavorted about the shaky boards in roof dust, peered between the stone blocks in the wall down on the long barn roofs and pale red shingles of the houses, peered down at the pattern of light plaster between the gray or brown beams of the half-timbered buildings, floated in my pillow over the farms and gardens and at the same time tugged as hard as I could, first on one then another rope, as if I wanted to make my peace forcibly with the clanging vibrations, as if the bells were an instrument I could actually command.

For some moments I was able to hear nothing but harmonies and be caught up in the swing of the bells. I flew on with the tones of the bells, below me lay the street intersection with the three story tavern, with the advertisement *Beer makes thirst fun.* I sailed over men on tractors, over women with milk pails, over horse-drawn wagons, rack wagons, and cow herds. I sailed up into the forests, the people becoming smaller and smaller beneath me, as I followed their steps to the rhythm of the bells. I felt revived by the exhilaration of seeing everything without being seen, and for a little while I could still hear the strict, rhythmic call of the strokes beckoning me to leave everything as it is, to accept the noise of the bells and the thundering power that came from up above like a protective, fatherly caress. Then the feeling changed into a bashful rage at being so far away from my own fantasies, and in the peals of the bells I heard both violence and warmth, repulsion and allure, slaps and music.

As the clapper strikes wafted towards me in irregular fashion, as they feebly ebbed and the last, lightly tapped deep tone of the large bell hung lost in the air and the last vibrations brushed my ear, relief finally settled in. I would like to have detained this tone, which the tone modulated, because the thunder diminished into something tender, the noise into stillness, and the stillness felt as pleasant as an ease of pain.

I stretched and looked for a different sleeping position, disturbed only by the uncertainty about whether my grandfather really could wander over water like Jesus or whether he wanted to be saved by me. I, eleven years old and non-swimmer, could never have saved the ship's commander, but perhaps the dream would have bestowed upon me unknown abilities. The picture was not restored, the bells had spoiled everything. I listened to the morning silence, swallows, sparrows, and soon, as they stood one last moment together, the voices of the boys who had rung the bells resounded from the church door and over the church yard. Without seeing them I knew who they were, roughly how many there were, some I recognized by the sound of their voices. I heard my father talking, telling a joke that elicited tired laughs, before they all dispersed.

I DIVED DOWN UNDER, searched for sleep, without knowing what I was searching for in sleep or what I was missing in being awake, dived down under the covers, down under all the noises, stretched my legs, pressed into the pillows. Only now did I hear my brother, with whom I shared the room. He turned over in bed and wanted to go on sleeping after the disturbance. I did not want anything from him just then, did not speak to him, dived back into the warmth, the bell racket still in my ear, and finally relaxed after the fifteen minute tirade. Not because I was tired, rather because I wanted to extend a rare moment of happiness, I tried to reach the condition of being half asleep and to enjoy the opportunity, for a brief moment, of not being subject to any pressure, any expectation, any severe gaze.

It was the only day in the week I was not awakened at six o'clock in the morning, the only day the bells tore me from slumber instead of the cheerful voice of my mother with her "Good morning!" (with extend intonation of the "oo" and then the "o"). The only day on which I did not start to think, by breakfast at the latest, of the Latin or math horrors of the school day looming before me like a giant obstruction, of my poor memory for vocabulary, of the half-digested formulas and my pitiful memory for figures, of the diligently memorized differences between moss and liverwort or my unstable memory for biology. The only day in the week on which I was halfway protected from the realization of how bad and weak I was in everything, so quickly set in panic when grown ups—with a certain overbearing expectation—asked any sort of question at all, and I would react only with stuttering and hesitation. I dived away from all the usual imprisonments of the week and looked forward to the relief that Sunday brought, although even this day was fraught with mild threats and commandments, prayers, and rules, which began already on Saturday evening when my brother and I had to sweep the street and courtyard for a nickle's worth of pocket change.

Just the thought that I did not have to sit in the bus at this hour was a triumph. That one hour long trip through hill and valley, from Wehrda to Scheltzenrod to Wetzlos to Stärklos to

Kruspis to Holzheim to Hilperhausen to Kohlhhausen to Asbach to Bad Hersfeld, I would be hunched over some Latin grammar book or a history textbook, and I was the first to have to stand because as one of the youngest and son of the pastor I was expected to give up my seat for my elders, at each hole in the road or curve I would be shoved about in a bus bouncing along. A day of rest stood before me, on which no answers were expected from me, a day on which I would not have to reveal myself and on which my frightened, pained silence went less noticed because everything was supposed to proceed quieter, calmer, and without emotional outburst.

Steps on the floorboards in the hall, motherly steps down the stairs, grandfatherly steps on the way to the kitchen, where the wash basin was filled, and then back into my grandparents' room. Water pipes in the walls, chickens in the yard below, birds chirping in the trees, these were the most noticeable sounds. The pigs had already been fed by now, so it was quiet in the neighbor's sties, a horse whinnied, dog barks in the distance, cows outside in the meadow, tractors stood in garages and barns—I could have recognized Sunday even by what was not heard. It was light out, summer, judging by the rising sun through the thin blue curtains—still I dived down one more time, trolled for a dream, wanted to dream everything away that could spoil dreams, and yet those Sunday rules of behavior pushed ever stronger into my consciousness, as though the echo of the bells or some other unseen power was commandeering me for the day's main purpose: *Honor the Sabbath!*

This commandment was paramount over not only both church services, for children and adults, not only over the ceremony of singing, praying, listening, but also over every impulse, every step. Playing cops and robbers and other such group games in the barns, on the streets, and in the fields was forbidden, playing in your room was permitted, rough housing and fighting forbidden, hammering and sawing on your own homemade wooden hut next to the chicken coop forbidden, sitting in the hut permitted. School assignments counted as work, even a quick peek in the Latin book on Sunday evening, and work was forbidden because even God rested on the seventh day, but reading other books was permitted. Lederhosen forbidden, corduroy pants permitted, riding your bike mornings during church services forbidden, riding in the afternoon permitted, playing soccer in the yard or around the church in the morning forbidden because Sunday was a day of rest, in the afternoon too, because of your Sunday clothes, but going to the stadium was permitted, where the varsity team of the soccer club, F. C. Wehrda, played its games every second Sunday. I had all these rules in my head, which seemed so shamefully clear to me because I had grown up with and into them. I did not like them, but I accepted them, and the longer I lay in bed, the later they would go into force.

I could have read or gotten the TRIX construction set out of the closet or talked my brother into playing a game or made him mad. I could have gotten dressed and gone outside, but I stayed in bed because I did not want to do any of that, did not want to be committed to anything, did not want to be observed by anyone. However, my own wishes were compromised more and more by the suspicion that my freedom to forestall the Sunday rules was running out minute by minute, and I did not have much longer than the luxury of an hour between waking and getting up, since soon everything would come down to the usual folded hands and the *Thou shallt.*

Sunday was not there for me or for the family, but rather for that bearded Father above my father whom we had to thank for everything. I just could not imagine a life without bells, without the *Sabbath,* without Christian schedules full of praying and singing. Even less could I imagine escaping the looming, omnipresent eye of God that hung somewhere in Heaven and saw everything without being seen. I could try to avoid His gaze, but I could not unburden my conscience because the eye of God was reflected in the eyes of my own father, of my mother, my grandparents—their eyes flanked and multiplied the eye of God. Too many eyes were looking down on me.

In such half-awake, uncontrolled moments I was overcome by an inexplicable shame, by a fidgety depression and immobilization, even if I had neither done nor thought anything forbidden. I was afraid and did not know what or whom I was afraid of, did not know a remedy for my fear, defended myself with extended dreams and had some idea just how limited my power of fantasy and of multiplying my dreams was. My head was besieged and the little bundle of my body was consumed with the incomprehensible power of God, a power that governed all thoughts, determined my stymied, stuttering life, a power that was supposed to be clement and strict at the same time and that as the highest tribunal of love seemed to direct my father and mother like marionettes. I became discouraged and exhausted when a nagging thought about that *dear God,* threatening and blessing from Heaven on high, brushed against me. I would never get used to this unpredictable *Lord,* not through prayer, service, gratitude, faith, song. Even worse was the image of emptiness, of damnation, of feelings of guilt with which God pursued those who did not manage to subject themselves to his commandments and who became *pagan.* Confused, I abandoned the beginning of such ideas, I did not want to, could not, must not suspect or guess into what kind of devilish, vicious circle this God was shoving me.

I had slept an hour longer than usual, did not want to lie in bed as though I were tied down, defenseless against the premonitions and fears that wafted through my head like light, deceptive breezes. Hands glided back and forth over my body, the slight scent of soap from Saturday evening bath time still lay upon my skin. I felt wide awake, saw myself storming across the soccer field, running after the ball, passing the ball, stopping, and shooting. I knew I was kidding myself into believing I could move so gracefully and with such control, my child's body was not strong, not fast, not big, and not athletic, and yet I wanted to count myself one of the better players, the winners. Just recently during Sports Day at school I sang *When the bright banners wave* with a clear voice and then scored pitifully few points, was singularly noticeable due to my pale white, peeling skin on my elbows, knees, and ankles, the illness with the horrible name of psoriasis, which made me seem closer to fish, frogs, insects than to the height of the victor's block. And while I scratched at the scales with quiet rage and ignored the warning that even more skin could flake off, I ran faster and faster over the soccer field and dribbled, quick and skillful, until no one noticed my scaly knee or elbow any more. I had to overcome the fear and the flakes. A mighty striker, I ran over two, three, four opponents and shot a goal, the deciding goal for me, my team, the students from Wehrda. As I was joining in the cries of celebration of my teammates and the applause of the spectators, it occurred to me which day it was, the day of the final play-off game. I could see myself in black pants and white shirt among the German strikers, the ball initially faster, then slower than the men who were in control of it, head balls, passing to the flanks, corner shots, every movement quickened by the magical certainty that these men had reached the final play-off game for the world championship. I saw myself there, wanted to be there. In the afternoon I would be allowed to listen to the radio broadcast of the game, I finally jumped out of bed, washed myself, got dressed in my freshly washed Sunday best.

THE BREAD, the bread in the middle of the table, around the bread was margarine, marmalade, currant jelly, a milk pitcher, *Kaba Cocoa, The Plantation Drink,* eggs in egg cups, six place settings around the edge of the table, in front of each were high-backed, stark chairs. Good-morning-faces around the bread, mother hovering over the bread and smiling in her blue Sunday dress, my two-year-old sister as well as the five-year-old in freshly ironed dresses and with polite little hair cuts next to the bread, my brother in a white shirt, his hair wet combed, and the girl who was learning to be a cook and housekeeper, puff-cheeked, waiting, servile. The chair next to me was empty because my father breakfasted in his study on Sunday as he leafed through his sermon notes, before he rode the motorcycle three kilometers down the road to the neighboring village Rhina to hold early services.

Before breakfast on Sundays no one had to wait for a prayer, a song. I took a piece of bread out of the woven basket, a slice perfectly cut by a machine. I spread margarine onto *our daily bread.* On Sundays my breakfast was not regulated by the bus schedule. I tapped open the top of my egg, stirred the chocolate powder into the milk. I stirred, I spread, I fit right into this circle of people sitting around the bread. I did what the others did, sought sweet comfort in *The Plantation Drink,* nodded when I heard the usual useless exhortation to enjoy my meal. The bread was fresh, the egg was warm and soft, I was hungry and was not sitting under my father's gaze. I observed the Sunday rule about not smearing marmalade on the bread I ate with the egg; like the others I bit and chewed pensively. I drew attention only when I wanted to—I could put on airs as the oldest with my eleven years, or I could retreat into the role of the quiet one without drawing attention to myself,—*don't talk with your mouth full.*

The bread, all eyes fell on the evenly, thinly machine-sliced grayish bread that lumbered towards five mouths with almost silent devotion, buttered, lifted, bitten, chewed, following the example Mother was providing with almost disturbing slowness. After she cut up the piece of bread for the youngest, she spread margarine on the bread, carefully pushed the knife into the margarine and then distributed it onto her slice evenly thin over every edge and bump, every tiny uneven spot and little hole with a puzzling dedication. Occasionally she would look up and tell the older sister not to dribble the marmalade dangling on the edge of the bread, and as she herself spread a paper-thin layer of red jelly, a little attention was directed my brother's way, a warning uttered nonchalantly to use only one spoon full of Kaba instead of three, and also my way, to me who should be setting an example for the rest, came the stock command also meant for everyone, *not too thick, not too much, not too fast.* And when she finally took a bite, she did it so carefully that one could think she was afraid of breaking another living creature's bones.

We pensively chewed, with almost the same rhythm, the identically shaped, similarly thin pieces of bread, fidgeted little, hardly squabbled, abstained from poking, pushing, kicking, needling, braid pulling. Although everything was a few degrees more informal than on other days, the Sunday rules and Sunday clothes demanded even more that we sit still and well-behaved. After all, the white shirts seemed to have special magnets woven into them that attracted marmalade and chocolate milk, and no one wanted to be branded with a splotch all day. Even when we spoke, we kept it down. We spoke little, as though a danger emanated not only from the marmalade, but also from talking, as if the meal were demanding inmost devotion. It could have been warmer, more relaxed, more fun, but relaxation was more the province of our father. Instead, we remained steadfastly stiff, imbued with a Sunday caution and jelly depression. We ate our bread without smacking our lips, drank the chocolate milk without slurping, and acted as if the bread we had just eaten immediately consumed whatever energy it gave us, and as if it contained minerals that lamed our tongues.

Bread was holy. Although baked in the village bakery, upon every loaf lay the blessing of the Savior, upon every slice, as though it had not been run through the bread machine, but rather broken personally by Jesus, the reflection of a miracle. *Our daily bread,* for which we prayed daily, did indeed appear daily on our table. The feeding of the five thousand and the bread of the Last Supper were so present that even a dry crust was the distant reflection of a piece of two-thousand-year-old bread from the Bible, *Manna,* heavenly bread on the journey through the desert. One lay hand on the bread cautiously, as if a rough movement or too much pressure would squash the bread, destroy it, as if it would disappear at the slightest touch of force and then punish him who dared to hold it carelessly, ungratefully, or to play with it—damn him to eternal hunger. By chewing the bread, we chewed the reverence for the bread with it, and although I was not old enough to take communion, the teachings had progressed so far, were so deeply stamped into my mind, that I felt the flutter of the Holy Ghost even here over our calm Sunday breakfast. Every mealtime prayer invoked the unity of bread and Jesus and God and that magical spirit, one of the three or all together they *gave* us the meal, and one should think of that upon seeing the wheat in the fields, the heads of grain, the flail and the threshing machine, the sacks of grain, the flour, the full baking trays of the farmer wives, and that's what we thought, even when we did not want to think about it, biting and chewing on the grace of the Lord, who had given us the bread and did not let us starve, who even let us live between fields full of wheat, rye, barley, oats.

We wasted no words about all this, because it no longer needed to be said and because we had been fed stories about the past war, how often just one piece of bread, and only bread, and always the final hope, salvation, a dried-out crust. Bread sated and destroyed something, bread ate at hearts, ate at tongues, bread suppressed something in me, bread separated us and held us together.

But on the Kaba label a palm did bloom, the desert shining golden, I found it comforting that chocolate milk was as yet unknown in the time of Jesus and was not mentioned in any prayer, and therefore could be drunk without suppressed devotion, I longed to be on the plantations, dreamed of a meal with nothing but food not poisoned by God's grace, and then I took my third slice of bread.

Seeking help, I looked over to Mother, who could have extinguished the destructive halo around the grayish bread at any time. She met my gaze because she was always smiling at the circle, but she did not look like I hoped she would, with a smile, a friendly joke of absolution. Maybe I was too bold to expect something of the compassion with which she cared for sick children, and of the comforting warmth that she radiated every evening while praying and singing as she struck the tender, loving tone of security in the melodies of lullabies. And maybe I held it against her that during the day she almost always lost that voice, the one I considered to be her true voice. I looked over at her and thought I could feel the bread separate us, the distance to her growing, and she seemed not to notice how she herself was increasing that distance every time her calm controlling gaze was replaced by a smile and that smile was directed towards me. But she did not mean the smile just for me, in any case, not me alone, because she was frozen in the earnest striving for kindness, when she divided things, when she divided her love among the four of us, not wanting to be unjust in sharing her love with any of her children. She wanted to show *her joy* for all four of us simultaneously. She did not seem to notice that I needed a kind of nourishment other than bread, her voice, her eyes, an embrace. A broach gleamed beneath her throat, the insect frozen in amber flashed black. Her gaze did not relieve the silent dialogue and left me questioning alone whether those eyes behind her gaze were really as well disposed towards me as they seemed. Speech could have helped, but since my mother's speech never found me, I sought the mistake in myself, felt deaf, speechless, mute. I expected perhaps just a soft, caressing, touching spark in her eyes, or I really did not expect it anymore and had to observe how her gestures, gazes, words halted, froze at mid-point: Everything is all right, we have enough to eat and can and must be thankful for that every minute.

When she rose out of her humility and finally spoke, then with long pauses, slow sentences, as though she had to examine every word, every sentence before she was allowed to utter it, as though an old fear of doing something wrong through just a few words had not been overcome, as though her father, the retired U-Boat captain and missionary, converted from Kaiser to Christ, still stood with his controlled looks on the bridge or as though he were eating with us at the table or looking down on us all. He lived one floor above us. The grandparents' room stood separated from my parents' bedroom by a sealed door, and when he was not on a speaking tour in church halls and tents earning his meager money by campaigning for God, he was present with his loud voice, critical gaze, witty friendliness and a sly smile in the corners of his mouth. The little man wore the royalty that his name bespoke like a medal. His family had seen better times, and worse ones, but everything was *providential dispensation* or *God's mercy*. He preferably referred to God as the *Lord*; the highest virtue was *Obedience*. So many sunken ships weighed heavily on his conscience, and whenever he saw me crying he would order: *Hold it back!* And even when I cried and he was not anywhere close, I would hear his military tone: *Hold it back!* Maybe he had also given my mother and her five siblings the same order. My grandparents never cried, but they did mourn the loss of the village Bad Doberan. Mecklenburg had been taken from them, their family had been Mecklenburgers since the time of Henry the Lion. And now grandfather feared the godlessness of modern times, which only the *Holy Scripture,* the *Frankfurter Allgemeine* newspaper, and the *Adelsblatt,* a paper for Germany's remnant nobility, could help to remedy. Grandmother would contradict him now and then, my mother never. He could laugh loud and rhyme poetry, the captain and missionary, staunchly footed on the ship of faith, steering through the sea of faithlessness, a defiant voice singing against the storms.

I saw my mother holding it back, saw his face in her face, his loudness mirrored in her stillness. She did everything to be good and to do *Good* thankfully and to perform her five roles of mother, wife, daughter, pastor's wife, and teacher of the house servant so perfectly that no one in this crowded house would get upset and everyone would be *satisfied.* As she was being quiet, she was planning, thinking about the remaining busyness of Sunday, children's service, lunch, appraisal of the sermon.

Suddenly she spoke, reminded us about the money for the collection plate at the children's service. I answered, briefly and decisively: "I would rather go with you to the regular service today."

She consented, smiled, a quick flash in her eyes beneath her high forehead and dark, parted hair. She was glad to take me with her to the adult service now and then. I chewed the last bite, the crust, asked if I could be excused, and left.

I WAS A FISH, and already caught before I noticed that I was a fish: the hook was in my mouth between tongue and cheek, the barb stuck in my flesh near my wind pipe, as long as I could remember, the wound around that sharp bit of metal in my throat was proof that the connection between me and the world had been disrupted. I did not always want to accept the situation, but when I tried to get rid of the hook, cramped up in anticipation of failure before I ever started, my whole body writhed, I shook my head, my half-opened mouth, I choked and pushed and pulled and could not free the hook and ripped it further into my flesh. The hook impaired my efforts to breathe, really breathe. I lost the beat and forgot my own breathing rhythm until I no longer knew with which bodily organ I should inhale air, exhale air, did not know whether I had lungs or gills, did not know where my gills were situated and whether my dry, scaly skin would even allow air to pass through. It hurt to speak without air, and I did not know whether it was ever possible to speak without pain, without tearing the flesh in my tongue. I refused to feel the pain as pain. I said to myself: That's normal, you alone are at fault. I did not know who had hooked me, I had no firm suspicion, not even enough to rule out those whom I hoped to love and who assured me of their love. My parents told me about the parable or the teaching of Jesus, the fisher of men, who wanted to catch humans in His nets for His congregation, for faith in Him, for redemption, and I was already so thoroughly ensnared that I did not cry at the thought: Jesus wanted to catch me too, hook me or trap me in His net, tearing me away from my own element and left to suffocate in the air, and I wondered only about what He wanted from me, the smallest of fish, from me of all people, a child. *Let the little children come unto me,* but He already had me, He was already visible in pictures and on crucifixes in almost every room I entered and gave me no peace. He wanted to catch me in His net or had already done so. I should let myself be caught, but I was not in the net, I dangled on the hook. I was well aware of the difference. The barb tore into my tongue, tore my body apart, separated head from body.

It would perhaps have been more comfortable in the net, despite it being cramped. There would be other prisoners nearby and touching. But I was alone. I dangled on the hook and did not know how long the line was or how large the hook in my mouth. I pulled and struggled and snapped, sometimes the line was longer, sometimes shorter, sometimes I could forget the line, forget about the barb in my mouth. It went on like that for years, and I fell mute like the fish, became the fish. Scales grew on my elbows and knees and ankles. Every gym class, every summer exposed the evidence for all to see: He's peeling, like a leper. And once it started, it could spread all over, arms, legs, gradually cover the rest of the body with flakes of skin and bestow upon the fish a seamless gown of scales. That is why I rubbed knee and elbow every evening with a stinky solution and got a nose full of sweetly foul stink during bedside prayer, but the medicine that was to ward off the fish skin helped about as much as the plea of *Make me pious!*

I could only hope for long, endless summers and exposed my afflicted body parts to the sun so that the scales would disappear; they did disappear a little bit, but soon returned. No doctor could say with certainty that the scales would not one day cover my whole body and consume it. And so it went for years, and I was a fish and remained a fish, mute, scaly, constantly gasping for air. I did not want to be a fish and was therefore afraid of the water, I became skittish around water and put up with the resultant teasing, did not want to learn to swim, did not want to be any more like fish, did not trust the water to hold me up, me who is neither fully child nor fish, and who could not breathe and wriggled on fear's hook. I saw the eyes of the herring on the plate, my eyes; they no longer saw anything; they stared emptily into the world, and I too did not want to see anything anymore, wanted only to get away and be rid of the hook and the muteness and the scales, but I could do nothing other than acquiesce to the tug of the fishing line and reduce the pain or shift it to other parts of my body, always expecting suddenly to be pulled up into the air and to have to give up breathing forever, I did not want to be mute and found a way to cope with it. I wanted to be rid of the scales and ceaselessly asked why my skin was peeling off of me and who could give it back to me on some far-off day. I wanted dry land under my feet, wanted to get away from water. I wanted never to be pulled about again and hated all hunters with rifle and tackle and did not know how to express any of it.

WHERE AM I? I am where the middle is. As the earth is in space, in the mid-point of the earth is Europe, in the middle of Europe is Germany, in its middle is Hesse, and, as far away from the pull of Frankfurt as from the outreach of Kassel, in the middle of Hessenland, just a bit to the east, in County Hünfeld, and even though my village was not quite in the middle of the county, it was at least an equal distance from Hünfeld and Bad Hersfeld, Wehrda was in the middle between both towns. It was easy here to picture the world and to determine a center point and from the window to see this point as a nest: in the middle of a place, in the middle of the middle were house, yard, church, churchyard. The house to live in, the yard to play in, the church to work in, the churchyard the point around which the world turned, a round village green with eight linden trees surrounded half-way by a low sandstone wall, like an island it was raised slightly above the four streets that met here, without cutting it up or reducing its size.

Sure of the middle, I defined the circle step by step, ever larger and out away from my house. It was easier to breathe outside, outside something new was starting, the world a sport field. An open house door, leaps down three steps, five, six long strides through the narrow flower garden, *close the gate, the chickens!,* across the yard and, past the elderberry bush and the courtyard linden tree, the thick wall—no barrier to me, the driveway gate open, quickly under the linden tree in the churchyard, at the benches, hardly visible to my parents, just barely within earshot, but already closer to my friends and closer to my other life, at the meeting place in the middle of the middle.

Four streets, ten neighbor houses, what's he up to, what is she doing now, where should he be, what is that? Always active between barns, stalls, house, and garden with buckets, pitchforks, shovels, pitchers, brooms, baking tins, water hoses, or farm machines, busy with cows, pigs, horses, chickens, in the cycle of feeding and butchering, of plowing and harvesting, slightly hunched over and shaky from hard work, the farmers looked up nonetheless when I, alone or with friends, turned from the street to their farms. You had only to say *Good Day!,* then they would greet you back and share a terse, uncomplicated friendliness with you. Sometimes I made my way into their dark kitchens, observed them as they ate with coarse, bent movements, hard, rough hands, shamelessly powerful arms and the men's white brow lines that shone in contrast to the reddish brown of their faces when they removed their work hats. In the warmth of the kitchen, beneath the sticky flypaper full of black fly remains, between the smell of manure, potato steam, and cow-warm milk, here I could put up with hearing the phrase *miller's cattle and pastor's children turn out well but seldom* more easily than other places, because a hidden recognition, a wink of the eye, conveyed the message: It's not your fault.

A child's game, claiming the world to be your very own possession. I was tolerated in all the neighbors' houses, they were all good folks in the village, almost all of them neighbors, no one locked his door. Wherever I ran, with friends or alone, between farmyards and doors, across gravel roads or behind houses along clay dirt paths and garden paths, even the forbidden meadows and gardens, everything belonged to my middle, everything belonged to me that I could reach on foot, reach with my hands, behold with my eyes.

Here they let me ride on the tractor, there they lifted me up onto a horse. I knew in which stalls I could go at what times, who milked by hand, who used the shiny aluminum milking machines from Miele. On every stall door hung a blue sign with the Hesse State Lion reading *Cattle Free of Tuberculosis.* Manure mounds did not stink; irksome were only the cow patties and the puddles of liquid manure. The milk cans made comfortable stools, fence pickets made good vaulting poles, hay was there to sink into and hide in. Potato beetles and quack grass were also my enemies. The commandment not to trample through meadows and wheat fields did not need to be explained to me. I could distinguish hay and aftermath by smell, and standing next to the giant threshing machine in the neighbor's barn, I would watch during late summers as six, seven, eight men worked, engulfed in the noise of the diesel motors, next to leather drivebelts and shaking sieves, trickling the kernels from the grain heads and sheaves into sacks and pressing the stalks into hay bales. I stood in the chaff dust and received something from the fruit of our labor when the reward for hard workers and onlookers was distributed, huge trays of pastry or fruit pie with whipped cream.

Among the people with wooden shoes and kitchen aprons, on milking stools or at public celebrations, in front of gardens and stalls, a different, a simpler language was spoken, an earthy dialect reflecting the rhythm of work, often three, four syllables and an appropriate gesture were enough. They needed, it seemed to me, only the one certainty: If you wanted to have enough to eat, you had to *work,* as farmer or as carpenter, blacksmith, cobbler, wheelwright with a couple of cows and pigs. Life's motto could just as well be that of the Raiffeisen Bank, *One for all—All for one,* and of the Fire Department, *Praise our Savior—Help Your Neighbor.* And the old women who need more nourishment for the soul found every day a Bible quote in the *sayings* from the Neukirch Calendar. They had the calendar hanging on their kitchen pantries; it hung in the study in our house. The same quote that I had heard in the morning in an atmosphere permeated by the Holy Word lost some of its awesome, proscriptive power when I saw it on the same calendar in one of the farmers' kitchens.

As son and grandson in my own house I stuttered and was afraid; as a child of the village I did not suffer. But both types of relationships belonged together, I needed the change, here and there, inside, outside, and in the streets of the village I emulated my father, who found entrance everywhere, was welcomed almost everywhere; he listened to the people and spoke to them. In the movement from the middle to the outside and back lay all possibilities, lay the certainty that I was truly in the middle, everything belonged together like the beams in the timber-framed houses. One beam supported the other, wood notched into wood in right and pitched angles; the wood is alive, they said; the wood worked the paint off in flakes, between the beams of crumbling plaster or brick, but the timber frame continued to stand, was repaired, protected its inhabitants, protected me.

I am where the middle is, everything moves toward the middle. Every one or two weeks the houses became stage props, the rhythm of work halted, and a modest drama, a wedding or a funeral, began. The people would move in double file towards the pastor at either the church or behind him from the house in mourning to the cemetery. I was proud of the fact that none of these ceremonies could occur without an actor in the leading role, my father. But more than in the man in a cassock, more than in the couple or the coffin, I was interested in the people who formed the wedding party or the mourners who played a double role: They mourned or celebrated an important event, they were related with the happy couple or the deceased or knew them well; at the same time they were actors on a stage, the streets of the village, subjected to the curiosity of onlookers. The men had laid aside their faded work clothes and, parodying the pastor, appeared in gleaming white shirts and ill-fitting black suits that had been passed down to them. The women, when with rosy cheeks they were not dressed in dark apparel, suddenly resembled my mother in their flowery dresses and white stiff collars. But they could not hide the wrinkles in their faces, and in the appropriate earnestness, in the awkward festiveness as participating performers, there remained something rather cunning, as if the mourners as well as the wedding guests knew that no metamorphosis was perfect and final, as if they needed to change their roles between work coat and tie, the up and down between work and celebration, drudgery and drinking.

Thus did they move past me, with their ambiguous faces and monosyllabic last names, Hühn, Röll, Vock, Zinn, Mohr, Roos, Trausch, Quanz, Lerch, Heinz, Trapp, Hahn, Stock, Lotz, Manns, and mixed in were Berlet and Billing, Opfer, Adolph, Sippel, Stuckardt, Gerlach, Döring, Bolender. They passed by and then disappeared into the rhythm of rollicking company upon the living-room stage, where plates were always fuller and voices grew louder, and the play led to a finale in the darkness of evening that excluded the younger audience.

Where am I, I am where soccer is played, on the playing field when eleven men dressed in white shirts and green pants entered, their club name F. C. Wehrda 1922 (which was painted on a board on the roof of the grandstand). They played with a ball against other men in black or red or blue gym shorts racing across the grass, defending the reputation of the village. They had been county champs of the A-League, they carried the name Wehrda into the villages of the Vorderrhön region and exhibited their artistry every second Sunday. I wanted to be as fast and agile as they; I stood at the fence around the field and cheered them on; I was the one who got the ball when it flew onto the playing field; I ran after them when, often still in their game shoes, they walked the kilometer to the Lotz Tavern. I heard the clacking of the cleats on the asphalt—I so wanted to have shoes like those. I was not with them when they celebrated a victory or an undeserved loss or the unjust tie with Auerhahn-Bräu, I heard only their singing resound across the churchyard *Drink, drink brothers* and *In Polish land, there dwelt a girl* and *The church fair has a hole, hole, hole.* I was far away from these men between twenty and thirty, coached by a former National Team player who had come to the village as a refugee and then stayed. I would never have dared speak to one of these heroes who carried the name Wehrda into the fray, Billing or Gerlach or Stock or Manns. I could not imagine that they would answer my questions, not even about what they thought the chances were for the world championship game and where they were going to listen to the broadcast.

I am where the middle is, where there is singing. Men formed a choir, the teacher raised his arms, swung his hands and was called the director; standing in a half circle, the men hummed the base note and sang at special birthdays in front of house doors *In the beautiful meadow,* or *Wonderful evening time*; at the monument they sang *I had a comrade,* at weddings in the church *I pray to the power of love.* They stood crowded together between graves at the cemetery and sang *Life rushes by*; at every ceremonious occasion, the Choir Club set the appropriate tone with hearty basses and dauntless tenors. Whenever on Saturday evening in the Lotz Tavern hall the singers began to rehearse *In snowy mountains* and *In the coolness turns a mill wheel,* whenever their songs drifted over the churchyard to our house, into my room, *Falling in love on the river Rhine* and *Down in the valley,* I lay in bed already and let my feelings go with the songs, for the melodies and lyrics (which I understood less and less as the evening wore on), bound me closer to the village than the melodies and lyrics of hymns. In the forests and valleys sung of by the men, I saw my forests and valleys, saw the cool bottoms and the snowy peaks in the nearby Rhön mountains, saw the Rhine in our own Haune River and saw myself wandering on the heights above our village. The choir was transported into the landscape and took me with it. I hummed along, wanted to be a singer—singers don't stutter. The harmonies of *Evening Bells* and *Moonlight* were meant for me too, removed my burdens and made it easier to sink into the waves of slumber.

I am where the middle is, but where does the middle stop? In the evenings, when the wind was still, I heard the commuter and freight trains race by behind the woods on the stretch between Hamburg and Munich or Frankfurt, only two or three kilometers away from my center point. Next to the tracks, drive heavy semi-trucks and ever more colorful cars, so much traffic on Highway 27 that the *Hersfeld Times* was screaming for an interstate highway to be built. The north-south traffic through the counties of Hünfeld and Hersfeld was becoming intolerable, in the neighboring village of Neukirchen, which had begun to take on the hues of Exxon-red and Aral-blue, the cars were killing children, but my middle was protected from all that. In Wehrda there was no major misfortune, no flood waters as in Rhina or Langenschwartz, no freight trains jumped the track, spilling gasoline in our Haune River, nothing sensational happened.

There was only one threat: Just beyond the closest mountains loomed the Evil Empire, behind the barbed wire was the desolate East Zone of Walter Ulbricht. But the Americans were protecting my middle, they had the stronger tanks with a white star; just before you got to Hersfeld the bus went by the army base. I saw those "Amis" at their posts, I saw them on maneuvers; they commanded the ground; they commanded the air; they radioed; they protected my forests; they chewed with open mouths; they laughed as though everything were a game.

High, thick forests, protective walls of beech, spruce, oak held back the storms and surrounded on three sides the place where I never felt lost. In a northerly direction, spotted with hilly fields and dull-green meadows, lay a broad opening that narrowed funnel-shaped into the middle of the village, and even the four streets—lined with apple trees, coming from Rhina and Schletzenrod through the unforested landscape and from Langenschwarz and Rothenkirchen, with many curves through the forest—fit into the slightly descending funnel, demarcated by three forest edges, as though the landscape were supposed to lead visitors from neighboring villages or travelers from afar directly here, in this valley, in this middle, as though all roads ended here or could start here. Spaciously enclosed by spruce green and beech green, between houses, church, and castles, with chestnut trees, linden trees, and birch trees contributing their own diverse greens, the village in the hollow lay in the lap of the landscape or was like a lap on which I curled up again and again. I was so sure of my place in the wide world that at the age of ten I had used my father's typewriter to type a *World Plan* on a big piece of paper. In it, the exuberance over being fortunate enough to be in the middle, and to able to perceive everything from that middle, took the form of an endlessly towering list. Following my first name and last name came eight lines: *Profession: Poet. Place: Wehrda. County: Hünfeld. State: Hesse. Country: Germany. Continent: Europe. Planet: Earth. World: Universe.*

THE BELLS RANG. I stood in the hallway beneath the decorated text: *He who goes in and out this door / Should consider evermore / That our Savior, Jesus Christ / The true door to heaven is.* The letters were in an old style decorated with gold points. I ignored the warning *Should consider*—I had seen it too often, too often considered. I was wearing a gray jacket over my shirt because of the summer chill in the church, was freshly combed, my hair half wet, was holding tightly onto a hymn book, and waiting for Mother, who was giving the maid instructions concerning lunch and the proper care of my little sisters.

I went where the bells beckoned me to go. I was doing something to which I was not obliged or pushed. I went a couple of steps beyond what was expected of me, perhaps to get attention or secure permission to listen to the radio in the afternoon, perhaps to elevate myself in the world of adults for an hour or to be near my mother, perhaps out of curiosity or a mixture of all these reasons. The bells rang louder and friendlier than earlier this morning, resonant magnets drawing me in and driving me away, driving me away and drawing me in with three-toned force, more beautiful than the suppliant hammering of an individual bell when it was time for the Lord's Prayer or at midday peals or the *ringing in* that informed the village of someone's death.

Through the house door past the blooming garden, first under the linden tree in the churchyard, then coming closer behind the courtyard wall, I saw the heads of the churchgoers. Men took their hats off at the door, a woman drew her head scarf tight, almost all of them looked up briefly, as if they needed to catch one last breath of air before submerging themselves in the thin, solemn, rarefied air of the church. There were no children to be seen, children had their own special service. I heard the bells, thought about the children who did not go to church, and recognized again in the bells a rhythm, the rhythm of a poem that we had just learned in German class: *There once was a child who never wanted / To attend church,* verses and rhymes that intermingled ever more clearly with the bell tones and bothered me somehow. Although I often *attended* church, even when I was not *ordered* to do so, I understood all too well the child's desire in the poem, *to take the path to the field.* No one needed to tell me that church time was not the right time for *the path to the field.* Nonetheless I understood the conflict and, although my mother was never so severe, sensed the threat, the curse of the mother in the poem: *the bell will come to get you.* I knew that the bells hung securely from beams up in the tower, and still I could not get the image out of my mind that was as horrible as it was funny, rhymed to the rhythm of the bells: *The bells rang no more, / The mother was hesitating. / Horrible to the core, / The bell came wobbling.* I felt the surprise, the horror of the child chased by a bell that had torn itself free and was hunting him down: *It wobbled wild, who would believe it, / See the frightened child, / As if the child in flight did dream it, / The bell will cover it anon.*

The three bells were calling. I obeyed, I was ready, everything was all right. I did not dissent, I was not in *pasture, field, and brush,* but I could see myself in *pasture, field, and brush,* I saw the picture in the school reader, how the bell pounced on the child and was about to *cover* it, trap it, smash and suffocate it. I saw myself suffocating, smashed, trapped, covered. I could not afford such disobedience, yet felt it along with the punishment that followed: I understood the poem, understood perhaps no other poem better than this one. I hated the poem, saw familiar dangers past the lines and rhymes. I cursed the poet, who was said to be our greatest poet, because he toyed with the *frightened child,* and I was disappointed that the subjugation to the will of the parents and their dear GOD was demanded and glorified in a school-reader poem. *And every Sunday and Holiday, / As the bell first rings your way / Don't let it worsen, / Or make the bell invite you in person.* The collusion between the poet and the German teacher strengthened the collusion of father and mother and the bell and the church; the poet did not allow the child any way out, he even attacked it with the *wandering bell* until it obeyed. What could one expect from poetry when it formed a coalition with those before whom I had to tremble and stutter; and the hope of something new, a better future that I had begun to discover in soccer, on my bike, in the arithmetic of lies, and in flights of fancy closed up—I was thinking something like that without noticing it and without saying it, because it was but a second's thought, vanished like the bell sounds of a minute that had long been drowned out, enshrouded, smashed by the new sound of bells.

My grandparents came down the stairs, I said "Good morning!" They repeated the greeting. Grandfather, dressed in a black suit, inspected me, although he wanted to avoid any impression of strictness; he smiled and seemed satisfied with the posture and clothing of the first of his eleven grandchildren; he had worn a uniform at my age and still thought it just fine that he had already been a soldier as a child. Grandmother smiled more tenderly; she was more inclined to balance out the strictness of her husband. She came towards me, removed the hymnal from her right hand and placed her arm around my shoulder. She did not expect me to say anything, no thank you's, no obedient stance, and with that brief gesture, she was able to shake me out of my thoughts.

I watched them as they went out the house door, off to church, slowly to the rhythm of the bells, she taller than the retired ship's captain. Tomorrow my grandfather would be off with quick steps to catch a bus, then in Neukirchen a local train, in Bad Hersfeld or Hünfeld a faster train or in Bebra or Fulda a commuter train, always with the exact connections in his head and a schedule in his pocket, and then to Bad Kissingen or Bad Pyrmont or Schleswig-Holstein, all in order to *evangelize.* When my grandmother was alone, she had more time for surprises from her drawer, for games and stories about the pictures of Mecklenburg that hung on the wall.

"Come!" said Mother, took my hand, and the ringing bells allowed us enough time to make the pilgrimage, those few steps between house door and church door, beneath the ringing that was like a ceiling of sound, through the entrance gardens, to arrive before father, who was the last to enter.

MY FATHER THE PASTOR WAS SPEAKING. He commanded the language and directed all attention to himself with the compelling black of his cassock and with his loud, friendly voice. The whole village, it seemed to me, was listening to him, the women below in the church nave, high above in the gallery the men, and in the middle gallery, where I sat with my mother in a row with my grandparents, other youths, and some people who did not acquiesce to the accepted sitting order. He had his *dear congregation* sing the chosen hymns, *The bright sun shines forth, joyful we awake from slumber,* and he had sung the loudest of all. I had also sung; next to the steady soprano voice of mother and close to the powerful voice of my grandfather, I never stuttered when singing. From the altar, he directed the *dear congregation* through the liturgy, with text and response, song and response song, standing, sitting, standing, and, having climbed up into the wood-paneled pulpit, now delivered the sermon. The pulpit was supported by a stone column on which grapevines, leaves, grapes, and an angel head with the panel LEX ET EVANGELIUM chiseled into it. The top of the pulpit was adorned with a woven green cloth on which stood the phrase *HE is our peace.* Between both phrases, above and below, my father's words moved, I saw his words framed, rising and falling between the woven and the chiseled sentences.

Up on the pulpit he was closer to us, his head no longer under the crucifixion before the altar, rather at the level of the gallery, *HE is our peace.* I followed the irregular movements of his Adam's apple, of the band beneath his throat, and in his broad black sleeves the arms and hands with which he gave impetus to the words. He spoke, speaking freely using notes, of Joseph and his brothers, about forgiving and forgetting, and he sent the sentences outward, downward, and upward. He sought faces to speak to, then he would change conversation partners; it seemed as if he left no one out, the diligent-devout farm women, the nobility in their family pew, the restless young men on the upper benches, refugees (who were still called refugees), mechanics and workers, dour farmers and quiet young girls, the engineer, the teacher playing the organ, my grandparents and my mother—he tried to give apt words for the week to each of them. He often looked up towards the men who sat left and right beneath the ceiling on the long benches along the balustrade, leaning on their arms, half asleep. Separated from the serious center of the service, they were on the *bench where the cynics sit*; my father's gaze hardly held them in check, to keep them from whispering and inspecting the women below.

He sought or caught my face as well. I could not look him in the eye, perhaps because once in such a situation, when five or six years old, at the solemn beginning of the Christmas Eve service, I yelled out loudly and cheerfully: *That's Father up there!,* and they still teased me about it. I did not want to embarrass myself again in church with an emotional outburst. Across the chasm between gallery and pulpit, every glance could cause an incorrect reaction, a grin; I looked to the side, studied the vine pattern on the green-gray cross beam, looked away from my father, who was inspiring or boring the people with the story about Egypt and the good Joseph who forgave his wicked brothers. The story sounded like all the stories, like the *parable* about the helmsman guided by the star of God, about the farmer who did not look back as he plowed, about the farmer sowing, about the olive tree; he always had at hand one of these unambivalent stories derived from the tortuous world of agriculture in the Old or New Testament and, in contrast to fairy tales, Good always won immediately.

I listened to my father's voice and yet did not listen to it, heard only the carpet of words upon which I spread out my own thoughts, tried to relax upon it. I could not lose myself in the

Biblical stories and interpretations like I could in a book. They were only the powerful linguistic adornment for rules, which is why they both attracted me and put me off. My father did his best to give the stories a human tone, tried to communicate the redeeming, the liberating, the joyful aspect of the message, but in his relaxed striving, in the strenuous intonation of some syllables, there still lurked some of the fear of speaking to no avail and of not being able to reach the people with his words or to inspire them for longer than the length of the sermon, a Sunday, a week.

I could see that my mother was gratified by the words, she in a cocoon of pious certainty, with an inner pride and a quiet glow in her eyes. Even during his sermons the two were close to one another; it seemed to me that he spoke sometimes directly to her, and that as she listened to the words she *preserved them in her heart*. She noticed my glance, she looked at me soothingly, asking for patience, but I looked away, down at the altar that she decorated with flowers every Sunday, at the burning candles on both candelabra, and at the black cross in the middle, at the orange-red carpet with vine pattern in front of it, at the wooden candelabra above, everything fixed, often seen—like the INRI shield—and yet pervaded by mystery. I shied away from looking at the pain-ridden, dying face and the horrible nails in hands and feet, then stared after all at the image of the dead, naked Savior about whom too many miraculous tales were told. Of all faces, why should this particular one be the expression of the highest love? *He suffered for you as well*: This rationale did not suffice. I could not and did not want to understand why one feasted on a dying figure, drew so much life from one who was tortured, why we had to pray to someone dead.

I looked away and did not want to stare into any faces; I saw on the walls the red-colored decorative script, the flaming script of Psalm verses, saw the diamond pattern in the windows, small red and blue squares glowed on the edge of the glass, and I examined whether the numbers of hymns and verses on the two sign boards—which I could see from my seat—agreed with one another and the confirmees had not made any mistakes.

I did not pay any more attention to the meaning of the sermon's sentences, which were meant for adults anyway; I heard only single words, listened to my father's voice, which alternated between highs and lows, between cleverly emphasized and non-emphasized syllables, a now softly, now loudly modulating voice, and I wondered whether a strange, a God-given voice might not really be speaking out of him, a strange power controlling his hands and measured gestures, whether maybe the oft-invoked Holy Ghost had not given his face that almost exalted, devoted expression. If it was not the acoustics of the church that gave his voice this strong and somewhat threatening tone that seemed to float down from above, if his voice really was nurtured by a foreign voice, I wondered, did he possess this voice only during church services, baptisms, weddings? Is there more warmth in the preacher's voice than in the father's? And if the foreboding, comforting power of his voice were noticeable only during his performances while on duty, then does he not have to think, I contemplated further, not in words, but possess two voices, two powers, two souls, one human and one divine?

HE is our peace, the pulpit phrase meant Christ; I watched my pastor-father speaking and his left hand lying next to the cloth on which the phrase was inscribed. I transferred the words, as if I had to heighten my confusion, to my father also, because he was not my peace, but rather exposed me to the most terrible dissatisfaction of these questions. In the dismay of such conjecture, I was lost, stranded forever with the uncertainty of whether I was dealing with the paternal-human or paternal-divine side, and as a result, I did not trust either—not the divine, because it was to be had only through faith, and not the human, because it was mixed with divine splinters and shards or could flip over into the divine at any time.

What kind of man was it who could speak *in the name of the Father* with his own voice, in his name and *in His name*? Why did he push me back into the deceptive ambivalence of every word with such formulations, why did he corrupt even the simple word *father*? I did not know whether he was fomenting this ambivalence intentionally and why he did not help me by letting me call him daddy or dad or papa like other fathers, why he had us address him like his wife did her father, my mother my grandfather, why he insisted on the title with which we addressed the Lord God, and why I did not dare to call him something else, or at least to try it.

I tried to help myself by imagining him without the black cassock, pictured him sorting postage stamps, putting slides into frames, taking an extra turn with me on the motorcycle, telling jokes from his school days in a Kassel dialect, bent over in the garden. When there was some distance from church and official duties—on trips, with relatives—he was a different person, and I especially liked to picture him kneeling down next to the train track that chugged around in his study on Christmas days, and for a moment, lying on the carpet, the turn key to the locomotive in hand, revealed the child in him and the fleeting regret at having grown up, before he put back on his invisible or his black cassock and spoke from on high.

On a bench behind the altar along the wall sat the church elders, who had passed around the collection bags just before the sermon. Above them hung plaques commemorating the dead soldiers of 1870–71, *They fought for king and country,* and next to it the one for 1914–18, *Heroes, fallen in the struggle for Germany's honor and existence, Never shall their names be forgotten, holy shall they be to us.* The name of my father's father was also on some chiseled plaque in Westphalia; I had been lucky; my father had only been taken prisoner, interned almost three years by the French, returned without serious wounds, thanks to *God's blessing,* lucky, had not turned up for five years, unlucky, and—as if he sprang up from the earth—he suddenly appeared as *the* father, how lucky, and having stepped into his dark vestments was unapproachable, unlucky, no, lucky, when I thought about the children whose fathers had died.

Down next to the benches for women, the nobility had their *box,* the baroness and her family, who owned everything except father. The five of them huddled there as though in an open crate, and at the same time on display in those seats that no one could take from them, the upper half of their bodies subject to the mustering gaze of the remaining congregation below, above, and in the middle and always close to the pastor, but they sat in their box on seat cushions because the baroness was the patron of the church. They were owners, more than two-thirds of the surrounding forests belonged to them, the other third belonged to the other aristocratic families, who had their own *box* in the middle level, next to our seats. They lived in the palace, they had opened up the palace to refugees, refugees of nobility, they had more power, more money than all the others in the village; they tried to get along with everybody and work like everybody, they opened the village for the first visitors from the United States and Finland, but the most important thing was that they sat on cushions in church. I envied them that luxury but still would not have liked to sit there on display like the baroness, the queen of the village, who made an entrance into her box every Sunday, in sturdy pumps with tire-tread soles, green-brown skirt, dark-green jacket, not quite forest ranger, not quite hunting garb. For a whole hour she had to sit across from the stony knights, her ancestors who were kneeling on their sepulchers in the church wall, in their armor or lady's gown in front of a bleeding Christ above skulls and the snake of the devil. When I saw her children and relatives next to the baroness, girls with pretty, confidant faces, with an aristocratic blond in their pigtails, I wondered whether it would not be simpler to be a child of these better-off people, not only because of the forests or the seat cushions, but rather because a different, livelier rhythm of discipline and gaiety was the rule in the palace more than in the pastor's house. Against that though was the fact that these children no longer had a father—the baron was shot in the last days of the war, he died in battle; this shadow alone was enough to make me not want to change places.

I had a father; alive, powerful, loud, even one who brought together lots of people, people who looked up to him, listened to him, and now groggily or attentively awaited his final sentences. I was proud of him again, envied his command of the language and the assuredness of standing in the middle point once a week and, without getting red in the face or struck by lightening, to speak *In the name of the Father, Son, and Holy Ghost.* Perhaps I could learn from him, perhaps even speaking, perhaps I just needed to listen better, breathe better, or wait the three years until my voice broke. Or was it praying, faith, that gave his words magic. I did not know. Again I had failed to discover which magic abilities were the driving force behind his oratory, in which now that one, monosyllabic word God occurred more frequently, the mystery word, the central word, the beginning word, and the key word *God*.

One thing I knew: Where God lives, it is not warm. I was cold, the church was always cool. In summer no heat came from the heater. I pulled my jacket together tighter. Beneath the pulpit and next to the baptismal font, the dark, black heating vent was in the middle of the church, and it had only one vent cover over the hole, entrance to hell. Beneath it smoldered the fire in winter; I could picture a rather large oven. Coal was shoveled there, everything was black there. And in autumn, toads gathered in the garden on the damp cement in front of the door to the cellar where the heater was. No, I did not believe in Hell, it was only a playfully heretical thought. In winter it got exciting because the pastor had to avoid the vent if he did not want to look like a bugaboo when the rising warm air puffed up his cassock like a sack, a joke of the congregation. In the summer, the devil played no pranks, and nonetheless he spurred my fantasy that there was more than a heating unit in this black hole. I had no fear of Hell, I was in good company between all the faithful and pious faces that now, relieved and thankful, celebrated the end of the sermon with a prayer and a new hymn. Despite all the uncertainty and inability to believe, despite all the unclear sins and mistakes, nothing much could happen to me, I was sure. As the son of the pastor and grandson of a missionary, I belonged to those in the better part of the world who were destined for Heaven.

The *dear congregation* lowered heads again, we prayed *together the Lord's Prayer,* my father and grandfather prayed loudest of all, almost competing, but my father had the advantage of declaiming the well-known sentences with his commanding voice from the altar. A booming, grumbling, defiant, triumphant chorus of women and men in the entire church saying the prayer; in addition, the bells rung, and I could hear quite distinctly the words that my mother said with tender intensity. I felt protected in this chorus, kept my head down, behaved nicely or wanted to behave nicely, and when we got to *the power and the glory,* I thought of Fritz Walter and the German soccer players, I quickly added a message to Heaven asking for victory, *Amen.*

After the voices rose to the rafters in song one more time, with every last ounce of effort in anticipation of the finale, belted out with a sense of relief over the end of the most wonderful and, for some people, comforting hour of the week, the man in the cassock raised his arms, his hands, right and left together, to the level of his face, holding up the open palms to the now wide-awake congregation. Everyone could see that he had no wounds there, no Jesus but His representative, and perhaps only my eyes could see from afar shadowy dark places, in the furrow of the lifeline, something that could be taken for wounds. Depending on how he held his hands or how the shadow fell, one simply could not discount the thought that he, now back under the Cross in front of the altar, incorporated something of that man who could walk on water and change water into wine, although the golden wedding ring glistening from his hand betrayed otherwise, and although lots of Hoffmann-brand starch was necessary in order to keep the cuffs on the sleeves beneath the cassock white and rigidly shining. He raised his large, sanctifying, miraculous hands, delivering his last exhortation, the climactic moment of his performance, and he spoke: *"The Lord bless your coming and going, now and forever. Amen."* In that moment his right hand cut down through the air just about a vertical meter and then defined a short horizontal line, so that we might imagine a cross now standing invisibly between us.

It was not so much this magical gesture, which ritual demanded, but rather the act itself that I admired: with signing the Cross, which was also used against the Devil when all else failed, drawing us one last time into his spell and releasing us with a blessing. The amazing thing was that he could extend this blessing *forever,* and then close with the thunderous word that we dared utter only in the Lord's Prayer: *forever. Amen.*

There I stood with my eleven and a half years, encased in the space of time between this Sunday morning and *forever,* and an unimaginable, future, endless time opened up before me in which my unimaginable, future possibilities lay concealed. The arch of these words reached far beyond my small life, reached beyond all life, all worlds and galaxies, and was now, as if the contemplation of *forever* were unwelcome, halted by the word *Amen.* We sang wholeheartedly *Amen Amen Amen,* before everything relaxed, stances, faces, hands, and everyone hurried, carried forth by lively organ music, to exit the nave of the church without noticeable pushing, but as quickly as possible—beneath the jeering applause of coins as they clanked onto other coins in the collection plate—and step out onto firm ground again.

I, HOWEVER, how often did I sway and fall, stumble with my speech, tighten my vocal cords, clamber onto rising sound fragments and find no secure hold, and fell: When an answer was expected and a hint of fear played a role, the consonants remained stuck in my throat or knotted up between my tongue, teeth, and gums, and took my breath away. The syllables flagged and stalled before they were formed, pieced together into nonfricative words, I trembled, twisted my mouth, punished vocal cords and tongue and still was not able to intone the syllables.

As soon as I took a breath to speak, there was a burning in my gums or between my teeth. I was afraid of all words that began with Z or with T or D, P or B, K, G or Q, did not want to capitulate before these cliffs, tried anyway and hung tight. I hated words like bell, belief, blessing, especially the insurmountable double consonants, and I tried to maintain my composure before the abyss of dangerous consonants. I had to avoid all these hurdles at the beginning of words and could do it only on rare occasions. I had to weigh the words before I attacked their pronunciation, and until I had found my way through the thicket of plosives, aspirated and non-aspirated, labials, dentals, palatals, examining, cheating, gulping, smoothing, the shame over the embarrassment of my own mouth making a fool of me, and I hesitated and gave up.

It was easier in front of women to speak the language, in front of children it was still somewhat easier, but in front of men, in front of teachers and fatherlike adult figures there was no exception: I sank between their expectations and my inability or unwillingness to meet the expected expectation. At every hesitation, there was the threat of impatience on the part of the one standing opposite me. Beneath those eyes, demanding, disapproving, or annoyed at my stammering, I felt in the wrong, in the wrong place; disfigured by the heat of a blush, I felt useless and already devoured. Too many of my forbidden feelings rushed up at the same time, shoved the simple answer—which was already on my tongue and expected—aside and occupied the narrow space next to my vocal cords. They rendered my vocal cords useless, blocked my mouth, and I felt like someone wanted to tear the consonants, with which I was still struggling, out of my gums with his bare hands in order to prove to me how simple the simplest thing in the world is: speaking.

The more I gave in to perspiration and hesitation, the more I saw myself from the outside: the boy is giving in to perspiration and hesitation over simple words. I saw the observer observing me, saw myself from the perspective of my teacher, of my father or some other challenger, stuttering, stuttering with a red face, choking on language, caught in feelings of guilt, and I knew at the same time that this strange look, in which I assumed was disapproval, saw correctly, because I felt guilty myself, long since saw my mistakes, my ignorance, my lies and excuses through the eyes of the other person and confirmed every negative suspicion with my fearful search for syllables, with repeated attempts to overcome the hurdle of a hated consonant.

Even when my parents tried to calm me down: *Speak slower!*—and I tried to speak slower, maybe a couple of words came out better, but then I got stuck again. My mother, too, could find no accompanying sentences or gestures that would free me from this linguistic hell, the flames of contrary and pointy consonants gripped me nonetheless and burned in me until I cried and tearfully gave up. I had to accept it: I was incapable of speaking normally, it was my fault. (Where did it come from?)

There was the Biblical example of the Tower of Babel, they had wanted *to make for themselves a name,* they had wanted to build a tower *whose top may reach unto heaven,* they were punished, did not understand each other's language, had to *disperse;* language was made confusing because they had committed a *sin:* Which *sin* had I committed, why was I being punished? I did not know. I knew only that I had no chance, I too would have bitten into the forbidden apple, I too fought with my brother Abel. There would have been no room for me on Noah's Ark; I would have been condemned to drown pitifully. Why should I learn to swim? I too would have turned around in Sodom and been changed into a salt pillar. I too would have helped build the tower in Babel; such a tower was a good idea really and, in any case, quite an achievement. I did not escape the judgments of the Bible, I saw the distraught faces of those fleeing, murdering, crying, raving, praying, half-naked muscular figures of the Old Testament on the woodcuts by Schnorr von Carlsfeld in the illustrated Bible. I had no chance before this God, when even the intensely God-fearing men and women did not survive the trials. There was then no escape from this tortuous God, who had it in for the disobedient and wicked people he himself had just created.

What salvation is there when everything is predestined? When the *loving* God *visits the iniquity of the fathers upon the children unto the third and fourth generation*? Why must I, with my eleven-year-old worthlessness, grapple with a God for whom everywhere in the word, not only in my little village, thick church walls and towers were built, for whom so many books were written, before whom everyone folded their hands? What separates me from the House of the Lord, in which my father and mother and uncle and grandfather and grandmother and an infinite number of ancestors had found the meaning of life? Why can I not just brush all that off?

I knew only that language left me speechless. My stuttering was the proof that I, at least in thought, had been in Babel. Did I want *to reach to heaven,* did I want *to make a name for myself?* Was I as presumptuous and childish as the people in Babel? I did not know, but was confronted with the result daily: My speech was confused and diffused; I carried the story of Babel around with me, carried it on within me; I felt the Tower growing in my body, felt how it was forced against my throat from the lungs, made my breathing difficult and cut off the air: I was scattered, scattered throughout the world, because my words, syllables, consonants, and thoughts did not fit together.

Soon I no longer believed that anyone expected anything good or successful from me. I settled into my linguistic hell, and discovered what power I won over the witnesses to my linguistic misfortune when I paralyzed a paralyzed situation even further and caused the abyss between thoughts and words, the gap of inappropriate pause between sounds to widen even further, and thereby caused what was embarrassing to me to be a source of embarrassment to the one posing a question and other listeners. In this way I was able to assure that they increasingly did not want to run the risk of renewed embarrassment, leaving me in peace—and thus I could find something good in my own fault and could diminish the oppressing sense of shame about stuttering with a secret pleasure.

I discovered what attention a speech-impaired child could garner, but I was not lying sick, cared for and spoiled. I had to work hard with the stutter, begging, making myself understood: Look at me friendlier, have some confidence in me! Set me free from the condition in which I am suspect, culprit, accuser in one! Let me speak my own text! So, I said in my own way: No! or: Help me! or: What are words compared to what is! Perhaps I spoke in my inner conflict in a topsyturvy way unambiguously about myself, perhaps I was never so close to myself as in the heat of embarrassment, perhaps I therefore never let go of the hope of frictionlessly becoming one with my words and thoughts in a later life, far away from all damnations and defeats, that is, among the victors. I dreamed of other, easier, clearer languages, of a language that consisted only of vowels, in a pinch enriched with a few of the less bothersome consonants like F, H, L, M, N, S, W.

I stood in the courtyard, mute, listened to the loud swallows in their nests on the barn roof and the sparrows under the linden. To be able to fly and chatter like the swallows in their language of nothing but vowels, that would also be a possibility. Mother had gone into the kitchen, Father—in his black robe—was talking with some churchgoers. I turned my back to him, snuck off to my bike in the barn; on the bike I could forget my stuttering, but bike riding was not allowed so soon after church services. My black-painted used bike was leaning up front against the others because no one rode a bike as much as I. I was saving for a new one, dreamed of more than one gear; it was not affordable. I wished for a bike stand; it *was* affordable, if I saved long enough; but father had decreed: *A bike stand is nonsense, I know because I had one myself once, and it broke right away.* I dreamed of my own soccer ball, a leather ball; I played only with rubber balls. I dreamed of the smell of fresh leather, of my hand on the soft, firm leather skin, a ball that one just had to kick and be fond of and take care of with shoe cream (better than the Sunday shoes). Anyone who had such a ball was popular and was allowed to decide who could play and who not; anyone who owned such a ball had already almost won. The ball was expensive and as unattainable as the bike stand. I wanted to go out, into the fields and onto the soccer field or listen to the radio broadcast this instant. Just a few hours left; the excitement over the final game grew. I fought it back, caught between church services and lunch, alone with my only strength, my only weapon—my disrupted speech.

I took advantage of the fact that people dared less and less to speak to me. I had an easier time lying. I learned to accept the shame of stuttering. Perhaps I wanted to disrupt something and not function without friction, as the model son of the pastor was supposed to function. Perhaps I wanted to put a lump in my father's throat, lame his remote-controlled tongue, limit his magical abilities, and let him know: It serves you right that I stutter! Perhaps I wanted to unlearn the foreign language of my parents and was nonetheless thrown back into it, thrown up against the cliffs again and again by the breaking waves of prayers and hymns, worn down between Mother's language poverty and Father's language power, until I lost my breath, until my voice failed even at easy-to-say consonants, and I had to seek out more decisive diversions in order not to sink in suppressed pain, suffocate in choked speech.

I went slowly back into the house, too mute to cry for help, and rejecting the help recommended in the saying, written in the old script on the ceiling beam in the hallway: *Jesu iuva iugiter. Jesus, always help!,* I had learned to translate it. Still I repeatedly forgot the exact translation, because Jesus did not help me either in overcoming the barriers of sick communication and my stricken skin that separated me from *people closest to me.* It seemed to me though, that it was more help when I was out of His immediate sphere of influence, really far away: At the place where I no longer had to stutter, where no Tabulet of Commandments–God lived, where apples were not poisoned by prohibition and snakes, where I did not have to drown as a sinner and slay my brother, and where no new Babel threatened.

THE CUCKOO CALLED TWELVE TIMES from the hallway, just a half an hour until lunch. The cuckoo heightened my anticipation, thirty minutes lay hidden still in his wooden nest of time, when he pushed open his little door, when the big hand reaches the VI or XII, he called out hastily the hours or half hours, he brought the starting whistle in Bern thirty minutes closer, with his call cut a little bit off of the waiting time, at each appearance he seemed as if he were about to fly off, though he just flapped back closing his little door behind him after the rapid double tone, a quick, aggressive referee of minutes, unreachable up on the wall.

The aroma of the roast had reached the hallway, my hunger grew with anticipation of the game. I could talk to no one about my expectations of the big event—my siblings were too small for the soccer world, my parents wanted nothing to do with it, and my friends were sitting down to eat at home now. I went and got the newspaper out of the study where my father and a church elder were tallying the collection, a lot of small change and a few mark coins stacked in little columns.

I took the newspaper, the *Hersfeld Times* from Saturday evening, July 3, went up to our room, where my brother was reading the new edition of *For you!* (a little pamphlet for the children's service) and working through the puzzle page, *Uncle Smart gives nuts to crack.* I did not participate today in word puzzles, picture puzzles, and funny questions—with which the Word of God was rounded out for children—I sat down at my desk like an adult and opened the paper. The first page with large photos of the foundation building ruins and of the President. Theodor Heuß had come to Bad Hersfeld for the opening of the festival, the festival was the only news on the front page and did not interest me. I looked for the sports page and read again what I had already read on Saturday afternoon.

"What question can never be answered with Yes?" asked my brother. I did not know, I said: "Let me read the paper!"—"Do you want to know?"—"No." — "Are you asleep?"—"Oh."

Can the Hungarians be stopped? That was my question. *The German National Team wants to storm Heaven's gate.* Even reading it a second time, the sentence still irritated me. Heaven was for the pious, the angels, and God. I read the article about the game slowly now, the chances, the hopes. *A soccer dream has become reality,* I followed the reporter's tale of the path to the playoff once again, relived the joy over past victories against the Turks, the Yugoslavs, the Austrians. I read and agreed with the author that we had no chance of becoming World Champions: *The Germans' chance is small, paper thin, nonetheless,* a game was not over until those ninety minutes went by. I read and tried to memorize phrases such as *physical condition, most consistent defensive work, super offensive game.* Like the reporter, I was proud that the team had reached the finals, *the sensation,* and was satisfied that Herberger had kept the same team *that beat the Austrians,* hoped that the players *rise to the challenge of the Hungarian ball-handling magic,* and hoped further *that one can without a doubt put some trust in this team.*

But it no longer mattered what I read and which opinion I had, more important was that I knew I was not alone when I read that others thought and hoped the same as I and had already formulated what I could not formulate, and that I recognized in these sentences my thoughts, and this form of appropriation occurred without me having to put out much effort. It was far more that I felt the quaking happiness of the reader: to find so much of my own ideas in the text of another, even on the sports page.

To meet in a book a boy or young man who showed up with my wishes and from page to page lived through the adventure and emerged as victor, with a stronger will, greater power, and a cleverness better suited to the situation, was maybe more gripping, but the newspaper delivered here and there enough stories in which I could play a small role. Not every day was as dramatic as a year ago, when I lay sick in bed with the measles and discovered what a tank was, a giant steel monster with cannons and merciless chains, which was headed for me, me who did not even hold a rock in his hand, and almost flattened me. The pictures in the newspaper had become so alive and loud that, although I had never really heard shots before, the shots in Berlin rang in my ears in my sick bed in Wehrda, and I had run away, just like the others in the picture had run away on the Berlin street Unter den Linden. I had not been hero, but had been there and had survived. I felt the rage at Ulbricht and the Russians and the tanks and loved the newspaper, which conveyed such adventures, such emotions to me.

I flipped to the *Page for Kids.* There I saw something about the *Eight Golden Rules of Swiming,* about *Journey to the Moon* by Jules Verne, about the *Flying Dutchman,* a picture story about *A Man Who Conquers an Empire, Cortes in Mexico.* I passed over all that; the excitement about the game, intensified by the newspaper, was already so strong that I did not want to concentrate on anything else. The suspense about something that had not happened yet, that was supposed to start in just three hours and already be over in five hours, was the most exciting thing ever. *It all seems a bit unreal, but it's happened: The German national team stands tall . . .* an event in the game plan with day and time and yet nothing but fantasy: a game that would take place in far-off Switzerland without any contribution from me, and yet was impossible without my participation.

THE TABLE IS SET, *and everything ready,* I sang, right hand in father's hand, left hand in brother's hand, *oh look what the love of the Father bringeth us,* I heard our song even as I sang, *oh taste and see that the Lord is good.* We stood behind the chairs around the table, looked at each other encouragingly, lightly held each other's hand and welded ourselves together into a choir and sang the Sunday meal blessing in celebration of the roast and of God, *For the* LORD *will not forsake his people for his great name's sake.*

The table is set, I could see that, a fresh white starched tablecloth, ironing folds marked the middle and right angles, plates sparkled white, knives rested on knife holders, napkins in silver napkin rings, the soup bowls in the middle, *and everything ready.* That was straightforward, but something bothered me in the other words. The words were riddled with little barbs, and I sang strongly against them, *oh see what the love of the Father.* I looked at the table and knew that it meant the Father in heaven and not the one next to me, and yet also the father next to me, whose job it was to proclaim the love of the Father in heaven, to represent Him and in doing so earn the money with which the food was bought at the Edeekay grocery store.

I looked up at my father next to me, who, like I, like we all did, sang of *the love of the Father.* I searched his face, the side he parted his hair on, for a reaction and tried to find out how he handled those five words singing. He sang away undisturbed, his eighth or tenth song this morning already, and did not seem to notice the embarrassment that derived from the ambivalent address of f/Father, from the invitation to confusion, from the shame that came from the Father on high. He sang with mouth wide open, his Adam's apple danced in his throat, and the level of the ear pieces of his glasses from ear to eyelash showed that everything was in balance, everything in its place. The hand that held mine did not jerk when *the love of the Father* was sung, and it gave no indication that I could have interpreted as I would a blink of the eye. I did not jerk either, did not squeeze the hand that just an hour ago had extended from the cassock sleeve and pointed to God, the magic hand that described the sign of the Cross in the air, that had formed the bridge to *eternity.* I did not dare touch this hand, God's instrument, more firmly than was proper for me. I let the larger hand hold mine, warmed against my will. Had I squeezed harder I could have felt the ring with the family seal on it, the decorated rose, which symbolized the name that I, that we all had inherited from father, but I also avoided contact with the dark prehistory of our predecessors and their vague *love,* whose product I was, caught in everything, stumbling over the words and over the word *bringeth.*

Although it was explained to me that this was an old way of saying *bring,* I still could not help but think of booty and at the same time of the silliness of such thoughts in face of the white, empty plates, the Sunday soup, and the expected two thin slices of roast. At the same time, there was something ridiculous, remote, grandfatherly in the word that did not occur in real life and in books, yet once a week was used as a bad rhyme. The little word seemed so extraordinarily silly, that it could make me or my brother grin and change a choral song into a competition. It was not easy to sing the long, sung Sunday prayer without uncontrolled emotion breaking through, a totally different athletic challenge than the short prayers recited on workdays: *Come, Lord Jesus, be our guest and bless what you have given us,* while we folded our hands and closed our eyes. In the middle of the Sunday ritual, however, singing with mobile hands and eyes, the word *bringeth* became the decisive hurdle or excuse when my brother or I wanted to animate our siblings—through funny looks or faces—to giggle, the forbidden giggle during prayer, made easier through artificial stances and required joyousness. Stares were distributed and bearable, a game, to cause others to giggle without giggling yourself, to be outwardly in control and keep a level head at the onset of a grin while singing, to hide it behind an open mouth and the restricted field of vision, but I kept cool.

After the choral singing we changed to a chorus of voices and belted out the syllables *Bless this meal!* like a battle cry, louder than was usual in this house, and finally we could sit down and start on the cauliflower soup. *Oh taste and behold,* I tasted the tricky lines of the song on my tongue more than the soup and had to wait in order to see *how good it is,* the roast.

Because the maid had off, my brother and I carried in the bowls of potatoes, beans, gravy from the kitchen, and when mother had placed the roast in front of father, he paused for two or three seconds, as if in brief prayer for the piece of fallen animal, before he sharpened the knife and cut the roast. With thick fingers he guided the knife and shared the meat, just as he had distributed the appropriate Sunday words. I saw how he lay the slices on the serving platter, *how good* he was, as I was getting myself some beans and potatoes. I saw the meat and heard in my head the sentence *And the Word was made flesh, and dwelt among us.* I could not get this disgusting Bible sentence out of my head, saw the flesh become Word in the roast and yet did not get sick. I was hungry for the flesh, not for the Word; only with words had my father worked on this piece of flesh. I watched as he, relieved as after a victorious battle, guided the knife and distributed what *the love of the Father bringeth.* He was wearing the same shirt as in church; now one could see the silver-gray collar, beneath his neck a napkin now instead of the white collar band. On the hand that was cutting shone the golden wedding ring as it did before on the hand that blessed, and his movements—with which the Lord over Words became Lord over Flesh—were still those of a man, even without cassock and evocations of God, who had a role and filled it perfectly.

He himself got the largest portion of the meat that *He bringeth* because it was his hardest work day, two church services, one baptism, several meetings. He had shaken lots of hands, maybe thirty people in Rhina, seventy in Wehrda, had made clear to them all the difference between Good and Evil, had paved their way to the Heavenly Kingdom, and prayed for good weather for the harvest, and had tried to give everyone who came to him a lift into the new week. Since I concealed my envy at father getting such a big portion, I loomed all the more over my brother's plate, took jealous measure of his slice of roast, always afraid that he, the smaller, weaker, more sensitive one, would get more of the *love of the father.*

Once every plate was finally filled, once fork and knife were in hand and poised to strike, mother chimed in with the phrase *Hope you like it!* She was not trying to anticipate or avert praise for her cooking, rather she just wanted to emphasize the decree *Taste and behold!* that we had sung and half forgotten as we smelled the mouth-watering aroma of the roast. Obediently, I gave in to the taste. Even before the first forkful of potato and gravy reached my mouth, it tasted like it was supposed to taste, tasted good to me. The last sprouted potatoes from the long-gone autumn tasted now, in early summer, like they looked, bland and wrinkled, but they had to be eaten up. I searched for that good taste. The old potatoes tasted good to me without stressing my taste buds and without allowing any contradiction between what I tasted and what I was supposed to taste.

Oh taste and behold!: I was not supposed to taste and behold either the potatoes or the green beans or the roast, rather I was supposed to taste in the beans, *how good* the Lord in Heaven was, supposed to taste *the love of the Father* in the slab of roast beef on the table, on the plates beneath the gravy, on the forks, regardless of how it was seasoned and how little of it I got. I was supposed to appreciate it as a visible sign of the grace of God, *who will not forsake His people,* that is, me and the others at the table. That is what I was supposed to taste, and I did taste it, God's flesh and God's gravy and God's potatoes, until I could not taste anymore, but just ate and ate as much as I could and forgot and unlearned tasting. At the same time, I was supposed to *see* what I tasted, and I saw what I ate and ate up, saw the food on the plate and did not see it, because everything, even the gravy, salt, and potatoes, was woven into a higher context, into Christian conviction. Seeing did not count, *blessed are they that have not seen, and yet have believed,* it was not about seeing. On everything that there was to be seen lay a fog of faith. I did not see what was, but rather saw what should be; my sight was distorted or muddied by God's sight, perception skewed in advance by what I was supposed to perceive. My eyes were not my eyes, but rather manipulated organs in which too much of the viewpoint of my parents had been implanted. I did not see, I did not believe, I dreamed.

Why adults repeatedly found comfort in the existence of an omnipotent being, *who will not forsake His people,* I could slowly understand because they had survived the hunger, flight, imprisonment of the war only a few years before, and they often spoke of past hardships. But they were not the only ones who had survived, and still they considered themselves *His people* without turning red in the face. It was embarrassing to me when I allowed these kinds of wayward thoughts to creep up, for how did they know that they belonged to the Chosen, *His people,* why could they so loudly and shamelessly proclaim themselves among those whom He will *never* forsake?

I did not ask, held tight to the handles of fork and knife, cut, stabbed, loaded, lifted, bit, chewed potatoes, beans, meat, saw the others doing the same, abject in Sunday faces over Sunday shirts and Sunday blouses, captives to a muffled Sunday caution. I sat straight, or tried to sit straight, to avoid reprimand at having poor posture. I listened in the concert of silence to the scraping and clinking of the silverware on porcelain, and although extended talking and laughing were allowed and desired at the table, as long as no one else was the butt of a joke, no lively discussions ensued because talking was not allowed while chewing because you were not supposed to talk when others talked, and because the events of the morning did not entail very much. The confirmees had posted an incorrect hymn number, no complaints about the man behind the organ on the billows pump, nothing about the bells, about the motorcycle, nothing new about school, no argument, no anger, no exciting news from the village. My brother repeated the joke from the *For You!* pamphlet, "What question can never be answered with Yes?" We both got excited when no one knew the answer. There was still the question about afternoon activities. It looked like rain, for days now the rain following the June heat wave. My parents were invited to a baptism party in Rhina, it was decided that only father would go. None of this interested me, I had permission to listen to the radio in the office, that had been promised and was certain, I wanted nothing except the playoff game.

After the sweet reward, dessert, bright-red sugared currants in a bowl, the mouth, the sugar hardly licked from the lips, had to open in song again. On Sundays, the short post-meal prayer was insufficient, *We thank you Lord for food and drink, Amen.* We grabbed each other's hands again, this time while sitting, as if the bond of family between us were not strong enough, and sang *We thank you, thank you, oh good Savior, your grace and truth will last forever.* The simple song was not enough. We split up into two groups and sang forth our thanks in two-part canon, from the dining and living rooms through the house, up the stairs to the grandparents' room, as if they needed to be reassured that this Sunday dinner ritual that they had enjoined upon their children was also being continued in the family of their son-in-law, that generations and traditions fit together harmoniously and the grace of the Lord would last forever, and we sang three rounds, but now in the fourth fell off key and out of rhythm and in the last minute, shortly before giggling broke out, all our voices joined in a long, sustained, and relieved *Amen.*

I WAS ISAAC, the son, the father grabbed his son and *took the knife,* because God had ordered him *to slay his son.* I saw Isaac with terrified, obsequious eyes on the woodcut of the illustrated Bible by Schnorr von Carosfeld. I was Isaac, bound, fearfully leaning pressed against his father Abraham, held by his father's left hand as his right hand raised the knife, broad at the handle and narrowing to its tip. Isaac could not believe it: His own father is stabbing him. I could not believe it: What kind of God would order such a thing, what kind of father would actually do it without so much as a question. I shuddered, I bled, saw myself burning on the altar, on the pyre. I did not know what was happening to me, and even if my father had no similarity to Abraham, no beard, no long hair, no cloth complicatedly wrapped into a gown, and even if burnt sacrifice was no longer the custom, he was the father, I the son, above us both was God, and I knew no more than Isaac what kind of prayerful conversations with his Lord God my father was having, how close his relationship was with this Being who knew everything, could do everything, foresaw everything. I did not know whether my father received instructions and orders from God in Heaven, like the great figures of the Old Testament. I was not afraid of being actually stabbed by my father. The idea of it though was enough, hearing the biblical story, gazing at the woodcut: There is a God, a loving God, who forces one of his most pious and loyal worshipers to slaughter his own son, his only son. There is a father who obeys, or wants to obey this command without grumbling or question, has his son drag up the firewood, lies to his son when he asks about the sacrificial animal, ties up his son and forces him to the altar—the altar is the place of both the sacrificial slaughter and the sacrificial fire—*and stretched forth his hand and took the knife to slay his son,* had not the angel appeared at the last second and saved the son from the father, who in turn was profusely praised, *for now I know that thou fearest God, seeing thou hast not withheld thy son, thine only son, from me.* Then the happy ending—a ram is sacrificed and burned. But where is the son, what does the terrified Isaac think, what did I think, how could I feel safe and accepted and comforted by the *Good News* of a Lord who demanded of my father similar tests. How far would my father go in a similar situation? Would he choose God over his children, over me? Wasn't there somewhere in the Bible the sentence: *He who loves son or daughter more than me is not worthy of me*? And why would each of us on his birthday be awakened early in the morning to the hymn "Praise the Lord," sung by the rest of the family in pajamas, bathrobes, or in day clothes, a hymn that reminds us of the knife between father and son with the lines *the name of Abraham* or *the seed of Abraham.* My father had the hymns and the power on his side, he wielded the knife to cut the roast on Sundays, sometimes he hit me, with his hand on my rear end, with the rug beater on the seat of my pants, until I screamed and screamed and he considered the lie or petty theft sufficiently punished. Or he and my mother consulted on whether I should receive five or ten or twenty licks, and then he administered the judgment despite my whining and screams. Just how violent must power become before *he would slay his son.* We lived in different times, pigs were slain on a farmyard, pulled by the ears and driven out of the barn with a pitchfork. The butcher numbed the pig with a bolt shot to the head, split open the pig's body and crucified it with the head down. We paid Mr. Mücke, refugee from Silesia, a few pennies to kill our chickens and rabbits. Nonetheless, I saw the knife in my father's hand, and yet I could not imagine a butcher knife in his hand. What kind of God was that who tortures the children of the pious with the idea that they could be slain at any time just because the Lord of Heaven and Earth has problems with the fidelity of his followers? What kind of God—who otherwise forbade lying—here forced a father to lie? What kind of God who tortures even fathers by ordering them to slay their own children, as though there were no other possible proof of their *fear of God*? What kind of joy does the great gruesome Unseen get in demanding killing as proof of love? The angel came too late, the knife did not disappear from the father's hand, Isaac did not resist. At the moment he understood the situation or did not, he sought refuge in the powerful father figure. The angel came too late, the pain could no longer be stayed. I saw the knife in Isaac's heart, saw him bleed, saw him dead, and the angel, floating against a mountainous backdrop, grabbed the ram—the son's surrogate—by the horns with one hand, laid the other sheltering hand on Isaac's head and checked the swing just as the father was about to stab the son. The angel came too late. The atrocity had already occurred; although the murder had barely been prevented, the atrocity was the gruesome game, playing with the life of the child, the Omnipotent's lust for torture and the sad obedience of his servant. The atrocity was that the child's terror played no role in the story and that I remained alone with that terror.

CAN THE HUNGARIANS BE STOPPED? What could I do to stop the Hungarians? I prepared myself for the contest with the Hungarians, all just a question of the right defense; I preferred playing defense because I was not quick enough to be a striker, because I did not want to embarrass myself as goalie or be cowardly. My imagination flew out to the distant game, I saw the Hungarians storming my position, five forwards against one defensive player; I saw myself on the playing field, it was not my game, but I played with the tension between the wrenching anticipation of the starting whistle and the timid defense against the unabashed hope, victory.

I had to take the tension somewhere. I ran outside, past the church around the corner in the direction of Wenzel's. The Erdal frog above the shop door with the Edeekay grocery store sign waved at me. I ran past five houses and four dung heaps on the road to Langenschwarz and Schletzenrod, then along the field path next to the Raiffeisen Bank, between grain fields up towards the forest. I did not want to go far, I did not have a watch, did not want to go any farther than where one could look down at the village from a raised hunting blind.

Just two hours till the radio broadcast. I had to keep moving, while away the time, escalate the excitement or disperse it. None of the usual children's games appealed to me right now, no book, and especially on a day when I was involved in a grown up activity like the World Cup. I simply could not bear wasting time listening to *Children's Radio in Hesse,* certainly not broadcasts like the fairy-tale lady and the choir of radio kids *Having fun and here we go, come play with us and Auntie Jo.*

Like every Sunday, every lunchtime, as soon as we had finished washing dishes and straightening up, mother had reminded us of rules about being quiet on Sunday, and today she added "and keep the radio down later on!" In the house, I would have had to sit quietly, hang around in my room without making any noise, because between the hours of two and four the only thing that counted was the nap taken by my little sisters, grandparents, and parents. They retired to their bedrooms and did not want to be disturbed by visitors, not by the telephone, and certainly not by children. No noise was allowed, no screaming, no quarreling, no door, no creaky floor boards or steps. As an eleven-year-old, I had had to fight long and hard not to be forced to take a midday nap, all the more reason to observe the rules and not to disturb the others in any way. I ran away from the ordained quietude, out into the air, among the larks beneath the clouds, out into summer, up Hutz Hill where the forest closed around the Wehrda valley along the ridge top like a horseshoe, in a small tongue of beech trees, pines and oaks that extended down the hill towards the village.

Sunday duties were fulfilled, Sunday dangers braved—nonetheless I wanted some distance between me and prayers and altars, knives and sacrifices, and away from forced quiet time. The grain stood high, I was about as tall as the golden-brown rye stalks and only a little taller than the wheat. My parents could have recognized me from their bedroom by my jacket and white shirt collar. I ran away from their field of vision, away from the asperity of the midday retreat, away from the sickening quiet, which was like the soundless echo of all commandments, the sum of all muteness. I did not know whether they really slept smack dab in the middle of the day and why they got so mad when a door accidentally slammed despite precautions, or when a sound came from the children's room or a visitor would not be turned away. Only once, when my grandmother complained about some man who just had to talk to my father, had my father snapped at his mother-in-law: *I am there for my congregation!* That did not change the usual rationale at all—they had to get up, also for me, at six and would not get to bed until eleven, and therefore needed a midday nap to even things out, that was just one rationale and did not erase the refreshed image every day of my parents slinking into bed under threat. The older boys grinned when ever someone spoke of the naps at the pastor's house, and when I defended my parents with that borrowed explanation, then it only made it worse, then they grinned even more, then they said that someone who did not work as hard as the farmers, certainly not physical work, likely had other reasons.

Can the Hungarians be stopped? I could not stop the Hungarians and ran, not rushed, but faster and faster down the path; I knew that I would turn back soon, would be sitting in front of the radio soon, and there would be only the game. And already the pressure to obey the house rules or circumvent them was eased. My running was not flight, only longing translated into motion, to throw off the dammed-up tendency to oblige God and to take a deep breath in green, bright surroundings. In the harvest ripe fields, blue swabs of the cornflowers, and red specks of the poppies, titmice hopping up out of the bushes along the field's edge; two spruce trunks lay along the path, branches and tips hacked off, and the muffled Sunday noises of the village drifted behind me.

I looked around, ran a few steps backward up the hill. The sun remained covered, the gray skies did not look like rain. *The*

German National Team Eleven wants to storm Heaven's gate. It was not far to the bench at the edge of the forest. The car tracks became deeper, the slope steeper, I was higher than the roofs, about the level of the church tower, and in climbing, happiness grew while looking down and recognizing the little world down there. When I was standing up there, beneath oaks and beech trees, above potato fields and grain fields in various golden colors, only the oats still green, when I stood still and heard my own breathing and the wind in the leaves, the wind in the grass, in the lupines and yarrow, and no sound from the village, the fear of being consumed by the quiet, of being ripped apart by the excitement, of being overcome by an unintentional hatred, finally vanished.

I sat down on the bench, and, as though of their own accord, my eyes photographed the wide panorama of fields, meadows, forests and roofs, the soccer field halfway to Rhino, not far from the Jewish cemetery, where no one was buried, and the ruins of the old moated castle, beyond that, half-hidden between spruce trees, was the Castle Hohenwehrda with lots of pretty boarding-school girls, across from that the cemetery on the other edge of the forest, the street below, recognizable by the barn roofs and house roofs in various shades of roof tile red over half-timbered patterns, between poplars and elms the deep warm red of the Red Castle and the washed-out yellow of the Yellow Castle, the four-storied Lotz Tavern, the church in the middle with the very broad, slate-covered onion tower, flanked by four side towers, the church, like a stone hen, crowned by a weather cock, and behind fruit trees the roof and the timber-frame of the pastor's house. It felt good to touch everything with my eyes and make it more beautiful, it felt good to view the power of my parents within the context of the village, the other timber-frame buildings, trees and roofs, and it assuaged me to look down upon the house of rules in which they now lay cooped up in midday quiet.

The Sunday quietude between the houses, carried to me by the light breeze over the grain fields, had something natural about it, not lifeless, not threatening, and even when a car motor, a cow, a rooster could be heard nonetheless, then the sounds seemed to fit into the quietude and make it clearer. Everything was there, nothing was changed, everything was as it should be, it was quiet, as though not just my parents and grandparents and little sisters, but everyone, was sleeping—the cows, the houses, and the three castles, like Sleeping Beauty. I was on the outside without feeling excluded, and I did not have the bold intent of the prince to wake them all with a kiss. I did not even know what a kiss was, I wanted to let everything stay as in static slumber, I was still asleep myself and was not even thinking of a princess. Too young to be tempted by the princesses in Castle Hochwehrda, too old for fairy tales, I sat in-between and numbly gazed down, as though I had to keep assuring myself that my place was still there, and I wanted to deal only with the foolish wish to halt time and simultaneously to accelerate it.

Sunken in the image that I already knew so well, or thought I knew, I looked for something in it like a mirror, could not get enough of what I saw, in love with the simple perspective from above, as though from atop a church tower, or in love with myself because roofs, timber-frames, garden-green, meadow-green, forest-green, and grain-yellow were like a mirror, and my gaze hovered over it all without faltering.

Above everything, more than five hundred meters high, was the hill called Stoppelsberg, with the castle ruins; beyond that lay the distant country that consisted of all those evil E's, East Zone, *red and dead.* Even farther past the barbed wire lived the Hungarians—I knew nothing about Hungarians, I only knew the sole question: *Can the Hungarians be stopped?* They were unbeatable on the soccer field, but one could stop them at this border, and Ulbricht too, I was sure of that. Because on our side we had the Americans, who every spring and fall celebrated maneuvers like cross-country games in the surrounding forests and camped between trees with their jeeps and tanks. We made pilgrimages to them on Hutz Hill, where I was now sitting, and stood pensively before their radios and tank treads, and they got a kick out of us marveling at their canned soup, chocolate bars, and cigarettes. The soldiers rode our bikes through the forests before they rewarded us with chewing gum and showed us pictures of naked women. It was peacetime, the Amis were dependable. Every morning and noon I rode the bus past the army tank encampment in Bad Hersfeld, where the guards loosely carried their submachine guns pointed downward.

The Hungarians, the Russians, the East Germans were stopped; I was not afraid of them. It was peacetime, the war still close but long gone, vivid in everyone's mind as the greatest experience, *In Polish land once lived a girl,* and the one-legged and one-armed men and the missing fathers proved that the war really had taken place. The last German soldiers finally released from confinement were escorted by torchlight from the entrance to the town all the way to their house doors and were greeted by a men's choir singing "We Thank You, God" and "I Want to Go Home Again." Stories about the first days of the occupation by the Americans, about plundered cupboards, being obliged to hand over potatoes, and fingerprints registered on file receded from memory. It was peacetime, even if the one party in Bonn wanted something different than the other party in Hesse. Adenauer's poster from the last election stayed up the longest on the bakery. People went about their business, interrupted only by Sunday, the farmer was needed, the factories were paying better and better, some worked at Zuse's in Neukirchen and Hersfeld on enigmatic, giant adding machines. *Life goes on,* though not in the East; in the East Zone nothing happened. That is why it posed no threat. But it was so close that a faint echo of political events still made its way into the valley.

I looked to the East, saw my village as a peaceful place, situated in fields and forests in the middle of the world. But the embrasures in the tower gave rise to the question about why someone would ever have used them to shoot through. Wehrdra had always defended itself well, I knew that, the village name derived from the Wehrkirche—or church of defense—and its tower with the thick walls. Yes, two hundred years ago or earlier, the village was the object of military dispute between the bishop of Fulda and Protestant Hesse. A border ran right through the middle of Wehrda, through our garden, directly by the church; mini-wars and decades-long battles were fought over this little speck of land. But why the high walls around the castle, and someone repeated what his grandfather had told him, that the lords of the village used to take away everything the farmers had and around the turn of the century still claimed the right of the first night with new brides, back then, and they paid the children who had to work for them with liquor, back then. All the battles were past, but the struggle survived beneath the harmony.

From far up on the hill, I listened into the houses, knew what most of them looked like on the inside. I knew that they had eaten, washed up, straightened up, and sat behind their timber-frame walls in the muteness of early afternoon. There in many of the parlors something dark and damp resided that had little to do with the hard life between stalls and field, dung heaps and pigs, hay making and trailer hitch. In the cold, stagnate air of these living rooms suppressed tales lay hidden—there was always a son or a father or brother fallen in the war pictured in uniform that had become embarrassing and in a picture frame placed on a little crocheted mat, staring at the survivors, staring accusingly at the crumb cake set out for visitors.

Every house, it seemed to me, had a secret, something about which no one spoke, not just opaque animosities concerning field paths or debts, not just rumors about who was a drunk, who had argued with whom, who had rejected a refugee as son-in-law, who was messing with other women. There was a stagnant rage, there were dark stories that did not belong in the world of a child, somewhere there was a chasm out of which terms like *Jew* were spoken with a contemptuously long EW and words like *Führer* with a high pitched Ü, or *Nazi* with a rebelliously intoned A turned up, then they were sneeringly and hurriedly swallowed, a fairy-tale world of evil terms and figures, a forbidden, dangerous mixture that one should not touch—but every fairy tale ended sometime, and *they lived happily ever after.*

That was not the way it really was, so many things were not, the dead men on the commode lived on, although they had died. They made accusations, they spoiled appetites. Amputees hobbled around potholes like living accusations against the healthy ones. Refugees lived crowded and gratefully in small houses or in attics; no one asked who had lived there before them. Again and again I heard the reproach of having been driven to injustice. The war had been a defeat and had left a dormant hate behind. The war was to blame for something with which everyone was involved but wanted to ignore, like the highway bridge behind me deep in the forest, across which no one ever had even driven because they had merely cleared away trees and begun setting up the bridge, which now in puddles and mud stood only as a monument to a wasted former future.

The German National Team wants to storm Heaven's gate, I wanted to be there and not miss a minute. *Can the Hungarians be stopped?* That was the decisive question. I ran back, with light steps down the hill, loosely like the players trotting out to midfield before the referee blew the starting whistle.

WELCOME TO THE JOINT BROADCAST OF ALL THE STATIONS *in the Federal Republic of Germany and West Berlin, including Radio Saarbrücken. Live from the Wankdorf Stadium in Bern: This is the final game in the World Cup Soccer Championship between Germany and Hungary, and this is your sportscaster . . .* the voice came from far away, strange and clear, every syllable spoken loudly, but I could listen only with the volume turned down, that was the condition. I scooted my chair closer to the radio, leaned over closer towards the far away voice. The announcer changed . . . *Germany in the final game of the World Cup Soccer Championship, what a huge sensation, what a genuine soccer miracle, which of course came about in a natural way.*

I entrusted myself to the strange voice. Glib and excited it carried the thrill from syllable to syllable and swelled to the word melodies of *huge sensation* and *soccer miracle.* I was immediately captured by the tone: Finally, an adult was saying with few words everything I was feeling but could not quite grab hold of. I inhaled the voice, let myself go whither it would, lifted and rocking sideways. The game had already begun, cries of the fans in the background. I set that little thin line precisely on the station. Frankfurt between curious names like Hilversum, Monte Ceneri, Sottens, and Beromüster, and my right foot jerked as the names *Fritz Walter* and *Rahn* were mentioned, and the first powerful shot at the goal, which the sportscaster imitated with a massive burst of voice. The miracle was there, I had a direct connection to that soccer field in Bern. It was raining there heavily. I prepared myself for the rain; how easy it is to slip on wet grass, and I ran after the ball, which I did not see, on the swivel chair, the office chair in front of my father's massive desk, turned towards the radio, as if I could see something in the radio, as if I, gazing at the brownish yellow cloth stretched over the speaker, gazing at the magical green eye, could influence the course of the game and direct the ball ahead of the right feet.

Without a moment's thought, I ran and I shot on the side of the German team, the *underdogs,* because I could not imagine myself here in the middle of Germany to be anything but opposed to the Hungarians, *the big favorites, the uncrowned World Champions who have not been beaten in thirty-one games over the last four years.* Besides, the Hungarians were Communists more or less, were among those I had considered hated enemies for a year now, since June 1953, and maybe, too, there was a quiet rejection of big favorites and unbeatable forces. I did not have the slightest sympathy for the *uncrowned* soccer world power. They had led in the preliminary round by 8 to 3. How they could massacre *us,* the little guys, their inferiors, the *underdogs.*

Our brave boys . . . had done it, were to battle this power, to challenge it, to stand up to it, and I tried to help *our brave boys* all I could with my good wishes. The sportscaster took my secret thoughts seriously. He drew me along onto the playing field, or into the first row of seats. It didn't matter to me, I was in the midst of the action, for with every *us* and *ours* or *we* I too was being directly addressed, and after only a few moments I belonged to the community of soccer fans. I was very proud that *we* had gotten this far. I felt myself becoming strong, ever stronger. Maybe the Hungarians could be stopped after all, and defeat be avoided. But with every passing second a new danger arose . . . *bad pass, and a second shot, goal!* Hungary leads 1 : 0 . . . *just what we were afraid of has happened . . . the lightning attack of the Hungarians.* At first I could not believe it, was completely surprised, and the worst part about the goal was that I felt found out because I had contributed to it: My swelling emotions in front of the radio in Wehdra had somehow set the counter attack in motion there on the field in Bern. A goal always occurs when you become too confident and easy going. Then you do not pay attention, and then it happens, that much I did know about soccer.

The sportscaster tried to be consoling . . . *let's not forget that Germany has never achieved such a spectacular feat* . . . but he did not console me; it was the beginning of the defeat, . . . *the Hungarian attack machine is on the roll* . . . and the shock of the first goal had not yet been overcome when . . . *Tschibor, like a tornado* . . . shot the second goal only two minutes later. Everything was lost, my trembling attentiveness, leaned over before the radio, my twitching foot did not help. Even the fiery voice of the sportscaster did not help any more. He had just gotten through saying that *it's a great day, a proud day, but we should not be presumptuous and think it might end successfully* . . . , now he had a calmer, more sober tone and was preparing me for the catastrophe. Two goals in eight minutes. It was all over. It was no use believing in the fine rainy weather that was supposed to be on our side, *the Fritz-Walter-weather. We* were losers again, once again I was one of the losers, the sportscaster was right: It had been *presumptuous* to allow thoughts of victory. And even worse was the fact that even the timid courageous hope of winning was being punished. I had already overstepped the bounds with my cautious delusion of grandeur and victory. I was ashamed, turned my body away from the radio, sought protection in apathy and convinced myself that it really did not matter, not a bit, how the game ends.

And GOAL! Goal for Germany! Goal! . . . Morlock's lunge blasted away everything I had just been thinking. The goal had rekindled my hope of not being totally defeated . . . *thank God, it's no longer two to nothing.* I concentrated, stared at the green eye as if it were the ball, and pushed it toward my players. They were battling on the field, battling on slippery ground, danger at the German goal, seconds later danger at the Hungarian goal . . . *the underdogs are on the offensive* . . . Every minute an attack on one side and then the other. The sportscaster's voice billowed back and forth between one *opportunity!* and then the next *opportunity!* It was as if the game's tempo made the playing field and the middle field smaller and I saw the white poles of the two goals very close to one another. The picture I had was in black and white, not only because the German team wore black shorts and white shirts, but also because to me the Hungarians had no particular colors, or because I just did not grant them any definite color. I saw only strong, rough figures with threatening names like *Puschkasch, Hidegkuti, Tschibor,* saw the grass gray, the sky gray, the fans gray, saw the movements of the game in the tempo of the names that the sportscaster passed to me, now a striker, now a defender. I became a part of the flow between the light and the dark, between offsides and out of bounds, had the ball, was the ball, kicked over here and over there, here the last save right at the goal, there at the other goal, but . . . *calm, unyielding Toni* stops the shot. Take a deep breath . . . *a corner for Germany, and . . . GOAL! Corner from Fritz Walter, Rahn kicks the goal! From two to nothing to two goals to two! Who would ever have believed it, we've tied Hungary, the best team of eleven soccer technicians that we know of!*

The voice trembled, I trembled with it, I did not scream, was not allowed during the midday rest period to lend my voice to the sportscaster's goal jubilation, because the stove was connected by a vent to the tile stove in my grandparent's room and carried every noticeable sound straight up there. *And it's Germany on the attack again* . . . the soft loud voice lifted me up, whipped me into a state of excitement that left me in voiceless abeyance. I felt the storm of emotions that the second goal set loose in me, but I had no outlet for it, was not allowed to, so I held it all in, collected my emotions, stored them, and remained still . . . *boys and girls, now* that's *excitement!*

I had never heard a soccer game announced on the radio before. Words kept coming up that had nothing to do with soccer . . . *miracle! . . . thank God! . . . This is what we all hoped and prayed for!* . . . and I was amazed that the sportscaster could say the word *believe* with more intensity than a preacher or religion class teacher. Almost a goal for Hungary again, almost one for Germany, and Toni Turek again stops an *unbelievable* shot at the goal, again a threat, the ball, in the goal, no, no its not . . . *Turek, you're a devil of a fellow, you're a Soccer God!*

I was shocked by these words, while at the same time I was overjoyed that Turek had stopped the shot, but the shock ran deeper. As the echoes of jubilation faded away I began to suspect in the most timid of ways just what kind of shouts those were: A new form of worship, a blasphemous, scandalous ritual, a pagan communion in which one person was addressed as devil and God simultaneously. Even if it was not meant literally, just jubilant phrases, I turned the volume down a little because I would have been embarrassed if someone had caught me listening to words like *Soccer God.* I resisted this blasphemy and mustered up all the arguments against it that I had been taught: *Thou shalt have no other gods before me. Thou shalt not take the name of the Lord thy God in vain.* And yet still entranced by the echo of the three syllables, *Soccer God.* I was pleased that this god was very human, that gods stood there in the goalie box or shot goals, instead of hanging bloodily on the cross. I was pleased that they struggled in the pouring rain and fought like *Liebrich, Liebrich, and its Liebrich again,* and I slowly began to realize why my parents did not care for my timid enthusiasm for this sport, that here they feared the possible competition of other gods who were more alive.

The excitement of the game eased my intractable feelings of guilt about violating the First Commandment by just listening. From minute to minute I liked it better and better, having a secret god, a *Soccer God* alongside the Lord God. The Commandments man hung directly behind me on the wall. I looked back at him, at the postcard-sized, gold-framed picture of the dark, bearded Moses with quill in hand jotting down the Ten Commandments. But he was looking to the side, at the Lord, was busy writing with his goose quill and not paying any attention to the blasphemy of the sportscaster and my momentary complicity.

I was alone, but surrounded by pictures and objects that are part of what makes up a pastor's office, a place where sermons are written, devotionals recited, instructions given to engaged couples and godparents, where books were stored in the shadows behind glass, awaiting their resurrection, where the sternness of two crucifixes characterized the walls, and the family coat of arms, the triple rose, was a decoration. We had to come here every day at eleven in the morning for a short prayer; here my father interpreted the miracle of Jesus of the Holy Land for the farmers of Wehrda, Rhina, Schletzenrod, and Wetzlos; here he radically changed the word of God and came up with new ideas, citations, important points; here he did not want to be disturbed and here he played all the well-known church songs on the piano; here is where he administered punishment and doled out presents: If there was anywhere in the world where the Ten Commandments ruled, then in this room. The shouts of the sportscaster: *A miracle! . . . prayed for . . . Soccer God!* rang in my ears and defied everything I saw in this room. But the crucifixes had not dropped from the walls, and glaring out from below the Cross was the halfway understandable Latin: VENI SANCTE SPIRITUS / PASCE PASTOREM / DUC DUCEM / APERI APERTURO / DA DATURO, meant as encouragement for the shepherd of souls, each word written with an exaggerated flair, but the Holy Ghost had not intervened, the thick Holy Scripture lay like a child's black gravestone on green felt upon the desk, and when the sportscaster spoke of our *guardian angel,* the music angels above the piano remained as motionless as the angel Messenger of God on the opposing wall, stiffly raising a hand in blessing before the kneeling Mary. This blasphemy was looking better all the time, and in those minutes I moved away from that triadic occupation force of God, Jesus, and the Holy Ghost, and began to believe in a *Soccer God* and an Underdog God, and not just one, for if Turek was a *Soccer God,* then the other ten had to be gods, too.

In Bern the game went undecided . . . *it hit the goal post, the goal post! Turek surely would have missed it* . . . changing with astonishing rapidity from one penalty area to the other as I hung on every name the sportscaster uttered, *Kohlmeyer, Posipal, Otmar Walter,* who were running with the ball, shooting the ball, heading it, intercepting it, stopping it. I breathed easier when the good names were mentioned, *Eckel the greyhound, May with the incomparable warrior's heart, Rahn from Essen, Fritz is everywhere,* while I flinched at the mention of the Hungarian names, expecting the worst from the likes of *Puschkasch, Hidegkuti, Lorant, Butschanski, Zakarias,* each of these hissing, tricky names stabbed into me . . . *here come the Hungarians again . . . the Hungarians are pressing towards the goal . . . the Hungarians in full force.*

I leaned back in my chair, turned towards the desk with the telephone, ink well, pen holder, pencils, red markers, and letters . . . *a frantic pace* . . . unconsciously picked up the letter opener, held the ivory handle, looked for my opponent, whirled around to every side, saw crucifixes and angels and Jesus and Moses and the large photograph of the portal of the cathedral in Chartres . . . *the Germans with another miraculous passing combination* . . . and laid the letter opener back down. I was so excited that I wanted to pace through the room, past the bookcase, to the sofa in the corner, or around that fortress of a desk, but I stayed where I was, right there in the seat of patriarchal power from which my father ruled the parishes of four villages. I could not tear myself away from the radio, the source of my Good News. The voice had drawn me back close to the loud speaker. Beneath the radio were the *Stuttgart Biblical Reference Book,* the *Evangelical Church Lexicon,* sermon books, commentaries, files, tools of my father's trade. My father, who was asleep, or maybe was not sleeping anymore—I had lost track of the time, only the minutes left on the game clock mattered . . . *six minutes to go, two to two, that's more than our wildest expectations.*

Above the radio the triumphal arch, a copperplate print from Rome with a scene from the edge of the Forum . . . *a day like no other in our soccer history . . . and Germany has the ball again* . . . I did not want to think about Rome now, but in the growing excitement I had to fix my gaze on something. Rome was much farther away than Bern. The picture did not move. *Veduta dell'Arco di Settimio* was written beneath it, in the foreground a partially sunken triumphal arch and endless stairs in the background, a few tiny people, a donkey, no color, gloomy and empty despite delicate lines dominated by tall buildings with dark walls, dark doorways, a world of stone . . . *Schäfer should shoot! Blocked! And a follow-up shot! Blocked!* . . . I could not understand why my father anchored his memory of Rome on this particular picture . . . *my dear Hungary, were you ever lucky, gotta admit it! Boys and girls, girls and boys, two minutes to half-time and Germany almost took the lead!*

The sportscaster thought about me too, thought about all those boys and girls, and I could care less whether it was just a figure of speech, he was including me, he knew how I felt and what I hoped, knew better anyway than "Auntie Jo" on *Children's Radio in Hesse* or *Having fun and here we go,* but now I was really happy, all knotted up in the moment's tension, guided by a voice that brought the game to me and me into the game. What I heard warmed me differently than my father's voice, it warmed me from inside, it seemed as though everything that had blocked me was loosened, as though I could finally feel like I wanted to feel, despite the growing proximity of all those thick black books and the pastor's briefcase. But the game was not over yet. I gazed at the picture of Rome, at the stairs, up and down, at the black and white structure of the copperplate print. A woman in the foreground reached out her arm, towards the triumphal arch, which with the stony burden of its lines and its stony pattern, matched so nicely my black and white perception of the distant game. The game was not over yet, the last word on my emotions not yet spoken, one shot, one defensive mistake could destroy everything . . . *header by Kotschitsch! Just missed the goal!* Someone is hurt, Eckel is hurt, how will it go on? . . . *Sepp Herberger, he seems cool as a cucumber, but what must be going on inside the man* . . . will Eckel have to leave the game, is he bleeding, is the team bleeding? . . . *here comes Hungary again* . . . and again . . . *but the whistle will be our savior* . . . The whistle saved me, time was called, ten-minute time out . . . *We ask you to take what our team has done into your hearts and give it the credit it deserves.*

BLOOD DID NOT STAY in the veins, blood did not stay in the wound, it did not dry, it flowed without stopping. Where did the blood go, who caught it, where did the bloodless body fall, who caught the body? I did not want to know what the teacher up front was saying about a bleeder, a boy, a bit older than we, who had to die because of his blood and could not be saved, and I did not understand why the story, which had already appeared in the

Hersfeld Times, was being told in German class. Maybe I had not been listening closely enough again, again had not grasped the most important point. It only took a few sentences before the teacher's story came alive. I saw the boy bleeding and becoming increasingly pale. I resisted the story, resisted the ever more vivid pictures, could not stop the blood, the blood would not stand still. I saw the bleeder lying in a white bed and around him clueless doctors and parents catching the blood in a bowl. Blood ran out of the wound, I saw the source of blood on the arm of the boy. There was no medicine that would make the blood clot, they could only cover the wound, plug it up, keep it elevated, but that was of little help. The blood kept overflowing through the plaster and bandage, and I thought, that's enough now, the teacher should finally stop now. I don't want to see it in such detail, I cannot look at blood, I don't want to see it, and the thirty boys around me were quite excited about the bloody story, it seemed to me, as they listened to the teacher, who now said that this ailment was inherited and frequently occurred among nobility, and I did not want to listen anymore. I already knew all that from nosebleeds, when warm red heavy fluid dripped out of the nose, and towels and handkerchiefs and nose pressure and neck cooling did not stop the bleeding, and it took several minutes before the blood began to clot and I, bloody handkerchiefs in the hand on my nose, lay on the sofa and, enervated, I could no longer avoid the question of whether I too was a bleeder or almost one, and why it always took so interminably long before this embarrassing torture was over. It was enough. I saw the blood, I smelled it, I felt its familiar, deceitful warmth. It was enough. The teacher finally stopped telling the story, but then someone asked something and it started all over again with clotting and transmission. I could not listen to it anymore. The information about nobility did not placate me, not at all, I was half aristocrat myself, stemmed from people who deceived themselves into thinking that the noble "von" added to their name really meant something, and so it was with our blue blood, bleeder's blood, that led directly to death at the slightest danger and smallest injury. I was afraid of blood, knew the blood on the depictions of Jesus, blood on His forehead beneath the crown of thorns, blood finely painted on the wounds on His side above the loincloth, Jesus with the suffering face, with traces of blood on His body hanging heavy in the throes of death, which was supposed to prove to me: life is in death, in blood, and the vulnerable, guilty body is a place of suffering and pain, which is necessary finally even for my salvation too. The blood that Christ had *shed* was supposed to have been *shed* for me, too, was supposed to be for me, but the blood that was *shed* and did not clot, only tortured me. It made my body empty, weak, pale, dead. Christ tortured me with His blood. It flowed out of His body, out of the bleeder's body, it flowed into the room, it flowed towards me, it was against me, the blood made me fall, I could not swim and drowned in the image of flowing blood. I could not stand the sight of blood and had often fainted when I saw blood. I felt my weakness and did not want to faint, especially not in school, a proud sixth grader, a Latin student at the Old Monastery School, the school of Konrad Duden. You already stick out because of your quietness and stuttering, you already stick out because of your poor performance in almost every subject, don't stick out, don't faint. I did not want to hear anything about blood, every new word about this bleeder hurt me, every syllable made me weaker, as though someone were forcibly pumping out my blood, as though I were as bad off as the bleeder, or even worse off, because the simple, monosyllabic word blood made me weak, me, someone in whose mind the images could not coagulate and who passed out as a result. I felt my head ache, emptyheaded, and saw no escape, did not trust myself enough to expose my weakness and leave my seat, the room, out into the sweaty, floor-wax smell of the hallway, into the schoolyard. I was always trying to run away whenever I didn't want to see or smell blood or hear stories about ailments; now I wanted to be strong and for once win the battle against blood, but someone chimed in with another question, and the teacher once again got going. I did not listen, held my ears, and tried to find refuge and escape in other fantasies, thought about buying ice cream for ten cents at the sports tavern before the bus left, but the blood had spoiled my appetite, thought about the blossoming cherry trees on blossoming meadows and yet still felt the blood pulse through me even as it ebbed away, and I felt ashamed that a simple story from the newspaper could make me sick, and ashamed at having such a cramped, unhappy relationship to the stuff that flowed through my body and kept me and everyone alive. The wound would not close, the wound remained open, it dripped and poured and flowed on and on. My veins were empty, my legs, arms, my whole body becoming weaker and limper, and my head floated lightly downward like a balloon, as the images toppeled—

and I woke up amid a bustle of voices, my vision awoke to garden green. I was standing at the open window, the teacher and two other students were holding me tight, the teacher said: "Breathe deeply!" and was relieved that I came to, and behind me, beside me, thirty boys with excited voices: I stood in the middle, breathed in the fresh air, and was the sensation of the day.

"YOUR SOCCER GAME ALREADY OVER?" asked my father.—"No, halftime. It's tied! Tied at two to two!"—"Hey, that's great!" The tone of his voice was not completely convincing, but before I had found out whether he really thought that a tie score was such a big deal, I was stunned: I had suddenly said "two to two," my tongue had negotiated the most difficult words without stuttering. I did not know whether my father noticed and maybe meant "Hey, that's great!" in reference to me. I was so confused over my achievement that I quickly ran from the bathroom back to the office.

Dance music spilled out of the radio, in the living–dining room mother was setting the table for coffee. I could have turned the sound up, the midday nappers had gotten up now, but I kept the music volume low. The fast, quick sounds were strange to me, did not seem to fit here, did not fit to this radio that played only religious broadcasts or *The Bells Ring in Sunday,* children's radio, and sometimes a symphony concert. The Word ruled here, and even the piano, which stood imposingly in the corner next to the hall door, was used only to accompany the words in songs, as if Felix Holzweissig of Leipzig had made the keys, in church colors of black and white, just for hymns.

I did not want to sit down yet and ran back and forth in front of the bookshelf, waiting for the second halftime, for the end of the music—my steps did not match the rhythm from the radio. In order to get to the books, touch them and open them up, one first had to open the wood-framed glass doors in front of each side of the shelf, pulling up on two handles and, when the doors hung horizontally, push them back. Besides newspapers, books of homilies, Bible commentaries, and Karl Barth *Ecclesiastical Dogma,* heavy books commanded the space, the ones with leather bindings my father had inherited from his father, Gregorovius's *Years of Travel in Italy,* Hiltebrandt's *The Battle for the Mediterranean,* O. Jäger's *World History,* Meyer's *Little Conversation Lexicon,* Ranke's *Princes and People of Southern Europe,* Hamann's *History of Art.* All the *good books* behind the glass doors held no appeal for me. I was looking for some diversion with ordered pictures of script, color, and patterns, farther down was the black-and-gold-embossed cover of the *Collected Works* of Raabe, Keller, Reuter, a more remote and inherited world of novels with burdensome Gothic letters, *Shakespeare, Schiller, Goethe, Storm,* then the bindings with more recent covers and curious titles like Gollwitzer's *Lead Where You Do Not Want to Go* or Klepper's *The Father* or Glasenapp's *Wisdom.*

The music stopped . . . *You've been listening to the dance band of Radio Hesse under the direction of Willy Berking* . . . I sat down again on the swivel chair between window, radio, and desk, beneath the postcard-size Moses, beneath the family heraldic rose, beneath the Roman triumphal arch, and I was ready for anything, victory, defeat, eternally tied.

We're reporting once again from Bern . . . distant cries of fans, announcements over the PA system, excitement in the air. The sportscaster immediately again found the tone that best suited my excitement and enthusiasm, led them with his voice onto the playing field and fed my ears with thrilling and reassuring sentences, to which I had already become addicted . . . *the underdog has an even chance* . . . The page had turned, the underdog was no longer an underdog, there was hope of more than merely a tie game, and without saying it directly, the sportscaster thought that a victory was possible . . . *Puschkasch is by himself! Eight meters in front of the goal!* . . . immediately the Hungarians dashed any intrepid, tiny thoughts of hope. No, we should not get overconfident, the team, I, and the sportscaster, who quickly changed to a careful, timid voice . . . *should remind us too that despite all the happiness, all the effort, it is only a game* . . . A game! There he was wrong, I knew better, it was much more, a game was everything that had nothing to do with school or focused on God, something that one played with friends or siblings or alone, but what I was listening to was much more than all games put together.

Two to two, and the Hungarians are on the attack . . . the scenes changed again . . . *like lightning! Deflected! A second shot! Deflected again!* . . . *and Hidegkute—misses a shot!* . . . I saw the ball that I did not see, in front of the German goal, in the German goal, twice, three times, but . . . *Liebrich, always that Liebrich* . . . *and Rahn to May and May to Eckel. Eckel to Rahn, let's hear it for the German attack* . . . and again . . . *Danger!* . . . *saved at the edge of the goal* . . . *Liebrich saves, saves, saves us* . . . *what a fantastic piece of teamwork by our German defenders!*

I liked playing defense best, right fullback, Kohlmeyer, but from minute to minute I more and more became Liebrich, center half-back, more and more a picture of Liebrich was coming together, whose name I had gotten to know only a few days ago and who was emerging in me. Whenever it got dangerous, *Liebrich, the Blond,* cut it off, and I, the fullback, the blond, focussed my liking, my hope, increasingly on this one man . . . *eighteen players in Germany's penalty area* . . . and Liebrich saves it. The sportscaster celebrated the *luck and ability* of the defensive team, I was part of that team and was happy about our ability. There was, evidently, an ability independent of obedience and prayer, an ability that was not blessed and approved from above, and luck existed, just plain old luck without ifs ands or buts, a happiness without shame and without the disturbing assaults of a conscience I participated in this luck, this happiness, about which no one else in the house knew anything, I was allied with distant people, other forces; nonetheless, I ran and got myself a piece of cake and hastily swallowed down the mouthfuls, as if I had to be ready to leap onto the field at a moment's notice.

Yes, whether in Hamburg, in Munich, in Bonn, in Cologne, in Frankfurt, all of you, everyone of you with a radio speaker now, hopefully you'll stayed tuned and cross your fingers for our brave boys . . . I obeyed, crammed the rest of the cake in my mouth and crossed my fingers, did not know exactly how one did that most effectively, a finger on the left hand over a finger on the right hand, crossing fingers on one hand, both hands, I tried it this way and that way, summoned up all my energy against the Hungarians, who were besieging the German goal again and shooting from all sides . . . *Header! Hit the top bar! No goal! Two to two, and that after Turek seemed beaten!* . . . I was crossing my fingers a little too hard, I had to let up some . . . *my compliments to you out there, ladies and gentlemen, crossing those fingers helped us there in the last three minutes, otherwise it'd be three to two in favor of Hungary.*

The crowd calmed down in Bern, but I could not calm down. I heard coffee cups clink saucers, in Bern it was still raining, outside the clouds were gray and blowing past. I had turned up the volume some and jumped up suddenly, because I noticed my father standing next to the desk. It was not so much him or his large shape that gave me such a start as just the fact that he appeared so suddenly, his encroaching presence . . . *Liebrich, Liebrich, if we didn't have you!* . . . those kind of sentences so full of enthusiasm, to which I had abandoned myself, were embarrassing to me in front of my father, who politely smiled and nonetheless might have detected the voice of a distant competitor in the sportscaster's voice . . . *and Liebrich, Liebrich, get him!* I did not want him to hear such sentences, his presence was a distraction; I did not want to be disturbed, I was ashamed. I said: "Still tied!" and pushed farther down into the chair, his chair, and acted like the game really was not getting to me, at the same time I was devoutly listening to the phrases coming from the radio. Whenever the name Liebrich was mentioned, I was Liebrich, whenever Kohlmeyer was mentioned, I was Kohlmeyer, and in the same way I was busy being Fritz Walter and Turek and Rahn. I could barely catch my breath when the sportscaster shouted *Posipal!*—I was not responsible for the defense on the left wing—or *Eckel!* and *May!*—I was too slow to be a sweeper; I was no good as left wing like Schäfer or a striker like Otmar Walter or Morlock. I was Liebrich and more than Liebrich, in five-fold shape on the wet grass in Bern, *everywhere* like Fritz, *airborne* like Toni, *fast as a bullet* like Rahn, *steady* like Kohlmeyer, *a fighter* like Liebrich. Father took a book from his briefcase and announced his departure for Rhina. He stayed only two or three minutes, but every second he was there and every word he spoke bothered me. I was impatient, the diversion meant danger for my team and danger for me, that someone would find out I had turned my back on his crosses and altars in front of the radio, that I entrusted myself to other voices and practiced a different faith. I took a deep breath when he left the room, took a deep breath because no goals had been made on either side in those few moments, and sentences like . . . *Liebrich, Liebrich leaps into the air like a world class high jumper* . . . helped me change into the hero of the day all the faster.

The second half was half-way over . . . *Germany's giving a fine showing* . . . again and again *the melodic names of the Pußta sons* were mentioned, did not sound melodic to me, because they always meant danger, because their sole purpose was to inflict the inevitable defeat upon me, thrusting in the last minute, even though they did not have knives and were not exactly Abraham. They were *unbeaten,* they were the *attack machine,* the winners, even though it was all tied up so deceptively until now and the game rocked to and fro with the rhythm of the sportcaster's words: *He could shoot! He shoots! He shoots! Deflected! Shoots again! Deflected! The ball would've gone in!*

I heard the motorcycle outside; father was getting ready to go. Through the window I saw him leaving, I saw the players, a whirling motion, running, jumping, diving, heading, dribbling. Now and then the agile pictures tore or washed away, because my imagination was dependent upon what I knew about the soccer movements and style of players on the local team F. C. Wehrda, and on that basis I had to construe—from mention of names and the abbreviated descriptions of play flow or duels over the ball—just where on the field in Bern Stadium the ball and the players were. Germany and Wehrda were similar—the former champions of the A-League wore white jerseys too, though they wore green trunks rather than black like the national team. The players from Steinbach, Eiterfeld, or Hünfeld were the Hungarians. I saw the Wehrda soccer field extending horizontally over the Hessian mountains and forests and on into Switzerland. The heavens poured their merciful rain upon the players below, the *Fritz-Walter-weather* was remaining constant, but otherwise Heaven, Father, Son, and Holy Ghost had no business here. No one beseeched them here, here nothing was certain or preordained, here nobody from the hierarchy of God, father, mother, and grandparents poked their nose in. Here I gazed into the distance, forward, and here not just an individual but a whole team with a captain prevailed, an altogether different kind of captain than my grandfather in his U-Boot. Here eleven men were going at it *with enormous gusto,* each one had to play well, all were dependent on each other, no one could stand *on the sidelines,* the principle of obey, acquiesce, fit-in, or fade away had no validity here. The only thing that counted was the vigorous alacrity of a *dribbling king* and the player with *dynamite in his feet.*

Despite all that, I knew that all efforts were useless—the defeat at the end was as certain as the power of the Hungarians, the Undefeated . . . *twenty-one players on the German half of the field* . . . a counterattack, recovery . . . *and now an attack by the Hungarians, Turek to the outside, second shot Hidegkuti!—Toni, Toni, you're worth your weight in gold, you're a regular Fort Knox* . . . gold, pure gold, money in the bank, a fortune, and yet another repulsive comparison, a human like gold, what a sin to think that way, to say something like that out loud, what did the game have to do with gold, I was not supposed to strive for gold and money, *easier for a camel to go through the eye of a needle, than for a rich man to enter into the kingdom of God,* money was the beginning of the path to Hell, the temptation, materialism, gold was acceptable in a fairy tale, in rings, in teeth, everything else lead directly to the *golden calf* that the Israelites prayed to and danced around, instead of waiting for Moses and God's Commandments. And now my heroes were weighed in terms of gold. I tried to imagine it in order to hide my confusion: a scales, a pile of gold, happy golden shiny faces in the sun—the picture was blinding.

Suddenly he said . . . *ten more minutes* . . . every second counted now, and the pace, the back and forth sped up again, the reporter's voice skipped a beat, and again it was Hidegkuti, and again Fritz, and again a corner kick for Germany . . . *our Fritz moves to kick, cross your fingers out there at home! Keep 'em crossed, as tight as you can, even if it hurts, it doesn't matter, do it!* . . . and again nothing, and again it was Eckel, and again Hidegkuti, and again Puschkasch, and again Hidegkuti, and again Todt, and again Kotschitsch and Puschkasch, and . . . *Liebrich blocks it with his head, always that Liebrich* . . . and again applause, and Rahn and Otmar, Fritz and again Schäfer, Morlock, Zakarias, and again Puschkasch, and again Eckel, and a free kick, and again there is danger, and again Kotschitsch, but Turek, and *the German attack machine,* and again Lorant and . . . *six minutes left, no one is wavering, the rain's been coming down incessantly, it's hard, but the fans, they're sticking it out, when have you ever seen this kind of play-off game, so evenly matched, so exciting* . . . I was sticking it out, I could not bear the excitement any longer, I almost did not care anymore what the final score would be, the main thing was that the strain of the game would be over in a few minutes . . . *Schäfer, outflanked towards the middle, header, deflected, Rahn should go ahead and take a shot from farther out, Rahn shoots! GOAL! Goal! Goal! Goal! Goal for Germany!*

While the screaming, electrified voice was almost tearing the radio apart, the hidden metal in the radio case vibrated from the screams of *Goal!,* and the cloth speaker cover trembled, while the radio crackled in every nook and cranny and the sportscaster fell silent as if he had been shot, Cries welled up from the background, underscored by applause and jubilation, direct from the Bern stadium to my ear, and although I had not fully fathomed it yet, I threw up my arms triumphantly and cried more softly than I intended to: "Goal!"—softly because I had not yet perceived my own joy, it was more a reaction to the cries from the vibrating case before the sportscaster finally recovered his voice:

. . . three to two, Germany leads, five minutes left in the game! You must think I'm crazy, you must think I've lost my mind!

I did not think he was crazy, did not think he had lost his mind, I was not prepared for the goal, was not prepared for victory, I cried out "Goal!" again, a little louder this time, as though with my voice I had added certainty to the fact that a goal for us had really been made. No one answered, neither my mother nor my siblings nor my grandparents came running, but I should not start to doubt now . . . *keep those fingers crossed, for four and a half minutes more.* The crosses on the wall shrank, the holy ghosts kept still as though defeated, the angels, always looking for an opportunity to praise or exalt, did not cross their fingers, they stood placidly in their golden pictures, frozen in their heavenly gestures, their trumpets provocatively quiet . . . *three to two, and the Hungarians acting like a tarantula bit them.* I crossed my fingers and could not understand why I pressed them together so hard. The Hungarians were about to lose, they shifted *into seventh or tenth gear . . . no goal! No goal! No goal! Puschkasch is offsides!* . . . the powerhouse was faltering, almost beaten, and the lowest became the highest, suddenly the Bible phrase made sense, *So the last shall be first,* and it depended on my crossed fingers, on my willpower, whether this dream persisted, whether it would become real . . . *still four more minutes . . . Hidegkuti . . . Turek's down* . . . what I was hearing could not be true, *the uncrowned World Champions* were losing, were almost beaten by one goal, it could not be true, to come out victorious against the favorites, who had not lost in four and a half years.

Three more minutes . . . cross those fingers, keep them crossed . . . and Germany is on the attack! . . . The second hand is moving so slowly . . . the voice wavered, I stared at the green eye. All of the angels and Moses had made their play or were defeated, the holy and black script sunken, devoid of power over me. The voice catapulted against the cloth over the speaker, my heart beat to the tempo of the voice . . . *now the Germans are playing out the clock . . . the Hungarians don't know what to do, Germany has the ball again* . . . I had been cast into a tempest of breathlessness, had to stay calm, very calm, even though the second hand ticked so slowly, ticked and ticked, we will, we can, we are, I or

Liebrich, we are, I and Liebrich, we, I, Liebrich, *the entire German team is using up its last ounce of energy, last bit of concentration* . . . I saw nothing more, no playing field or players blurred in the whirl of excitement, in the rain, I saw only the invisible second hand . . . *Tschibor, he shoots—caught, Toni held! And Puschkasch the Major, the best soccer player from Budapest, he pounds his fists on the ground, as if to say, how is it possible, just a seven meter shot! It's true, our Toni beat him out! And the forty-fifth minute is past, at most there can only be a minute adjustment to the clock for lost time* . . . I held my breath, I did not know what *adjustment to the clock* meant . . . *Danger!* . . . *It's over! Over! Over! Over! Over! The game is over! Germany is World Champion, has beaten Hungary three to two in the final game here in Bern!*

The voice flipped from *Over!* to *Over!*, whirled from syllable to syllable with its final gasps, collapsed, fell down and yet was still there and announced the unbelievable news, the miracle that I did not comprehend, and still could not comprehend when I repeated with my own voice, "We won, three to two, we won!" because there was no echo, no questions from the adjacent dining room, where they had finished coffee and cake and had dispersed. I still needed the connection to the voice in Bern, which, somewhat less excited, but unsure, almost stuttering, repeated the unbelievable . . . *the German team, World Champions 1954* . . . and it searched for the appropriate words for me too, who in that moment, plunged into the intoxication of a new speechlessness, could only stammer the result and the words "We won!"

The sportscaster described the scene on the playing field, how the fans, the photographers, and the teams reacted, the Hungarians, defeated, *composed* themselves and the Germans celebrated . . . *our pride, our joy, and our heartfelt thanks to these eleven players in white jerseys and black shorts, as they run over to the presentation platform and greet the German fans* . . . I could not stay in my chair, I had to shout my joy, my thanks to the world, to the rest of the house, to the village, and yet I could not tear myself away from the radio, wanted to know what would happen next, where the jubilation was coming from . . . *we can see black red gold flags over there in the crowd, and we're swept up in the excitement too* . . . I too was swept up in it, a shudder went down my back and made my body shiver. I wiped away the tears, wanted to show my joy but did not know to whom. I felt clearly that for almost two hours I had succeeded in escaping the Sunday state of alarm, the father-cage, the invisible divine traps, and I knew that the exception afforded me in this time, in which I could forget my failings, would soon come to an end, I wanted to preserve this paradise if possible, and so I ran out to find my friends and soccer friends, whose hearts had to be just as *swept away* as my own.

We shouldn't forget right now that it is only a game, a game, but the most popular game in the world . . . it had long ceased being just a game, because I had become what I had secretly and shamefully wished for—I had become World Champion, and I did not want that diminished by calming words . . . *the players are acting like they just stormed a castle* . . . I had won more, tears ran down my face, the victor's reward, an old man's voice in the background tried to speak over the noise of the celebration, the sportscaster spoke on, ignoring it . . . *the proud triumph of our German World Champions* . . . *this is a high point* . . . he named off the players once again, the coaches, I grew calmer . . . *I can just imagine how you at home must be feeling part of all this* . . . *now comes the ceremonious presentation of the Cup to Fritz Walter, the captain of the German World Champion Team* . . . Fritz held up the Cup that I did not see, the national anthem was played, I listened as the words *Deutschland, Deutschland, über alles* were screamed more than sung, Germany before anything else—I did not understand the words exactly because there were evidently two versions being sung at the same time, the prohibited first and the permitted third strophes. Only a few days ago, before the holiday on June 17, we had been taught to sing *Einigkeit und Recht und Freiheit* and not *Deutschland, Deutschland, über alles.* I could clearly understand the part about *fraternal unity* and the voices rising in combination at the words *über alles in der Welt,* muffled cries of jubilation as it was repeated from liberated throats, *Germany, Germany, before anything else in the world.* Before the singing ended in wild, loud yelling that sounded like *Hey!* or *Yes!* or *Hurrah!*, and applause and screams were over, as the other sportcaster's voice, which had uttered the first sentences before the first half, excitedly and seemingly afraid of another wave of cheers, that other voice said . . . *You have been listening to the joint broadcast of all the stations in the Federal Republic of Germany . . . Your commentator was Herbert Zimmermann. Our broadcast is now concluded. We're switching you back to Germany.*

BENEATH THE LINDEN TREES, in the church yard, over the little wall, three steps across the streets that converged here, as the tempo of the national anthem continued to reverberate in me, I stood and looked in all directions, paths, and yards and hoped that my friends would storm out of their homes after the end of the broadcast and themselves look for people so that we could celebrate together how each of us, *each of us,* was now World Champion. I was the first, had the shortest path, stood in the center. The soccer fans would have to gather here, behind me the church and pastor's house, where there was no room for my excitement, in front of me and around me, the village, the wide-open world.

It was like I was standing there naked in my emotions of victory, alone beneath the lowest branches of the linden trees, waiting impatiently to be discovered with my pure, bouncing joy. I was not ashamed, on the contrary, I was enjoying the intoxicating moment: the sportcaster's voice reverberated throughout my body, and the victory elevated me to a state of happiness in which I forgot about stuttering, psoriasis, and nosebleed, and conscience, and the vise-grip of God lifted away from me. I had never felt so light, and beneath the pulsing emotion of victory was a deep desperate hint of what it would be like to be liberated from the curse of a world divided between Good and Evil, liberated from the occupying forces, from an insatiable God, and perhaps also a hint of the limited duration of this happiness at being able to say one time an unchecked *Yes!* By suppertime this evening the victory would only be half as valuable, at the latest by the time Brahm's merciless lullaby was sung, *Morgen früh, wenn Gott will, wirst du wieder geweckt,* I would be driven back under the Will *of the Lord,* reminded that only if He wills it, might we awaken, forced back into downcast acquiescence and avoidance, and the exile of my helpless *No!* would begin again. That is why I wanted to savor this moment between the linden trees as long as possible. I would have liked to cry out, laugh, dance, have a good time, ring the bells, wake up the whole village with the siren on top of the Lotz Tavern, cap off the day with a big celebration, like Christmas, birthday, the start of summer holidays, the Song Festival, the Fire Department Festival, when someone became a master craftsman, church fairs, all that combined.

But the village remained torpid, nestled in warm stalls, in the Sunday afternoon quiet time, and in the aromas emanating from flowers and dung heaps, from hay in the barns, from grain in the fields, from milk in the stalls, from the sawdust in the carpenter's shop, and from the linden trees. When I turned around, I could see about ten doors, maybe fifty windows, but no faces appeared. All that I saw was the placidness of the timber-frame buildings, the rain-washed gray of the boards on Heinze's barn, the iron fence-post tips in front of sunflowers and vetches in Hahn's garden, the silent hydrant next to the short stinging nettles, the empty milk bench next to the wall with advertisements. The enamel sign *Drink Coca-Cola* shone red from the stone steps of the Lotz Tavern, I would stand underneath that sign tomorrow morning again just before seven o'clock and have to wait for the bus to Bad Hersfeld.

Whenever there was important news to be announced, the beadle would stand in front of the hydrant with his cap tilted, his bike leaned against the fence, and ring his hand bell and read out in a loud voice what was on the paper, what everyone should know, but now, there was not a soul to be seen despite the momentous occasion. On workdays, cows, horses, and tractors crossed the intersection next to the churchyard, pulling piles of dung, wagons with liquid dung, farm machines, wagons piled high with hay or sheaves, now and then there was Walter Scholz's truck, Franz Richter's van, and a few delivery trucks, seldom an automobile, but now there was not even a wagon pulled by cows in sight. Perhaps the drowsily tapping, swinging gait of two cows in time with their chewing mouths and a farmer who led them in reins and with a switch would have sufficed to have let me, as a World Champion, not be seen completely alone in the world.

It was as if nothing had changed because of the World Championship, as if now of all times, someone had enchanted the village, put it to sleep, or as if the people in the village had, just in the moment of my triumph, separated themselves from me for always. The disappointment stung like nettles, except that stinging nettle was bearable, if you held your breath. I no longer knew in which reality, in which dream, I was. Sparrows twittered in the branches, chickens clucked, lots of stinging nettle grew along the courtyard wall. I had been abandoned to a stillness that, after the boisterous jubilation in Bern, was painful, and it almost changed the victory into a cheap lie. The world stood still, although it should have been spinning faster around the circular churchyard with its eight trees, with the chains between the stone pillars around the edge, like a carousel spinning and spinning, with me as the axis.

I grabbed the linden branches, pulled one down, held tight to the swaying branch, the perspiring leaves, breathed in the already fading aroma of pollen, seized upon the belief in soccer gods, and wished that nothing would take the victory away from me, regardless of the way my friends in Wehrda and Hersfeld acted: Bern was a part of me, I was Liebrich, I was World Champion, the proof was in the sportscaster's voice, the proof was a new energy beaming over the radio, here was the glimmer of a way out that extended farther than the black-yellow street signs to Neukirchen, Langenschwarz, Hünfeld.

I stood like that in the churchyard for three, four, five minutes, ready to embrace the whole world, to show my friends and to share, ready to turn in any direction except towards the house I had just run out of, any direction from which a person might come who might be able to understand my emotions, and then, finally, three men staggered out of Senning's Bar. Despite their Sunday clothes I recognized them to be three soccer players on the F.C. Wehrda team, and they ran, avoiding cow patties and holes in the street, past the post office, to the churchyard, just as I had wished for, they ran towards me, and after them, from one direction and then another, appeared my friends Herwig, Horst, Gerhard, Helmut, and Wolfgang, and as we screamed like idiots to each other phrases like "World Champion!" and "Germany!" and "Three to two!" scaring off the sparrows, and, carried away by the unaccustomed might of the words, we fell out of our normal Sunday behavior and laughed and shouted, and in that moment I was, without really understanding it myself, the happiest one of all, happier maybe than Werner Liebrich or Fritz Walter.

Translated by Scott Williams

Titles Available in The German Library

All titles available from Continuum International
370 Lexington Avenue, New York, NY 10017
www.continuumbooks.com

Beginnings to 1750

Volume 1
GERMAN EPIC POETRY: THE NIEBELUNGENLIED, THE OLDER LAY OF HILDEBRAND, AND OTHER WORKS

Volume 2
Wolfram von Eschenbach
PARZIVAL

Volume 3
Gottfried von Strassburg
TRISTAN AND ISOLDE

Volume 4
Hartmann von Aue, Konrad von Würzburg, Gartenaere, and Others
GERMAN MEDIEVAL TALES

Volume 5
Hildegard of Bingen, Meister Eckhart, Jacob Boehme, Heinrich Seuse, Johannes Tauler, and Angelus Silesius
GERMAN MYSTICAL WRITINGS

Volume 6
Erasmus, Luther, Müntzer, Johann von Tepl, Sebastian Brant, Conrad Celtis, Sebastian Lotzer, Rubianus von Hutten
GERMAN HUMANISM AND REFORMATION

Volume 7
Grimmelshausen, Leibniz, Opitz, Weise and Others
SEVENTEENTH CENTURY GERMAN PROSE

Titles Available in the German Library

Volume 8
Sachs, Gryphius, Schlegel, and Others
GERMAN THEATER BEFORE 1750

Volume 9
Hartmann von Aue, Wolfram von Eschenbach, Luther, Gryphius, and Others
GERMAN POETRY FROM THE BEGINNINGS TO 1750

Eighteenth Century

Volume 10
Heinse, La Roche, Wieland, and Others
EIGHTEENTH CENTURY GERMAN PROSE

Volume 11
Herder, Lenz, Lessing, and Others
EIGHTEENTH CENTURY GERMAN CRITICISM

Volume 12
Gotthold Ephraim Lessing
NATHAN THE WISE, MINNA VON BARNHELM, AND OTHER PLAYS AND WRITINGS

Volume 13
Immanuel Kant
PHILOSOPHICAL WRITINGS

Volume 14
Lenz, Heinrich Wagner, Klinger, and Schiller
STURM UND DRANG

Volume 15
Friedrich Schiller
PLAYS: INTRIGUE AND LOVE, AND DON CARLOS

Volume 16
Friedrich Schiller
WALLENSTEIN AND MARY STUART

Volume 17
Friedrich Schiller
ESSAYS: LETTERS ON THE AESTHETIC EDUCATION OF MAN, ON NAIVE AND SENTIMENTAL POETRY, AND OTHERS

Volume 18
Johann Wolfgang von Goethe
FAUST PARTS ONE AND TWO

Volume 19
Johann Wolfgang von Goethe
THE SUFFERINGS OF YOUNG WERTHER AND ELECTIVE AFFINITIES

Volume 20
Johann Wolfgang von Goethe
PLAYS: EGMONT, IPHIGENIA IN TAURIS, TORQUATO TASSO

Titles Available in the German Library

Nineteenth Century

Volume 21
Novalis, Schlegel, Schleiermacher, and Others
GERMAN ROMANTIC CRITICISM

Volume 22
Friedrich Hölderlin
HYPERION AND SELECTED POEMS

Volume 23
Fichte, Jacobi, and Schelling
PHILOSOPHY OF GERMAN IDEALISM

Volume 24
Georg Wilhelm Friedrich Hegel
ENCYCLOPEDIA OF THE PHILOSOPHICAL SCIENCES IN OUTLINE AND CRITICAL WRITINGS

Volume 25
Heinrich von Kleist
PLAYS: THE BROKEN PITCHER, AMPHITRYON, AND OTHERS

Volume 26
E. T. A. Hoffmann
TALES

Volume 27
Arthur Schopenhauer
PHILOSOPHICAL WRITINGS

Volume 28
Georg Büchner
COMPLETE WORKS AND LETTERS

Volume 29
J. and W. Grimm and Others
GERMAN FAIRY TALES

Volume 30
Goethe, Brentano, Kafka, and Others
GERMAN LITERARY FAIRY TALES

Volume 31
Grillparzer, Hebbel, Nestroy
NINETEENTH CENTURY GERMAN PLAYS

Volume 32
Heinrich Heine
POETRY AND PROSE

Volume 33
Heinrich Heine
THE ROMANTIC SCHOOL AND OTHER ESSAYS

Volume 34
Heinrich von Kleist and Jean Paul
ROMANTIC NOVELLAS

Volume 35
Eichendorff, Brentano, Chamisso, and Others
GERMAN ROMANTIC STORIES

Titles Available in the German Library

Volume 36
Ehrlich, Gauss, Siemens, and Others
GERMAN ESSAYS ON SCIENCE IN THE NINETEENTH CENTURY

Volume 37
Stifter, Droste-Hülshoff, Gotthelf, Grillparzer, and Mörike
GERMAN NOVELLAS OF REALISM VOLUME 1

Volume 38
Ebner-Eschenbach, Heyse, Raabe, Storm, Meyer, and Hauptmann
GERMAN NOVELLAS OF REALISM VOLUME 2

Volume 39
Goethe, Hölderlin, Nietzsche, and Others
GERMAN POETRY FROM 1750 TO 1900

Volume 40
Feuerbach, Marx, Engels
GERMAN SOCIALIST PHILOSOPHY

Volume 41
Marx, Engels, Bebel, and Others
GERMAN ESSAYS ON SOCIALISM IN THE NINETEENTH CENTURY

Volume 42
Beethoven, Brahms, Mahler, Schubert, and Others
GERMAN *LIEDER*

Volume 43
Adorno, Bloch, Mann, and Others
GERMAN ESSAYS ON MUSIC

Volume 44
Gottfried Keller
STORIES: A VILLAGE ROMEO AND JULIET, THE BANNER OF THE UPRIGHT SEVEN, AND OTHERS

Volume 45
Wilhelm Raabe
NOVELS: HORACKER AND TUBBY SCHAUMANN

Volume 46
Theodor Fontane
SHORT NOVELS AND OTHER WRITINGS

Volume 47
Theodor Fontane
DELUSIONS, CONFUSIONS AND THE POGGENPUHL FAMILY

Volume 48
Friedrich Nietzsche
PHILOSOPHICAL WRITINGS

Volume 49
Hegel, Ranke, Spengler, and Others
GERMAN ESSAYS ON HISTORY

Titles Available in the German Library

Volume 50
Wilhelm Busch and Others
GERMAN SATIRICAL WRITINGS

Volume 51
Bach, Mozart, R. Wagner, Brahms, Mahler, Richard Strauss, Weill, and Others
WRITINGS OF GERMAN COMPOSERS

Volume 52
Mozart, Beethoven, R. Wagner, Richard Strauss, and Schoenberg
GERMAN OPERA LIBRETTI

Volume 53
Luther, Heine, Brecht, and Others
GERMAN SONGS

Volume 54
Barth, Buber, Rahner, Schleiermacher, and Others
GERMAN ESSAYS ON RELIGION

Twentieth Century

Volume 55
Arthur Schnitzler
PLAYS AND STORIES

Volume 57
Gerhart Hauptmann
PLAYS: BEFORE DAYBREAK, THE WEAVERS, THE BEAVER COAT

Volume 58
Frank Wedekind, Ödön von Horváth, and Marieluise Fleisser
EARLY TWENTIETH CENTURY GERMAN PLAYS

Volume 59
Sigmund Freud
PSYCHOLOGICAL WRITINGS AND LETTERS

Volume 60
Max Weber
SOCIOLOGICAL WRITINGS

Volume 61
T. W. Adorno, M. Horkheimer, G. Simmel, M. Weber, and Others
GERMAN SOCIOLOGY

Volume 64
Heinrich Mann
THE LOYAL SUBJECT

Volume 65
Thomas Mann
TONIO KRÖGER, DEATH IN VENICE AND OTHER STORIES

Volume 66
Benn, Toller, Sternheim, Kaiser, and Others
GERMAN EXPRESSIONIST PLAYS

Volume 70
Rainer Maria Rilke
PROSE AND POETRY

Titles Available in the German Library

Volume 71
Hermann Hesse
SIDDHARTHA, DEMIAN, AND OTHER WRITINGS

Volume 72
Robert Musil
SELECTED WRITINGS: YOUNG TÖRLESS, TONKA, AND OTHERS

Volume 78
T. W. Adorno, W. Benjamin, M. Horkheimer, and Others
GERMAN TWENTIETH CENTURY PHILOSOPHY

Volume 82
Einstein, Heisenberg, Planck and Others
GERMAN ESSAYS ON SCIENCE IN THE TWENTIETH CENTURY

Volume 83
Lessing, Brecht, Dürrenmatt, and Others
ESSAYS ON GERMAN THEATER

Volume 87
Plenzdorf, Kunert, and Others
NEW SUFFERINGS OF YOUNG W. AND OTHER STORIES FROM THE GERMAN DEMOCRATIC REPUBLIC

Volume 89
Friedrich Dürrenmatt
PLAYS AND ESSAYS

Volume 90
Max Frisch
NOVELS, PLAYS, ESSAYS

Volume 92
Peter Weiss
MARAT/SADE, THE INVESTIGATION, THE SHADOW OF THE BODY OF THE COACHMAN

Volume 93
Günter Grass
CAT AND MOUSE AND OTHER WRITINGS

Volume 94
Ingeborg Bachmann and Christa Wolf
SELECTED PROSE AND DRAMA

Volume 96
Rolf Hochhuth, Heinar Kipphardt, Heiner Müller
CONTEMPORARY GERMAN PLAYS

Volume 98
Hans Magnus Enzensberger
CRITICAL ESSAYS

Volume 99
I. Aichinger, H. Bender, G. Köpf, G. Kunert, and Others
CONTEMPORARY GERMAN FICTION

Volume 100
P. Handke, F. Mayröcker, Uwe Timm, and Others
CONTEMPORARY GERMAN STORIES

Complete Author Listing in The German Library by Volume Number